The RESURRECTION *of* EVANIA JAMES

Books by Jaime Jo Wright

The House on Foster Hill
The Reckoning at Gossamer Pond
The Curse of Misty Wayfair
Echoes among the Stones
The Haunting at Bonaventure Circus
On the Cliffs of Foxglove Manor
The Souls of Lost Lake
The Premonition at Withers Farm
The Vanishing at Castle Moreau
The Lost Boys of Barlowe Theater
Night Falls on Predicament Avenue
Specters in the Glass House
Tempest at Annabel's Lighthouse
The Bell Tolls at Traeger Hall
The Bookshop of 99 Doors
The Resurrection of Evania James

The RESURRECTION of EVANIA JAMES

JAIME JO WRIGHT

BETHANYHOUSE
a division of Baker Publishing Group
Minneapolis, Minnesota

Published by Bethany House Publishers
Minneapolis, Minnesota
BethanyHouse.com

Bethany House Publishers is a division of
Baker Publishing Group, Grand Rapids, Michigan

Printed in the United States of America

Library of Congress Cataloging-in-Publication Data
Names: Wright, Jaime Jo, author.
Title: The resurrection of Evania James / Jaime Jo Wright.
Description: Minneapolis, Minnesota : Bethany House Publishers, a division of Baker Publishing Group, 2026.
Identifiers: LCCN 2026009645 | ISBN 9780764246258 paperback | ISBN 9781493455478 ebook
Subjects: LCGFT: Christian fiction | Detective and mystery fiction | Novels
Classification: LCC PS3623.R5388 R47 2026
LC record available at https://lccn.loc.gov/2026009645

Scripture quotations are from the King James Version of the Bible.

Cover design by Jennifer Parker

Published in association with Books & Such Literary Management, BooksAndSuch.com.

Baker Publishing Group publications use paper produced from sustainable forestry practices and postconsumer waste whenever possible.

26 27 28 29 30 31 32 7 6 5 4 3 2 1

To my real-life Grandpa Don

From an orphan to a war hero.
From a dairy farm to a Bronze Star and a Purple Heart.
From a motorcyclist to a front-lines messenger.
From a pitchfork to a flamethrower.
From a small town in Wisconsin to the Asiatic war front.

To you and the three things you loved most in life:
God, family, and your country. I salute you. HOOAH!

1

Eloise James

Because I could not stop for Death –
He kindly stopped for me –
The Carriage held but just Ourselves –
And Immortality.

Emily Dickinson

September 1879
New Jamestown, Indiana

She had always been led to believe that the Grim Reaper rode a horse as dark as the bottomless fathoms of hell, when in fact it was a brougham carriage rolling on four wheels, as enclosed as a prison and pulled by a dappled-gray mare. The Grim Reaper himself sought sanctuary inside its depths, and when the carriage finally jostled to a halt outside their expansive home, he dared to show himself by first giving a glimpse of his pompous silk top hat.

Eloise James hated Dr. Merriweather, and hate was no exaggeration of her feelings. Regardless of his profession's promise of healing, he instead wielded a scythe of death, invisible to the eye but well known to the women of New Jamestown.

This was the man who had so quickly penned his signature to Lucy Addlethwaite's sentence of imprisonment at the Corinth Asylum for the Chronically Insane. All because Lucy's reverend husband claimed she had lost her senses, so visceral were her arguments against him and his theology. She was his wife, he defended, not a theologian, and the fact that she dared to lead a women's Bible study and teach things of a nature that caused wives to question their husbands' spiritual leadership was itself the epitome of lunacy. In the end, it had nothing to do with the accuracy of scriptural interpretation and everything to do with a man's threatened pride and authority.

Eloise raced through the hallway of James Mansion, her hip knocking into a side table, sending the decorative vase on it wobbling and then falling with a dramatic crash. Ignoring the chaos she left in her wake, Eloise took the staircase one horribly slow step at a time, hoisting her dress so as not to trip. Had she wings, she would have flown with fervent urgency, but as it was, all she could do was rely on her two feet, and with the excess of petticoats, skirt, and layers of underthings required to be a proper lady, her athleticism—what little she had—was therefore hampered.

Eloise careened past the master bedroom belonging to her widowed father, her own room, and on to the bedroom farthest toward the back end of the house. She was met with a closed door, its deep mahogany enhanced by a scrolled brass plate and doorknob, which she grappled for and twisted, pushing the bedroom door inward.

"Evania!" Eloise cried.

Her wan sister looked up at Eloise from her chair by the window, which overlooked the back lawn of the manor. Eloise noted that Evania's eyes seemed to have sunk further into her head, darkening the circles beneath them, and only hurting Eloise's vehement defense of her sister's faculties.

"Evania." Eloise dropped to her knees beside her sister, reaching for her hands. Evania was younger than Eloise by a mere ten months. Many thought they were twins when growing up. But between Eloise's tendency toward intellectual endeavors that left her on the more homely side—or so she'd been told—and Evania's brilliant blue eyes and effervescent personality, it was made apparent that while close in age, they were very different from each other.

Now, if just meeting Evania for the first time, one wouldn't believe the word *effervescence* had ever been used to describe sweet Evania. Her expression was blank. Lifeless. She stared down at her hands folded in her lap, and Eloise wanted nothing more in this moment than to shake life back into her sister. That impetuous old life that had led Evania to dance in the hallways when everyone was looking, to laugh so melodically it would make a music box envious, and to live with an abandonment Eloise could only be jealous of.

"Darling, you must come with me." Eloise squeezed her sister's hands.

In response, Evania managed only the whisper of a smile.

"Dr. Death and Doom is here." Eloise used Evania's old nickname for Dr. Merriweather. "Please, we must go."

Escape. *Escape* was the word she should use. Father—for Eloise and Evania had never dared to call him anything more affectionate than that—had been the one to call for Dr. Merriweather. Eloise had known it was only a matter of time now that it was over. Now that Evania's babe had been born, as still as death could make it, and on as grievous a night as Eloise had ever known.

"If we go down the back stairs, we can hurry to the carriage house. Kenny will have a carriage waiting. We can leave immediately for Mrs. Shelton's. She will give us respite there until we can board the train tomorrow morning." At Evania's tiny glimmer of interest, Eloise hurried to explain further. "We'll take the train to Chicago, and from there we will board another one for Iowa to stay with our James cousins there. They haven't approved of Father for years, and they would give us respite until we can devise our next steps. Think of it, Evania! A new beginning. For both of us!"

But there was no more interest on Evania's face than there was initiative to rise from the chair she'd convalesced in for four days since the birth of her stillborn child. Eloise had been reticent to make her move so quickly, but now there was no time left.

Eloise shook her sister's hands again, and this time she was not gentle. She made no effort to hide the stern demand in her voice. "Evania, get up at once!" She pushed herself to her feet, using the arm of Evania's chair for support. Staring down at her sister, Eloise urged her again. "Father and Dr. Merriweather will come. They will take you away. I will never see you again!"

Evania merely turned her head to look out the window. She didn't care, so it seemed, and that stung Eloise in a way she was not prepared for. If for no one else, she'd assumed Evania would fight to be with Eloise. To stay together as sisters. They had always been inseparable. Evania, the spirited sprite, and Eloise, the sister whom no one understood, least of all herself.

Firm, manly footsteps sounded down the hallway, echoing of impending doom. There was no use in veiling the truth from Evania. Eloise bent, taking her sister's chin in her hand and forcing Evania to look at her.

"Father is going to have you committed to an asylum. He only needs Dr. Merriweather's signature, and you will be taken away from me. You are grieving the loss of your daughter, yes, but then you will grieve the loss of a sister, of your freedom. Of a life you've known. Of a life you can have again! *Please*, listen to me."

Evania raised her eyes, empty of hope, and whispered three words that confirmed to Eloise that the war was lost before it had truly begun.

"Let them come."

The following hour had been nothing but furious chaos. Eloise had locked herself in the bedroom with Evania, defying her father's angry knocking and Dr. Merriweather's cajoling. It wasn't until a ladder had been positioned outside beneath the window, where Evania sat immobile and unreactive, that Eloise flew into an all-out panic.

Of course, Father would have no reservations at all about ordering the use of a ladder to gain access through the bedroom window. However, it wasn't Father who appeared in the frame. No. It was Kenny who climbed the ladder. The estate's handyman. His expression was nothing short of horrified apology. While Eloise vowed never to hold him responsible for doing her father's bidding, she still slammed the window shut, locking it firmly against Kenny's halfhearted attempts to gain access. He stared at her through the glass with a beseeching expression that suggested he might lose his job over this if he failed to retrieve Evania. To Eloise, that was the least of her worries. Kenny would not be held responsible. No. *She* would be.

"Evania!" Eloise cajoled. But her sister remained unmoving, her hands curled around a lace-edged handkerchief and her eyes fixed on some distant point outside the window. Grief had stolen Evania's spirit. Shame had robbed her of her father's respect. And her absent lover had absconded with her future.

What had Evania left to hope for?

Eloise sagged onto the edge of the bed, the mattress sinking beneath her weight. She met Kenny's eyes, the window between them a thin barrier of safety against the inevitable. There was small comfort in their shared look of defeat.

Another series of commanding knocks on the door.

"Open this door immediately or I will be forced to break it down." Father's tone held no room for negotiations or patience.

Dr. Merriweather's "Come, come now, child" irritated her like a hand rubbing the fur on a cat backward.

Then Evania stood, her nightgown draping her body like a shroud.

Eloise was shocked into wordless horror as her sister padded on bare feet across the wood floor of her bedroom and twisted the lock on her door.

It flew open, and Evania stepped aside as Father and Dr. Merriweather marched into the room. Father did not spare Eloise from his dark glowering, which promised she was not out of danger from his fury. But it was Dr. Merriweather he addressed.

"As you can see, Evania is not herself."

Dr. Merriweather's monocle exaggerated the size of his eye. His assessment of Evania took mere seconds. "Ah, yes. I see."

Evania did not defend herself, nor did she say a word.

"As you can see? You see nothing!" Eloise cried in repulsion. This man called himself a doctor? How could he assess with one look that Evania was better off institutionalized?

"Silence, Eloise." Father lifted his hand, palm forward with commanding authority.

Eloise lifted her hand to her mouth to keep from protesting more and ruining any possibility she might have to get Father to see reason.

Motion at the window told her that Kenny was descending the ladder to give the family their privacy.

Dr. Merriweather clucked his tongue. "It's a shame whatever fractious bent in your daughter has brought us to this point, but it is very apparent that she is not in her right mind."

Eloise launched to her feet, but a severe snap of Father's head in her direction silenced her.

"You see where my concern lies?" Father's low timbre was smooth and calculated.

"Oh yes, yes." Dr. Merriweather nodded. "I fear there is no coming back from this condition. Not without medical assistance. I've seen behaviors in women like this before. Licentiousness is incurable, I'm afraid, and without supervision it will only be allowed to flourish in its sinful progressions. Add to that the loss of the child . . ."

Eloise noticed Evania's eyes grow watery with remembrance.

Dr. Merriweather continued, oblivious. "It's apparent Miss James's mind is in turmoil to say the least." He sniffed, causing his handlebar mustache to twitch as he did so. "I shall sign off on the paperwork immediately. She must be committed to a place where she can receive proper treatment."

"No, please!" Eloise rounded the bedpost. "Father, you cannot—"

"You've nothing to say about this, Eloise." Father's retort was clipped.

Dr. Merriweather ignored Eloise's outburst. "There are experimental treatments that may help your daughter. If nothing else, the hospital will be able to temper her illicit impulses, which only prove she does not have the right mind of a proper lady."

"I agree." Father's nod carried with it an air of relief. Not the kind of relief that came from a soul being unburdened, but the sort that accompanied a scheme to be rid of a troublesome problem.

Dr. Merriweather nodded. "We can transport Miss James immediately. There is an opening at the Corinth Asylum, and they were quite eager to ready a bed for your daughter."

"Good, good." Father shifted to Eloise, who stared at him with disgust. She debated flying at him to claw at his eyes and face, but then he might have her committed as well, and then what use would she be to her sister? "Eloise," Father said, ending her frantic attempt to arrive at a solution, "gather your sister's things. A small travel bag will suffice. We'll be moving her to the hospital today."

Eloise would go to war on her sister's behalf. She would stand before the Grim Reaper and return his life-stealing blows, strike for strike.

If only she knew how . . .

2

Tilly Thompson

Death, be not proud, though some have called thee
Mighty and dreadful, for thou art not so;
For those whom thou think'st thou dost overthrow
Die not, poor Death, nor yet canst thou kill me.

John Donne

Present Day
New Jamestown, Indiana

He was going to die. But before that happened, her grandfather was going to lose any recollection of her. Her name would become an elusive whisper in the back of his mind, teasing but never revealing, until one day even that whisper would be silenced, and all Tilly would see in the eyes of Grandpa Don was emptiness. But that time was not now. And Grandpa Don was adamant that they lived today and not tomorrow, for tomorrow would take care of itself.

"I don't understand." Tilly positioned herself next to her grandfather as they stood on the cracked cement sidewalk on the historic street of New Jamestown.

Grandpa Don perched on his electric scooter, a satisfied smile on his face, his buzz-cut gray hair reflecting the afternoon sunlight off its white tips. "You've always loved this place," he observed. True to form, Grandpa Don was ignoring the fact that he had the onset of Alzheimer's. Instead, he was studying the massive structure that loomed before them. A Queen Anne, château-esque home featuring two stories and attic windows, culminating in a gabled roof with chimneys and a turret.

"James Mansion? Yes, I've always loved it." Tilly couldn't help but give a contented smile. She absently rested her hand on her grandfather's shoulder. "The limestone architecture and that lone attic window at the top? You know, I firmly believe I saw a ghost peeking out of it when I was a little girl."

"Of course you did," Grandpa Don said kindly.

"I love this place," Tilly continued, because once she began talking with Grandpa Don, her words ran loose and unfettered. "The James Mansion has been a centerpiece of New Jamestown for over a century."

"Longer," Grandpa Don corrected.

"Yes." Tilly surveyed the mansion, not ignoring the little pangs of sadness as she noticed the unkempt front lawn, the flower gardens barren of any vegetation but sticks and dead leaves, and the weeds that grew through the cracks of the brick and concrete Victorian retaining wall that bordered the walkway. She couldn't ignore the sadness. This house had spoken to her soul since she was a girl. If a house could speak, Tilly was sure this one had many secrets to spill. Secrets of the family that had occupied it until fifteen years ago when the last James family member abandoned it. "I was sad to hear they sold it recently," Tilly mused.

"Hmm?" Grandpa Don hadn't taken his eyes off the great house.

"They sold James Mansion. Didn't you hear?" Tilly informed him. "It was a private sale—that's all I know. They didn't even donate it to the New Jamestown Historical Society, which is what the community had hoped."

"Mmm." Grandpa Don nodded.

"Isn't that just like a James?" Tilly issued a soft laugh that wasn't unkind but also wasn't admiring. "I don't know how Luke James thinks he'll ever be elected mayor this fall. The James family has never been known for playing nice. His brother has been mayor long enough, and now we need *another* James son to take office?"

"Don't be too hard on the boy," Grandpa Don reprimanded, giving Tilly a gentle look. "He is merely the result of a family that has long been a part of our town's tempestuous history."

"Mmm." It was Tilly's turn to mimic her grandfather's contemplative reaction. She had reasons for not being fond of the James family—not like she was their ancestral home.

"Do you know who bought the place?" Grandpa Don led.

"No. Like I said, the paper printed it was a private sale." Yes, she still read the local newspaper. That was one reason why Tilly loved her small-town home, population 6,000. It was quaint, old-fashioned, and it still held on to the last remnants of the past. Just like she did. Tilly didn't even own a cellphone, much to Grandpa Don's chagrin. As for the internet and social media, Tilly had concluded that compared to paper and ink, they were of the devil.

"You'll want this." Grandpa Don reached into the inside pocket of his sport jacket and tugged out a thick envelope. He lifted it toward Tilly.

"What is this?" Taking it, she turned it over in her hands, noting a professionally printed name in the top left corner. The name of a law office. "Grandpa?" She dragged out the word, scared to think what she was thinking for fear she was wrong while also worrying she was right. "What did you do?"

Grandpa Don grinned smugly, gripping the handlebars of his

scooter as if preparing to take off on an electric run if Tilly protested too vehemently. "I bought it."

"Bought it?"

"Yes, I bought James Mansion." He looked up at her with faded blue eyes. "It's yours, Tilly Renee Thompson. My gift to you. Well, after I'm dead, of course. I've adjusted my will, and your parents and brother all know. They agreed that this place should be your inheritance from me."

"Grandpa!" Tilly had no words. Grandpa had always been one to invest in real estate, but she had never imagined he'd pull something like this! He'd retired years ago and sold most of the properties he'd invested in as part of his retirement plan.

Tilly caressed the envelope with her palm, not bothering to doubt the legal papers that were inside. She knew they were already signed and sealed. Apparently, the manor had been sold to Donald Edward Thompson, Vietnam War veteran, her grandfather, her best friend, and the man she was loath to think of ever losing.

"There are three conditions," he continued. "One, you don't argue with me about it. Two, you reserve one ground-level room for my model trains and tracks. And three—and this one is more costly for you—you agree to be my caregiver."

"I'm already your caregiver!" Tilly exclaimed with a small laugh. She had quit her job as an administrative assistant over a year ago to be Grandpa Don's companion and caregiver. It had caused some friction between her and her parents. They were preparing to pull up roots from their retirement home in New Mexico to come care for Grandpa Don. Their other alternative was to move him there to be with them. Tilly had been adamant that being with Grandpa Don was what she wanted to do, and she would never survive if he moved halfway across the country from her.

"That you are, but . . ." Grandpa Don grew contemplative, seeming to search for the right words, until finally he composed his thoughts. "But I would like you to promise that my care will ensure I'm not moved from this place. When I'm unable to be the man I am today."

Don't put me in a nursing home.

Those were the words she knew Grandpa Don was trying to speak. When he forgot who she was, when he could no longer care for himself or his hygiene, when he became a soul encased in a body that no longer served its master.

Never. Never would she have Grandpa Don moved to a nursing home facility. He had been there for her since her earliest memories. Her grandmother had passed away when she was only two, so Tilly had no recollection of her. But as a toddler, she became Grandpa Don's reason to continue, and he had been Papa Bear to her.

She'd never been good at making friends, and in school she was the proverbial girl who wasn't even average. She was ignored, and when that didn't work, Tilly was tolerated. There were no sleepovers or birthday parties or best friends. There was only Grandpa Don, welcoming her in from a world that was all angles and sharpness into his embrace where she fit perfectly. He had taught Tilly to have confidence when the world around her pegged her as different. Which was also interesting to Tilly because she found her thought processes and sense of reasoning quite logical. The rest of the world seemed to be the ones who lacked common sense and organization. Regardless, Grandpa Don was the one she came home to after school and put model train sets together with and talked about history. Tilly knew all the facts about the Vietnam War. It was one of the most heartbreaking periods of American history. The war had contributed to the framework of Grandpa Don's life story and many others like him, and so it made sense that Tilly would know as much about it as she could. But no one else seemed to grasp the importance of it. Well, no one except Grandpa Don.

And, God bless her parents, while they lived in New Mexico

now, they had always encouraged Tilly's relationship with her grandfather. And her older brother, Erik, had understood that there was no favoritism being shown by Grandpa Don toward Tilly. They had both filled a need in each other, Tilly offering purpose to a widowed man, and Grandpa Don offering purpose to a child who was always on the sidelines.

Tilly bent to wrap her arm around his shoulders, pressing her cheek to his. "You know I'll never leave you," she murmured to the man who held her heart and would always be her number one.

"I wish I could say the same, my dear. I wish I could say the same."

Two days later, Tilly could hardly believe her good fortune as she stepped inside James Mansion. It was like an American version of Downton Abbey. The front doors opened to greet her with dull but still remarkable parquet floors in intricate, multicolored geometric patterns. Her eyes widened in awe at the dizzying design. Whoever had chosen the combinations of patterns had to be a kaleidoscope of personality. The walls were covered in equally busy patterned wallpaper, and when she stood in the foyer, Tilly could look all the way through the front hall, past arched ceilings, to the back exit that opened onto a glorious veranda.

She stood there now, cardboard box in hand, angsty over the fact that it held her modern belongings like a digital clock and her collection of LP records. They didn't belong here. Instead, she should be hauling in an old phonograph, vintage photos of her ancestors, and piles of lace doilies. It was a collision of time periods that begged further planning on how to merge the two.

"Move it, pup."

Her brother's voice broke her out of her admiring stupor. She looked up at her six-foot-two older brother, craning her neck to see his mischievous grin. He'd inherited their mother's height, while she'd inherited her father's more diminutive form. Tilly could only boast three inches over five feet. Dad had never been diminutive in personality, though, and that Tilly had not inherited. The Thompson family was made up of strong personalities, starting with Grandpa Don, her dad, and then her brother, Erik. It was the family joke that when God finally got around to creating Tilly, He'd run out of His reserves of spunk and instead turned her into the shy one. It was meant to be complimentary and was always stated with affection, but the fact that Erik had called her "pup" since she could remember was a bit annoying. Especially now that she was staring down thirty in two years and he was married with two kids.

Erik kneed her backside.

She hadn't moved yet.

"You may own James Mansion, but you don't have any house staff. Your belongings aren't going to move themselves in." Erik laughed.

Tilly gave him an awkward smile and entered the 7,000 square-foot house. Maybe she *should* get house staff. She considered it, then thought of the finances, the implications of the intrusion of strangers in her home, and a conclusion was quickly drawn. Even if she had the financial wherewithal to hire staff, there was no way she would want them in her home, nosing through her life and Grandpa Don's.

"I always said you had Grandpa Don wrapped around your finger, but this is a bit much. I mean, a whole house? He bought you a whole house!" Erik's jesting echoed through the foyer. He waited to the right of Tilly, holding a stack of boxes. "I don't know where you want these."

She hesitated. Erik was planted at the foot of the four stairs that led to a short landing, then turned at a ninety-degree angle to climb to the second floor. The entrance space where he stood was square and, amazingly, still had an original table at its center, waiting for a potted fern to adorn the room. To her left was the sitting room, where, Tilly imagined, guests of old would have been seated as they anticipated the host or hostess to join them. There was the bay window, a fireplace with checkerboard tiling of gold and maroon, and a massive mahogany surround with a square mirror in near-perfect condition.

From the foyer, Tilly could look past the fireplace through a large doorway with mahogany molding and a bridge of stained glass at the crest. The dining room was beyond it. That, too, had Victorian-era furniture, no doubt original to the house, and the high-backed chairs were covered in red velvet brocade. Matching red velvet curtains had been pushed to each side of the doorway but could be pulled shut for privacy's sake. So many dinner parties must have occurred in that room over the decades. The walls would have soaked in the conversations, the gossip, the old town—

"Earth to Tilly Thompson."

Tilly jerked her head back toward Erik. "Sorry. I'm—"

"In la-la land. Got it. But that doesn't help me at the moment." He shifted the boxes in his arms.

"Sorry. Those are books."

"I figured as much—they're heavy."

"They go in the library."

"Which is where exactly?"

"Upstairs." Tilly gave him a perplexed expression. Erik had already toured the house, so he should remember where the library was. She pointed to the stairs. It wasn't that difficult to recall the layout of a house, was it? She could envision the blueprints in her mind. But then maybe that was why she and Erik could tolerate each other so well—her with her reasoning skills and her brother with his feelings and impulses. They were different enough to appreciate that they would never be similar. Tilly didn't always understand Erik's teasing, but she never doubted his affection for her. So while she didn't know how to tease him back very well, she accepted his sense of humor like one might accept a warm embrace.

Erik eyed the stairs and then turned his attention to the boxes of books in his arms. "Of course the library is upstairs."

"Sorry," Tilly mumbled. She felt as though she should apologize even though she wasn't the one who had put the library on the second floor.

She took the lead and began to hike up the staircase. Four steps up, turn sharply, go up nine scuffed wooden stairs and another landing, then another right, nine more stairs, and they were on the second floor. Tilly glanced behind her at Erik, wishing she could stand in awed silence at the arched stained-glass window that cast light onto the stairs in a vibrant array of colored petal patterns.

She hiked down the hallway, her soft-soled shoes quiet on the wood floor, and then turned into the library. Floor-to-ceiling bookshelves. Every bookworm's dream.

"Here?" Erik said, nudging Tilly.

"Yes. You can put them over there in the corner."

Unfortunately, or perhaps fortunately—she hadn't determined which yet—the house hadn't included the original library of books. The shelves were empty, dusty, and home only to spiderwebs and some mouse droppings. While Tilly bemoaned the fact that old Victorian books would be delightful to have here, she was also intrigued by the idea of building her own library of classics: Dickens, Shelley, Austen, Eliot, Frost, Poe, Tennyson . . .

"Look, I love ya, pup, but you really need to focus."

Tilly lowered her box to the floor. She *was* focused. There was more to life than just surface tasks that needed doing. Books. Books required attention, appreciation, and exploration. But she acquiesced anyway because, again, she knew she was expected to. "I'm enamored by this place. It's as if it's *alive* and just waking up."

Erik blinked. "Sure." It was his only response. "Okay. The rest of the books go here then?"

Tilly nodded.

Erik left, the sound of his boots clapping against the floor growing distant as he bounded down the stairs.

How many feet had done that over the decades? The James family's time here had spanned from the mid-1800s through two world wars, the Civil Rights era, Vietnam, and into the 1980s. The house had been closed up since 2011 following the deaths of Rodney and Trisha James in a car accident.

To Tilly, this house had always been a place of mystery, even before the James family had closed its doors for good. Its gables and corners promised stories, with windows that were like openings to the mansion's soul, and voices that had been silenced long before an automobile ever drove up the drive. Those were the tantalizing unknowns and the unremembered that had always fed Tilly's curiosity. History was like that. Not only did she appreciate dates and facts, but the story behind the walls, or underneath the soil, or infused in the essence of a place like this. And now? Now it was *hers*—well, hers and Grandpa Don's.

They would make the parlor downstairs into his model train room, and the study next to it they would make his bedroom. Which meant the second floor was all hers. And the attic. And the turret. And—

A door slammed down the hall.

Tilly spun around. She'd thought she was alone up here.

"Hello?" Tilly peered down the hallway, taking tentative steps in the direction of the sound.

She passed two doorways, both to bedrooms, both with furnishings that had come with the place, each covered with protective sheets. They were ghostly mounds of antique memories. Yet they were inanimate pieces that would never speak of who had slept in them, sat in them, or stared into their mirrors.

Tilly remained in the corridor as she calculated the logic behind the door shutting. It was the door at the far end of the hall and to the right. That room had likely once belonged to a lady's maid, who might have attended the woman of the house in the adjoining and much larger bedroom. The little hairs stood at attention at the back of Tilly's neck, and bumps raised on her arms as if in anticipation of something—something unseen—that was drifting down the hall toward her. She could dodge out of its way, if only Tilly could see the ghostly memory of what had once been. A memory that had slammed a door shut in order to be heard?

No. Tilly blinked to clear her focus and bring her mind back to the present reality. Memories did not have voices. Walls did not talk. Spirits did not inhabit old rooms and shut doors.

Doors slammed in old houses all the time, and there was no anomaly in it at all. There were drafts, uneven floors, and even hinges that just gave in to the need to move after being stationary for a time.

Still . . . Tilly bit her bottom lip to hold back a tenuous smile that no one was there to see anyway. There was something intoxicating about it. Something that gripped at the places inside her that no one besides Grandpa Don seemed to understand. It was difficult to explain, so Tilly never really tried. That intrigue of uncovering secrets and details and a story. She could spend hours, intensely focused, just to learn every nuance and crevice and crook and cranny of a place. She would sometimes sit with her eyes closed, trying to hear the silent voices of the past. Tilly never really did, not audibly anyway. But she liked to believe that in the stillness, she could. That time could be bridged between the past and the present. She believed it could. But not through mechanisms or science. Instead, through memories. Through the clues left behind by those who had gone before.

James Mansion was one of those places that had beckoned to Tilly for years. This place breathed the stories of the ones who had passed through it. Those people who had left invisible marks, like unseen fingerprints that tempted Tilly to rediscover them.

The slam of the door might be explained by the shifting of a house or a draft that came and went. But Tilly believed that memories shouldn't be forgotten. They should be resurrected. To remind the living of good to be repeated and, more so, to warn them of the bad that should be forever forsaken.

IF WALLS COULD TALK

I am watching.

Each moment ticks by. Seconds on the hands of a clock.

One.

Two.

Three.

Four.

Five.

Each second has slipped into the past, and it will never be touched again. It will likely be forgotten. It will become a lost moment embedded in the walls, breathed in by the air, felt so briefly that it has neither emotion nor event to anchor it.

Instead, the seconds come to live within me, and I store them away somewhere deep and shadowed. In a place where no one will likely find them. I hide the seconds in the walls, beneath the floorboards, under the beds, and behind closed doors. I slip them into drawers and pockets, I attach them to mementos and photographs, and I stuff them away into corners that are covered in the webs that collect.

Time.

Time collects itself as memories.

There are times when a jolt occurs, and I return against my

will. There are moments when tears dampen my visit, yet there is a sweetness in their salt.

But more often, I am the walls that cannot speak. I have hidden myself there.

Yes.

I am there.

I am watching.

I am watching her now as she travels down the hallway, looking for the door that I closed. I am watching her now as she questions if she even heard me, let alone if she will see me.

I am watching her.

Because that is what memories do.

We watch, and we wait. And sometimes we come back to life.

3

Eloise James

Death is nothing at all.
It does not count.
I have only slipped away into the next room.
Nothing has happened.

Henry Scott Holland

October 1879
New Jamestown, Indiana

Rain. It rained and rained, and it didn't lessen in its torrential downpour, bathing her world in tones of gray and black and the effervescent color of liquid blue. Eloise wore black taffeta. Her sleeves were puffed at the shoulders, her bodice trim to her waist, her neckline choking her throat like strangling hands. The cemetery was empty, save for the many dead who soaked up the rain along with the earth. Stone after stone, marble towers, markers chiseled with names and dates and epitaphs that would make the most hardened of souls weep.

This was the future.

This was *her* future one day—and sooner if she wasn't careful. There were many things that could take a person's life, and in this moment, Eloise was sure her reason for death might be grief itself. Grief and the horrible realization that no matter her efforts, she made little difference in the life of the one she loved the most.

Evania.

Eloise paid no mind to her shoes as they squished into the sodden earth. Her black velvet hat with its swooping black netting wrapped around her face did nothing to keep the rain from soaking her hair, her skin, her shoulders.

The rain was relentless.

Her path through the cemetery was equally so. And she was not alone. The undertaker accompanied her on this grim walk.

"There." Eloise pointed to an empty plot positioned between two elaborate headstones. One for her grandparents, Eugene and Temperance James, and the other for her mother, Marjorie Staten James.

"I beg your pardon, Miss James, but—"

"Will she be buried there?" Eloise interrupted the undertaker, pointing with a wet, gloved hand to the empty section of earth.

"I'm sure it's not my place—"

"My father has already prepared for my sister to be interred here, has he not?" Eloise leveled her stare on the thin man, with an equally thin nose and cheekbones a person could slice cheese on, if they were of a mind to.

"I do believe that is something to be taken up with your father, Miss James."

Had he ever taken anything up with her father? Eloise surmised Mr. Lipping hadn't or he wouldn't have suggested the futile endeavor. It was why she was here, after all, to find out for herself.

Eloise was grateful for the rain. The fact that it hid the tears that hadn't stopped falling since she'd intercepted a letter from the Corinth Asylum for the Chronically Insane.

Dear Mr. James, Esquire,

It is with great concern that we write to inform you of the condition of your daughter, Miss Evania James, who has continued to decline to such a degree that we express our admonitions that she is not long for this world. . . .

There had been more, but Eloise didn't need to go on reading. Evania was dying, and the letter had been dated over six weeks ago. Father had done nothing, to the best of Eloise's knowledge. It seemed he was waiting for his daughter to die. It was as if he anticipated the missive that finally brought the news he was free of his wayward daughter. The daughter who had once brought joy to everyone she met. The daughter whose spirit had been stolen from her under the moral judgment not of God, but of society, of Father, and anyone else who knew she'd borne an illegitimate babe.

Was Eloise expected now to wait for Evania to return home, with only her body left as an empty shell to bury beside their mother? Eloise suspected Father had more than likely already made the arrangements. He was proactive when he wished to be. He would not be caught by surprise, nor would he be unprepared when the day of Evania's death arrived. That was who Father was, and that was what Eloise most despised about him. Still, she needed to know to be sure. There was always some small part of her that hoped she was wrong about him. That there was something salvageable in her father.

So now Eloise had come to the New Jamestown Cemetery not only to visit her mother—oh, how she missed her mother!—but to confirm if her suspicions were correct. That Father was waiting for Evania to die. A problem that he could easily bury and move on from.

It was almost too simple to read Father's mind, and she wished she was wrong, but knew that she wasn't. Father would expect for Evania to be laid to rest between her mother and grandparents. Then Father would likely imagine that Eloise would be the doting, grieving daughter who was always obedient. Eloise would bring Evania flowers in the spring. Tulips were Evania's favorite. She would bring her orange tiger lilies in the fall. In the winter, she would adorn Evania's grave with evergreen boughs and dried cranberries, so that in Evania's eternal slumber, the wild birds could be fed. Birds that flew free as Evania still should. That would be Father's plan. That would be what he pictured.

Something was breaking inside Eloise, something that had been brittle—fragile—for a long time. Her respect for her father, born out of training and expectation, was shattering into a million shards. Eloise was not finished questioning the undertaker. She knew he would eventually confirm that arrangements had indeed been made for the impending passing of Evania James.

"Has my father already chosen a coffin as well? A hearse? Will her name be etched on my mother's stone, or has Father arranged for Evania to have her own memorial marker?" Eloise had no intention of allowing Mr. Lipping to walk away. She knew her interrogation of him was unfair. The man would only do as he was hired to do. It wasn't Mr. Lipping's fault that Father was merely waiting for Evania's death like one anticipating relief.

Mr. Lipping blustered, raindrops rolling off the brim of his black hat. "I-I have not finalized arrangements with Mr. James." His admission was laced with an undisguised tone that it was not Eloise's place to demand answers. It was apparent he didn't appreciate that she'd insisted he show her the plot waiting for the next James family member who needed to be laid to rest. "I do extend my sympathies regarding your sister's unfortunate illness, but I must urge you to speak to your father. He will be of far more help than will I."

On that note, Mr. Lipping rudely turned away and walked back toward the carriage that awaited him. They had come separately, and Eloise knew that Mr. Lipping was probably very glad he had.

She ignored the fact that he'd abandoned her by the place where Evania would be buried if she were to pass away. Instead, Eloise stared down at the earth, challenging herself not to accept this as the final answer. Yes, she could speak to Father, but he would offer her no satisfactory explanation, and Eloise had no delusions that he would have a change of heart and seek to retrieve Evania to bring her home to be nursed back to good health. But if she did speak to Father, she knew he would be offended that Eloise dared to question his decision. It was, after all, the role of the women in the James home not to question, but to comply and, ideally, not even ask questions.

Eloise began her own slog toward her transportation. With the ground spongy beneath her feet, water bubbled with each footstep. She managed to make her way to the stone path that wound through the gravestones until she reached the wrought-iron fence. Pushing open the gate, she walked through, shutting it with a resounding latch.

Her driver opened the carriage door, and Eloise climbed inside. It was dry there, and her clothing dripped onto the leather seat and floorboards. She lurched forward as the carriage began to roll. The horses' clip-clopping on the brick road mixed with the pounding of the rain on the carriage roof.

Evania was dying.

God forbid, she might already be dead.

More than a month, Evania had been ill, and Eloise was learning of it only because she'd accidentally seen the missive lying open on Father's desk. Was there another letter telling of Evania's death, and Eloise had simply not found it yet? The horror of that thought made tears sting Eloise's eyes. The days and weeks since Evania's departure had been torture in James Mansion.

The hallways were empty. The rooms echoed with memories of Evania's infectious laughter. The windows remained closed at night, instead of sliding open to allow the rebellious but delightful young woman back inside long after dark.

It was only Father, herself, and the household staff. Eloise had little to do with her time except to volunteer at the Ladies' Guild and attend a few teas with women she had no endearing friendships with. They were society women, who judged each other with narrowed eyes and competed to be the best Christian woman in the church. A ludicrous idea, as all of them were sinners in God's eyes, and Eloise highly doubted God would be overly impressed by their efforts. If *she* had little patience for such piousness, surely the Lord felt the same. Even so, Eloise buried her own stubborn and tempestuous impulses deep inside herself. It was the right and proper thing to do, though she ached to be free of the restraints. She had always been what Father had trained her to be. Obedient. Submissive. Squashing her own spirit to allow his to be the authority. Wasn't that how it should be? And yet these last few weeks without Evania had made a startling impact on Eloise. She had considered her sister, compared herself to Evania, and even—God forbid—*admired* Evania's defiance.

Evania had rebelled against their father through her actions. Through behaviors that, if Eloise were frank, even she didn't approve of their morality. Yet how could she judge Evania for her desire to live, to love, and to be free of all constraints? Evania was bearing the consequences of those actions not only by the loss of her babe and the abandonment of the father whose name Evania never spoke, but now by Father's rejection and the obvious fact that he saw her as a problem to be rid of, not a daughter to be restored.

Eloise could not squelch her own stirring. The awakening of an anger she had not experienced so viscerally before. Not until Evania had been taken away, and not until Eloise had read the letter stating that given her condition, Evania was not long for the world. Was it rebellious to defy Father on behalf of and for the sake of Evania? Was it sinful to raise her chin and refuse to allow Father to forsake his daughter because of her sins? Was it immoral for Eloise to have her own mind, her own opinions, her own convictions? When God issued Scriptures commanding submission, did He truly mean for a woman or a child to be dominated and silenced?

Whatever the answers, Eloise was certain of one thing, and it was that Mr. Lipping was right. She must speak to her father. Regardless of the outcome and the consequences, she must hold him accountable. She might not be able to demand answers like a son, but she was owed them nonetheless, wasn't she?

Evania had been ripped from her. She had been imprisoned in a hospital where she was to have received care for a malady of the mind that Eloise believed should be attributed to grief and nothing else. Instead, Father was willing to stand back and let Evania die.

Eloise sat upright in her seat, the cold dampness of her dress chilling her. There was no comfort in a time like this. She mourned her sister. She had mourned her from the day Father had taken her away. That day had been its own sort of death. And now?

"O death, where is thy sting?"

Eloise knew exactly where death's sting had gone.

It had lodged in her heart, and it was not going away.

The only sounds in the dining room were the clinking of utensils against china plates, of Father chewing, his jaw cracking now and again, and his ever-present sniffing, as if some travesty had settled in his nose and he was offended by it.

There was a small fire in the fireplace. It, too, snapped and popped. The smell of roasted chicken filled the room. Sam, their footman, stood in the corner by the sideboard, waiting to be called upon or to refill their glasses. Father was drinking wine with his dinner. Eloise was not. She knew as soon as their meal was over, Father would retire to his study and pour himself a serving or four of brandy.

Her time was now, if there ever was one, and yet the silence was so heavy and so suffocating, Eloise was desperate to find the words.

Father found them for her. He speared a potato and eyed her as he chewed it. His dark eyes, dark hair, and peppered beard were expertly cared for. He was elegant and commanding.

"You were out in the rain this afternoon," he observed.

Eloise nodded, her throat tightening out of instinct and choking her words.

"Where did you go?"

Eloise rested her fork on the edge of her plate. She hadn't been very hungry to begin with. "I went to the graveyard."

"With as often as you go, your mother will never be lonely."

When Eloise didn't respond, Father considered her for a moment. "Or is your mother the reason you were there? It's obvious you have something to say, so say it." He took another bite, chewed, and waited for her to answer.

It was hardly a welcoming invitation, but she pressed on nonetheless. "Are you going to send for Evania so that we may care for her? I saw the letter—she is very ill."

Father swallowed. His expression did not change. "You needn't inform me of something I already know. You should also mind your own matters and not nose around in my personal papers."

"May we send for her?" Eloise tamped down her rising anxiety. "I will gladly tend to her, and I will—"

"She is already in a hospital. The asylum has the best of resources. We've nothing to offer your sister that they cannot see to there on our behalf."

"So you intend to let her die?" Eloise bit down on her tongue. She had surprised herself by her defiance.

Father, on the other hand, seemed unperturbed. "I intend to let God do as God sees fit."

"You're already making arrangements with Mr. Lipping at the cemetery," Eloise stated, this time tempering her tone so it was less accusatory and more inquiring.

Father set down his fork and heaved a sigh, indicating he was trying to be patient with her when she should just accept that he knew what best to do and she did not. "I am doing what is wise. It is unfortunate that your sister has not been well since . . . her behaviors of the past few months. But I cannot stand in the way of God's judgment, nor will I be unprepared when it comes. As should you. It is biblical, you see. One must not argue with God's disciplines."

"It also says that God disciplines those He loves, so I cannot imagine he would strike Evania dead. That hardly provides room for potential reconciliation. Besides, I cannot prepare for the death of my sister when it may be preventable," Eloise retorted, then bit her tongue from the sheer shock of her audacity.

Father lifted his napkin and dabbed his mouth before wadding it next to his plate. He was so casual, so undisturbed by it all, that Eloise wanted nothing more than to scream at him.

She didn't dare.

He sniffed, choosing to ignore further spiritual debate and instead address the matter at hand. "I gave the hospital permission to give your sister the best care that money can provide. Take comfort in that I've not yet received word that she has passed, so I can only assume she is still among the living."

Eloise couldn't help but respond, "Why prepare for her death at all, then?"

"They have their own cemetery at the asylum. If Evania were to pass away, she would be buried there unless we have made other arrangements. So I have done so." Father rested his elbows on the table and steepled his fingers, eyeing her. "You should be pleased I don't intend to allow your sister to be laid to rest in a communal cemetery set aside for the feeble of mind without a marker or a ceremony."

"With your permission"—Eloise found the words but delivered them carefully—"I would like to go to Evania. I would like to bring her home."

"Oh, Eloise." Father's look was one of pity. "From the moment your sister was sent away, she was never meant to return here. You know this. Her maladies were never going to be cured, only managed."

"Managed?" Disbelief weighted her question.

"Yes. Unfortunately, very few patients admitted to hospitals like the one Evania is in are ever released. Mind sicknesses do not just go away. If God sees fit to give Eloise passage to the beyond, then look upon it as a mercy, not a grief."

"As a mercy?" She shouldn't be so stunned at the callousness of Father's declaration, and yet Eloise was. "Were you even going to tell me that Eloise is very likely dying?"

"I didn't want to pain you." Father took a sip of what remained of his wine. "We have moved on with our lives, and I felt it benefited your constitution not to be burdened with it."

"Benefited my constitution?" A warning went off in Eloise's mind. Father had used words like that about Evania not long ago.

Constitution, condition.

Dare he begin to insinuate that she, too, was of a mindset that required more care?

Eloise treaded carefully with her following words. "My melancholy for Evania is that of a sister's loneliness. I wish to see her again. I wish to have her home."

"Perfectly understandable." He pushed up from the table. "But perhaps not beneficial—for either you or Evania. Allow your sister to rest in Fate's hands, Eloise. We must push forward. It may be difficult, I acquiesce, but it is necessary." With that, Father offered her a thin smile. One that indicated the conversation was over, and Eloise was to respect that boundary.

She watched as her father stood and left the dining room.

The candlelight flickered from the candelabra in the middle of the table. The food she had eaten soured in her stomach. Eloise took her time folding her napkin, attempting to collect her thoughts, if not her emotions.

A rustle from the corner snagged her attention, and Eloise realized she was not yet alone. She looked to Sam, who still remained in case service was needed. He did not give her direct attention but had politely fixed his eyes on something across the room.

Eloise couldn't help herself. She needed a listening ear, and while Sam was not typically someone she would confide in, at the moment he seemed her only option. "Did you hear my father?" The footman's eyes shifted to her; his expression was one of surprise and discomfort. "Uh . . . yes, miss."

"How am I to sit here and go about my evening as if my sister does not have need of me? As if my sister isn't dying alone without me?"

Sam blanched at her words.

Eloise continued unburdening herself to the footman, hoping Father wouldn't hear, but wishing she could find some relief from the feelings locked inside her.

"I've heard stories about places like the hospital Father sent Evania to. Awful, horrible things. Has he no mercy for my sister?" Eloise struggled to hold back the tears burning her eyes. Tears of fury and pain. Tears she never wanted Father to see and certainly hadn't intended for Sam to witness. Such vulnerability would be chatted about among the house staff if Sam decided to gossip. But that really didn't matter. What was a little gossiping behind her back compared to the wrongs committed against her sister Evania.

And they *were* wrongs! Regardless of Evania's behavior and any ownership she had in her actions, Father never should have condemned her to a hospital.

"Do you see any mercy at all in my father's decisions?" Eloise pressed the footman.

His eyes flickered—probably with fear lest he say something that might get him dismissed.

Eloise recognized the spot she had put him in. "Never mind," she added, taking pity on him. "It is unfair of me to ask you to question your employer's decisions." She considered, then tried again. "But if you were in my shoes, what would you do, Sam?"

The footman couldn't be much older than she was. In fact, they were likely the same age. Yet because they held such different stations in life, Eloise knew that Sam would respectfully make the assumption that her question was rhetorical. Yet it wasn't. She truly wanted to know. "Please. I promise your answer will not go beyond this room. I just . . . I have no one to ask, no one to—" Eloise let her sentence drop.

Sam succumbed to his discomfort and ran a gloved finger between his neck and his collar. But when he spoke, Eloise lifted hopeful eyes toward him. "Your father knows what he's about, miss."

"So you believe I must acquiesce to his decisions regarding my sister's care?"

He cleared his throat. "It's not my place to say, miss."

"But I've given you leave to be honest with me," she urged, and this time a desperate tear slipped down her cheek. "Please, Sam." Eloise pushed back in her chair and lifted pleading eyes to the footman. "I know we have our social ranks and all that nonsense, but what should I do? What would *you* do if you were me?"

Sam looked toward the door, then across the dining room to the other door. Seeing they were alone, he took a half step nearer, and his expression sharpened. Now that she had given him license to speak his mind, Eloise wasn't certain what he would advise.

"If I may," he began quietly, "were it me, Miss James, I would board the next train and go to the hospital myself. I would demand to see my sister. I would make an assessment regarding her well-being with my own eyes."

"I wouldn't dare," Eloise whispered.

"I never meant to imply that you would, miss." Sam straightened, returning to the proper pose of a footman at work.

Eloise turned back to the table, the candles still flickering like silent witnesses. Go to the asylum? It was surely run by a man, perhaps a board of men, and in serious matters like this, women had no voice. Even if Evania was well enough to be transported from the asylum into Eloise's care, that responsibility would never be allotted to her. Whatever Evania's condition, she was still subject to the authority of their father, and Eloise had little sway.

Swallowing back tears of frustration, she pushed to her feet, leaned forward to pick up a brass candlesnuffer where it lay beside the candelabra. She settled its cup over each of the candles, extinguishing their flames. When finished, six curls of smoke rose toward the ceiling, an omen of finality. Eloise started to leave the room but then hesitated, turning back toward Sam, who waited for her to exit before moving on with his duties. Only this time, the footman was confident enough to meet her gaze.

"I cannot go to my sister," Eloise admitted. "It is like a prison, and one must have a key to get in. The key is my father."

Sam didn't respond. He simply held her gaze, and Eloise wasn't sure if the look in the footman's eyes was pity or the wish that she would leave him and he would be released from having to express any opinion on a family matter that was none of his business.

At last, Eloise exited the dining room, slipping down the corridor toward the back entrance, which would lead her to the veranda and the gardens. She needed fresh air. She needed to escape the suffocating confinement of James Mansion, and the oppressive reality that there was likely nothing she could do to save Evania—even if she were brave enough to try.

4

> Time does not bring relief; you all have lied
> Who told me time would ease me of my pain!
>
> Edna St. Vincent Millay

Eloise had tossed and turned to such a degree that her bedcovers were torn from their tucks beneath the mattress and balled into a pile at the foot of the bed.

Go to her.

Go to her.

She could not free herself of the repetitive command that refused to let up. Was God himself urging Eloise to go to her sister? Or was she hearing her own internal voice, which warred to be given the freedom to think for herself, do for herself, and therefore go to Evania no matter what the outcome?

Sam the footman had said he would go were he in her position.

But Sam was a man.

But this was Evania. Her sister. If the situation were reversed, Eloise knew that Evania would have let nothing stand in her way. She would have gone to Eloise even if she had no plan or idea how to help Eloise leave the asylum.

Eloise rose at half past midnight.

Go to her.

She would go. She *had* to go. For Evania's sake.

Eloise was cautious as she moved about her bedroom. There was a small room just off her bedroom where her lady's maid, Ida, slept, but Ida had the hearing of a restless spirit, and Eloise wasn't sure she trusted Ida not to alert Father. While Ida had been a faithful maid, she was brusque and there was no affection between them. If Eloise was honest, Ida intimidated her because she was severe like a Puritan matron. She looked like one too. Ida was pasty and thin with dark, deep-set eyes, and when Evania was still at James Mansion, she teased behind her hand that Ida looked like a raven might if its feathers had been plucked. It was highly uncomplimentary, but it was also terribly accurate.

Eloise tiptoed across her room, her feet comforted by the velvet softness of the Oriental carpet. She lit a lamp perched on a gilded stool by her dressing table. Eloise paused, sure that somehow, in her sleep, Ida would see the lamplight and come to investigate. When she didn't stir, Eloise lowered herself onto her chair and looked at her reflection in the mirror.

The glowing lamplight was not particularly friendly to the image that stared back at Eloise. Her brown hair—almost pretty but not quite—hung in waves over her shoulders. Eloise had always considered it unfortunate that women were expected to pin up their hair to avoid a wanton, disheveled appearance, because she thought if she could leave her hair down, perhaps she would look prettier than she was. Her face was narrow, and some might say it tended to be a bit long, as was her nose, and while her eyes were a pretty green, they were usually hidden behind round, gold-rimmed spectacles that gave her a decidedly schoolmarmish appearance.

However, as Eloise assessed her face, she also admitted that being average or plain was to her advantage now. She could travel without being afraid of untoward looks as she strolled down the street, as Evania had. She didn't wish to draw attention.

For by this time tomorrow, she should be a few hours away at the Corinth Asylum for the Chronically Insane. And those in charge would be made to acknowledge Eloise's anger as well as her determination to see her sister. She only hoped upon her arrival that she would be able to muster the courage necessary to face them and not back down.

They *would* let her see Evania.

They *would* make arrangements with Eloise for Evania's care, even if that meant allowing her to return home in spite of Father and his wishes.

"May I assist you with something, miss?"

The nasally voice spoken over Eloise's shoulder caused her to yelp, and she startled backward as Ida's face suddenly appeared in the mirror's reflection.

"Ida!" Eloise splayed her hand across her chest. "You terrified me."

The maid, likely in her early forties—Eloise had never dared to ask—looked as apologetic as a skeletal, featherless raven could.

"My apologies, miss. I heard movements and thought perhaps you were ill?" The woman blinked.

Eloise sometimes wondered if Ida was required to give regular reports to Father as to her goings-on. She met Ida's eyes in the mirror. "I'm not ill, no. Merely restless," she explained. She intended to pack some clothes and necessities for her trip, which Eloise of course did not mention.

"Would you like me to get you some chamomile tea to help you sleep?"

"No, no." Eloise waved her off. "Truly, I'll be fine. Go back to bed, Ida."

The woman considered for a moment, then gave a short nod. She turned and walked back toward the open door that connected her sleeping quarters to Eloise's expansive room. For a moment, she thought Ida looked like a ghost. Her white nightgown glowed in the lamplight, and her peppery-brown hair melded into the darkness.

If she could only find kinship with Ida or believe the lady's maid truly had her best interests at heart, then Eloise would have brought her into her confidence. As it was, she waited for the door to close, the latch to click, and the seconds to tick by.

Reassured that Ida was not going to offer further service, Eloise moved to retrieve a carpetbag from her wardrobe. As she packed a few belongings, she considered the ramifications of her actions. Getting to the train station to take the train two hours south of New Jamestown would not be difficult but was probably not safe. She would need to walk there in the dead of night. Or she could awaken Kenny and ask him to drive her. Yes. That would be the wisest option. But then she would need to pray that Father would not awaken, and Ida would stay in her bed.

However, from there, she would be on her own. And to travel unchaperoned? Eloise knew *that* was not wise. A well-bred lady did not travel alone. In which case she should perhaps consider bringing Ida into her confidence and taking her along.

Eloise winced. What was she thinking? This behavior—sneaking out of the house in the night—was what had led Evania down the dark road to the asylum. Of course, she wasn't slipping out under cover of darkness to meet a man, but would Father see it as anything other than outright rebellion? Once Eloise had departed on the train, it would be too late to return without him knowing she had left James Mansion. Her leaving would be discovered by morning.

And then Father might never let her back into James Mansion. In fact, he might disown her entirely, or worse, purchase a permanent residency for her at the hospital where Evania now suffered. Dr. Merriweather would no doubt be glad to add another deranged feminine mind to his tally. If he kept it up, New Jamestown would incarcerate all of its women in asylums for being ill of mind and body. Under his watchful eye, a woman already had enough to do to temper her emotions during the time each month when they threatened to spiral into unpredictability.

Eloise caught sight of a reflection in the mirror of something behind her. She blinked, thinking her eyes were playing tricks on her, then looked around the room, going from corner to corner. She thought she had just seen another person in her bedroom. The figure had moved so quickly. A shadow.

"Ida?"

The room was empty but for Eloise.

She stared into the mirror again, which now reflected only the furniture behind her. But there had been something, *someone*, Eloise was sure of it! For a split second, a face had been barely legible in the far corner. Eloise had seen its shape, the eyes, and she blinked only to have it vanish.

"Hello?" she whispered so as not to awaken Ida. Her heart pounded as she craned her neck to peer into the corner. Eloise then eyed the draperies. A window exposed the night outside, the drapes having been pushed aside that morning and not closed this evening on Eloise's request. She liked to lie in bed and look out the window, up at the stars and the moon. But now she wished she'd had Ida draw them shut. They wouldn't collect then in thick folds, and her imagination wouldn't picture someone tucked behind them, discreetly watching her.

Was the room spinning?

Eloise grabbed the post at the foot of her four-poster bed, hugging it to steady herself. Fear heightened her senses, and she blinked rapidly as her vision blurred and then cleared, even as an urgent horror squeezed her heart.

She was not alone.

Go to her.

Someone was hiding behind the drapes.

Eloise stumbled, reaching for her bed and sinking against it for stability.

Go to her.

"I'm coming," Eloise whispered, yet her voice sounded loud in her ears. "I'm coming, Evania."

With hesitant steps, she made her way toward the imposing draperies, which swayed in, out, around. Or perhaps it was the room that swayed? Eloise could see the draperies come to life, waving back and forth, arms extending out from behind them, reaching for her . . .

Eloise tumbled to the floor, her knees giving way.

Her room fell into an abysmal darkness, and she saw no more.

"Miss James!" Ida's hand tapped Eloise's face. "Miss James, are you all right?"

A heaviness pressed against Eloise. It felt as though someone was squeezing her head between their palms. It was hard to breathe. She tried to see who or what it was, but her eyelids were so heavy, and when she did manage to open them, the room was warped. The walls were moving inward and then out, as if they were breathing. Her body was falling, and she could feel the floor giving way beneath her.

Eloise grabbed at the lady's maid, taking hold of her arm and clinging to it.

"Miss James! Shall I call for a doctor?" Ida's voice grew more urgent.

Eloise shook her head, attempted to open her eyes again, and this time the room had righted itself. The walls were back in place. The draperies were limp. The heaviness had lifted, and Eloise blinked several times to reorient herself. "Help me sit up," she gasped.

Ida positioned herself so she could boost Eloise into a sitting position. As Eloise leaned back against the wooden bed frame, Ida hurried over to the window and opened it wide. "Fresh, cool air, Miss James. That's what you need."

A wave of crisp, autumn night air wafted into the bedroom.

Ida was right, Eloise did feel a bit revived. She drew in a deep breath, drinking in the fresh air. "I don't know what came over me." She swiped a hand over her eyes, willing them to see clearer. "After you left me, I thought I saw someone else in here. Then the room began to spin and–"

"Left you?" Ida turned a knob on the wall, causing the gaslights to illuminate the room, bringing it to life in a way the lone kerosene lamp could not. "I was never here, Miss Eloise."

"But you came to check on me?" Eloise argued. "You offered to get me some tea."

Ida frowned, looking peckish that Eloise didn't believe her. "I promise you, Miss Eloise, this is the first I've been in your room since we retired."

The women exchanged looks, and Eloise shrank against the bed.

"You were walking in your sleep again," Ida added, resting her hands at her thin hips.

"But . . ." Eloise bit her tongue. What could she say? She had wandered in her sleep for years. But this time it had seemed so real. She had been sure someone was in the room. She could recall so clearly speaking with Ida.

Ida stood over the bed, gazing down at the carpetbag, clothes laid out beside it–stockings and undergarments, even a dress that Eloise had been intending to put on before sneaking away from the house.

"And were you packing to go somewhere in your sleep?" Ida asked. The question wasn't accusatory but more of an inquiry.

"No!" Eloise protested, pushing up from the floor onto her knees. That was an error. The room spun for a moment, and she squeezed her eyes shut against the whirling. "Please, no. I wasn't sleeping when I . . ." Or had she been? Eloise remembered her fitful attempts to fall asleep. Then her sudden surge of resolution to leave the house, to awaken Kenny for a ride to the train station. "I . . ." She struggled to explain as she used the bed to pull herself to her feet.

Ida gave her a sideways look. "What about the carpetbag, Miss Eloise?" She reached out and lifted one of its handles. "If not packing in your sleep, then . . ." The words hung between them, unfinished but indicting.

Eloise jerked the bag toward her. She began stuffing her belongings into it, wanting to put a stop to Ida's questions. "I was just curious, if I were ever to travel, how much I could fit in my bag." A paltry excuse, and Eloise knew it the second it left her mouth.

Ida's birdlike eyes met Eloise's. She was not fooled. She lifted her chin, and her nose became even more like a raven's beak at that angle. "Ever to travel? Are you considering going somewhere?"

Eloise tried to be firm. Kind, but firm. "That really is none of your business, Ida." She heard the quaver in her voice and knew she had been unsuccessful.

Still, Ida seemed to understand her place. "You're right, Miss James."

Eloise managed a smile to offset her sternness. Ida was always proper and careful, mindful of her position in the house, and yet there were times Ida seemed more like a governess and Eloise a young child. Those times were much like tonight. When Eloise would wander in her sleep. When she was vulnerable and disoriented. When they were all trying to keep Father from realizing how often the wandering occurred. Especially when Eloise was anxious about something. Father mustn't know, Evania had insisted. Father would think Eloise was losing her mind.

Which was ironic now that Evania—the sister who was most in control of herself, the most confident, and the most likely to succeed at independence—was the one taken to an institution.

"Please return to bed," Eloise assured her maid. "I am quite all right now, and I apologize for giving you a scare." She stuffed a nightgown into the carpetbag.

Ida watched her.

Eloise paused.

Their eyes locked.

Hesitation mixed with suspicion in Ida's. "I realize I am overstepping," she began, "but I do sense something more is amiss and you need my assistance."

Amiss?

Oh, everything was amiss, that was certain. If Ida had been a friend, Eloise would have confided in her that Evania was dying in Corinth Asylum. That Father had no intention of going to rescue her. That Eloise was gathering her courage to defy him and bring Evania home. And that she had no idea how to do it, save getting herself on a train and going there.

5

Tilly Thompson

When I am dead, my dearest,
Sing no sad songs for me;

And if thou wilt, remember,
And if thou wilt, forget.
Christina Rossetti

Present Day

She had wiped down every windowsill, molding, wall panel, and railing. Finials had been polished. Windows had been cleaned. Spiderwebs had been eradicated. Even so, Tilly's never-ending to-do list seemed to be growing longer by the minute.

Yet she wasn't stressed. No. Now, as Tilly leaned against the doorframe and watched her grandpa, she was grateful that she could be his full-time caregiver. Between his retirement and VA benefits, there was allowance for it, and when Grandpa Don asked her last year if she'd be willing to be his companion and aide, it had been a no-brainer.

"Just goin' to stand there and watch me play with my trains?" Grandpa Don's back was to her as he bent over the long table Erik had helped set up as the platform for the model train.

"No." Tilly took a sip of her coffee. "I have plans."

"Are you going to share them?"

Would he remember them if she did? Tilly processed that question before she answered. His Alzheimer's was going to get worse—it was inevitable—but if the worst she had to process today was fear of what was to come versus what was, then she would accept that and not borrow trouble.

"I can get you a copy of my to-do list," she offered, pulling her phone from her pocket. She could print it out using the printer she'd already set up in the library upstairs.

He waved her off without looking at her. "No, no." Grandpa Don chuckled. "You go on and do what you need to. I'm good here."

Tilly took him at his word and left him. He would keep himself entertained for hours in the downstairs room. Tilly was fairly certain it had once been used as a parlor and later converted into a family room in the 1990s. Now it served the purpose of Grandpa Don's model train room, and the man who had gifted her with James Mansion was in his glory, surrounded by boxes of track and train cars.

Tilly's to-do list today, though, was less task-oriented and more of appeasing some curiosities that had been building in her the last two days of living in James Mansion. She rested her coffee mug on a small table in the parlor by the front door, then sat on the landing of the main staircase leading to the second floor. She eyed the arched stained-glass window facing her at the top of the wide, wooden stairwell. With her love of history, Tilly had studied enough old homes to know that in Victorian times, people often relied on windows to light their homes' staircases.

And this was why her curiosity was piqued. The way the stairs were positioned, along with the elegant glass window at the top of the first landing on the eastern wall, led them to turn left and continue upward. Which meant the wall to the right of the stairs was an exterior southern wall. It would have made sense, then, considering the architectural design and need for natural light, for a window to have been placed there too. But there was no such window. Tilly could have let it go, but then she was sure she had seen evidence of what looked like the framework for a potential window in the limestone outside wall.

Bounding down the stairs, she made her way to the main entrance and stepped onto the front porch. The chilly October breeze didn't faze her as she hurried down the steps and onto the expansive lawn. Heading toward the east side of the property, Tilly stopped to face the mansion.

The entrance occupied the eastern side of the grand front porch, where it curved around and jutted back to a side entrance. Tilly knew that if she entered through that door, she would find herself in a small room with stairs leading to the basement and a confined entryway opposite, one that had a door leading to Grandpa Don's conservatory train room. The porch ended at the side door, and the wall that extended upward to the roofline of the second story boxed in the stairwell.

Tilly perched her hands on her hips. It was the chimney that jutted out from the main structure that captured her focus. If she took several steps to her right, she could see the stained-glass stairwell window into the east side of the house. It was as tall and beautiful on the outside as it was on the inside. But if she returned to her original position and faced the stairwell wall that ran at a ninety-degree angle to the stained-glass window, there was definitely the limestone outline of what looked to have once been another window. Just as she had imagined it would have been. But where a window may have been, it was instead filled in by gray stone.

Tilly frowned. It didn't make any sense as to why someone would have either framed in a window and then decided against it, or if there really had been a window installed at one point, and for whatever reason, why someone had decided to remove it.

"Can I help you?"

Tilly startled at the intrusion. She turned toward the sound of the woman's voice, which came from the sidewalk beyond the ornate limestone retaining wall. She looked to be in her mid- to late thirties, dressed in a wool plaid skirt, a navy peacoat, and a jaunty beret perched on short brown curls.

Tilly didn't recognize her, nor did she have any idea why this stranger would be offering to help her. "No, thank you." As the stranger remained with a perplexed look on her face, Tilly decided to add, "I live here."

"Oh!" The woman's face brightened, and she helped herself to hiking up the three stone steps that led from the sidewalk to James Mansion's yard and cobblestone path that led to the front entrance. She hurried toward Tilly, her hand outstretched in greeting. "*You're* the new owner!"

Tilly took the stranger's hand with reluctance, returning the handshake.

The woman's brown eyes flashed with life and energy. "I had *no idea* someone so young had purchased the mansion. I thought for sure it'd be a stodgy, middle-aged couple with grandiose plans to turn it into a bed-and-breakfast." She stopped, bit her bottom lip, and winced. "You aren't turning it into a B and B, are you?"

"No," Tilly reassured her.

"Oh, good." The woman laughed, a soft trill sound that eased some of Tilly's discomfort. "I'm Daphne, by the way." Finally. A name. "Daphne Dover." She waited as though Tilly was going to recognize it. When Tilly didn't react, she finished, "From Dover Memorials."

"Oh!" Awareness flooded Tilly. "The funeral home." The primary funeral home in New Jamestown. It had been in existence almost as long as James Mansion.

"That's right." Daphne's smile was bright and friendly. "I grew up alongside the last family to live here. It's been years since a James lived here." She clucked her tongue. "It's sad to see the family wither away . . ." She let her sentence hang and gave her head a slight shake as if to chase away unwelcome thoughts. "But now you own it! How wonderful! You can bring life back into this place, and God knows it needs it. Is it just you, then, living here by yourself?"

Tilly was digesting Daphne's chatter, but she managed to piece it together and respond, "My grandfather and I live here together."

"And you are?"

Tilly felt the blush creep up her neck. She far preferred interacting with inanimate objects or Grandpa Don than being sociable with strangers. "I'm Tilly Thompson. My grandfather is Don."

"Yes." Daphne snapped her fingers and pressed her lips together in a satisfied smile. "I thought you looked familiar. You're Erik's sister, aren't you?"

"I am."

"I graduated with your brother. Daphne Morrow. Daphne Dover now."

The space between the women was filled with the expectation that Tilly would respond with warmth and realization as to who Daphne was. Instead, Tilly tried to avoid the unease that filled her. *This* was Daphne? From high school? Sure, she was three years older than Tilly, and even though it seemed Daphne didn't recall her clearly, she certainly remembered Daphne now. She was the girl in her brother's class who had ghosted him on prom night. Tilly had never liked Daphne. Even though their town was small and their school average-sized, she'd avoided Daphne. Daphne had been known for being spiteful.

She was also known for having dated Luke James, who'd been

part of the last family to live in the mansion. Luke was currently running for town mayor, and he had made Tilly's life miserable in school. Why would the star senior on the football team target a lowly freshman girl who had made it her goal to stay out of everyone's way? Tilly had never really understood it. At the time, Erik said it had something to do with the fact that he and Luke had been rivals, and making Tilly his target was Luke's way of getting to Erik. Tilly wondered if it was because she had somehow threatened Luke's intelligence. In spite of their three-year age gap, she was in two of Luke's classes because she was advanced. History being one of them. She knew Luke had barely passed with a C average, which was necessary to play football. So maybe that was why he'd picked on her incessantly? Among other things. Yes, Tilly avoided Luke James as if he were the Black Plague. And Daphne wasn't much better.

Daphne's eyes clouded at Tilly's silence. Tilly had a feeling that similar realizations were dawning on Daphne at the same moment Tilly was trying to reconcile the fact that high school was more than a decade ago. They should all have outgrown the drama, right?

"I've changed since high school." It was a little pitiful the way Daphne pushed the words out so quickly, as if she wanted to convince Tilly without giving Tilly a chance to see it for herself.

Tilly believed she should be polite, but she wasn't going to offer forgiveness for Daphne standing Erik up on her own doorstep at prom. She didn't have much patience for people who didn't treat others kindly. Tilly would never forget how Erik had skipped prom. He'd come home, corsage thrown in the trash, and clomped up the stairs to play video games instead. Tilly learned later that Daphne had gotten back together with Luke James right before prom night. She'd failed to tell Erik. Eventually, Daphne had broken it off with Luke again, and that was that. But it didn't change what had happened so many years ago. To Tilly. To Erik.

"Erik is married now." Tilly grimaced. That wasn't exactly what she'd been thinking she should say.

"I know!" Daphne's smile was surprisingly kind. "We've grown up and changed."

So apparently, Daphne had kept track of Erik, Tilly concluded.

"I'm married too," Daphne continued. "To Mitch Dover."

Of Dover Funeral Home. Yes. Tilly had deduced that. She shifted her weight to her other foot, casting a glance at what she thought might once have been a window. She'd have to rip out the south wall on the stairwell to confirm it. But–

"I have two kids." Daphne's announcement broke into Tilly's wandering thoughts. "A boy and a girl. Jacob and Lily."

Tilly nodded politely, wishing that Daphne would leave.

Instead, Daphne shifted her attention back to the mansion. She crossed her arms in a relaxed stance and issued a nostalgic sigh. "The hours I spent in this place growing up. Luke and I were best friends since we were in third grade."

Tilly hadn't known that. She dared to ask, "Do you know if there was ever a window there?" She pointed to the outer wall.

Daphne frowned, considering. "No. I don't think there was. That's the stairwell, isn't it?"

Tilly nodded.

"There was always just the one big stained-glass window. Such a gorgeous example."

"Ah." Tilly nodded. It could be that what looked like a window frame was in fact just a design feature.

"However," Daphne continued, shaking her index finger, "I do remember when Luke was maybe ten or eleven, his mother went on a redecorating kick. That's when they added that garish wallpaper."

"Actually, it's authentic to the era the mansion was built," Tilly offered.

"Maybe." Daphne smiled patiently. "But I recall them stripping off the old wallpaper, and there was discoloration on the plaster underneath. They talked of the possibility of mold, but Luke's mom just papered right over it anyway."

"Mold?" Tilly shuddered. That wouldn't be good, especially if it'd never been addressed.

"Or something, I don't know. You could ask Luke." Daphne's declaration was stated matter-of-factly.

Ask Luke James? Tilly had no desire to approach the man who looked and acted like he'd walked out of a political version of *GQ* magazine—the man who'd never apologized for being the stereotypical high school jerk.

"If you want, *I* can ask Luke for you?" Daphne offered. She tacked on a sheepish smile. "Time alters friendships. My husband and I are good friends with Luke. Luke has changed. Especially with his brother Kyle . . ."

The words hung between them. Everyone in New Jamestown knew that the current mayor, Luke's older brother Kyle, had been diagnosed with stage 4 lung cancer. Of course, that meant Luke would pick up the mayoral baton that seemed to almost belong to the James family. It *was* New Jamestown, after all. Their history had been long in this place.

Daphne continued when Tilly didn't reply. "I feel awful for Kyle and Luke. They've always been so close, and now . . . well, you know. I just feel bad."

The ironic thing was that the man running against Luke James for mayor, the man Tilly intended to vote for, was Will Morrow, Daphne's brother. The dynamics of a small town were always a bit like a soap opera, Tilly admitted. While Tilly had never been a fan of Daphne, Will's entire grassroots campaign claimed it was time for fresh blood in leadership in New Jamestown. The James family had dominated the town for over a century.

It might be petty, but with the memories of Luke James's actions toward her when in high school, Tilly was totally willing to post a *Vote for Will Morrow* sign in her front yard.

"It's so awkward!" Daphne kept chattering. "I mean, my own

brother running against Luke, who's my friend?" She turned wide, dramatic eyes on Tilly and waited for a reaction. When Tilly didn't give her any, she dialed back the intensity. "Anyway, if you want, I can ask Luke about the house for you."

Tilly didn't want Daphne to butt her way into the business of James Mansion, let alone invite the one remaining James family member into it. Sure, Luke's input might be helpful as it pertained to the history, but it was *their* house now. She didn't need Luke James to express any regrets about selling his family home, nor did she want him involved in anything to do with her. So what if high school was over a decade ago? She could still feel the ache that Luke James had instilled in her.

Besides, it was just a window. A window that probably never existed.

No, it wasn't worth the hassle.

"If there was evidence of mold two decades ago, then we should get that wall checked out." Erik planted his feet on the glass-topped table on the back veranda of James Mansion. He exchanged looks with his wife, Ashley.

Grandpa Don rocked in his wooden rocking chair, tendering a cup of coffee in a Corelle coffee cup circa 1984. He'd used it for as long as Tilly could remember. It had mushrooms decorating it in shades of brown and orange.

Tilly regretted bringing up the conversation with Daphne. The last thing she wanted to do was start ripping off wallpaper and inspecting for mold, but it was also going to eat at her now. Another line item on the to-do list. It was something that should be investigated at the very least. But it could open up a whole can of worms, and as she considered the tick marks of things still to get done, Tilly tried to reassure herself as much as her brother.

"I'm sure it's fine," she stated.

"A mold inspector may not be a bad idea," Ashley interjected.

"The place was inspected before I bought it," Grandpa Don retorted, sipping at his coffee, which had to be lukewarm by now.

"Inspected for a home sale, yes, Grandpa, but that didn't include an expert mold inspection. I wish you had, to be honest. These old homes can be filled with toxic—"

"We're not getting a mold inspection." Grandpa Don's interruption of Erik was sharp. It was inconsistent with his traditional way of reasoning with others. This was a side of Grandpa that was beginning to rear its ugly head more often. Alzheimer's was increasing his lack of patience and heightening his need to show everyone he was still in charge.

"Maybe just that wall?" Erik pressed.

Grandpa Don flung his mug toward the yard, tossing out the remainder of his coffee. "Who put you in charge of my home?" His blue eyes snapped as he leveled a glare at Erik.

"Well, you asked me to help with decisions as they related to your finances and investments."

Grandpa Don shoved up from his chair, the rocker swaying back and forth with vehemence. "Biggest mistake of my life!" He hobbled away, disappearing into the mansion with a fluster of swinging open the door and then banging it shut.

Silence ensued for a bit before Ashley reached across to squeeze Erik's arm in reassurance.

He looked at her. "I'm fine. It's the disease speaking."

"He didn't mean it," Tilly said.

Erik shifted his attention to her. "Are you sure you're up to this? I mean, long-term care for Grandpa is going to be demanding. As the Alzheimer's takes over, he could become someone else completely—someone we don't recognize."

"He's worth it," Tilly answered without hesitation. And he was. He was her safe person, no matter the disease.

"You're so devoted," Ashley said with a smile. "I admire that about you."

Erik shifted in his chair. "About that wall—"

"Let it go, hon," Ashley admonished.

"I want to take a look at it first." Erik eased out of his chair and headed inside. Tilly and Ashley shared exasperated looks.

Tilly followed him inside, Ashley motioning that she was going to check on Tilly's nieces, who were playing in the backyard. Tilly glanced into the train room, and sure enough, Grandpa Don was hunched over a table, tweezers in hand, settling Spanish moss around a model building. He was mumbling to himself, the picture of serenity. His cranky outburst seemed forgotten already, and he'd put a cassette tape in his old player. Neil Diamond's music lingered in the air as Tilly hurried to catch up with Erik.

Erik was already at the landing, silhouetted in the dusk by the arched stained-glass window. He faced the southern wall, running his palm over the gold damask wallpaper.

Tilly perched on the steps below him.

"I don't see any signs of mold." Erik's words were no consolation. He began picking at the wallpaper.

"Don't rip it!" Tilly protested.

"There's a corner here that's come loose." Erik leaned in closer, his fingernail lifting part of the aged wallpaper that was indeed detached from the wall's surface.

Tilly regretted ever bringing up the possible mold issue. She also regretted mentioning Daphne Dover. Erik had chuckled and waved it away as a silly high school memory. Right now, her older brother was making her anxious, and Tilly wanted to stop him. Frankly, she needed Erik to go home. He was getting nosy, and she knew him well enough to know that if she let him continue, he'd end up ripping the wallpaper off entirely. And she'd never be able to find replacement wallpaper to match the pattern. "Please don't—"

Too late. Erik pulled back the paper, which tore upward, leaving some of its backing stuck to the plaster behind it.

"Erik!" Tilly exclaimed. He was going too far. She'd never match the wallpaper to repair it, and he was too flippant about everything.

"Sorry." Erik's apology was the typical empty apology of an older brother. He was placating her. "Check it out."

Nose to the wall, Erik ran his index finger across a patch of black dots of something. "Mold."

"You don't know that it's mold." Tilly's anxiety was fast-growing. "Erik, you're wrecking the wallpaper!"

"Mold is serious business." His look of concern should be endearing because Erik was only this stubborn when he was worried about her. He had always been protective of Tilly. But he was also irrationally insensitive without realizing it. "You and Grandpa will want to look into it if you'll be living here."

"Erik!" The ripping sound of more paper turned Tilly's anxiety into frustration.

He ignored her as older brothers who know better do. "Yeah. It's definitely mold."

Tilly eyed the small black dots. "Leave it be."

He pushed on the wall and raised his brows, giving Tilly an I-told-you-so look. "It's not good, pup. The entire wall here is yielding to my hand pressure."

"You're going to put a hole in it!" Tilly proclaimed. She hurried up the remaining steps. "If there's mold, then yes, we need to have it treated, but please don't ruin the wall." Things were getting out of hand.

"It's weakened." Erik pressed again to prove his point, looking at Tilly.

A snap and a crunch filled the air between them, and the wall caved in sickly soft submission as Erik's hand pushed through.

He cursed, snatching his hand back.

Tilly moaned, throwing her head back toward the ceiling. "Erik!"

"I'm sorry!" This time he sounded a little more contrite. "The wall just–"

"Please, leave it alone!" Tilly grabbed at her brother's arm. He wasn't wrong that the mold needed to be addressed, but he was doing things out of order. There needed to be a system, and Erik just charging in and breaking things wasn't part of it.

They wrestled like siblings back in grade school for a moment until finally Erik stepped back, dropping his hand.

The hole in the wall gaped at them as though the house itself was offended at the defacement.

Finally, Erik turned to her with a sheepish expression. "You're gonna need to get that fixed."

6

Death is the veil which those who live call life;
They sleep, and it is lifted.

Percy Bysshe Shelley

The house talked after the lights went out. Tilly was sure of it. She could hear moans in the walls. She was being watched. And yet she wasn't. Inanimate objects were spiritless, and dead people didn't hover in the corners. But now her senses and her reason were conflicted. She was hearing whispers. Not audibly, of course, but it was as though something in the house—in the walls—were desperately trying to speak. They were strangled by time and had no mouthpiece. Still, she heard the house and sensed its eyes on her. The inaudible voice was louder now that Erik had shoved a hole into the stairwell's wall.

Tilly sat up in her bed, pushing herself against the headboard and drawing her knees up to her chest. The room was dark, except for the essential oil diffuser in the far corner. She had set it to a red light at first, but that had felt devilish, so Tilly had long since opted for a soft green glow. It filled the room now.

No.

Wait.

She squeezed her eyes shut and then reopened them. The light was purple. When had she switched the light to purple? It had been green, Tilly was certain of it.

She ran her palms down the side of her face. Her skin was sweaty. Tilly realized her shirt stuck to her back, and her sheets were damp.

Help me.

She heard it as clear as day. But it also seemed far away, a distant echo.

Help me.

Tilly slipped from her bed, her bare feet hitting the cool wood floor. It was twelve steps to the doorway, this she knew. And she tried to ground herself in the reality of it as she counted off the steps.

One.

Two.

A door slammed.

Tilly stopped. Was it a door? It sounded more like a shutter banging against a window.

A trickle of sweat traced a path down her temple. Tilly swiped it away. The room seemed to breathe, the walls pressing in and then expanding.

Help me.

Make it stop. Tilly wanted to make it stop. The voice. But she couldn't. Tilly found herself standing in her bedroom doorway. The second floor was dark, all the lights turned off with the exception of a glow that came from the staircase. Had she left a light on downstairs? Was Grandpa Don awake and moving about?

Slowly, Tilly moved toward the stairs, the light beckoning her. It flickered on the ceiling. Someone had lit candles. The sconce. At the bottom of the stairs. A century ago, it would have been a source of light for the stairwell. But now? Who had lit candles?

She smelled candle wax and smoke as she reached the top of

the stairs. Looking down, she saw the stained-glass window was dark, but the wall where she'd thought a window should be but wasn't shone with a golden light.

Her vision drifted to the hole in the wall. Was the voice coming from inside the wall?

Tilly tried to take a step forward, but instead she grabbed for the railing as the stairs seemed to move beneath her feet. Steadying herself, she managed to descend them, her eyes fixed on the hole in the wall.

Help me.

The stairs were dark. The ceiling was high here, and for a moment, Tilly could almost envision a wraith hovering above her in the chimney-like space, its ragged black cloak hanging from it.

Watching.

Always watching.

Tilly's breaths came shorter and faster now.

Help me.

Why wouldn't it stop? There was no voice—not really. If anyone were to stand next to her now, they would hear nothing but the very normal ticking of the grandfather clock downstairs.

But Tilly could *feel* it—the cold whisper at her ear.

Help me.

It was coming from the hole in the wall.

It pulled Tilly toward it, almost against her will. She reached for the hole, her fingers shaking as they traced the gap. The ragged plaster edges. It was dark behind it. The secret innards of the mansion.

Tilly peered into the hole, straining to see inside and into the framework. Without thinking, she hooked her fingers on the plaster edge and pulled. Earlier in the evening, she had wanted order and a plan, but now? Now there was an urgency that filled her and awakened her nerves. The need to save—save something or someone.

Help me.

The wall released a chunk of plaster with a shower of debris crumbling onto the tops of her feet. The hole was bigger now. Tilly could see the old brick of the outside wall. It was blue in the darkness. The deep navy blue of night. She breathed in the smell of mildew and a faint tang she could only assume was dust mixed with moisture from the outside wall.

Tilly clawed at the wall again in a frantic gesture coupled with inexplicable urgency. She was trying to free whatever was calling to her soul. Whatever it was from the years that filled the chasm and was locked in the wall by the mansion's secrets.

Tilly reached with both hands now, the hole the width of her head. She pulled, and a large piece crumbled beneath her grip. It landed in a pile at her feet, some of the chunks bouncing off her toes.

Help me.

This time the words came with clarity. They filled the distance between Tilly and the wall. They exhumed decades that had been held captive there. They spoke, though their plea was too late.

Tilly stared into the hollow eye sockets of a dead woman.

Stumbling backward, her hands came up to cover her mouth and stifle the scream that released in a suffocated choke.

The body's jaw hung low, the mouth gaping in its desperate plea. The ragged remains of a woolen Victorian dress clung to the skeleton that was a combination of bone and brown leathery patches. Where the dress had disintegrated, metal buttons, green with corrosion, clung to the unmistakable outline of the rib cage.

Help me.

Help me.

Help me.

But Tilly was well over a century too late.

"Tilly. Tilly, girl."

Grandpa Don's voice came from a distant place.

Tilly moaned, her head pounding and her body aching. She moved to readjust but was met with hands holding her back.

"No, Tilly. You'll roll down the steps."

She wrestled to open her eyes. Heaviness weighed her down. Tilly reached up to push it off her, but there was nothing there.

A hand patted her cheek. "There we go," Grandpa Don murmured as Tilly finally managed to open her eyes.

Disoriented, she looked around her. She lay on the landing of the staircase. It 1was lit only by the modern electric light Grandpa Don must have turned on himself. There were no candles burning in the antique wall sconce below the stairs.

"Wait. I . . ." Tilly struggled to sit up. There were pieces of plaster lying on the floor around her legs and on her body. "What happened?" She lifted her eyes and met the horror in her dreams.

The dead woman's remains gaped at her from behind the wall.

Tilly scrambled on her backside to get away from it.

"It's all right." Grandpa Don reached for her to help quell her panic. "Shh."

"There's a . . ." Tilly pointed.

"I know, I know." Grandpa Don eased his aged frame into a sitting position on the stairs. "I heard a ruckus and came to check on you. And there you were, tearing the wall apart with your bare hands."

Tilly looked down at her hands. Her fingernails were broken, plaster stuck beneath them. "Was I–?"

"Sleepwalking?" Grandpa Don filled in for her. "I think so. You used to sleepwalk when you were a kid."

"I haven't done that since . . ." Tilly tried to remember but couldn't recall exactly.

"Well, whatever the reason, something got into you, and then you got into the wall." Grandpa Don eyed the corpse through the hole. "Seems as though you're not the first either."

"W-who is she?" Tilly asked, knowing full well that Grandpa Don wouldn't know any more than she did.

He met her eyes and declared without compunction, "She's someone really old, and really dead."

She was huddled in Grandpa Don's train room, the old parlor, trying to keep herself calm while strangers traipsed in and out of the mansion as if it were a crime scene. Well, it was a crime scene—sort of.

First, it was a call to 911 inspired by Erik, who'd taken the reins when Tilly had finally called him once the sun broke the horizon. The coroner was here now, along with the Division of Historic Preservation & Archaeology, or as Erik referred to them, the DHPA. The moment the coroner had determined the remains were old and not evidence of a recent crime, a whole other avenue had to be followed. Yellow tape cordoned off the stairwell now, and people who were essentially archaeologists had been called in to catalog every inch of the corpse in the wall. When they were finished, they would remove the body from the wall and transport it to the coroner's office. The weight of responsibility for such a discovery and its aftermath weighed heavily on Tilly's shoulders, and she couldn't stick around to watch any more than she could get the image of the dead woman out of her head.

So here she sat, no longer the authority in her own home, trying to remain calm after her sleepwalking excursion had left her with vague recollections of glowing lights and whispers in the air, and the terrible knowledge that a woman had been buried in the wall for decades. It had been hours now, and while Grandpa Don seemed calm and unaffected by the night's events, Tilly was questioning not only what had been discovered, but what in her memory of the night prior was real versus what was merely the remnants of a dream.

"I need to see it, please."

The unfamiliar male voice coming from the main entrance of James Mansion snagged Tilly's attention. She met Grandpa Don's eyes as he lifted his head from where he was dabbing touch-up paint onto the side of a model train car.

Still feeling possessive of the situation, Tilly hurried to the foyer, turning her attention to the front door.

The unfamiliar voice belonged to a very familiar face. Tilly cringed and melted against the doorframe. Luke James. He was in her house? No, he was in *his* house. Or what *had* been his house until the James Estate sold it to Grandpa Don. This was where Luke had grown up, where his father had grown up, and no doubt his grandfather as well.

Memories of Daphne's recent visit mingled with recollections of Erik on prom night—alone because Daphne had returned to her ex, Luke James. But more unnerving were the memories of Luke James and herself. He had always made her feel inadequate, less than. He'd made a practice of deliberately misunderstanding Tilly's literal statements, making her feel even worse about her struggle to communicate with social tact and ease.

To make matters worse, he'd caught wind that she had a crush on him—why she had, Tilly knew, was because he could be convincingly charming when he wanted to be, and he was good-looking and confident—and then Luke had exploited the opportunity. Genuine apologies for his prior behavior led to tender flirtation, which built her trust in his unexpected friendship. Then, in his ultimate act of awfulness, Luke James had denied all of it in front of everyone at school, making a mockery of Tilly.

Why would an awkward freshman ever believe someone like Luke James would be interested in her? She had become obsessed with him like she was with her history and her weird little hobbies and hanging out with her grandpa.

Tilly had never forgiven Luke James. She didn't hate him, but she certainly didn't like the man, and never would she trust him again.

Now Luke was here. Had Erik let him inside? With the doors wide open and people coming in and out, nothing was orderly at that moment. The stress of the chaos, mingling with her discovery of the body, had frayed Tilly's nerves to the point of breaking.

Tilly started down the hallway, and just as she reached the main room, she took in what looked like a mob of people gathered on the stairs, equipped with cameras and other devices to catalog the remains. When she met Luke James's surprised look, she wilted.

"Tilly Thompson." Even now, her name on his tongue made her feel as if she had all the insignificance of a carrot stick on a charcuterie board. "Do you live here?"

"I . . ." she faltered.

Erik's voice from behind saved her—and made her feel like she was fifteen all over again. "Hey, Luke."

Tilly shot Erik a bewildered look. He was being friendly. The men shook hands. There was an air of respect between them.

"Do you mind if I take a look at what you found?" Luke pointed toward the staircase.

"Sure." Erik nodded, seemingly oblivious to her surprise. "It's fine with me, but you'll have to run it by the coroner or the DHPA. They're in charge at the moment."

Tilly grabbed Erik's sleeve and tugged.

Erik glanced at her, realization filtering through his eyes. "Oh, uh . . ." he stammered. He couldn't backtrack on his permission now without causing a scene, but Tilly made sure Erik knew she wasn't happy with him by leveling a stern glare at her brother.

Erik knew their history! Just because he had moved on or grown up or whatever the reason was that had him acting so chummy with Luke, *she* hadn't. Not to mention, this was Grandpa Don and her home, not Erik's.

Luke shifted his attention to the scene on the stairs.

A camera flashed.

"I heard about this when someone from the police called the mayor's office. My brother sent me a text. I can't believe it." Luke ran his fingers through his hair, obviously bewildered by the secret the walls of his old home held. "How old do they think the . . . victim was?"

Tilly caught the catch in Luke's voice, and it made her study him, which was easy to do since he was giving Erik all his attention.

Wavy, blond hair—she'd always preferred darker men herself—with ocean-blue eyes, the epitome of a California surfer. Tall, athletic, and . . . Tilly frowned. *Troubled* was the word that sprang to mind. Yes, Luke James was troubled.

She glanced at the stairs illuminated by the stained-glass window. Tilly couldn't see the woman's remains from where she was, but she could envision the tattered, rotting remnants of a dress from days of old. She could also picture the leathery patches of skin, the gaping mouth . . .

"She's old," Tilly blurted out, then clamped her mouth shut as Luke turned toward her. He had to be a foot taller than her. His presence was intimidating.

"You mean she was most likely elderly?"

Had his face lost a little color? "No. I mean she's old. As in over a century old."

"She's over a hundred?" Luke's eyebrows winged upward.

"The coroner believes the *remains* are at least a century old," Erik interjected. He gave Tilly a curious look. The kind that was the unspoken equivalent of *What's going on with you?*

"Oh! The remains!" Luke parroted.

"The coroner said he believes the deceased to have been female, but they haven't yet suggested the age of the person at time of death."

"She's wearing a dress," Tilly offered, regretting her impulse to share the additional detail. It didn't really matter if a dress identified the victim's gender or the bone structure. Luke hadn't asked why the coroner had come to the conclusion that the body was that of a female.

"I appreciate your stopping by, Luke," added Erik.

Tilly looked up at her brother. She was still trying to reconcile the congeniality between the two men. High school was a long time ago, sure, but Erik had never been fond of Luke, and theirs was a small town. Since when had Erik and Luke become friendly, not to mention, why didn't she know a thing about it?

"It's been less than a month since the sale of the mansion to your grandfather went through. I was hoping . . ." Luke paused as if to consider his next words. "I was concerned." While he seemed genuine, she recalled being duped by that before.

"Well, seeing as the poor soul has been trapped in a wall for over a century, you're hardly responsible." Erik grinned. "I doubt you're on anyone's suspect list."

"I appreciate that vote of confidence." Luke gave Erik a nod.

Ah yes, the election. All the pieces fell into place for Tilly, and she couldn't help but stare up incredulously at Luke James. He was here to make sure the body in the wall wasn't going to cast a shadow over his mayoral campaign. This wasn't the concern of a prior owner, worried the new owners had perhaps been saddled with a messy crime scene. This was a man who wanted to get ahead of a potential scandal. His interest was purely self-centered—and Erik had fallen for it.

Tilly decided to take control of the situation. She cleared her throat, drawing Erik's attention and then Luke's.

Luke gave her an uncomfortable look.

"If your only concern is for the dead body in your family's old house ruining your reputation somehow, I'm sure you'll find a way to spin it in your favor." Tilly stated her feelings out loud—like she often did unfortunately—before filtering the words.

"What?" Luke asked incredulously.

"Tilly." Erik's warning barely pierced her consciousness.

Tilly didn't miss the look Luke had shot Erik. For a second, she almost would have identified it as desperation, but it flashed so quickly that she couldn't be sure.

"I really didn't—" Luke started.

Tilly held up her hand with more gumption than she'd ever had with respect to Luke James, but then finding the remains in the wall of her home had done something to her. It had changed—or maybe awakened—a part of Tilly. The nameless person had been a victim. She had to have been. There was no reason anyone in a loving home would shove someone's body into the cavity of a wall and plaster over it. Whatever her story, in the end, she'd been stuffed there to be unremembered. To disappear into history, unnamed. Tilly might not have had enough courage to stand up for herself, but for the poor soul in the wall? Yes. She could.

"Since this isn't your home anymore, it's not really your concern," Tilly concluded. "You can feel free to leave."

"Tilly!" Erik's sharp rebuttal sliced through her.

She looked at her brother. His eyes told her she'd overstepped, that she was out of line.

Well, what about Luke? He'd just walked into her house uninvited and expected access to the remains. The James family had always lorded over the people of New Jamestown, and it didn't matter that this place had belonged to their family since the mid-1800s. It was hers now. Hers and Grandpa Don's.

"I think maybe we need to take a moment." Erik's attempt to keep the peace meant he was summoning his skills from his day job.

Tilly could see the deep concern in his eyes. She also noted the tone of voice he adopted when trying to calm down an irate patient. But she wasn't a patient at the rehab facility where he worked and counseled. She was his sister.

Tilly didn't bother to look Luke's way. "He has no right to—"

"I can't believe Luke is trying to assert any authority here."

Erik's glance toward Luke inspired the uninvited guest to shake his head.

The apology in Luke's eyes seemed real. *Seemed* being the issue at hand.

"I didn't mean anything other than to show concern for your family," Luke said, trying to reassure her. "I couldn't believe it when I heard, and the fact that our family's trust just sold the place to your grandfather . . . well, I didn't want you all to have to be saddled with the responsibility of . . . of whatever this becomes."

He was attempting to be nice, to smooth out the edges of their past. Well, it wasn't that simple.

Tilly had lost confidence that day, all those years ago, when Luke had shamed her in front of everyone at school. It wasn't that he had just been a jerk and made up lies and mocked her; it was that he had made a show of her deepest fears—whether he intended to or not. That she would never be worth someone's intimate affection. That she was clueless in reading other people, their thoughts and feelings. That she was someone worth forgetting . . . just like the woman in the wall.

IF WALLS COULD TALK

I have seen things.

I have captured them in pockets of time and held them there. I have fingered them over the years, the decades, even the century. I have considered releasing them to be remembered, and then something holds me back.

They walk the halls, they sleep in their beds, and I see them at the dining table, feasting on meals that fill them. Yet their spirits are not filled. Their spirits are broken. Cracked or shattered. Some have attempted to glue their pieces back together, but with a single nudge, they can crumble.

Now dreams whisper in their ears.

Help me.

Help me.

They will no longer pass by like others before them. They will reveal the forgotten.

Yes.

Bring the truth into the light. Bring her into the air and let her rise again. After all these years of staying silent, locked behind a wall by a will that shunned her into stillness, it is time that she be allowed to speak. That someone listens to the one who was hidden within my shell. Who will find her? Who will return to her what was taken?

It has been too long.

She is weary of waiting.

7

Eloise James

As once I wept, if I could weep,
My tears might well be shed,
To think I was not near to keep
One vigil o'er thy bed. . . .
Lord Byron

October 1879

The Corinth Asylum for the Chronically Insane loomed over Eloise like a miniature castle positioned between two groves of oak trees, its windows reminding her of the eyes of goblins, glaring down at her with a distinct air of unwelcome. It was not a pleasant place. Not at eight o'clock in the evening, although Eloise could hardly imagine it would be kinder at eight o'clock in the morning. She pushed her spectacles up her nose, but they did nothing to improve the view.

This was the place where Evania convalesced. This grave above ground. This prison for the troubled. A preacher, a missionary, and an angel could have exited the asylum and declared that only goodness resided within its walls, and Eloise would not have believed them. Anyone in their right mind could see this was a place where the tormented were left to die. Anyone in their right mind would never be committed here, or so it was said. But Eloise knew the truth of it.

Evania had been in her right mind. She was merely grief-stricken and shamed into silence. The loss of her child was worse than the loss of her purity or the loss of her lover. That terrible triad was enough to send any woman into silent agony. The kind of anguish that begged forgiveness while one hoped there might still be a future. The kind of sorrow that stole the breath from a mother's body and caused her to throb with the ache for the babe missing from her arms.

"Watch your step, Miss Eloise."

Ida broke into Eloise's growing discomfort. When Eloise boarded the train, she was horrified to see Ida sliding into the seat next to her, her chin tilted in the air, with her pale-as-death features and hair making her black eyes spark. Ida's sudden appearance on the train was a conundrum Eloise didn't know how to process. Had her lady's maid followed her out of concern over Eloise's welfare? Or had Father somehow caught wind of Eloise's nighttime sneaking from the house and sent Ida to follow her, to keep an eye on her, to send him missives as to what Eloise was up to?

Eloise didn't trust Ida, yet she couldn't deny there was some strange relief at having the older woman beside her, and part of her had always *wanted* to trust Ida. She had at least two decades on Eloise, and with that came a sort of worldly wisdom that might be beneficial to Eloise—especially with no mother there to guide her. But knowing Ida as a person and not a maid was like attempting to see inside a sealed coffin. One must break the seal first, and that was a difficult problem, not to mention what lay inside might not be a welcome sight.

Now a full rotation of the earth had taken place since Eloise had left James Mansion, and like it or not, Ida was accompanying her. They had arrived at the hospital, and Eloise was determined to see Evania today—if it was the last thing she did.

"Miss Eloise," Ida said, her tone sharp, "you've almost tripped twice over this godforsaken excuse of a sidewalk." The maid toed a crack in the cement. "Do be careful," she added.

Eloise was taken aback at Ida's assertiveness now that they were not at home. She seemed more disposed to play the role of a governess. Eloise clutched her reticule, her gloved hands twisting around the delicate silver chain more than they should.

"I will be just fine, Ida." Eloise attempted to sound in charge, but instead she sounded put out, even to her own ears. She made no apologies, however. Ida had not been invited along, and Eloise was not only on a mission to retrieve her sister but to find her own footing as a woman of independence. Well, if she was bluntly honest, that was what she would probably be forced to become after this venture. Father would be furious at her rebellion. His predictable response was already inspiring Eloise to make decisions to protect herself. This she knew and also dreaded.

The two women hiked up the steps to the double doors of the hospital. A distinct smell of loneliness permeated the air. Eloise could never have described it otherwise, and while she knew it fell short, it was the only way she could categorize it. The door opened beneath Ida's push, and they entered as though it were a public building and they needn't wait for an invitation.

The hospital looked clean. Sparkling really. And though the gaslights cast an eerie glow about the entryway, Eloise couldn't deny that the stuffed couch against the wall, the coat tree, the table with a potted fern on top, and the woman behind the front desk, there to bid visitors welcome, all gave an unexpectedly pleasant first impression.

The woman stood, her starched gray wool dress adorned only

with a watch that hung from a gold chain, clipped to the dress's breast pocket.

"Ladies," she greeted, her smile warm. "Welcome. I am Matron Rourke. I'm afraid visiting hours ended a few hours ago."

There were visiting hours? Had Eloise known that, she would have come here the same week Evania was committed. Another fact Father had seen fit to withhold from her. That very idea bolstered Eloise's commitment to her cause.

"I'm here to see the head of the facility, please." Eloise had practiced that line over and over again in her mind on the train here.

"Oh, I'm so sorry. Dr. Holzer is not here in the evenings. Would you like to set up an appointment, Miss . . . ?"

"James. Eloise James. I am the sister of patient Evania James." Her words rose in pitch as she spoke, insinuating that the woman should know who Evania was.

"I see." The matron's face remained expressionless. She folded her hands in front of her, the epitome of calm and professionalism. "The best I can do for you this evening, I'm afraid, is to recommend you return in the morning. At that point, I can see if Dr. Holzer is available to meet with you. Or I can arrange an appointment, although his schedule is quite full."

Moments before she'd said Evania's name, there had been no mention of a full schedule, only an invitation to make an appointment.

Ida remained stiff beside her, but Eloise noticed there was a slight frown between her brows. A panic sliced through Eloise. If Ida took it upon herself to insert herself into the conversation, Eloise would lose all credibility. It would communicate her inability to speak on her own, to assert any authority, or to be even the tiniest bit intimidating. While it would be tantamount to insubordination for Ida, a lady's maid, to do such a thing, Eloise wouldn't put it past the woman if she was acting on the behest of Father. A lady's maid speaking on behalf of her mistress would be ludicrous, and it would sabotage the entire visit.

Eloise plunged ahead without giving her words much consideration. "My sister is very ill. A letter was sent over six weeks ago, and I only just received the news. I must see her at once."

"I see." Matron Rourke's mouth thinned in sympathy, tinged by her emotional distance from the circumstances. "I apologize for the inconvenience, but I simply cannot allow visitors after hours, and certainly not to enter the sick ward, not without Dr. Holzer's express permission."

Eloise pressed on. "Then I would like to request Evania's discharge immediately so that I may take my sister home."

"Her discharge? Take her home?" Matron Rourke cast a perplexed look at Ida and then back at Eloise. "I'm sorry, but I cannot issue any authorization of such requests."

"Please take into consideration that my sister's health hangs in the balance," Eloise said, trying to stay strong—sure of herself and confident. "Evania shouldn't be alone, not when family is near to attend her."

Matron Rourke snagged a lace-edged handkerchief from the pocket of her dress and dabbed her nose. "I'm afraid that is quite impossible."

"Which is why I must speak with Dr. Holzer," Eloise insisted.

"Which returns us to my initial declaration, Miss James, that Dr. Holzer is not here." Again, the matron glanced at Ida. Did she expect to find reason in the lady's maid where she didn't find it in Eloise?

Realizing she wasn't going to gain admission, and afraid the matron would ban her from the property altogether for being so ridiculous as to demand Evania be released into Eloise's care, Eloise lifted her chin and asked, "What time should I return in the morning?"

Matron Rourke's polite smile evaporated. Her face was pinched now, her response guarded. "You may return no earlier than ten o'clock."

That seemed late. Eloise made the quick assumption Matron

Rourke had padded the time, so that Dr. Holzer could be advised about her visit. Why it mattered, Eloise had no idea. Surely her circumstances were not that unusual. Evania couldn't be the only patient in the hospital to be at death's door, with family and friends at hand to show their care and concern.

"Very well," Eloise acquiesced, though she was determined to arrive at the facility no later than nine in the morning.

"Good evening, ladies." Mrs. Rourke moved toward the door, a clear sign she wished for them to leave now.

Eloise and Ida did just that, exiting and being bid farewell by the resounding thud of the door behind them.

Ida took several steps in the direction of the carriage they had hired to transport them to-and-fro. When Eloise didn't follow, the lady's maid turned back.

"Are you coming, Miss James?" she inquired.

Eloise debated, then shook her head. "You go on. I'll be but a moment."

"Miss James?" Ida tipped her head, her brow furrowing.

"Please do as I say," Eloise responded with an admitted snap of irritation in her voice.

Ida stiffened.

Eloise knew her blunt order was out of character for her, but she also didn't want Ida to follow her. She had intended to make this trip by herself, and just because Ida had superseded those wishes, it didn't mean the maid had license to do as she wished.

Without waiting for a reply, Eloise turned and strode away, taking the path that led from the hospital's front entrance to what appeared to be the side gardens. Even in the growing moonlight, Eloise could see that the gardens were beautifully manicured. The picture of a pleasant place to reside, hinting at afternoon pastimes for the patients as they meandered the lawn. Eloise suspected that was merely what visitors were *supposed* to believe. She had no proof of such, yet it weighed on her spirit nonetheless.

She dared to cast a look over her shoulder and was pleased to see Ida had chosen not to follow her. Of course, she was flirting with trespassing on the hospital grounds now. But perhaps if she wandered around to the back of the expansive rectangular building, she could see into the windows? How unseemly would it be if she pressed her nose to the glass? Very. And the idea made Eloise cringe, and yet,there might be staff, an aide or a maid perhaps, whom she could convince to allow her entry through the back of the building. The idea she was so close to Evania and yet unable to see her added even more determination to Eloise's steps.

Surveying the grounds, she shivered as she noted the farther a person strolled toward the back of the facility, the more shadowed and darker the place became. The stone pathways branched into several directions, most leading to sitting areas. But one path skirted the edge of the gardens and led toward a brick outbuilding, and beyond this was a field lined by woods. The area must be where the grounds staff worked, for it was separated by some distance from where the asylum's patients or their caregivers might walk to take in the fresh air.

Beyond the outbuilding would be an ideal place for a cemetery. Eloise's stomach curdled at the thought. Death, burial . . . that which Evania was in imminent danger of. But whether a lonely asylum cemetery or a morosely beautiful one such as where their mother had been laid to rest, the grave remained an awful reality altogether.

A look to see if there was such a thing as an asylum cemetery might behoove her to know. It would also delay the option of peering through windows and trying to summon a friendly aide, which seemed futile and desperate. She would attempt that *after* she investigated the woods.

Eloise snuck along the edge of the woods, looking back toward the hospital, a mere outline in the dark of night. She didn't want to admit she was more relieved to go in search of graves than to be seen trespassing outside the direct vicinity of the asylum. Besides, she thought she'd seen someone moving among the trees. A groundskeeper perhaps? If so, Eloise justfied her shift in direction that the person might be just the staff member to allow her, a patient's family member, access into the hospital. After all, a groundskeeper might not be as concerned about the rules of visitation. Eloise hoped they would be willing to bend the rules and show her inside rather than deny a family member from seeing a patient, especially one who was nearing death.

Crickets chirruped, and the crisp scent of the autumn evening met Eloise's nose. Her shoes crunched the fallen leaves as she strained to see in the fading light of dusk. The pounding of her heart matched her quick breaths. If she didn't hurry, Ida would most likely come looking for her, and who knew what the woman's response would be to Eloise nosing around the property without permission.

Her toe stubbed on a root that jutted from the ground. She stumbled forward, bracing herself by placing a palm against the trunk of a nearby oak. The woods were silent, and only the sound of the wind whispering through tree branches announced their presence. She must have misjudged seeing someone, and even her intuition that this might be a place for a cemetery seemed wrong. She saw no gravestones and certainly no groundskeeper.

Her worst fear was that she would be too late if she didn't press forward tonight, for Evania's sake. What if her sister passed away during the night? That horrible thought warred against her instinct to flee back home, to admit she was in over her head when it came to Evania's care. Eloise remained propped against the tree as she considered it. An even worse scenario would be if Evania did pass away, and they rushed her lifeless body to wherever it was they buried unclaimed patients. She might never find Evania's body, never be able to return her sister to be buried properly beside their mother. And if the asylum's graveyard wasn't here in these woods, then where was it? Perhaps the cemetery was one of those affiliated with a church in the area, with the patients being buried according to the rites of their denominations. A

Catholic would wish to be buried in a Catholic cemetery, as would a Methodist in a Methodist cemetery, and so on.

But what about Evania?

They espoused no association with a particular church. Father was a self-proclaimed Darwinist who had no time for the things of God. The graveyard in which Eloise wished to have Evania was the New Jamestown Cemetery, which wasn't connected with a church or denomination. She wondered if God held an opinion on the matter. Once dead, she highly doubted that when she arrived at the gates of heaven, she would be questioned about her denominational leanings.

"But she is not dead," Eloise proclaimed to the night with a vehemence that shook her from her worries and her rambling thoughts that borrowed trouble before it had fully arrived. "Evania is alive, and I will come to see you in the morning," Eloise addressed the hospital, its rows of windows like glowing eyes. "One more night, my sister," Eloise whispered, praying that her words would float across the grounds to Evania's bedside.

With a sigh, Eloise turned and began to hurry back toward the carriage. Now was not the time to be deliberating such things. It was growing darker. She was trespassing. If she were found out, it would be the ruination of her own mission.

Movement in the woods just ahead snagged Eloise's attention, and her heart leapt. Whether a groundskeeper, a hospital steward, or a guard, none of those options seemed to be good ones any longer. Not to mention, the idea that the asylum might have a guard on watch at night had not occurred to Eloise until just this moment. She hurried back to the protection of the oak tree, praying her dark dress provided enough camouflage that she wouldn't be noticed.

She had not thought this through. She couldn't just pop out from behind a tree and introduce herself to anyone without it appearing suspicious. And if this was in fact a guard, she might be arrested!

Under those circumstances, there was no possibility Dr. Holzer would grant her request come morning. This was why Father never entrusted her with anything of importance! He maintained that, as a woman, she simply did not see or understand the reasoning behind the decisions he made. She could hardly argue at this moment that Father was in error. She had failed to take into consideration the consequences of being caught tiptoeing the grounds of the asylum at night. The mortification she would suffer as a result. Logically speaking, this manly shadow skulking her way in the night was either looking for her, or he was destined to discover her.

Eloise considered the form as it slunk along the edge of the woods.

He was alone.

Saying nothing.

Not even calling her name.

With no lantern by which to see.

Secretive. Much as she was.

Eloise frowned. The man truly *was* skulking. He dipped into the woods and vanished.

She was not alone in her subterfuge! While that brought her small comfort, it also increased the danger of her being found. If she wasn't the only one trespassing tonight, her situation could become far more dire if she were caught and aligned with whoever this man was.

With the moon hidden behind the clouds, she could only pray the darkness would provide enough cover for her to hurry back to the carriage. Assuming Ida was still waiting for her to return and not taking matters into her own hands, she and Ida would then return to their hotel a mere three miles away. All would be well. After enjoying a cup of hot chamomile tea to calm her nerves, she would retire and try again in the morning.

She released her embrace of the oak tree. A few minutes and she would be back in the carriage and–

A hand slid over her mouth even as an arm snaked around

her waist. Yanked backward, Eloise yelped into the palm of the man's hand as she kicked against his forceful tugging of her into the trees.

"Keep your mouth shut, lass."

Her captor's breath was warm in her ear.

"Stop strugglin'," he ordered.

Eloise obeyed because that was her instinct. As the man felt her resistance wane, he loosened his grip.

"I'm goin' to let you go now. Don't scream or you'll be the death of us, ya hear?"

Eloise nodded vigorously, though mentally she convinced herself the moment the man's hand fell away from her mouth, she would scream.

He removed his hand.

Eloise opened her mouth to scream.

"If you want to find yourself a place in the jail, then go right ahead and wake the dead."

She snapped her mouth shut, straining to make out the man's features in the dark. He wasn't much older than she was. His hair was long in the front with wavy strands pointing every which way, and a jaunty cap was smashed down over them. His angular face was shadowy.

"Smart." He gave a curt nod. "Now, lass, the best way to take our leave from here is through the woods. If we go west, we'll reach the property line and the road. From there, you can find your way back to town."

"I've a carriage waiting, out front of the hospital."

He offered her a patronizing grin. "Ah, well then, m'lady, off with ye. An' watch out for security. I s'pose you didn't know that the hospital has a man who walks around at night. He'd love to find a lass like you, take ya inside, and ne'er let ya out again."

"Who are you?" Eloise whispered, appalled it sounded so loud and frantic.

A grin split his face, a flash of white teeth. "You'd like to know, wouldn't ya?"

"Do you work here?" Eloise pressed, ignoring the way the lilt of his brogue sent little butterflies fluttering in her stomach. That was altogether unnecessary and ridiculous, considering the circumstances.

He snorted. "Work here? Are you daft? I don't make deals with the devil, miss, though me mum used to say I flirt with him now and then." He chuckled low in his throat. "Come quick now. Before we find ourselves tied with our sleeves behind our backs and bangin' our heads against the wall. This place won't be kind to a lady like you, nor a so-called penny-a-liner like m'self."

The man grabbed her hand and began to tug her after him. Stunned into obedience, Eloise followed, ducking under branches, squeezing around underbrush and, in what seemed like fifteen minutes, finally breaking free from the woods into the open area of the roadway. Lined as it was on both sides by forest and in the meager moonlight, Eloise was sure that if the headless horseman of Sleepy Hollow came barreling toward her on his black horse, she would have found it perfectly fitting.

The man stood a few inches taller than Eloise, and he was lean in his trousers, shirt, suspenders, and jacket. He looked both ways and then gave a nod. "All right then. You'll be wantin' to go that way if you need to reach town." He pointed left. "And you'll go that way if you wanna head to the countryside where the farms be. The cows don't charge much to share their beds in the pasture, mind ya, but it's a trial to find a pillow for your head. Bein' a fine lady, I'm expectin' you'd prefer to go to town."

Bewildered was too kind a word for how Eloise felt in this moment, standing on a deserted road at night with this cheeky stranger for a companion. Still, she didn't want him to leave her alone to her own wits and wiles. They hadn't seemed to serve her well up until this point.

"I don't . . ." She gathered her thoughts. "Sir, I don't understand who you are, and why you were at the asylum tonight."

He tilted his head and eyed her, a smile tipping the corner of his mouth. "I could say the same about you. The last thing I was expectin' was a wee lass sneakin' through the trees. What were you about then?"

Eloise blinked. He seemed to be enjoying their little nighttime adventure, while she wanted to go back in time to two months ago when all was right with the world, when Evania was at home and none of the tragedy had befallen them.

"I was looking for my sister," Eloise answered. She felt she must. It was only polite.

"In the backyard of a madhouse?"

"I was trying to find a way into the hospital," she clarified.

"In the woods? Aye. Makes sense, it does." He was teasing her.

"I wanted to see . . ." Eloise hesitated. Nothing she said was going to add a bit of credibility to her actions. Eloise opted to tell a falsehood. "I wanted to see the graveyard. To see if she's already passed on." It was half true, she supposed.

He drew back, and even in the darkness, Eloise could see the disbelief on his face. "Find her grave? If she's dead, that won't happen. Not ever, I'm afraid."

Eloise stared at him. He'd stolen any words from her with his bold statement. The man seemed to understand this and so continued.

"They don't mark the graves of their dead at the asylum. It's just dig a hole and put 'em in. There's no pomp and circumstance. No marker. No prayers. Sweet Mother Mary herself would be hard-pressed to find someone's grave there. And I'll say, you weren't even lookin' in the right place for the graves to begin with. Seems you'd be lost as well."

This was becoming worse and worse. Eloise wanted to ask another question, but the sound of wheels and the clomping of horses alerted them that they were not alone.

He grabbed her arm, and in spite of Eloise's yelp, the stranger pulled her into the trees once again.

"Unhand me!" Eloise shook him off, indignant now.

He did as he was told, but then gave her a saucy wink. "Best make sure it's not the police comin' to find us before you announce yourself. They come round once a night to keep an eye on things, even though the hospital has its own man. I think the captain is sweet on the asylum's matron. They'll not be pleased to see me. An' you bein' with me won't be good for you."

8

Tell me not, in mournful numbers,
Life is but an empty dream!
For the soul is dead that slumbers,
And things are not what they seem.
Henry Wadsworth Longfellow

It was most disconcerting. The jovial and self-assured man who had all but careened her through the woods and hid her in the trees from the oncoming wagon now wrapped his arm around her waist and held her to his side as if she were his and he were hers. Eloise squirmed, but his grip only tightened. He kept his gaze straight ahead, and his mouth tipped in a sideways smile. He spoke through gritted teeth.

"Pretend you like me a wee bit, love."

"Whyever should I—?"

The wagon—definitely of the law-enforcement type—rolled into view, and a lantern was held high enough that in spite of any attempt to remain hidden, the policeman was still alerted to the fact they were in the woods.

"Dobbs?" the officer shouted from the wagon. "That you?"

Her captor, or rescuer, or whatever he was, took a step into the light, hauling Eloise with him. She stumbled, and it caused her to grab for his chest to steady herself, and he took the liberty of wrapping his other arm around her as well.

His laugh split the night air. "Ah, Captain Farber, ya found me again!"

The captain remained in his seat, with another man beside him holding the reins and watching with obvious curiosity. The road was lit by the lantern in the captain's hand and another that hung from the back of the wagon.

"What *are* you doing out here, Dobbs? You know you've been warned!"

Eloise could feel the lean muscle of Dobbs's arm twitch as it held her. He was perturbed. She peered at him now that she could see his face better. His face was chiseled, handsome even, with a look of sheer mischief and a rebel's edge merging into a devil-may-care grin. He was covering his genuine emotion; she could tell by the way he held her even closer. Eloise wondered if he thought he was protecting her from the police.

"I'm here with my girl, Captain. Can't you see?"

Eloise stiffened as she felt his mouth peck her cheek in a kiss. She bit back a yelp when she heard him whisper, "Say nothin'."

The light swung toward Eloise.

"You're with Dobbs, then, miss?" The captain's eyes were narrowed. They doubted him. As well they should!

Eloise cast a glance at Dobbs, who didn't look at her but continued to smile up at the policeman.

"I-I . . ." She fumbled to find the words.

"Are you with Silas Dobbs, miss?" the captain repeated.

Eloise nodded quickly. "Yes. I—"

She received a reprimanding shake of the law officer's head. He had to be in his fifties, with a round stomach and a burly set of shoulders that made Eloise not want to be on his bad side.

"Best watch your reputation, miss. Dobbs here loves to dally where he's not wanted, and the next thing you know, you'll find your name in the paper and his, and it won't be in the byline but in the arrests column. You'll never be able to lift your head in good society again, and then where will you end up?" Captain Farber's tip of his chin in the direction of the institution sent an unwelcome shiver through Eloise.

For the first time since she'd come into the company of Silas Dobbs—whoever he was—she was thankful for his supporting arm and his all-too-possessive posture.

"I tell my daughter all the time: stay away from the scribblers. And this one is the king of them."

"The truth tellers, you mean," Dobbs retorted.

Captain Farber waved him off. "Keep telling yourself that, Dobbs. Meanwhile, best get your girl away from here. You know you've been warned, and if I catch you on the hospital grounds, I'll have to arrest you."

"I'm not on the grounds," Dobbs replied flippantly. "Last I looked, 'twas a public road."

Eloise stilled as Silas Dobbs spun her in front of him without warning and wrapped his arms around her waist, pulling her back against himself. He nuzzled her ear, whispering "shh" once more, then stole her breath while igniting her outrage as he planted another kiss, this time against the sensitive skin of her neck.

"There's no way I'll be toyin' with this one's affections, Captain. She's the love of me life, an' we're just trying to find a way to be together so her da doesn't catch wind of it."

Captain Farber shook his head in apparent disbelief, then exchanged glances with his partner. "Be off with the both of you. And, Dobbs, I'd best not see you around here again."

Dobbs reached up and swept his cap from his head, swinging in an exaggerated bow, even as he retained his hold on Eloise. "You've my word on my mother's grave," he declared.

Captain Farber snorted. "You don't even know who your mother is." He dropped onto the wagon seat, and the reins slapped against the horses' backs. They rolled away into the night, and only when the tiniest glow of lantern light remained did Silas Dobbs release Eloise.

She staggered away from him, wrapping her arms around herself, her eyes wide. "Mr. Dobbs!" It was all Eloise could manage. She was befuddled, verklempt, and at a loss for words. In the last hour, she had done more in her life than she'd ever dared to do. She had trespassed, she had darted through the night with a complete stranger—unchaperoned—and now she'd received her first kiss—her first *kisses*—ones that left her reeling with emotions she didn't think were wise or proper. And all this was so she could recover Evania and take her sweet sister home.

The man raked his fingers through his black curls before smashing his cap back on his head. He was agitated, that much was clear, even though he tried to hide it behind a lopsided smile. "Now that I've all but asked for your hand in marriage in the eyes of the captain, best be tellin' me who you are and why you're sneakin' around in the dead of night."

Eloise swallowed, averting her eyes because his smile was too disarming and his words too laden with an edge that made her nervous. "I told you—I'm looking for my sister."

"Aye! The dead sister."

"She's not dead! She's ill. Very ill." Eloise rammed her spectacles up her nose from where they'd slid down, cursing her watery voice and the tears that stung her eyes "My father had her installed at the asylum, and she became ill some weeks ago. I intend to take her home."

Silas Dobbs rested his hands on his hips. The blue-black of the night closed in around them like a blanket. "You won't be seein' your sister, Miss . . ."

"James. Eloise James," she provided without thought.

"And if she's off and died while you've been makin' your way here, ya won't find her ever again," he finished. "They don't mark the graves for more reasons than one."

"What do you mean?"

An eyebrow lifted. "If I told ya, I'd have to marry ya, an' I don't plan to do that."

"Pardon me?" Eloise didn't try to hide the offense rising in her voice.

"Oh, I'll pardon you, but it don't change a thing." He tipped up his chin in defiance. "I don't tell my secrets to anyone but my kin. An' you're not that, nor are you my wife, so no secrets tonight. Just a word of warning. You'd best make your way back to where you come from. The captain will recognize you now, an' he's not wrong—I *do* have a bit of a reputation." A handsome wince with little real apology followed. "It seems I gave the impression you might be my girl for good, which we both know you aren't. An' bein' caught out in the dark with me, well . . . the captain and his men like to chat up the town. Makes them feel important. Such gossip keeps my secrets hidden. And you don't want to be the center of gossip, now, do ya?"

Eloise could almost feel the color leaving her face. It was enough that she'd left home and taken a train to the asylum, accompanied only by Ida, who by now had to be beside herself with worry. That the captain hadn't mentioned they were looking for Eloise told her Ida hadn't alerted the authorities yet, but she could hardly doubt it was coming soon. If she were aligned with an Irishman with a questionable reputation, a penny-a-liner as he'd so blatantly maligned himself, well, Father would conclude she was on the same path as Evania. Penny-a-liners were not employed by the newspapers. Instead, they sought out news in hopes of selling it. That was all. This man Dobbs was more than likely a man trying to scrape by on his bad grammar and wits.

"I will walk back to town now, thank you." Eloise lifted her skirts and started heading up the road to the right.

"Eloise James."

"What?" The sound of her name on his lips stopped her cold. She turned to face him.

He pointed to the left. "I think you mean to go thataway."

The man was following her all the way back to Corinth, Indiana—home to the Corinth Asylum for the Chronically Insane. Eloise guessed the walk back to her hotel would be approximately two miles. That was what their hired driver had indicated when he'd transported her and Ida what seemed like hours ago now. If she were lucky, she would find them looking for her, and Eloise wouldn't have to hike the entire way there. In the dark. Listening to the owls hoot and other strange noises coming from the woods nearby. Not to mention, being followed by a man who was far too jovial for a nighttime jaunt.

"Why are you following me?" Eloise sent her question over her shoulder, straining to see in the darkness as she walked along the road.

Silas Dobbs shadowed her. "I live in Corinth."

That made sense. Still, the fact he was mere yards behind her was disconcerting. Not to mention he'd yet to tell her why he'd been on the asylum's property, how he claimed to know what they did with the patients' remains, nor why the police had threatened to arrest him if he was spotted on the property.

"Where are you from, Eloise?"

He was cheeky too, using her given name.

"Miss James." Eloise corrected, managing to maintain her propriety even as she stumbled over a rock in the road.

"Why so formal when you're practically m'wife now, love?"

"I am *not* practically your *wife*. Nor am I your *girl* or whatever nonsense you try to convince the police of. You said so yourself, Mr. Dobbs." Eloise almost choked on the words.

"Silas. I much prefer it, and so will the police if they ask you more questions. Why would ya call a man you're in love with 'mister'? Be a tad strange."

Eloise didn't even know what to say to that. The entire situation was altogether ludicrous. She stopped in the middle of the road and whirled to face her shadow. "Captain Farber called you a scribbler."

Silas stopped also. They stood like two people in a duel, facing each other down. "He called me the king of it too. Now that I think of it, that might be the first time he's paid me a compliment."

"Do you work for a newspaper?" Eloise was already pretty sure she knew the answer, but she challenged him anyway.

Silas shrugged, his hands in his trouser pockets. "I'd like to say I do, but I'm a free man, as no paper will hire me seein' as I come from nowhere and have no pedigree. A street urchin—that's what I was called as a boy. But now I write stories, and I sell 'em by the line if I can. An' the only way to do that is to find the *good* stories. The ones folks'll wanna read."

"And the asylum fits into that how?" Eloise hadn't quite wrapped her mind around it all yet.

"That's my next story, Eloise." Her name on his tongue was disarming. "See, people go there and then they're no more."

"I don't understand." She tried to convince herself of that, but Eloise didn't appreciate her instant intuition.

He shrugged. "If you can't figure it out, might be for the better. 'Specially seein' as you don't know how your sister fares."

Desperation coursed through Eloise. If this had something to do with Evania, she needed to know. "Please tell me."

He was quiet for a long moment, either deliberating or taunting her, she wasn't sure. Finally, he cleared his throat as if preparing to make a grand announcement. "I don't know about your sister, so don't take this too personal. But there are those who go there that ya never hear from again. I know they die. I've been told that by those who work inside the place. Problem is, I keep looking for fresh graves, an' there are none. No graves. No stones. No earth turned over like a garden."

Eloise felt her throat close in on his words. No graves anywhere for the patients? "You mean they're not taken to a cemetery somewhere in town?"

"Therein lies my question, love. Where do they go? What becomes of them? They certainly don't rise from the dead like the Lord Jesus did, now, do they? It's a big story, an' I'm aimin' to find out how it unravels. Once I do, I'll sell it to the newspapers."

"You're looking to profit, then, from others' misfortunes?" Eloise inhaled at the gall of it.

"Well, a penny is a nice thing to have in a man's pocket. 'Specially if I'm lookin' to settle down with my girl like I inferred to the captain tonight."

Warmth crept up her neck and cheeks without invitation, and she was glad it was too dark for Silas to see it.

He kept on chattering. "But no, it's not just for the coin. It's so justice can be served. You see, I grew up in the orphanage with my cousins, Penny and Seamus. We were inseparable, we were, until some fine folk adopted the two of them and took 'em home. Put them in school. Bought them fine clothes. But Seamus told me it wasn't a fine family after all, not behind the doors that stayed closed. Soon enough, they said Seamus was sick in his mind. Said he made all sorts of claims about them that weren't true—only I knew they were. My kin didn't lie to me. 'Twas no reason to. Seamus was taken to the asylum, with Penny left behind by herself. Then one day they said Penny was sick too. An' before I knew it, both my cousins were stuck behind those prison walls. Convenient way to be rid of them, since neither Seamus nor Penny knew how to hold their tongues. The family didn't want the scandal, so they called them crazy and sent them there when Penny was no older'n sixteen and Seamus just shy of eighteen. 'Tis been four years."

"Are they still there?" Eloise was holding her breath.

Silas drew closer to her. "All I know, they disappeared. Just like the others. Leastways that was what I've been told."

"You don't believe they're dead?"

"I'd like to believe not, but I don't trust them that run the place." Silas's response quelled her surge of optimism. "I know it in my soul—there's somethin' wrong in there. Where are the sick? No one ever tells of visitin' the sick. An' the graves? Where are the bodies? Where are their belongin's? Why is it no one seems to care enough to ask questions? They're just throwaway people. Treated like the trash. Well, I might earn a penny if I sell the story, but I'd gladly trade the copper to know what happened to my kin."

9

Tilly Thompson

We were so happy, you and I,
So happy, you and I.
And then the world is always too much for me.
Edna St. Vincent Millay

Present Day

It was unusual for Tilly to want to be away from home. Especially now that home was at James Mansion. Her childhood dreams had been realized because of Grandpa Don, but following the gruesome discovery in the staircase, Tilly wanted a break from the place. In this moment, she was thankful she could leave Grandpa Don alone for a bit. How life would change sooner rather than later, she wasn't unaware of. For now, Tilly sucked in a steadying breath of fresh air and uttered a silent prayer of gratitude.

She made her way down the sidewalk of sleepy New Jamestown, the morning bringing a dense fog that hovered along the pathway and mingled with the orange leaves of the maples.

Her sleep had been restless last night. If she was being honest, she was afraid to sleep for fear she would dream as though awake and end up in another part of the house, uncovering more of its secrets. Knowing she had been sleepwalking was a small comfort, and in many ways it was more disconcerting. It was out of control. She had torn away at a wall from which in her sleep she thought she'd heard someone calling to her. If that wasn't creepy enough, the last thing she wanted was to find out the James family had a history of hiding bodies and there were more in the basement or something equally as awful.

Her conversation with Erik earlier that day had also unsettled her. He had encouraged her to give Luke James some space to prove he was no longer the person he'd been back in high school.

"I don't understand." Tilly's confusion was difficult to navigate. "You aren't friends. You never talk about Luke, and I never see you two together."

"I know you don't understand." Erik's obtuse response told Tilly nothing. "Maybe you can just trust me?" He had tried to be gentle, so Tilly had accepted his words with a nod. She did trust her brother. He didn't look at her differences as weaknesses or something to be tolerated, but as gifts. But she also didn't find solace in incomplete answers.

"Just remember," Erik said as he draped his arm over her shoulders in a sideways hug, "not everything is black and white, Tilly. Sometimes there are layers. You have to peel them back to understand."

"I don't like peeling things back. Things don't need to be so complicated."

"And yet they are," he said with a regretful smile.

She'd let it go then and made her way to bed, going upstairs using the back staircase, as the main one had been cordoned off.

Now, this morning, she was still uneasy. Coming to terms with a dead woman hidden behind the wall of her new home was heavy enough. Peeling back the layers that were Luke James? She had neither the time nor the energy for that. It wasn't on her long task list, and she had no intention of adding it even to the bottom.

Tilly drew in a deep breath of the fresh morning, laced with the scent of wet, fallen leaves from last night's rain and the kiss of cold air. She was praying. Hard. This was her attempt at a prayer walk, something her mom had suggested for years she should do.

"Go for a walk with the Lord. Clear the air every morning."

She thought again of Erik's words from yesterday.

"Not everything is black and white, Tilly. Sometimes there are layers. You have to peel them back to understand."

That was where she and her brother walked separate paths. Lists, tasks, order, framework—those were the things that brought continuity and reason to her world. She didn't understand how someone could walk into their home and toss their keys in one spot, deposit their shoes in another, and throw their coat over the back of a chair. No. Everything had its place, and life was so much simpler if a person put things where they belonged. She approached life like this as much as she could. Tilly well knew not *everything* could be straightforward, but there was so much a person could do to make it so. Even one's emotions. Yes, they were real, but compartmentalizing and processing her feelings made them easier to manage, or if she was lucky, to leave behind altogether.

But Erik had told her that compartmentalizing could also lead to avoidance of issues that needed to be addressed. And while Erik rarely talked about his work, Tilly knew his position on staff at Morning Song Recovery, New Jamestown's drug and alcohol rehab center, had given him an entirely different perspective on life. It was a place of anonymity. All those treated at Morning Song were nameless to the rest of the world. They came from all over, and they left in secrecy. All because they needed to process vices—to peel back the layers, so to speak. Emotions were complicated. Life was a maze. A person's influences were stronger than their ability to control in many cases. The world spun, people spiraled, and very little was as simple as it seemed.

This morning, Erik seemed more right than usual.

Sleepwalking?

Luke James reentering her world and reviving *very* deep emotions she'd packed away years ago?

"Maybe you can just trust me?"

Erik had asked that of her last night, and it took Tilly a good bit of time before she realized what he'd meant. He meant that he couldn't expound on why things had changed between him and Luke. He couldn't tell her why she never saw them together, or why he'd never spoken about Luke.

When it dawned on Tilly, it was like being hit by a charging bull.

Erik's request that she trust him was his unspoken cue that he'd worked with Luke James. He had worked with Luke at Morning Song Recovery. The idea that Luke had at some point been one of their anonymous patients not only floored Tilly but left her questioning everything she had assumed about Luke. It was in a way that left her feeling irritated at him and at Erik for hiding things, but even more so, stinging with conviction that she was being judgmental and hard on a man whom she'd never given room to redeem himself.

Did the town have a clue that Luke had a past that included rehab? Probably not. He was a James after all. Such things were swept under the rug, silence bought for a price, ensuring Luke's anonymity was protected. Which was necessary in the event he decided to run for mayor in place of his dying brother.

A dog trotted toward her. It was a little black dog with a yellow collar, floppy ears, with curly well-groomed fur. Tilly crouched as the dog approached, its black eyes snapping with happy greetings.

"Well, hello!" She petted the squirming dog as it licked her fingers and nudged her wrist with its wet nose.

"Pickle!"

The dog's head jerked around, and then the dog spun and ran to its owner, who was jogging toward Tilly.

She straightened, lifting her eyes.

God had a really ironic sense of humor this morning. Even Tilly couldn't hold back her small smile, which was directed toward heaven, not Luke James.

Tilly crossed her arms over her chest as Luke, wearing basketball shorts and a T-shirt, bent over the dog and hooked a leash onto its collar. He raised his head—a charming, stupidly handsome grin across his chiseled face—and looked ready to campaign his way into her heart as a citizen of New Jamestown. Then Tilly saw the change occur the moment he realized who she was.

The twinkle dimmed in his eyes.

His smile dissipated.

"Good morning, Tilly." Luke's voice was flat.

"Hi." Her response was a bit delayed, and it made the awkwardness worse. Tilly scrambled for something else to say. She pointed to the dog, sniffing the grass at the edge of the sidewalk. "Her name is Pickle?"

"*His* name," Luke corrected. He shifted his weight. Why he didn't just carry on with his jog, she had no idea.

Tilly cleared her throat. "Cute."

"He's a French poodle," Luke offered.

"I figured as much."

"About yesterday—"

"I'm sorry—"

They both spoke simultaneously, then stopped, then gave each other a nervous smile. Tilly looked down at her shoes and toed a dandelion growing through a crack of the cement.

Luke beat her to being the bigger person. "Yesterday, I wasn't trying to butt in on your business."

"I know." She didn't, but it was the easiest, most polite thing to say considering the circumstances.

"I heard about the discovery and . . ." Luke faltered. He was remarkably insecure, and it made Tilly uncomfortable. The Luke she used to know would never have shown vulnerability. "Well, I . . ."

"Your family has over a century of ties to the place," Tilly said, rescuing him. "I understand your wanting to check things out." Did she? She supposed she did.

There was gratitude in his eyes. "It's such a crazy thought that I lived there all those years with no idea someone was in the wall!" He squinted in disbelief, shaking his head. "It's unnerving."

"Do you have any idea who it could be?" Tilly had to ask. Maybe Luke might actually have something to offer the investigation.

Luke tugged on the leash as Pickle investigated a hole in the earth that looked like a mole had been busy tunneling. "I . . . don't, no."

The brief catch in his voice told Tilly that he wasn't being one hundred percent honest. That didn't surprise her. Luke's "layers," as Erik called them, were becoming obvious very fast.

"Well, I guess we'll leave it to the experts." Tilly knew it was a flippant thing to say, but she was anxious to get walking again.

"It's going to be in the paper today." Luke's statement was delivered as if warning her to be prepared.

Prepared for what? Tilly met his frank look and thought briefly that the Caribbean could take a lesson from Luke's eyes on how to be blue.

"I don't understand." The minute she admitted it aloud, Tilly waited for a typical Luke James retort, no doubt mocking her.

Smartest girl in school when it comes to classwork. Stupid when it comes to life.

But the old Luke seemed to be missing. Instead, he shifted his weight again, and Pickle rounded his leg to sniff Tilly's shoe. "It's newsworthy because of me," he added, "and my family. Human remains found in our old home? That's interesting even if I wasn't running for public office."

"It'll bring you publicity," Tilly stated.

Luke nodded. "Unfortunately."

"What do you mean, unfortunately?"

Luke slipped the leash out from under Pickle's leg where it had become tangled. "Well, my family history is rich with all kinds of stories, and while we've done a lot of good for this town since we helped found it, some of the stories are not so . . . complimentary. It may not be good publicity is what I'm trying to say. People might latch on to old stories of proud and arrogant James men from the past and even make accusations."

Tilly nodded. There wasn't any reason to pretend he was wrong.

He chuckled at her affirmation. "You make me laugh, Tilly Thompson."

She made him laugh? Tilly didn't know what to say.

Luke continued, "Anyone else would have tried to make excuses for my family. We're the Jameses. Rumors of affairs, illegitimate children in our family tree, the proverbial family crest of entitled arrogance? You've heard them all. You just admitted I'm right. That this could look bad."

Tilly waited.

Luke's smile faded, and now he worked his jaw back and forth. "This is a new addition to the collection of James family fodder. Anyone against my campaign is going to try to twist it into something sinister. Something relevant to today."

"You mean they'll say the body points to a recent crime?"

"I'm afraid so."

"But it's obviously not!"

"I know that. You know that. And no doubt the authorities will confirm it to be the case. But that doesn't change how people talk. Will Morrow is running for mayor. You know he'll jump at the chance to leverage this discovery as just another reason not to trust a James family member in the mayoral seat."

Tilly frowned. She assumed Luke was running for mayor

because of his brother's illness. She wondered if he was running *because* he was a James and that was what was expected, or if he truly wanted the position of prestige. Then she remembered her conversation with Daphne from the other day and asked, "Aren't you friends with Mitch and Daphne? That's got to be awkward with her brother running against you."

A shadow flickered across Luke's face. "Sure. We're friends. On and off."

Just like it always was with him and Daphne back in high school.

Luke had never married. His parents had died years ago in a car accident. Luke and his older brother, Kyle, had moved out of the mansion after they'd graduated from high school. That was when they closed up the house, leaving the place to the ghost of memories. Kyle was almost eight years older than Luke and had been mayor just like their father, but now? Luke would be left alone when Kyle died, the last remaining James in New Jamestown. Against her will, Tilly was hit with a sudden sympathy for Luke. What would it be like to carve out a life in the world with just a French poodle as your companion?

For some reason, she couldn't stop the words from coming out of her mouth as she blurted, "If it'd help for you to come over and take a look at the staircase, or if Grandpa Don and I can help in any way . . ."

She figured if they could somehow ascertain the identity of the body, there might be less gossip for Luke to have to deal with. With the mystery of the woman in the wall solved, the upheaval surrounding the discovery would quickly settle down. Or so she hoped.

"Really?"

Tilly hadn't expected Luke to sound so hopeful, if not a little relieved. He wasn't the self-assured mayoral candidate of this morning or the self-confident alpha male he'd presented himself as in high school. Maybe she wasn't the only one unsettled by the corpse hidden in the wall. Luke seemed to need something.

A friend perhaps.

People didn't have to make life so complicated, Tilly had assessed earlier, but now she admitted that sometimes it was life itself that made everything complicated.

Tilly studied the document that had been handed to her. Grandpa Don hovered at her right shoulder, peering down on it. Luke towered over her on her left side, also staring at the page. He'd taken her up on her offer to stop by James Mansion to see the staircase. He hadn't been able to get a good look at anything yesterday, partially due to the investigators and partially due to Tilly's lack of welcome.

The body had been removed. The document she held now was a copy of the coroner's report. A DHPA representative who'd introduced himself as Jeff Blatz had just given it to her and now waited as she skimmed it.

—— SUMMARY PRELIMINARY REPORT OF AUTOPSY ——

Case No.: 2025-IND-0291

Date of Call: October 10, 2026

Examiner: Dr. L. Florence, Ph.D., Forensic Anthropology Consultant

Sex: Probable female (based on pelvic morphology and gracile cranial features)

Age: Estimated 15–20 years of age (pubic assessment, dental wear)

Race: Indeterminate at this stage; further analysis recommended

External Examination

One (1) skeleton recovered from interior stairwell wall of Victorian residence, James Mansion, in New Jamestown, Indiana. The skeletal remains are largely complete; the preservation is moderate. The skeletal system is unremarkable and within normal limits. Pelvic bone measurements indicate the body belongs to a female.

Bones exhibit surface staining consistent with long-term damp environment. Some localized areas of the remains, including fingers and portions of the deceased's face, show partial leathering of remaining skin, indicative of the cold environment of the uninsulated wall portion where the remains were recovered.

No coffin hardware recovered; remains discovered in direct association with lath and plaster debris. No insulation as consistent with architecture built ca. 1860.

A perimortem fracture to the back of the skull consistent with blunt object trauma.

Multiple fractures to the right arm.

Evidence Collected

Upon removal from the wall, the remains were accompanied by corroded metal buttons (x2), fragments of wool textile (likely dress), partial cotton shift, silk stockings, leather shoes (right and left foot).

Time Since Death

Extensive mineral staining and adipocere remnants, along with historical construction context, suggest interment >100 years prior to discovery.

Remains likely date middle to late 19th century.

Opinion

Immediate cause of death to be blunt force trauma. Manner of death: Undetermined.

Recommendations

Submit tooth sample for mtDNA analysis; results may be limited due to age and environmental conditions.

Consult Indiana Department of Natural Resources, Division of Historic Preservation & Archaeology, for compliance with state burial law and final disposition.

Maintain chain-of-custody documentation for all associated artifacts.

"It's not conclusive, then, that the victim was murdered?" Luke's voice startled Tilly from her fixed staring at the document. She'd never read a coroner's report before today.

"No." Jeff crossed his arms over his chest. "She could have been struck from behind or fallen and hit her head. The broken arm bones leave questions as to abuse of some sort. Either way, the injuries indicate she would have been deceased prior to being put in the wall."

"So the body was purposefully hidden in the stairwell?" Grandpa Don interjected.

Jeff shot him a puzzled look for the obvious answer. "Well, yes. It didn't just accidentally fall into the wall and get plastered over."

Tilly winced at the man's abruptness. Grandpa Don was trying to put things in order in his mind. She couldn't blame him for asking the obvious, but she also couldn't blame Jeff for being confused. He didn't know Grandpa's Don condition or that it would lead to confusion.

Jeff continued, "Don't ask me why it was hidden there of all places. Maybe the house was undergoing renovations, and it was convenient?"

"Wouldn't it . . . smell?" Tilly ventured. She hadn't yet handed the report back to Jeff, mostly because she couldn't tear her eyes from the drawn outline of a human being and the marks the coroner had placed on the arm and skull indicating fractures.

"Likely," Jeff affirmed. He glanced at Luke. "Was there a time when the James family vacated the mansion for an extended period?"

Tilly realized again that Luke might be helpful in getting to the bottom of the mystery.

But he wasn't. "I don't know." Luke shook his head. "I don't recall anyone ever saying the place was empty prior to when my parents left it."

"We'll send a tooth in for analysis as the coroner recommended," Jeff continued, seemingly more concerned about the remains than the mystery. "Mitochondrial DNA is used when autosomal DNA is degraded and can't be used. What mtDNA will give us—hopefully—is a group of people that the victim is related to through their maternal lineage."

"So we won't know exactly who she is?" Luke verified.

"No," Jeff answered. "At best we'll determine lineage, and then we focus our investigation on the people she may have been related to and see what history might reveal. Who knows what will surface at that point. When it comes to the integration of modern science and historical records, one will likely provide a much stronger lead than the other."

Tilly reread the line about blunt force trauma to the back of the head. She cleared her throat. "So the girl in the wall was killed by being hit from behind?"

"Yes." Jeff reached over and pointed at the sentence beneath it. "If you want my opinion—and keep in mind it's speculation only—it looks like there was a struggle. Those types of fractures aren't caused by just falling. She may have been struck multiple times from the front and raised her arm in a defensive gesture." Jeff demonstrated.

Tilly winced.

"And then someone snuck up from behind and clobbered her," Grandpa Don summarized.

"Perhaps." Jeff shrugged. "It's difficult to know. If the victim fell, she may have fallen face-first, and her assailant then issued the final blow. Or she was pushed backward and connected with a blunt object like—" he glanced around and then pointed—"like that wall sconce made of cast-iron. I'm only speculating, of course."

"And we'll probably never know those details," Tilly concluded.

"Probably not. No."

That alone increased Tilly's anxiety. Odds were there wouldn't be much they'd learn for certain about the woman in the wall. Her story had decomposed along with her remains.

Tilly shuddered as she recollected the echo of the voice from her sleepwalking dream calling for her. Asking for help. Had the woman or girl called for help when she'd been killed? What if she hadn't been dead as suspected but merely unconscious and then had come to after being walled in? The idea made Tilly's skin crawl.

"We need to find out who she was. She deserves to have her name back."

Jeff cleared his throat. "Yes, well, unfortunately there wasn't anything to give a hint as to her identity. Although you can see by the coroner's report that she was a young woman."

One crammed into a wall and plastered over.

"Woman in the wall." Tilly mumbled the phrase. "Girl in the wall. Both sound so . . . alone." She sensed Luke's eyes on her, Grandpa Don's too.

Hadn't anyone missed her? Looked for her?

"There have to be news reports," Tilly muttered. She looked between Jeff and Luke. Then to Grandpa Don, who, by the expression in his eyes, seemed to understand her struggle. She focused on him. "Reports of a missing woman. New Jamestown was even smaller and more intimate in the nineteenth century. Everyone would have known if a woman disappeared."

Grandpa Don squeezed her shoulder. "She's finally been found."

Tilly knew he meant it to reassure her, but it didn't. She was agitated. Even though the remains had been removed from the mansion and Jeff was taking down the yellow tape and releasing the area for repair, she couldn't shake the feeling that the girl was somehow still there.

In James Mansion.

Watching.

Begging to be remembered after a century hidden out of sight.

How did one remember someone who no longer had a face or a name?

Tilly tightened her hold on the report.

I'll find your story. It was an unspoken promise. Tilly hoped that her thoughts could reach the young woman wherever her spirit resided now. *I'll find your story and make sure you can rest in peace.*

Tilly had no clue how she was going to do it.

But do it she would.

10

Death
Then suddenly I saw a cloud of gloom
Take form within the room . . .
Then from the shadows came the Dreaded Shape,–
The candle flickered out!

Carrie Williams Clifford

Tilly sat at the top of the stairs on the second floor, fixated on the far wall. The wall she'd not long ago been convinced should have hidden a window but instead hid something far worse.

It was past midnight. She had yet to go to sleep, though Grandpa Don had retired four hours prior, tucked in bed in his parlor train room. He'd had a rough afternoon after the excitement died down. It was all out of their hands at this point. Being that it wasn't deemed a current or even a definite crime, there was no active investigation outside of the government entity that would work it from a historical angle. Grandpa Don had seemed to crash after the adrenaline of the past two days. He'd retired to his model trains, and later in the evening, Tilly found him wandering the hallway looking for something he couldn't recall.

"What do you need, Grandpa?" Tilly had come up beside him.

The lost expression on his face, as compared to the coherent and independent man of earlier in the day, twisted Tilly's heart.

Grandpa Don had scratched his head, his face drawn into a confused scowl. "I-I'm a bit turned around." He scanned his surroundings. "I thought I needed to go somewhere, but I think my mind's not working right."

Tilly had reached for his arm and hugged it, giving him physical reassurance even as she answered frankly, "You're home, Grandpa. With me. Your mind is tired. It's time for bed."

Now that he was peacefully asleep, Tilly wanted to rest herself, but all she could do was sit and stare at the gaping eyesore of the wall she'd torn apart. The story that was untold and unsolved taunted her. Where to even start? She'd made a promise to a dead woman. A dead woman who, in all actuality, couldn't possibly know she'd been promised such a thing.

"Who were you?" Tilly whispered. Her words came back to her, a soft echo in the vast house. She shifted her eyes to look farther down the stairs. The ghostly remnants of the unnamed woman's life hung over James Mansion and transformed it from a beautiful historic home to something almost menacing. What other secrets did these walls hide? A shiver rattled through her. Were there more bodies? More victims? What if the James family history of wealth and power had a darker streak than anyone had suspected?

"Did a serial killer live here?" Tilly asked aloud, thankful no one answered yet feeling more anxious by the moment. She jumped to her feet and hurried down the stairs. She needed to move, to make some tea. Chamomile would be comforting. She needed to be busy doing something grounded in the present moment and cease mulling on mysterious people who were mere whispers of what they used to be.

The parlor was dark, making the foyer loom with its high ceiling. She avoided the sitting room as well because after midnight, the corners and bay windows and fireplace struck her as cold and intimidating. Instead, she rushed down the hallway that stretched the full length of the house, as if running from the unseen eyes she felt followed her. She resisted the urge to slide her stocking feet across the wood floor in an effort to speed up her journey. Pausing outside the pocket doors of the parlor, she pushed them open enough to see the outline of Grandpa Don's tables and trains, and then his sleeping form by the door on the south wall that led to a side entrance beneath the staircase where the body had been found.

The house was like a maze, Tilly realized, eyeing the small door. Openings and entryways. She could envision a servant using that entrance to avoid the family's hall. They could slip in and out without walking through the family's more formal spaces.

And if one wanted, one could haul a body through the narrow door. It connected to another door half hidden in the paneling of the entryway and parlor, which was adjacent to the alcove near the main staircase. Goodness! Tilly could almost see it play out like an old movie. The woman's body being maneuvered into the mansion, taken between the parlor and the hall by way of the hidden side entrance, then lifted up the stairs without much fear of being caught. It was all so simple, especially if done at this hour of night when the residents of the house would have been sleeping.

But of course, she was only speculating. It was entirely possible the woman had died inside the mansion. Yet none of this would answer the crucial question of why or how the act had gone undetected after that point. One had to imagine that if a body were placed into the wall's framework, the replastering and wallpapering necessary to hide it could not have been done covertly. And the smell of the decomposing body would have called attention to itself.

Tilly backed away from the conservatory and Grandpa Don's snoring. She continued down the main hall until she reached its end. A door to the back porch was straight ahead of her, another door to her right led to an empty room that might have been a study back in the day but had long since been converted into a laundry room and powder room. To her left stood another door that gaped to reveal a dark hollow in the wall ahead. The basement stairs. Which, if Tilly was being honest, had creeped her out even before she'd found the corpse in the wall.

She skirted the stairs, not at all tempted to explore the basement tonight. She'd been down in the dank, brick-walled recess of the mansion once since moving in, and that was quite enough for now. She turned into the kitchen, which had been updated sometime in the last decade. Tilly made for the gas stove and turned it on. The *tick-tick-tick* of the burner starting brought some reality into the room. She made fast work of filling the teakettle with water from the sink.

Now for tea.

Tilly rummaged through the cupboard selection. Peach, mint, Earl Grey . . . where was her chamomile? On seeing it tucked behind a few other boxes, Tilly reached for it, her eyes drifting to the window overlooking the backyard with its old stable and big oak tree.

A face at the window peered in at her.

The glass was foggy, but the eyes were unmistakably narrow slits.

Tilly couldn't move, as the being dissipated before her eyes, leaving nothing but a mist on the windowpanes, and—

A white hand slammed against the outside of the window, fingers splayed. The glass rattled, and Tilly screamed as she yanked her own hand from the cupboard, sending boxes and bags of tea flying. The hand slid down the window, an apparition that appeared to have no arm or body attached to it. A smear disrupted the moisture on the glass where the palm had wiped it away.

And then it was gone.

Tilly sucked in quick gasps, staring at where the face and then hand had appeared. It couldn't be! There was no such thing as spirits and specters and–

She sensed someone watching her from behind. Tilly whirled around. Sure enough, the door to the hallway that she'd closed behind her began to creak open. Slowly. The whine of its hinges was every haunted house's soundtrack.

Tilly was rooted in place, fear having paralyzed her. She stared as the door inched open. Then it was there. The hand slipping through the opening, extending toward her, reaching for the–

Light flooded the kitchen as the hand flicked the light switch. Grandpa Don pushed the door open the rest of the way, bewilderment painted on his face.

"What on earth are you screaming about?" he asked.

Tilly took that moment to crumple to the floor, her entire world dissolving into darkness.

"Tilly. Tilly."

A hand patted her cheek.

A man's hand.

Too large and strong to be Grandpa Don's.

Tilly startled into consciousness, scrambling into a sitting position on the kitchen floor and pushing against the man who hovered over her.

Luke James.

Luke James?

The face in the window.

The hand.

All of it came swooping back to Tilly, and she scooted even farther away from Luke, as she noticed Grandpa Don bending over her with a worried expression.

"It's okay," Luke soothed.

"Why are you here?" Tilly demanded, not meaning to sound as sharp as she did.

"I called him." Grandpa Don waggled his smartphone over her for Tilly to see.

"You called . . ." She tried to collect her thoughts and make sense of things. It made no sense for Grandpa Don to have called Luke James.

"Don't worry about it," Luke reassured her. He remained on the floor by her but kept the distance she'd put between them. His dark blond hair was mussed and didn't look remotely the part of someone running for mayor. In spite of it being October, he was wearing shorts and a T-shirt, none of which translated well for Tilly.

She crossed her arms over her chest to hide the fact that she was braless beneath her sweatshirt. She'd never been accused of being a lightweight in the front region.

"Did I pass out?" Tilly looked between the men.

"Yes, after you screamed like a banshee." Grandpa Don waddled to a nearby chair and sat down, still clutching his phone. "I think you were sleepwalking again. I came in and turned on the ceiling light—you just had that silly little stove light on over there. You fell to the floor when you fainted, and I tried to wake you without any luck. Ended up calling Erik."

Tilly frowned as Grandpa Don finished with a motion toward Luke. She still couldn't figure out why he'd called Luke "Erik," or how he even had Luke's number.

Grandpa Don thumbed through his contacts, and Tilly noticed he looked confused as he did so.

He mumbled to himself, and his eyes brightened. "I called Erik. See?" He turned his phone toward Tilly.

Sure enough. It was Erik's name, but not his number.

"Grandpa, this is Luke. Not Erik."

Grandpa Don's brows pulled inward. "No. It says 'Erik' right here. And that's his number."

"But this is . . ." Tilly's argument was pulled up short when Luke gave her a slight shake of his head.

"Why don't you head back to bed, Grandpa," he interjected.

Grandpa?

Tilly started to protest, but then as realization crept in, so did her understanding of the situation. A new sort of sorrow filled her as she watched Luke push off the floor and extend a hand to her grandfather. Grandpa Don waved the phone at Luke as he stood.

"My own granddaughter doesn't think I know how to use a phone." He smiled good-naturedly at Tilly, and she gave one back.

"I know," Luke placated as he played Erik's role with grace and without embarrassing Grandpa Don. "Tilly always thinks she can boss us around."

Grandpa Don chuckled, then hesitated as he assessed Tilly. "Your sleepwalking is getting worse. Maybe you should sleep in my room. I can bunk on the floor if need be."

Oh, Grandpa. Tears sprang to Tilly's eyes. He was always looking out for her. Always. Even when he was in the middle of confusion and didn't know it.

Luke shot her a look that all but begged her to stay put, and the two men disappeared down the hall.

Tilly remained on the floor and not just because Luke had implied she should, but because she was still woozy. Not to mention she had no desire to look out that window ever again, at least not at night.

A few minutes later, Luke reentered the kitchen. He wore moccasins, and he passed her on the floor and reached up to a cupboard where he pulled a glass down as if this were his home. He filled it with water and then crouched beside her, handing the glass to Tilly.

She eyed him warily.

Luke James.

She could say his name fifty times, and it still wouldn't make her feel any less uncomfortable.

Reaching for the glass, she mumbled her thanks and then stilled when her fingertips touched his.

Their eyes met.

"Sorry." He drew back his hand.

Tilly decided the safest thing to do was to drink the water.

"I gave my number to Erik yesterday." Luke's explanation broke the awkward silence. "Your grandpa was standing next to us. I'm guessing he somehow entered it into his contacts but put in Erik's name by mistake."

"I'm sorry he woke you up. You didn't have to come." Tilly tried to apologize. She felt like a ninny. Sprawled on the kitchen floor in a dead faint like some weak-willed Victorian female with the vapors? And then Luke had to be Grandpa Don's emergency contact of choice?

"I don't mind." Luke tipped his head toward the west wall. "I live only three miles that way."

"Oh." Of course he did.

"Any idea what happened?" Luke settled on the floor and leaned back against a lower cabinet.

Tilly eyed him as she took another sip of water. How was she supposed to tell him what she saw? No. That part was easy. How was she supposed to *trust* him with what she saw, to *convince* him she'd seen it? And *had* she? If she had been sleepwalking again, then what had been real and what had been a dream?

"I just . . . sometimes I walk in my sleep." That was all she could offer him at the moment.

Luke gave her a kind smile, and it made her squirm. This wasn't the Luke she remembered. Well, actually, it *was* the Luke who had led her on, toyed with her affections, and been nice in high school—right before he'd made a mockery of her in front of everyone. Laughing that she'd fallen for him. Scoffing at the idea he'd be attracted to someone like her.

But her instinct wasn't to be suspicious. It was to take things and people at face value. To be cautious now when he seemed so genuine was exhausting but necessary. Something inside Tilly had ached for Luke to appreciate who she was. To like her. To want her and . . . she had to knock this off. Ten years. High school was ten years ago, and Luke hadn't said "boo" to her until now.

"Do you sleepwalk often?"

"Not usually," Tilly replied.

"Huh. Do you remember why you screamed? Your grandpa said it woke him up."

Tilly shook her head. She wasn't going to mention the hand on the windowpane, the opening of the door, the fingers—anything she saw while sleepwalking but had no evidence for after was merely speculation.

Silence stretched between them, until Luke stretched out his legs, giving a deep sigh. "Think you can stand up?"

"Oh!" Tilly hadn't considered the fact he was hanging around just to see if she was all right. She was quick to get to her feet, grasping the counter and setting the glass on it. "See? I'm fine."

Luke followed her lead and was on his feet next to her. His height made her feel puny. "What *really* happened, Tilly?"

She stilled.

"Tilly?" He wasn't fooled, which was unfortunate.

"I just got a little creeped out is all. Sometimes in my sleep, I feel—awake. I see or hear things that aren't there." Hopefully that would suffice. Admitting she was seeing things outside the window was one thing, but admitting it to *him*? Nope.

Luke let it go. He turned toward the window—the same window the ghoul had been peering in—and studied the dark night outside it. "You know, when I was a kid, I used to think this place was haunted."

Well, that didn't help her relax.

Tilly didn't respond or encourage him to expound further.

"It wasn't." He turned back toward her. "At least—" Luke shook his head, biting off his words. "Well, I guess if you're all right, I'll take off."

Tilly felt sure he'd been going to say something. Something vulnerable. But he'd decided to keep his thoughts to himself. She realized he didn't trust her either.

"Yeah." Tilly hugged herself, still aware that she was wearing her pajamas and a sweatshirt. "I'll be fine."

"Okay then." Luke walked into the main hallway, and Tilly followed, very aware that he knew his way around the house. She noticed him glance at the basement door as they passed the stairs. She noticed the change in his expression, shifting from looking relaxed to a brief scowl. Then he turned the corner and started toward the parlor.

Tilly followed, glancing into the conservatory where Grandpa Don was curled up in bed again.

They reached the front door, and Luke opened it, hesitating as he stepped onto the front porch. "Call if you need anything."

"Thanks," Tilly replied.

They looked at each other. Wordless. Distrusting and yet somehow Tilly could feel they were tied together. By this house. By their unspoken secrets. By the girl in the wall.

"Good night, Tilly," he murmured.

"Good night, Luke."

IF WALLS COULD TALK

I can see things they cannot.

Tonight I could see their breath mingling in the room, their unspoken words and the trust that has never been shared. I could see there is much hidden in this place. Generations' worth of evil that lurks outside the window and pounds on the glass to be let back in.

But something keeps the wickedness at bay. A prayer perhaps? A presence? They won't acknowledge me—or maybe they don't yet realize I am here. But I will get their attention. I can only be silent for so long until I insist their secrets be told and mine along with them.

Death hides in this place, and I've held hands with it for decades. I hope for them to survive, while death waits to take them to itself. But I am powerless to hold death back. I can only observe.

I can see things they cannot.

She is afraid to be strong.

He is just afraid.

Have you ever seen a grown man live in terror?

I have.

Because he was once a boy who lived in this house.

He was always afraid.

11

Eloise James

No longer mourn for me when I am dead.
William Shakespeare

October 1879
Corinth Asylum for the Chronically Insane

These were the moments she missed Evania the most. When she sat ramrod-straight beside Ida, the censure in the carriage so thick that Eloise struggled to breathe. Had she been beside Evania, her sister would have taken her hand and encouraged Eloise to be bold, to be brave. But Eloise wasn't made of the sterner stuff Evania had been born with. She dwelled on her choices, dreaded consequences, bore guilt like a weight she was intended to bear, and felt shame before it was ever leveled upon her. Evania? She had lived. No matter the discourse over Evania's choices being right or wrong, her sister had *lived*.

Eloise could hardly breathe at the moment. She had arrived at the hotel late last night, the rapscallion Silas Dobbs leaving her at the door with a tip of his cap and an "I'll be seein' ya, love."

He wouldn't be. Eloise wouldn't seek out the self-appointed writer who had bandied her reputation about with the law itself. She was certain he had no intention of finding her again, either. They had been shoved together by circumstances, but regardless of their mutual mission to discover the whereabouts and condition of their loved ones, they had nothing in common. She was the daughter of a wealthy businessman who had an entire town named after him, while Silas was a man of no pedigree and little means.

"A rabble-rouser." That had been Ida's condemnatory proclamation when she'd met Eloise at their hotel room's door. "Your reputation would be sullied if anyone spotted the two of you alone together."

"You don't even know Mr. Dobbs," Eloise had argued, unsure why she felt the need to defend Silas. She certainly wasn't going to admit that the police had more than spotted them together.

"I don't need to *know* him. One can see it by merely looking at him."

Ida's disapproval had continued well into the morning and now filled the carriage.

"The fact you were manhandled and hauled through the woods is appalling." Ida at least had the grace to blame Silas for Eloise's disappearance instead of Eloise herself. For the time being, Eloise let her believe what she wanted.

She had explained to Eloise that it had been against her better judgment to leave the asylum in hopes that Eloise would somehow return on her own the few miles to the hotel, but the guard at the hospital had insisted there be no further loitering or the police would be summoned. That Eloise had turned up was a desperate relief, Ida had concluded, though it was hard from her birdlike features to believe she had any affection for her.

As she'd promised, Eloise was returning to the asylum this

morning to speak with Dr. Merriweather. Last night, there was no question in her mind—not after hearing Silas Dobbs's story about missing patients—that something troubling was going on. But with the sunrise, reason had returned, quelling Eloise's suspicions as the midnight delusions of a tired mind and an untrustworthy companion. The hospital had its policies, and visitors would not be admitted after hours. She had been loath to accept that, hence the brouhaha that had commenced with her impulsive traipsing about the property. But Silas's story—if it could be believed—spoke of a conspiracy. Something darker and more nefarious. Would she take the word of a reputable institution or the word of a freelance journalist looking for a sensational news story to sell?

"Here we are."

Ida's announcement made Eloise jump.

Eloise turned her attention to the looming gray-brick hospital. She adjusted her black gloves and tugged at her sleeve cuffs. The navy-blue wool of her dress scratched against her skin, but Eloise wore it in order to present the proper picture of a well-bred sister.

"I shall come with you?" Ida presented it as a question but also as an expectation.

"Of course," Eloise accepted, though a part of her wanted to resist. It would be better if she didn't go in unaccompanied. Having Ida with her would help make Eloise more respectable in the eyes of others, as compared to a single woman showing up alone miles from home.

Climbing from the carriage, Ida close on her heels, Eloise took in the asylum in the daylight. It didn't look much cheerier with the blue sky as a backdrop, and the fact that crows swooped down from the treetops, cawing out their warning, did nothing to ease Eloise's nerves.

On entering the building, they were met again by Matron Rourke, whose thin smile revealed she was none too pleased to see Eloise make good on her promise to return.

"Miss James," she greeted, "how prompt you are this morning. But as I indicated last night, Dr. Holzer is not available until ten."

"We will wait," Ida stated before Eloise could open her mouth.

Eloise gave her maid an incredulous look, yet Ida had turned her back to Matron Rourke and moved to a line of chairs along one wall. She sat, her chin lifted and her gaze fixed on Matron Rourke, as if expecting the woman to produce Dr. Holzer out of thin air.

Taking her seat beside Ida, Eloise tried to summon the words to rebuke Ida for overstepping. But before she could, Ida spoke in a low tone out of the side of her mouth.

"You must take charge, Miss Eloise, or they will never cooperate with you."

Eloise realized that by simply allowing no question, Ida had gotten both the matron and Eloise to acquiesce out of politeness. Matron Rourke had excused herself, so Ida and Eloise remained behind, the only sound in the front parlor being the ticking of an antique clock resting on the fireplace mantel.

"I will see Evania," Eloise said aloud to Ida, not because of a sense of camaraderie but because she needed to urge herself forward. "I will insist on it."

"And then?"

Was Ida challenging her because she was testing Eloise or because she was trying to help prepare her? Eloise didn't know, but she answered anyway. "I will demand to bring her home with me."

"And if you're told you cannot take Evania home?" Ida led. "What will you do then?"

"Then I will put up a fuss." Eloise shifted uneasily on her chair, repositioning her reticule in her lap.

"Well, that should do it." Ida's response was anything but reassuring.

She twisted in her seat to look at Ida. "How could they refuse me? Evania is my sister."

"Yes, but your father's word wields the authority here."

"Be silent," Eloise snapped, feeling at her wits' end. The fact that Ida raised such legitimate concerns brought to the surface every fear Eloise had harbored.

"There you go," Ida said. She nodded and gave Eloise a thin smile of approval for her peevishness.

Eloise didn't know why Ida approved, nor why the woman fell silent, but she did.

It was one in the afternoon before Eloise was invited into Dr. Holzer's office. Without asking, Ida followed. The doctor of the Corinth Asylum for the Chronically Insane was a debonair man, with hair pomaded into a fine side part and whiskers that drew downward on either side of his mouth, leaving his chin bare. He had fine eyes, soft and brown, and there was a pleasantness about him that took Eloise by surprise. She had come prepared for battle—especially after sitting for four hours waiting to meet with him. Now her nervous energy rushed back like an unwelcome foe.

"Miss James," Dr. Holzer began, "let me first offer you my condolences on the passing of your sister."

Eloise grappled for the arm of the chair next to her. Her face went cold as blood drained from it, and it was all she could do not to collapse right there. She felt Ida's hand at the small of her back—whether to reassure her or to catch her should she fall, it didn't matter. "What did you say?" Eloise managed to gasp out.

Dr. Holzer's eyes widened in consternation. "Miss James, my apologies. I thought you had received the word and—"

"Received word of what?"

"Your sister passed away. Four days ago, I'm afraid. I sent word to your father immediately."

"I don't understand." Eloise didn't want to understand. What the doctor stated could not be true! Wouldn't Matron Rourke have said something last night?

Evania glanced at Ida, who sat beside her, staring down the doctor as if at any moment he might morph into Frankenstein's monster. She averted her attention from the maid and back to Dr. Holzer.

His features were the perfect example of a doctor who had delivered horrible news and wished only to extend sympathy and understanding.

"How?" Eloise asked, even as her breath was stolen from her.

Dr. Holzer folded his hands and rested them on the desktop. "She had been quite ill."

"Yes. My father received that letter. It is why I've come. I wish to take my sister home." A tear trailed down her cheek, and Eloise swiped it away in frustration and shock.

"Miss James . . ." Dr. Holzer looked between her and Ida. "I'm afraid your sister is no longer with us."

Patients going missing.

No graveyard.

Silas's conspiracy rushed back to Eloise. She straightened, stiffening her shoulders. "Then I would like to see her remains, please."

Another compassionate wince settled on Dr. Holzer's face. "Your sister passed away four days ago."

"Yes? And? The dead are often cared for over a period of days until a proper service and burial can be arranged. We *are* her family, and I am here now to take possession of my sister's . . ." Eloise couldn't finish her sentence.

"That is true," Dr. Holzer said. "However, we telegraphed your father with the news, and he indicated that we should take charge of your sister's burial."

"Why would you think I'd have come all this way?" Eloise hated the tremor in her voice. It didn't fit. Father had indicated Evania would be buried at home—if she died.

Dr. Holzer cleared his throat. "I assumed you were here to collect her belongings."

"What use would I have of those?" Eloise heard the shrillness in her voice. "I demand to see my sister!"

"But she has already been buried—"

"Then you must dig her up!" Eloise shot to her feet.

Ida stood quickly as well, reaching for Eloise, who shrugged her maid's hand away.

Dr. Holzer took a moment to collect himself and then rose in a careful and gentle manner. "Miss James, we cannot exhume your sister's remains."

"Why not?" Eloise glared down her nose at the man, even as tears came unchecked down her cheeks. "My sister cannot rest in peace so far from the people she loved. I don't believe taking her home to be buried next to our mother would be of any further disturbance to her, that is, if she *is* dead as you claim."

"I understand, but—"

"I realize my request is not customary, but I must insist."

"It is quite unorthodox," Dr. Holzer stated.

Eloise had no intention of being dissuaded. "Yes, but it is necessary. For my sister's eternal peace and my own."

Dr. Holzer assessed her for a moment, then sniffed as he prepared to speak. "I have a telegram from your father clearly stating his wishes that your sister be interred here. I simply cannot override your father's wishes to appease your own. And while I am sympathetic to your loss, I must insist that his telegram be adhered to."

"I assure you, Doctor, that were my father here—"

"It is out of the question, Miss James." This time, Dr. Holzer's pleasant demeanor shifted into one of veiled impatience. "I cannot in good conscience authorize the exhumation of your sister. Especially without written consent from your father."

In that moment, all words of protest and persuasion fled from Eloise's mind, though she knew that later in the day, she would think of a thousand and one things she should have said. The mention of Father was enough to silence her. Dr. Holzer was correct. He wouldn't wish to counter Father's wishes any more than she normally would. And yet the loss of her sister had urged her to dare things she never would have before. She had come here for Evania. She must remember that.

Eloise rummaged through her reticule for a handkerchief, drawing in a few shuddering breaths to gain control. Grief and panic were not going to win her any influence concerning her sister whether she truly had passed away or was still alive. But what purpose would the doctor have to withhold Evania from her family?

"Dr. Holzer, I–"

"Forgive me, Miss James." He pushed to his feet. He had taken on the wan smile of a man attempting to placate a woman. "As I've already stated, I am *very* sorry for your loss. It is unfortunate that you were not aware of your sister's passing, and that you were unaware of your father's acquiescence to your sister's burial. I'm afraid the best I can do is have your sister's belongings gathered and make arrangements for you to retrieve them later tomorrow."

"Tomorrow?" Eloise squeaked.

"Yes." Dr. Holzer rounded his desk and made his way to the office door, opening it to indicate their deliberation had ended.

Beside Eloise, Ida cleared her throat meaningfully. Eloise caught the look her maid sent her. Gathering courage from Ida's determined demeanor, Eloise held out a hand to stop the doctor.

"Dr. Holzer."

The doctor offered her a blank look, but he waited, his hand on the open door.

"Dr. Holzer," she tried again, taking a step toward him, "I simply must insist that my sister's body be prepared to be transported to the cemetery in New Jamestown." And if Evania wasn't deceased, and Silas Dobbs's accusations had merit and something was indeed amiss here, she knew Dr. Holzer would refuse her once again.

"I will have your sister's belongings ready to retrieve tomorrow by three. That is all I can do for you, I'm afraid." He began to exit.

"She isn't dead, is she?"

Eloise's accusation stopped Dr. Holzer. He turned toward her, his eyes grazing her face with disapproval, and yet to Eloise's dismay, there was regret in them. Sincere regret. Something she had hoped not to see because it indicated honesty.

"I know this is beyond difficult for you." Dr. Holzer had gentled his tone. "Truly I do. But I've no reason to lie about your sister's demise. What would I gain from withholding your sister from you were she still living? As for her body, again, I cannot in good conscience go against your father's directives. Your sister should be allowed to rest in peace now."

"Evania isn't gone." Eloise's throat hurt with unshed tears. She was frantic. "She can't be gone."

"Come, Miss Eloise." Ida's hand on Eloise's elbow was no comfort, but neither was it unfeeling.

Eloise wrenched away from her maid. "No." She looked toward the hallway that led to the hospital's interior. She would go. She would look for herself and find Evania!

Eloise marched toward the closed door at the end of the hall.

"Miss Eloise!" Ida hurried after.

"They won't keep me from Evania. Silas said his cousins disappeared from here also. Something is amiss. They're taking patients from their families. I will not allow this to happen to Evania." Eloise gripped the doorknob and twisted it. It was locked. She pressed her face to the little window at the door's center.

"You don't know this, Miss Eloise," Ida insisted.

Eloise rattled the doorknob. "Evania is not dead."

"The doctor said—"

"I don't care what Dr. Holzer said. I don't believe him. I *won't* believe him!" Eloise pounded on the door with the heel of her hand.

A nurse hurried toward them, keys dangling from her fingers. Eloise stepped back as the nurse unlocked the door and opened it a crack. "You're disrupting my ward with this noise. Visitors are not allowed in this section of the hospital."

Eloise tugged on the door, but the nurse resisted. "Please," Eloise begged, "my sister is ill, and I'm here to see her. Please let me in. She *needs* me."

"I cannot do that." The nurse shook her head, gray eyes snapping with authority. "Now leave before I call the security guard and have you removed."

"But–" Eloise choked on the panic that stole her breath. "My sister–"

"I don't know who your sister is, but you must speak with Dr. Holzer," the nurse hissed, glancing over her shoulder. A few patients had wandered into the hallway. Eloise saw emptiness in their eyes. The vacant expressions reminded her of Evania just before Father sent her away. The purposelessness that had stolen life from her sister.

Evania.

Eloise let her hand slip from the doorknob.

The nurse shut the door firmly and keyed the lock. Her look through the glass was disapproving, and then she turned her back to Eloise and marched back toward the patients.

"Come, Miss Eloise." Ida was kind but firm. "There is nothing we can do at the moment."

Strength drained from Eloise, and she held on to the door in order to stay upright.

Evania . . .

"Miss Eloise." Ida's hand settled in the middle of Eloise's back, and Eloise didn't fight her this time. Ida took her elbow and gently helped her turn back in the direction they'd come. "We'll return to our rooms. You can rest there."

As they passed the doctor's open office door, Eloise glanced inside. It was empty. Dr. Holzer was nowhere to be seen. Matron Rourke rose from her seat as they entered the front parlor. This time, her expression bore pity, and Eloise looked away. She didn't want the matron's pity. She didn't want sympathy. She wanted the truth—and her sister.

Exiting the hospital, Eloise sucked in a sob, swaying on the front stoop. She grabbed for the railing. Ida guided Eloise to a chair on the veranda and eased her onto it.

"I will see that the carriage is brought around. Wait here, Miss Eloise."

When Eloise didn't answer, Ida took her leave.

The sun warmed the chair in which Eloise sat. The air was crisp with the scent of autumn, and a light breeze brushed across her skin, reminding Eloise that without the sun, she would be chilled. She shivered anyway. Evania was dead? Truly? Then where was her grave? Eloise realized she'd not insisted on seeing Evania's grave but only demanded her sister's remains be returned to her.

If there was no grave to visit, how could the hospital prove Evania had truly passed on? Intent surged through Eloise. If Evania, even now, convalesced inside the hospital, then the doctor's claim of her death could not be substantiated with a grave.

Eloise moved to stand but then stilled. What was a grave when one couldn't verify the remains of their loved one? It was just a mound of dirt marked by a stone. It was nothing but a facade with the truth buried beneath, just out of reach.

"Miss James?"

An urgent whisper from the corner of the veranda startled her.

Eloise swung her head around to see an unfamiliar man half hiding behind a potted fir tree. "Are you Miss James?" His voice was just above a whisper.

"Yes?" She leaned in out of concern.

He shot a glance over his shoulder as if afraid of being watched or followed. "You're Miss Evania's sister?"

"I am." Eloise rose and hurried toward the man.

He wore the uniform of a steward. His beard half covered his face, and he shifted nervously, scanning around him once again.

"What of Evania?" Eloise gripped her reticule, feeling the velvet fold beneath her grasp. "What do you know of my sister?"

The steward hesitated, and then, as if overwhelmed by the fact he was out of order, he hurried to speak before he lost his nerve. "You won't find your sister here at the asylum."

"Then she is alive?" Hope rushed through Eloise with the force of a thunderclap.

The steward dropped his gaze, and his silence was weighted with his unspoken answer.

"Please, sir! Tell me my sister is still alive!"

The steward shook his head vehemently. "I don't lie, miss. On my mother's grave, I'd never tell such an awful falsehood if it isn't true."

Eloise saw genuine honesty in the man's expression, but she wanted to deny it. "Tell me where she is buried."

"You could dig up every grave if you could find them, but you won't find your sister." The steward delivered his sentence with a gravity that stalled Eloise's grief for the moment.

A dark hand of dread clamped around Eloise's heart. Another worried glance over his shoulder. "They took her away."

"Took her away?"

He nodded. "I've worked here for three months now, and the things I've seen . . . I even told that newspaper man—Dobbs, is it? The one whose cousins have also vanished. But I *saw* what happened to your sister. They took her away. Along with others. Loaded them into the back of a wagon and rolled off into the night."

"I don't understand." Eloise could hardly comprehend what the man was conveying. "Did they take them to be buried?"

The steward shrugged. "No idea, miss. They took the bodies out the back door, just as they always do to lay them to rest. Two men put them in the bed of a wagon and covered the bodies with tarps. Disappeared into the night and took the dead with them."

"Why?" Eloise tried to make sense of it.

Another shrug. "How am I supposed to know, miss? I'm merely telling you what I saw. I liked your sister. She was kind to me."

Eloise heard a horse snort, and she glanced behind her. Ida stood there ramrod-straight, watching. The horse, hitched up to their rented carriage, bent to nibble at some weeds sticking up through the cobblestones.

She returned her attention to the steward. "How do you know my sister?"

"I worked on her floor. She was one of those patients who didn't belong here. And she knew it too."

"What do you mean 'one of those patients'?"

"Your sister was clearly in her right mind. She was just grieving, but after she arrived, she became friends with a few of the patients. She helped me tend to them. I believe it gave her purpose."

Eloise tried to steady her breath. That sounded like Evania! "She wasn't ill?"

The steward shook his head. "Not at the beginning, but then—"

"Evania fell ill." So anxious was Eloise for answers that she interrupted him mid-sentence.

"Please, miss," the steward said, "allow me to finish."

"Forgive me—you were saying?"

"Well, it doesn't take long for folks to recognize bad when they see it. And your sister did. She told me she'd never get out of this place unless she did something for herself. She *did* get ill, though, and that was not of her doing. She had pneumonia, and a few nights ago, she let herself die."

"I don't understand," Eloise stated.

The steward seemed to search for the right words. "She *pretended* to die. Two others passed away, and Miss Evania told me she was going to as well. The doctor wasn't tending. I told the nurses Miss Evania was dead. I covered her with a sheet. No one questioned me, and they took her away with the others."

"But I thought . . ." Eloise paused, trying to recollect what she'd been led to understand. "I thought you said her body was loaded into the wagon."

The steward nodded. "Her body was loaded, but she was still alive. They just didn't know it. She was trying to escape, to get free of this place. But she was so ill, I can't say if she even made it."

He made a move to leave, but Eloise grabbed his sleeve to stop him. "But there is hope! She left here alive—she escaped!"

He tugged his arm away. "I've told you all I know." He looked directly into Eloise's eyes. "Your sister never should have been here. But it was just as dangerous to do what she did." His words chilled Eloise. "Patients disappear from here, Miss James. Dead or alive, and no one ever sees them again. Your sister was trying to find her freedom, but I'm not sure that she didn't just jump into her grave of her own free will."

12

He 'scaped from all the cares and woe
That earth inflicts or manhood know
And enter'd with the blest.

Lydia Howard Sigourney

The telegram that had arrived that evening at the hotel lay on Eloise's lap as she sat on the bed.

COME HOME IMMEDIATELY STOP
WE SHALL TALK STOP FATHER

Even the moonlight that cast its ethereal glow across her bedcovers didn't make the telegram any more delicate. It had arrived with the force of a well-aimed blow. It also told Eloise many things.

One, that her father knew where she was and had probably known since two days before when she'd arrived in Corinth on the train with Ida.

Two, that his declaration that they would talk meant *he* would talk, and *she* would listen.

Three, she didn't really have a choice but to obey promptly;

otherwise, he would send someone for her. She would be *retrieved* like a wayward puppy.

Lastly—and Eloise fingered the telegram as she considered it—Father knew why she was here. If he didn't, his missive would have been less decisive and more interrogative. He expected that she would obey. Eloise crumpled the telegram in her fist. She slid her legs beneath the sheet and blanket of the hotel bed, thankful that Ida was staying in an adjoining room and not observing her from a dark corner with her uninterpretable intention.

Nighttime was the worst time of day. It was in these moments when the burdens of life that could be borne during the light of day—or so she fooled herself into believing—became insurmountable. And the grief? The grief was suffocating. The fear was consuming. She didn't want to allow herself to *feel* the potential loss of Evania, yet she couldn't just lie in bed and try to rest when it was still a possibility that her sister was out there, ill and maybe dying, as she sought her freedom.

"Oh, Evania." Her sister's name on her lips brought the reality crashing down even more. Evania had disappeared.

What was Eloise to do now? Return home immediately as Father had demanded? Or should she try to determine where Evania had been taken, lying in the back of a wagon next to the corpses of her hospital mates?

Eloise looked toward the hotel window, whose lace curtains allowed the moon to peek in and share its opinion. She was on the first floor, and a veranda stretched around the building. Her window was locked to shut out the night's sounds, although Corinth was a peaceful town, not unlike New Jamestown. Even so, Eloise wondered what lurked in the night. Wagons carrying bodies from the asylum, but to where? What other nefarious activities might be taking place under the cover of darkness?

Should she stay here in Corinth and seek to find out more? What would Evania wish for her to do?

If only her sister could speak to her. Come to her—a visiting spirit in the night. But there was no movement outside of her window, no ghostly presence anywhere.

It seemed there were no answers.

Even God had fallen silent.

Eloise felt very much alone.

Silas Dobbs.

He came to her in a dream, and Eloise startled awake, his image so alive that she half expected him to be there in her room. She blinked, her eyes thick with sleep. The dream had been so vivid, Silas and her together, sneaking along a path in the cemetery, gravestones on all sides of them. Bats winged and swooped overhead. Because it was nighttime, she couldn't read the names etched into the stones, but she saw the graves with mounds of dirt piled on either side of them. Caskets broken open and shattered. Bodies of the dead, pale and decaying, strewn about the earth like discarded vessels. Silas had grabbed her hand, and his clasp crushed her fingers. So tightly he gripped her that in her dream, Eloise knew they would never be separated from each other. In the horror of the nightmare, her soul was stitched to his. Bound together by the memories of the dead.

She was awake . . . or was she? Eloise had thought she was sitting up in her bed, her room darker now that the moon had shifted as the earth turned. She thought she was tucked beneath bedcovers, but instead her legs were bare, her nightdress pulled to her knees. There were no longer any sheets and blankets on the mattress, but instead, grass cuttings and dirt. They stuck to her feet and pressed into her knees as though she had knelt by the graves.

Eloise lifted her hands, and in the shadowy light, her fingernails were cracked and broken, dirt embedded beneath them. Had she clawed at the ground to rebury the dead?

Yes. She remembered trying to push one of the corpses back into its hole. Scraping at the earth to cover it.

It had been Evania.

Eloise could see her sister's face, her eyes frozen in a deathly stare as Evania gazed unseeing at the world beyond. She'd pushed dirt onto her sister's body, then tore at the grass, sprinkling it over the grave. Anything she could use to bury her sister. Her sister who had not been buried. Her sister who could find no peace. It had been stolen from her.

Eloise dropped her hands into her lap.

And Silas. He was there too. Beside her bed, grasping her hand. His grip had not failed.

"It'll be a'right, love," he whispered, gathering her hand and pressing his lips to her fingers.

Gone was his devilishly mischievous smile.

There was desperation in his voice.

Was she dying too?

Eloise wanted to cry out, to beg Silas not to leave her. To make sure she was tucked peacefully away in a coffin to sleep for eternity.

"Shh, love," Silas whispered. "You must wake up now."

Eloise moaned and looked around her bed. It remained in the cemetery, beneath the moon, beside Evania's grave. More dirt was scattered over her legs. It fell on top of her, onto her face. She clawed at her cheeks with her free hand while Silas kept hold of the other.

"Stop, please . . ." She begged the man who had come into her dream, shovel in hand, to bury her in her bed.

Another shovelful of earth landed on top of her, stinging her flesh.

"Stop!" Eloise whimpered.

She saw him then. The grim outline of his features.

Father.

Another shovelful. Father was burying her with no grief or

sorrow on his face. Just an empty, detached expression that bit into her soul.

Another shovel–

Eloise's scream was silenced as Silas lunged for her, covering her face with his chest, her body with his own.

He was sacrificing his life for hers. Something she had never known was possible. She cried out for the depth of his devotion, for the dream that was a nightmare, holding hands with hope.

But the weight of it was crushing.

She couldn't breathe.

She couldn't breathe.

She couldn't *breathe*!

Eloise's eyes flung open wide as she gasped, finally awake from the terror her mind had conjured. A terror all too real, and a premonition that offered no promise.

"You've got to wake up, love."

The voice was most assuredly that of Silas Dobbs. Only now he didn't cover her body with his own. Instead, he crouched beside her, the night sky expansive and star-filled. As awareness crept over her, Eloise felt the cold ground beneath her body. She realized she was clad only in her nightgown. Her hair hung in strands around her shoulders, leaves and debris snagged in it as if she had wrestled with a ghoul in the woods and barely escaped with her life.

As in her nightmare, her feet were bare and filthy. She held up her hands. Yes. Her fingernails were broken with dirt beneath them.

Frantic, Eloise struggled to sit up and succeeded only with Silas's assistance. As soon as she sat on her own strength, she shoved away from him on her backside, stopping abruptly only because her back collided with something cold and hard. She looked behind her.

A tombstone.

"What's happening?" Her voice was a hiss nearly stolen by fear.

"I found you. Here in the graveyard, half out of your mind." Silas's expression was drawn with concern and not a little curiosity.

Eloise looked around her. Yes. She was in a graveyard. Unfamiliar and cold in its slumber. Row upon row of stones marking the names of the dead. But unlike her nightmare, there were no bodies strewn across the ground, no mounds of dirt and open graves, and no Father to contend with.

Just Silas Dobbs.

"Where am I? How did I find this place? I've never been here before in my life." She pressed back against the gravestone rather than drawing near to Silas, who in real life didn't bring her the intense comfort she'd sensed in her dream. Instead, he frightened her. And the fact that she wasn't in her hotel room horrified her.

"You're in the Corinth Presbyterian Cemetery," Silas answered.

She had yet to see this man in the light of day. But he looked different tonight with his jaunty cap lying now on the ground beside him. His eyes were furrowed with such worry that she could hardly continue to be afraid of him, wary and suspicious though she was.

"H-how did I get here?"

"I don't have the slightest idea." Silas shook his head. "You came walkin' through the graveyard like a ghost, you did. Near made my heart stop, and not because of your beauty."

Eloise lifted a hand to her face. She forgot his remark the moment she realized she wasn't wearing her spectacles. That would explain why the world around her was hazy, edged in silhouettes, and making her see double.

"Did I sleepwalk?" she pondered aloud in disbelief.

"That might answer a lot if you did," Silas replied. "But a dangerous walk it was."

He wasn't wrong. She must have left her hotel room, wandered the streets of Corinth, and somehow arrived at this cemetery. The irony of waking in a graveyard wasn't lost on Eloise.

"I'm filthy." She pulled her knees to her chest, hiding her feet under the folds of her nightgown.

Silas shifted in discomfort. "You started to dig at a grave with your hands. You knelt on the ground over there," he added, pointing, "and you were crying out for your sister."

Eloise followed his line of sight. She squinted, unable to make out the name on the grave he was pointing at.

"Rupert Flidgett. Died ten years ago," Silas supplied. "Did ya know him?"

Eloise shook her head. The name was as strange to her as the idea that she had awakened in a cemetery she'd never before set foot in. A thought startled her then, and she shifted her attention back to Silas. "Why are *you* here?"

He eyed her for a moment before answering. "I'm looking for bodies."

Eloise studied him, wordless.

Silas continued, "The ones who have disappeared from the asylum. Did they die? And if they did, where are they buried? I've checked the Methodist graveyard and the Catholic one too. There are no unmarked graves or stones with names that match those of the patients who might have died. So where are they? Where're Seamus and Penny? And your sister?"

Eloise couldn't answer that any more than she could account for how she had gotten here.

"Thank the good Lord, I found ya." Silas hadn't moved from his position next to her.

"They took Evania away in a wagon," Eloise started.

Silas had been in the process of reaching for his cap. He jammed it on his dark curls and turned surprised eyes in her direction. "Say again?"

Eloise kept her arms wrapped around her knees. She was exposed. Vulnerable. Her only armor was her nightgown, which was flimsy. Still, something compelled her to tell Silas what had occurred at the asylum. From Dr. Holzer's claim that Evania had died and had already been buried to the words she'd shared with the steward stating Evania might still be alive.

Silas's frown deepened as she recounted what she'd been told.

"So they took your sister and other bodies away in a wagon?"

Eloise nodded.

Silas's shoulders lifted as he sucked in a sigh. "Ah, 'tis looking more and more as I've been fearin'."

She waited, sensing he was debating whether to tell her his theory and worrying that he would hold it to himself.

He didn't. "Body snatchers."

Eloise paled.

Silas gave a nod as though to verify what she hadn't even asked. "Men have been stealin' the dead for decades. What better place to take them from than the asylum after they die? I doubt they fight hard to save their patients, and when they're dead, who would miss them?"

"I don't—"

"You don't understand?" Silas gave a little laugh. "Don't you read the news?"

Eloise didn't read the news. According to Father, a woman didn't need to read the news.

Silas tilted his head and eyed her. "Well, love, just this year they passed a law making it a felony to steal a corpse or to sell one. It used to be a misdemeanor. Slap o' the hand, it was."

Eloise was afraid to ask him to explain further. There was such frankness in Silas's expression that she felt ignorant, and he seemed to notice her perplexity.

Sighing, Silas shifted where he sat on the grass. He rubbed a hand over his face. "I've been investigatin' it for a while now. I mean to sell the story one day and, in the process, expose what happened to Seamus and Penny at the asylum—and your sister. You see, dead bodies are big business. Haven't you heard of the rash of them being stolen? Fort Wayne gettin' the worst of it, they did. Resurrection men have been diggin' up the graves or smugglin' bodies from the hospitals and sellin' them."

"*Selling* them?" It was awful. Pure evil. The desecration of the dead! Eloise shrank back against the gravestone.

"Aye. According to the law, any cadaver used at a school to study anatomy needs to come with official paperwork stating cause of death and where the corpse was obtained."

Eloise was nauseated by the idea.

"Is this really new to ya?" Silas studied her. "Didn't you hear about the dead woman they found in the back of a wagon after the police ran off two of the snatchers? It made the newspaper because someone identified her as having been the body that went missing from the rich folk cemetery. That caused quite a stir. People like Seamus and Penny—no one cares about them if they die. But a fine lady? Aye. An' when her husband came to identify the body, he stated he'd been to his wife's grave an'—"

"And what?" Eloise could barely breathe.

Silas ducked his head, lowering his eyes. "I hate to tell you the gruesome facts, love."

"Tell me." Eloise might retch after hearing the details, but she had to know.

He nodded and went on. "Well, the fine lady had been buried with her newborn infant. The father found the poor babe lyin' at the bottom of the grave all alone—the casket was busted wide open. I'm telling you, Eloise, these men have no hearts. But they have deep pockets, and they want to fill 'em."

"Won't the law stop—"

"Do laws stop murder? Thievin'? Criminal acts?" Silas interrupted, an edge of steel in his tone. "No. They slow it down is all. Till men find a way around the law."

"Surely the schools will cooperate with the authorities—"

Silas laughed loudly this time. "Some mayhap. But by the time the bodies that are legally obtained for study are released, they're not in good condition. Too many records to keep, and all before the schools can get to them."

"You mean—"

"The business is in fresh bodies," Silas said matter-of-factly.

"Fresh bodies," she repeated.

"Aye. So my theory is that when a patient at the asylum takes sick, they pretty much just let 'em die. There's money to be had if they sell the corpse." He stopped as soon as he said the words.

Eloise could hold it in no longer. She scrambled to her knees, her legs tangling in her nightgown, and vomited onto the grave.

"There, there, love." Silas was by her side in an instant. He combed her hair from her face with his fingers, holding it back as she vomited again. "I shouldn't have said so. I don't know where they took your sister. I'm sorry, love. I'll bite me tongue next time."

Eloise shook her head, even as she wiped her mouth with the back of her hand. "But if Evania was alive when they loaded her into the wagon, then she might still be sick and dying somewhere!"

Silas considered this. "It's true, but she could be—" He bit off his words.

"She could be dead," Eloise finished. She rubbed her hands over her eyes, desperate to find sense in it all. "We just don't know."

"Or if they found her still alive, well—"

"We need to find her. Before they hurt my sister, or if she *is* gone, before they desecrate my sister's body! My father will stop it. He will." She was sure of it. The moment Silas helped her expose this to Father, his ire would focus on what really mattered: his daughter. He might not have cared that Evania was buried in an unmarked grave on asylum grounds, but to have her try to escape, as ill as she was, only to be carted off as if dead with the intent for her remains to be sold and then cut into as if she were a doll on display? That alone would cause Father's pride to suffer, if nothing else.

She reached out and gripped Silas's wrist, desperate to gain his cooperation. "You must come home with me," she urged.

"Why?" Silas frowned.

"My father will listen to you. He will review your evidence and pursue these men . . . these body snatchers. He will find Evania—and Seamus and Penny."

The look Silas gave her was full of pity and regret. "Oh, love, that's the problem. I've got all conjecture and no proof. You know how you can be certain of what's going on around you, but you have no basis to claim it but your own hunches? I just *know* in me gut this is what's happenin' at the asylum. The stealin' of bodies. But I can't prove it, Eloise. Not yet."

"Then we'll find proof," Eloise stated. "We'll find the men who took my sister. We'll tell my father and . . ."

Silas nodded slowly. "And if they haven't survived, then we'll bury the ones we love," he vowed.

13

Tilly Thompson

A bloody and a sudden end,
Gunshot or a noose,
For Death who takes what man would keep,
Leaves what man would lose.

William Butler Yeats

Present Day

"You going on in?" Grandpa Don asked as he paid attention to the paintbrush in one hand and the scuffed model train car in the other.

"To the basement?" Tilly eyed him. She was content to perch next to him today. There had been enough excitement the last several days to last her a lifetime.

"That's what we're talking about, isn't it?" He dabbed the tip of the brush at a chip in the engine's black paint.

"I don't do basements," Tilly retorted.

"I don't do Alzheimer's, and yet here I am."

Tilly didn't know how to respond to that. Grandpa Don seemed to maintain a positive attitude about it, but she couldn't always say the same for herself. She saw the shifts and changes. Mostly when he was tired or when his routine was disrupted. Which explained why he'd called Luke the other night instead of Erik.

She still hadn't lived that one down. Erik had actually *laughed* when he heard what happened. Of course, she hadn't told anyone about what she'd seen in the window, the face and the hand splayed across the glass, and the fear that something otherworldly was roaming about James Mansion at night. No. Erik—and everyone else—had concluded that Tilly had passed out due to the stress after discovering the dead body in the wall.

"Go check out the basement," Grandpa Don said. "Goodness knows there's plenty to sort through down there. The James family shut the place up years ago. Now you get to sift through what they left behind. I know your job is to take care of me, but I'm doing just fine right now." He turned the engine and stared down his nose through his glasses at it. "I snuck a gander at the basement the other day. It's rough down there."

"I know," agreed Tilly. "It's nasty and gives me the creeps! Besides, I don't know where to begin."

Grandpa Don looked at her over the rim of his glasses. "Last I looked, there's no dead bodies hanging from the rafters."

"I wouldn't be surprised if there were at some point," Tilly muttered.

"Now, hold on." Grandpa Don lowered his arms to his lap, still holding the train car and the paintbrush. "You mean to tell me you think this house has more dead folk hidden in it?"

"No! That's not what I'm saying." Tilly allowed herself a chuckle. "I was just being morbid. I don't care for creepy old basements is all."

"You know what I always say." Grandpa Don returned to examining his model train.

"What's that?"

"Feel the fear and do it anyway."

Tilly frowned. "That sounds like a motivational poster, Grandpa."

He shook his head. "It's an original."

"Fine." She got to her feet. "I'll go check out the basement." Tilly considered what she might need. She decided on a notepad and a pen. She would make another to-do list, this one pertaining to the basement.

It was a short jaunt from the train room to the kitchen. But she didn't go that direction. Instead, she crossed the parlor toward the door that led to the narrow servants' hall. It was another way to enter the basement, but for some reason, accessing the basement from this direction seemed less unnerving. That gaping black doorway from the other day was still a bad memory.

She took the stairs heading down into the bowels of James Mansion. Tilly could imagine a century ago the house staff using these steps to retrieve items stored in the area below the living quarters. It was where a cellar would have been located, along with a coal furnace. Access to a well perhaps, Tilly considered as she felt the air around her growing cooler and damper. Maybe it was just as she had imagined when she was a child, with secret passages in the basement leading to other areas of the house. Or old tunnels where folks ran liquor during Prohibition. Or maybe, she determined as she pulled the chain dangling from a lightbulb overhead, it was just a basement.

Light flooded the room. The foundation was stone and felt wet to the touch, even though it wasn't. The floor was uneven, a mix of old brick and patches of concrete. There wasn't much in the way of natural light since there were no egress windows to enable someone to climb out if need be. Empty wooden shelves lined the walls, which were probably used for storage at one time.

She made her way deeper into the basement, gathering her

bearings as she did so. If she pictured the floor above, she was directly beneath the stairs where the body had been found. She was moving toward the west side and the space under the sitting and dining rooms.

Spotting a wall switch, Tilly went and flipped it on, thankful for the row of bulbs in the ceiling that helped to illuminate the space. It was very 1980s and reminded her of a serial killer's basement. A place where someone would tie up their victim, the bulb hanging above them like a bad omen. Some electrical shocks powered by an old battery. Maybe a pair of pliers to pull a tooth?

"Stop it!" Tilly scolded herself for her morbid thoughts. She needed to stop this. Her imagination was going full speed ahead, and this was exactly why she hadn't wanted to come down here in the first place.

Basements were full of secrets, and she'd already discovered a massive one in James Mansion that even Luke, who'd grown up in the house, hadn't known about. Reason told her she had to assume it was a once-in-a-lifetime discovery, but her imagination was creating all sorts of monsters lurking about the basement. And she couldn't forget what she'd seen in the kitchen a few nights ago. She hadn't slept well since.

The next section of the basement was where Tilly observed the bulk of belongings that had been shoved down here to be forgotten. Wooden chairs stacked, boxes of old Mason jars, and several lamps that looked like the 1990s had at one point a very neon influence in at least one room of the house. Tilly spent the next half hour rummaging through boxes of old magazines and travel maps. She also discovered an old bottle of wine, its year 1981. That would be saved for a rainy day, or maybe the garbage if the things floating in the neck of the green bottle meant the wine had been contaminated. By the time she had at least a cursory understanding of what needed to be prioritized on her to-do list, she was ready to abandon the belongings.

Tilly moved farther into the basement and was relieved to find there was nothing much to see but empty spaces, stone walls that gave off the feeling of a tomb, and a musty smell that was sure to trigger a full-on sneeze attack soon. She could feel it in her sinuses.

She hurried down a short corridor, brick walls on either side, knowing it took her to the stairs that would lead up into the kitchen. Sure enough, they appeared—basic wooden stairs with no railing. The kind where a hand could reach through to grab your ankle as you rushed up them.

About ready to do just that, Tilly paused when she noticed a small cupboard-like door at the base of the wall near the bottom of the stairs. It wasn't tall enough to walk through, but it was large enough for a small storage area.

More walls.

More openings.

Tilly knew she'd never sleep tonight unless she opened it and checked to make sure whatever space was behind it was empty. She had no desire to find another dead body, but then she had no desire to find herself busting down the door in her sleep again either.

She squatted and tugged on the door. With a definitive pull, it popped open, the sound of wood against wood scraping and squeaking. Tilly peered inside, but the area behind the door was black. Pulling her phone from her pocket, Tilly flicked on the flashlight and pointed it inside the space.

Empty.

Thank the Lord.

No skeleton stared back at her. In fact, the alcove was barely large enough for an adult to squeeze into. She ducked her head inside. Spiderwebs. Yes. A nice collection of those. There was an old pencil in the far corner—weird—and a shoe. She lifted the light beam higher and noted it was an old tennis shoe, a popular brand, and nothing to worry about.

As Tilly ducked from the space, her light caught the edge of a brick that jutted out from the wall. It wasn't one of those loose bricks with treasure behind it. But Tilly had to check anyway. The brick slid out easily, and Tilly stretched her upper torso into the crawl space so she could shine the light behind it.

A book.

That was better than a severed hand.

She pulled it out and then quickly retracted her body from the tiny area and clomped up the stairs with speed—so that no one could grab her feet as she ran. Tilly would have loved to have found relief in the kitchen, but even that room creeped her out now. She ducked into the main corridor that stretched the full length of the mansion and hurried onto the back covered porch.

Crisp fall air greeted her. The sun reflected off a blanket of orange and yellow leaves in the yard. She collapsed onto an iron chair, far more out of breath than she should be, and made a promise to herself that the next time she went into the basement, she would do so with a higher level of courage than that of an eight-year-old kid.

Tilly set her phone on a side table and lifted the book. It was black, no title, probably a journal of some kind. Interesting. Opening the front cover, she smiled. A child's handwriting scrawled a sentence on the front page.

Don't read on pain of death.

I'm serious.

That made sense. The pencil. The tennis shoe. The basement alcove had likely been a secret hideaway for a child who had lived in James Mansion. Tilly could picture the person hurrying down the old steps, diving through the cupboard door like leaping into the rabbit hole in *Alice in Wonderland*. An entire new world would open up for them inside that tiny space. It could be a spacecraft, or a boxcar, or a time machine, or even a clubhouse.

Tilly ran her finger over the printing. Dare she risk the pain of death to turn the page? She smiled to herself as she did.

She instantly regretted it.

Her smile faded.

L. W. J.

The initials, also in a young person's scrawl, brought the truth slamming into her mind. She knew what children had grown up in James Mansion. Luke and his brother, Kyle. The initials didn't fit Kyle. The age of the journal and the fact that it had a printer's mark on the first page dating to 2006 made it only logical that this had to be Luke's handwriting.

She should return it to him.

Definitely not open it.

But Tilly opened it. Her curiosity was heightened as she quick did the math in her head. In 2006, Luke would have been eleven years old. He was thirty-one now. So if he'd been that young when he first penciled his initials in the book, then he certainly was not old enough to be scribbling high school secrets in its pages—which was when she'd first become aware of Luke James.

The secrets of an elementary school kid had to be entertaining.

Tilly turned the page.

A horribly sketched horse met her eyes, and she laughed when she realized it was wearing tennis shoes.

The next page.

I hate A.T.

Who was A.T.?

Another page.

It's dark in here. I'm scared.

She quickly flipped to the next page. Something about those two short sentences made her nerves taut. She scanned the words that followed. More hatred for A.T. and some missing Legos. The momentary relief Tilly had felt in the subsequent page or two dissipated as she turned to another. This time, the young boy, Luke, had written more than a few words, misspelled but agonizing in their honesty.

Evry time he comes home, Mom crys. So do I. I hate him. I hate him so much. He smells like beer but he acts like hes god. I dont think god drinks beer.

i hate my dad.

i want to kill him.

14

Death is nothing at all.
I have only slipped away to the next room.
I am I and you are you,
and the old life that we lived so fondly together is
untouched, unchanged.
Whatever we were to each other,
that we are still.

Henry Scott Holland

Tilly sat cross-legged in a papasan chair on the screened-in porch of Erik and Ashley's little house across town. Grandpa Don was playing with his great-grandchildren inside, and she took heart from the giggles she heard coming from her nieces.

"What's with the urgent visit?" Erik was lounging in an upholstered chair, his legs propped on an ottoman.

Ashley handed them both piping-hot mugs of apple cider, the perfect topping off to a pleasant autumn evening. She eased onto the chair beside Erik. "Is everything okay, Tilly?"

"I'm not sure." She looked between her brother and sister-in-law. She hadn't brought Luke's journal with her. It felt like a betrayal layered on top of her error of nosing into his childhood business. She took a sip of cider. It burned the tip of her tongue.

She probably deserved it. "I found a journal in the basement of the mansion."

"You keep on finding things, you're going to end up uncovering a chest of gold or something," Erik quipped.

"I wish it were that." Tilly measured her words. "I know you can't tell me much because of patient confidentiality at the rehab center, but what do you know about Luke James's childhood in the mansion?"

Erik's expression darkened. "Tilly." The warning in his voice was clear.

She held up a hand while gripping the hot mug in her other. "It wasn't hard to figure out. You left reasonable clues, and I followed the logical progression. Luke James was a patient at Morning Song Recovery."

"I will not confirm–" Erik started.

"Or deny. I know," Tilly finished for him. "I'm not trying to dig up dirt on him, but it was *his* journal I found. He had to have written it when he was around eleven."

Erik exchanged looks with Ashley.

"I read the first few pages." It felt good to admit her invasion of privacy out loud.

Ashley nodded as if she would have done the same, but Erik disapproved. "Why would you do that, Tilly?"

"Well, at first it was to find out whose journal it was." She hadn't set out to pry. "Then it . . . well, what I read wasn't good."

"What did it say?" Ashley leaned forward, invested in the conversation.

Erik shot her a look that caused her to sit back in the chair.

Tilly answered, "It said he wanted to kill his dad."

"*What*?" Ashley's shock was evident.

Yet Erik didn't appear at all surprised. He sighed and placed his mug of cider on the floor. He then leaned forward, forearms on knees, folding his hands and addressing Tilly in a voice that made her feel both reprimanded and appeased at the same time.

"Remember, he wrote that as a kid. The best thing to do is to return the journal to Luke. He doesn't need that getting in anyone's hands—especially with his running for mayor."

"But what about his dad? What happened to Luke as a child?" Tilly had a growing vision of little Luke tucking himself away in the alcove of the creepy basement, with his journal, pencil, and probably a flashlight. Hiding from his dad? His parents? Or was he being punished for something he did or said?

Erik looked down at his feet, and then after a moment of consideration, he raised his head. "Listen, I'm not going to say anything about Luke. I can't, and you know that."

Ashley interjected. "I'm sure if Luke was at Morning Song, he had the best of care."

"But if Luke was at Morning Song, that meant he was using or is an alcoholic," Tilly concluded. It was how her mind worked, and she couldn't not put the pieces together even if she tried.

Erik's gaze met hers, and it was stern. "Let it go, Tilly."

"But if his dad—"

"It's common knowledge," Erik went on, "that the James men have had their struggles along with their enormous successes."

"And Luke's dad was the mayor of New Jamestown," Ashley said. "It's a James family tradition for the men to be in leadership."

"That doesn't mean they aren't abusive or addicted behind closed doors," Tilly stated. She didn't mean to sound accusatory; she just wanted to understand. Things left hanging were unsettling to her, even if it wasn't her own story.

Erik shifted on his seat. "In my opinion, Luke is the first James I've known to try to live with some humility. He's changed tremendously over the years, and his faith has played a significant role in his life. He's made no secret of that. And I never thought I'd say this, but I'll be voting for the man in November. I never thought I'd respect Luke James—I mean, you knew Luke in high school."

Tilly nodded. Did she ever. "But for a kid to write something so *violent*."

"Kids say crazy stuff. Why is this so important to you?" Erik challenged. "If Luke wrote that, it was many years ago."

It was an honest question. She'd all but called an emergency family meeting over it, but in reality, it didn't affect her or have any influence on her future. Perhaps not even Luke's.

"She cares about Luke," Ashley observed.

"I don't—" Tilly bit off her words. She didn't want to sound cold or robotic. She had been accused of that many times. And she did care—not so much about Luke, but about the disturbing elements of James Mansion and its past. "I want to know who the woman in the wall was, and this journal—the cupboard beneath the stairs—it's all very unsettling. Something happened in the mansion, over time with the James family, something that wasn't right." She hesitated before adding, "Something that still isn't right."

Erik's forehead creased. "What do you mean?"

Tilly struggled to find the words. "It's hard to explain, but there's a wickedness that lingers in the house. I can feel it in my gut."

Ashley made no attempt to hide her shivering. She pulled her knees up into the chair and balanced her mug on them. "I couldn't sleep there knowing they'd just removed a dead body from the wall."

"I'm sure that helps Tilly feel better." Erik gave his wife a lopsided smile.

Ashley shrugged. "Just saying—I get it. First, a dead body. Now, a journal written by someone we know wanted to kill his father."

"Again, he wrote that as a kid," Erik countered.

"Still . . ." Ashley sipped her cider, and Tilly was grateful for her sensitivity. "My grandmother used to say that when a house has seen wickedness, parts of that wickedness seep into the walls and stay behind. She used to pray over her house every night."

"I don't know if wickedness has that much power," Erik stated.

"I do." Ashley nodded. "Only because I believe God says there's a spiritual world we don't see. So if Tilly is uneasy, it makes sense to me. I don't believe any of it can harm you under the shelter of the Lord, though." She met Tilly's eyes. "I mean, God is so much more powerful than evil, but there are shadows. Sin leaves shadows. We can't avoid that."

"If it makes you feel better," Erik said carefully, "we can come pray with you."

Tilly shook her head. It felt like an overreaction. An irrational one. Was it, though? The memory of the face in the window. Had it been real or just in her dreams? "I-I just wanted to talk it through. But I don't think I should talk to Grandpa about it." Yes. It would be too disturbing for Grandpa Don. His mind was already struggling to keep up. Adding the burden of more secrets and questions could exacerbate his confusion. She'd needed to express herself out loud. Now that she had, Tilly concluded, there wasn't much to do about any of it. The woman in the wall was gone—though Tilly still wanted to know who she was. Luke's journal was—well, it was Luke's story, she supposed. Erik was right. It wasn't hers to know.

Her conscience gnawed at her. "So should I return the journal to him?"

"No!" Ashley exclaimed just as Erik stated a firm "Yes."

They looked at each other. Erik frowned at his wife. "Why would you say no?"

Ashley's eyes widened, and she tucked her chocolate-brown hair behind her ears. "Why would you return it to him? It would only dredge up bad memories. What if reading it sends him into a tailspin, and he becomes tempted to start using or drinking again?" It seemed Ashley had drawn the same conclusion Tilly had, that Luke was recovering from something he'd been treated for at Morning Song.

"I understand your concern, but it's *his* journal," Erik said. "If it were mine, I'd want it back." He shifted his gaze to Tilly. "Life isn't as straightforward as you want to believe, Tilly. You have no idea what he went through."

"His father was abusive toward him," Tilly began, for Erik's dancing around the truth had already confirmed as much. "The James family's shady reputation dates back long before Luke and his parents. Luke aside, there have always been questions about whether they've conducted their business on the up-and-up—including whether their repeated campaigns to be elected mayor were legit."

"I remember my dad claiming Luke's father bought his way to the mayoral seat," Ashley provided.

Erik nodded. "I've heard that too. The James men have always been in charge. That's the primary platform Will Morrow is running on. His campaign motto against Luke is 'New leadership, new hope.' A lot of folks in New Jamestown are tired of the tradition of James men in leadership. It's not as though the family made their money through holding the mayoral seat. It was merely to emphasize their influence and position in town. But they're an old-money family, and with that comes the burden of reputation. It's been rough on Luke."

"Will Morrow is Daphne Dover's brother, correct?" Ashley was piecing together the small-town family tree.

"That's right." Erik shifted his attention to his wife. "Morrow is a good guy for the most part. But he's making Luke the main issue in his run for mayor rather than the issues that affect the town. His tactics have included personal attacks—not very classy."

"But another James family member in leadership *does* affect the town. I'm sympathetic to Kyle's health concerns, but just because he's unable to run for mayor again doesn't mean the seat is owed to Luke. I was planning to vote for Will Morrow,"

Tilly conceded. At Erik's look, she widened her eyes defensively. "What he says makes a lot of sense."

"I'm also considering voting for Will," Ashley admitted.

Erik sighed. "The fact that he isn't talking about city issues as much as he's been making a point to denigrate the James family and push them out of leadership—well, that bugs me."

"Luke was a jerk in high school," Tilly muttered.

"And you believe people can't change?" Erik countered.

Ashley inserted a new question that drew Tilly's attention back to James Mansion and its history. "Wasn't there a story about a James man who sent his daughter to an asylum?"

"Is that true?" If so, it was news to Tilly. Amid all the rumors of the James family involving rum running, the Mob, and tales of being in cahoots with Russians during the Cold War, it piqued her curiosity. She knew most of the stories were exaggerated and untrue, but a woman being committed to an asylum by her father? That could very well have happened. The victim in the wall in James Mansion was strong evidence that someone there, at some time, had potentially degraded and abused women.

"I don't know much about it," Erik was explaining. "I think it took place in the late nineteenth century. The old Indiana asylum was about twenty minutes north of here in Corinth. Luke's great-grandfather times however many supposedly had her committed even though she didn't have mental-health issues, or so the story goes. It was a way to be rid of her for whatever reason. Who knows if that's even true."

"I bet people didn't like *that* Mr. James very much," Ashley said.

"At least the women of the time. Can you imagine being institutionalized against your will?" Tilly and Ashley's eyes met in consternation.

"It's something people did back in the day," Erik stated, though he redeemed his blunt statement by adding an apologetic tone. "Sucks, but it's true. Elizabeth Packard, a woman who almost single-handedly changed the law in that regard, was committed to an asylum because her reverend husband thought she was too outspoken and their doctrines didn't mix. Back then what the man said, and the doctor signed off on, was the way things went. It didn't matter what the truth was."

"That's awful." Ashley shook her head.

Tilly considered it all as they fell silent, each lost in their own thoughts. A history of pride and dominance like that—she could see why Will Morrow was running against Luke. But she couldn't forget the words she'd read in Luke's childhood journal. Words of hatred and anger, and beneath it all, a pain that resonated with her.

Women weren't always the victims.

Too often, so were the children.

That Luke James was hiding a history of secrets was obvious.

Erik was right. She needed to return the journal to Luke, whether or not she voted for him for mayor. His childhood secrets were nobody's business—including hers.

Newspapers were still a thing in a cozy place like New Jamestown. And this autumn morning, with the color of fall at its peak, the rows of historic homes and the village of folks waving at one another from across the street made a newspaper seem like a must. The internet could never replace a good hometown paper.

Made even more evident by this morning. While the New Jamestown newspaper boasted a headline about the latest new business grand opening and heartwarming community news, while a local social media group had reared its ugly head. Tilly wished she'd opted for a book instead of doomscrolling. She also wished she'd stood strong against Erik's insistence she get a phone now that she was Grandpa Don's caregiver. She stared at the post in the community group on the neighborly app as she sank onto a chair on the outdoor patio of the Brew Shop.

The James family has more than a skeleton in their mansion's wall, someone posted.

She stared at the insinuating statement, being quick about skimming the post before Luke showed up to meet her for coffee. His childhood journal was burning a hole in her bag, and after last night's discussion with Erik and Ashley, Tilly just wanted to wash her hands of it. She was getting too immersed in the James family history. It was one thing to discover a dead body that was over a century old, but it was something else entirely to exhume the secrets of a person who was still very much alive.

Her eyes scanned the post.

It referenced a local woman who had disappeared in 2006, who had once been thought to be tied to the James family—an uncalled-for speculation that the body in the wall was hers.

"That's not even possible!" Tilly muttered.

"Exactly." Luke slid onto the chair opposite her.

Startled, Tilly's head shot up, and she frantically tried to tuck her phone away out of sight.

"Don't bother," Luke said. He sounded grim. He looked tired. There were shadows under his eyes. "Everyone is reading that app this morning. I thought the major social media apps were bad. No one warned me of hometown neighbor-to-neighbor watch apps. It's like the old-fashioned gossip party lines."

"I thought community groups were supposed to be about, well, community." Tilly's statement sounded futile the moment it escaped her.

"Have you met humanity lately?" Luke was jaded, yet she could hardly blame him.

Tilly noticed a few people glancing their direction. They probably would have anyway regardless of the post. Luke James cut an impressive figure, mayoral candidate or not, and he was sitting across from a woman who didn't fit the stereotype of a good-looking man's coffee date.

It wasn't a date, Tilly reminded herself, glancing at the bag. She was having second thoughts about giving Luke the journal. It felt like throwing another grenade in his direction, and for goodness' sake, if she wasn't feeling empathetic toward the man! But if she didn't hand it to him now, he'd want to know why she'd asked to have coffee with him and then things would get awkward very fast.

"Who is this other woman who disappeared that they're talking about?" Tilly blanched as the words tumbled out of her. One of these days she'd learn to have a conversation without saying something completely out of line.

Luke chuckled softly as he stirred cream into his coffee with a spoon. "Going for the jugular, huh? You sure you didn't inspire the article with a conspiracy theory about my family?"

"No!" Tilly protested.

He lifted his blue orbs. "I was kidding."

"Oh."

Luke tapped the spoon against the side of his glass. He seemed blissfully unaffected by the people stealing looks at him. "When I was a kid, there was a woman who was known around town as one of the few unhoused in New Jamestown. Do you remember her?"

"She was homeless?" Tilly clarified. She didn't recall her. But then, as a child, she'd spent most of her time with her nose buried in history books, not gazing out the window at the present day.

"Sure. We try to use 'unhoused' now so we aren't defining people by their situation." Luke didn't say it as a reprimand, but a statement of observation. He was in politics after all. "Anyway, she disappeared. Apparently, according to this anonymous poster, she's your girl in the wall, and my father killed her."

Tilly couldn't help thinking back to the day Luke had strode into James Mansion when the DHPA was there to examine and remove the remains. He'd seemed upset, worried, and hadn't he asked about the age of the victim?

"Obviously they're speculating," Luke went on. "Will Morrow supporters want to make the point that James men aren't trustworthy, that we've been in leadership for too many years. And linking us to a recent disappearance and possible murder would help his cause."

"But the remains are over a century old. There's no ground for that argument. As for being in leadership, if it's your calling . . ." Tilly let her sentence hang. The suggestion probably sounded silly, not to mention she'd just declared last night to Erik her intention of voting for Will. For the very reason Luke had just stated.

"Is it?" Luke's question was muted as he stared down into his coffee.

Tilly wasn't sure she'd heard him right, and she didn't know if it were wise to push him further. Instead, she opted for an equally sore topic of conversation because it was the only thing she could think of to quick change the subject. "How's your brother?"

She needed to stop talking.

Luke offered her a grateful smile. "It'll be good when he can step down from office and rest." He sipped his coffee absently. "The doctors have given him about a year . . . maybe less."

"I'm so sorry." And she was. Tilly couldn't fathom losing Erik. Family was family, after all, and regardless of their upbringing, it seemed that Luke was close to Kyle.

"Anyway," Luke said, sucking in a deep breath, "what did you want to meet about? You said you had something for me."

Tilly's stomach curdled. Luke had just pulled the pin from the grenade. There was no going back now. She reached down into her bag, hesitated, met Luke's expectant gaze, then lifted the journal and set it on the table.

Luke's attention became glued to it. She saw the color leave his face.

He coughed. Fisted his hand and covered his mouth. He cleared his throat and then nodded, blowing breath from between his lips. "I did not expect to see that again." Reaching for the journal, he picked it up, eyeing it as though it would come alive, grow teeth, and bite.

"I found it yesterday," Tilly admitted. Should she tell him everything? That she'd read the first few pages? "It was—"

"In the alcove under the basement stairs."

"Yes."

"How'd you find it?" Luke lifted questioning eyes. "I forgot it even existed."

"I noticed a brick in the wall was sticking out. When I moved it, this was behind it."

"Yeah. My old hiding place." Luke didn't bother to open the journal, but leveled a look on Tilly that suddenly transported her back to high school when Luke was less approachable. "Did you read it?" he asked.

There it was. She could lie and say no, but then she'd writhe in guilt forever. Tilly offered him a weak smile. "Just the first few pages." She hurried on to explain, "I didn't know it was yours, and I was trying to figure out whose it was and . . ."

Luke frowned. "You didn't read the whole thing?"

Tilly shook her head. "That would be dishonest of me. I wanted to," she admitted, "but I talked to Erik about it last night, and he recommended I return it to you."

"You didn't read it," Luke repeated as if unbelieving.

"Well, like I said," she felt she needed to make it clear, "I did read the first few pages."

Without another word, Luke opened his childhood journal. "I hate A.T." A light chuckle followed. "Adam Tibedeau. My fourth-grade nemesis. The kid was a piece of work. He stole my Legos one Saturday when he came over, then swore he didn't. And everyone believed him."

Tilly managed an apprehensive smile.

Luke turned the page. "Ah yes. The horse with tennis shoes."

Another page. His eyes skimmed the words Tilly had read. His mouth tightened, head bent even as he lifted his eyes. The blue of them slammed into hers, and Tilly knew he understood the gravity of what she'd read.

"There are times when kids want to kill their parents."

"I never wanted to kill mine." In retrospect, Tilly determined, she probably shouldn't have said what she was thinking.

Luke stared at her for a moment. "Then you were lucky." He shut the book, laying his palm over it. There was a long stretch of silence between them. The sounds of the coffee shop's patio grew louder. Conversations floated to Tilly's ears, but she tried to block them out. She could tell Luke was trying to figure out what to say. How to explain it. A look settled on his face that Tilly couldn't understand. Hurt maybe? Mingled with fear of the memories the journal brought with it?

"I'm sorry," she breathed.

"Don't be. You can't help what my family was like."

"I meant," Tilly corrected, "I'm sorry for reading that page."

"Oh." Luke gave a short laugh. "Well. There's worse if you'd kept reading."

Tilly wanted to make sure he understood. "I didn't keep reading. I didn't read past that page."

There was a thin edge of bitterness in Luke's voice when he replied, "If you had, then you'd already know about the unhoused lady who disappeared. Sometimes public opinion offers more truth than you think, Tilly Thompson." In a swift, unexpected motion, Luke rose, his chair scraping on the concrete pad beneath them. He dug into his pocket and took out a ten-dollar bill. "Here. This should cover the coffee."

"Luke—"

"Thanks for this." He waved the journal at her and then spun around, weaving his way between tables and ignoring the murmurs.

Tilly stared after him. Never in her life had she seen an expression such as the one plastered on Luke's face as he dropped the ten dollars onto the table. It was haunting. Or maybe haunted. It was the look of a man who was still emotionally trapped in that little basement alcove with his journal of secrets and a story he couldn't tell.

15

And that is dying . . .

Death comes in its own time, in its own way.
Death is as unique as the individual experiencing it.

Henry van Dyke

"Luke!" Tilly called out. Against her better judgment, she'd chased after him, leaving the coffee shop behind. But she didn't want to make a scene, and he was moving down the sidewalk toward the town park with such long strides that she couldn't keep up.

He crossed the street and beelined for the park. His feet ate up the ground so that in a matter of seconds, he was out of sight. Tilly stopped to catch her breath. There was no point in chasing him down. He obviously wanted his privacy right now. Could she blame him? No. But in the last several minutes, Luke James had shifted from someone she wanted to hold at arm's length to a man who was awakening not just her curiosity but her compassion. It was difficult to withhold compassion when a person deserved it, and from what Tilly was slowly learning, Luke James might never have had much of it.

Peeling back the layers.

She didn't like peeling back her own, but if she could help Luke . . .

Tilly understood the loneliness and helplessness she'd seen on his face. The fear that no one could understand the deepest places in him. The part that believed he wasn't valuable.

She made her way back to James Mansion. Grandpa Don was alone, and while he'd shown no signs of posing a threat to himself, she still didn't want to leave him for long. When the mansion came into view, Tilly trudged up the drive only to come to a halt as she neared the front porch. Beneath its roof, in line with the beautiful Victorian front door, sat Luke.

They stared at each other.

Tilly had not expected to find him on her front steps, and yet it seemed as though he belonged there.

"Why are you here?"

"Direct as always," Luke said, then added, "I'm sorry. I shouldn't have left you the way I did."

The words sliced through Tilly. She'd waited years to hear him say that, to apologize to her. Of course, he didn't mean for this to cover all the pain he'd caused when she was a teenager, but to hear "I'm sorry" coming from Luke James . . . it unsettled her. She wasn't sure how to process it.

As usual, her words came unbidden. "When I was ten, I borrowed Erik's skateboard. I fell, and it rolled down the hill and went into Mill Pond. It sank."

Luke furrowed his brow.

Tilly hurried on. "I never said anything to Erik. To this day, he thinks he left it at school and someone took it."

A small smile quirked Luke's lips.

"When I was sixteen," Tilly continued, "I hit the stop sign on Eighth and Jorge Street. I never told anyone it was me who hit it. I knew they'd be doing road construction in a few months and the sign would be replaced anyway." In retrospect, maybe she shouldn't have admitted that to her potential future mayor.

Luke tilted his head to the side. "That was you?"

She nodded. "Yeah. I've never been spatially aware."

"The whole sign was knocked over flat," Luke recalled.

"I thought I had more room between my car and the curb."

"Ah." Luke nodded as if that explained everything.

Tilly moved to sit beside him, and Luke scooted over to make room on the steps. "And another secret," she ventured. "I had my first taste of liquor, a rum and Coke, when I was nineteen, while at a party." She'd hated it. She'd hated the party too. In fact, it was the last one she'd ever gone to.

Luke gave her a sideways look. "You realize I'm not a priest."

"Of course."

"So why the confession?"

"Because sometimes it's good to get things off our chests." She felt bad for saying it, but Luke didn't seem to mind. He lowered his head and stared at his thumbs, which he began to twiddle. "My confessions are a bit heavier than that," he said.

"That's okay." And it was.

He stopped moving his thumbs, but didn't look up. "You know I was in Morning Song Recovery, don't you?"

"Erik didn't tell me." Tilly hurried to defend her brother. "I figured it out myself."

"Law of deduction, I suppose." Luke sucked in a shaking breath. "If that gets out, my campaign is shot."

"I won't tell anyone," Tilly promised.

"I didn't think you would," Luke replied. "But someone's digging. They're trying to find anything and everything they can. It won't be long till that comes out."

"Do you think it's Will?"

Luke shrugged. "Maybe. But as much as he wants to be mayor, I don't see him stooping that low."

Tilly felt her cheeks heat. She'd just assumed it was Will, and here Luke was giving his opponent the benefit of the doubt.

Luke reached down and picked up the journal he'd set on the

porch. He turned it over in his hands. "You were right to doubt me."

Tilly gave him a questioning frown.

Luke met her eyes. "The day I stopped by to see the remains you found in the wall, you were right to doubt me. I was here to find out if . . . well, I was concerned it was the woman from the post this morning. It's not the first time someone posed the theory about whether my family had something to do with her disappearance."

Tilly couldn't help but be straightforward. "Did they?"

"That's the thing. I don't know." Luke tapped the journal with his index finger. "I know what I experienced as a boy—my dad, he wasn't a nice guy. I know my dad *knew* the woman, and I know she disappeared."

"Your dad was the mayor, so he probably knew everyone," Tilly offered.

Luke stared out at the walkway that skirted the mansion's front lawn. He tipped his head toward it. "I saw my dad and that woman standing right there. They were arguing. A week later, she vanished."

Tilly had nothing to say to that.

"When I heard you'd found remains in the mansion, I have to admit, my mind went exactly to where today's post went. But even though the body in the wall isn't that woman's, there was still a body in the house I grew up in. A house my family owned for well over a century."

His observation hung between them.

Tilly twisted to face him as they sat on the steps. "You're saying someone in your family put the girl in the wall."

Luke nodded. "The walls of this house have seen generations of secrets, and it appears as though someone wants to resurrect them and bring them into the light."

"Secrets are usually kept for a reason," Tilly said.

Luke handed her the journal. "Put it back where you found it, would you?"

"Why?" She didn't understand why he didn't want to hang on to the book.

"It's what we do in this place." Luke gave the mansion a surveying look. "We hide things and trust that the walls will never speak."

"And if they do?" Tilly asked solemnly.

Luke locked gazes with her. "Then we might all get a peek into a darkness we're not ready for."

Tilly could sense them. The secrets. Especially as night fell upon James Mansion. Grandpa Don sat by the fireplace in the sitting room, his eyes fixed on the small fire they had built. It snapped and crackled with sparks shooting up into the chimney. Tilly thought of the people who had lived here, who sat in this very spot and stared into this very fireplace.

All of them Jameses.

Until she and Grandpa Don had moved in and made it their own.

Was she sensing the untold stories that generations of the James family had hidden inside the walls here? As a child, she had imagined this house to be a place of magnificence. She had pictured long-ago ladies in crinolines and skirts, with befeathered hats and corseted waists. She'd even imagined how they'd changed as the decades went by. Hats transformed to 1960s pillbox-style and miniskirts. Vietnam War news being reported through black-and-white televisions. Then the neon of the '90s as Luke entered the world. Only to do what? Hide in a storage space in the musty basement of an otherwise phenomenal example of Queen Anne architecture?

Perhaps his loyalty to Kyle stemmed from his older brother being someone who had offered him safety and security. She was beginning to see why Luke had been the person he was in high school. A teenager seeking to find himself at the expense of those weaker. It was classic compensation. And then he'd fallen into the clutches of addiction.

Tilly held Luke's journal in her hands. She hadn't opened it, but neither had she put it back in the basement alcove like he'd asked her to. Something inside of her couldn't do it. Not in that lonely, dark place beneath the stairs. It was like a little prison to her now, and returning the journal felt like returning Luke to his hiding place too. Instead of a fun childhood hideout, the place had taken on a darker role. Perhaps that was why Luke didn't wish to read his own words. He'd written them during the darkest of days. He'd left them behind as if to erase forever the memories he never wanted to resurface.

But as with the woman in the wall, they were being revealed to the world. Tilly and Grandpa Don's very presence here was bringing the mansion's past—and that of the James family—into the daylight.

A door slammed.

Tilly jumped.

Grandpa Don snapped out of his silent study of the fire. "What was that?"

"I don't know," Tilly responded. She did not wish for a repeat of what happened the other night in the kitchen. She avoided looking at the windows. *Stay away from the windows.* The last thing she needed was to see another flash of a face or have another hand squeak its way down the windowpane as it dragged against glass.

"Did you leave a window open?" Grandpa Don looked over his shoulder at the open pocket doors of the front parlor.

"I don't think so." Tilly remained frozen in her chair. The little hairs on her arms rose up, and a chill went through her.

"I'll go look." Grandpa Don struggled to stand; his legs were always tired at this time of night.

His action snapped Tilly from her fear, and she popped up from her chair. "I've got it. Let me go check."

Grandpa Don settled back in his seat, not arguing, which told her he was weary.

Tilly didn't want him to try to climb the stairs to the second floor, for that was where the sound seemed to be coming from.

She hurried up the stairs, sprinting like a little kid afraid of the bogeyman when she passed the hole in the wall. At the top landing, she paused. The library was to the left, and while it had once been the primary bedroom years ago, it now served a better purpose. Its door stood open. Tilly turned to look down the corridor. Her bedroom door was also open, and beyond that was a smaller bedroom. She walked toward it, eyeing the door. It was always shut. At one point, someone in the James family had placed an entertainment cabinet in that room in front of the door, making it useless and only accessible through Tilly's room.

Another shudder passed through Tilly as she neared it.

There was no plausible—no, *possible*—way for it to be open and yet it was.

Tilly tiptoed to the opening and peered in. The entertainment cabinet had been shoved away, allowing the door to open and enough room for her to slip inside. She closed her eyes as she squeezed into the opening. She should call the police. But not yet. Maybe there was a reasonable explanation . . .

She couldn't think of one, though, and Ashley's comments about houses holding wickedness in their walls suddenly came back to Tilly.

Praying the Lord's Prayer seemed like a good idea. She started whispering the words as she peered through the adjoining door that led into her bedroom. It was empty. She scanned this room, eyeing the twin-sized antique bed pushed against the far wall. Aside from that, the room was empty, save for the entertainment cabinet.

Tilly saw it then. Lying in the middle of the floor. A pile of three hardbound books that had fallen from the cabinet. That would explain the bang, but it didn't explain how the cabinet had been moved.

She looked around her, alone but feeling oh so not alone.

"Hello?" she whispered.

Silence.

Tilly dared to peek behind the cabinet that no longer abutted the wall. She stared, not believing what she saw. Scribbled on the antique wallpaper, once hidden behind the entertainment cabinet, written in black script were the words that chilled her to her core.

Help me.

You are not alone.

IF WALLS COULD TALK

I watched while it happened, those nightmares inside this place. There was love once, but mostly nightmares, and it's the nightmares that I keep. Even now I see her discover one of them. It is old. I can tell she's wondering who wrote it and why. I could tell her, if only I could speak louder. But I am not given a voice that transcends time or space or breaks the barriers of sound. Instead, I am here, mute and desperate. I want to speak. To tell her. But I can only guide her and steer her to what secrets she must uncover so that the truth can be laid to rest.

I remember when those words were etched into me. I have kept them carefully all these years. They were hidden in anger, hidden with fury, a testament to the fact that no matter how they try to erase the past, it still visits. Even now.

It has been exposed.

She still speaks, even though she is dead.

She is not who they think she is.

And now? Perhaps they will begin to search. What more can be done to inspire? I have revealed some of the darkest secrets, and still they only consider listening.

But I can see it on her face now. This one. This woman. She resists, but she is listening. Finally. She has heard the voices.

She is listening.

16

Eloise James

When spring, to woods and wastes around,
Brought bloom and joy again,
The murdered traveller's bones were found,
Far down a narrow glen.

William Cullen Bryant

October 1879
James Mansion

She had never felt such disapproval in all her life as she did after facing the cold, infuriated glare of Father. Eloise had arrived home just this morning, Ida sweeping off to her room as though her work was done now that they'd returned. Of course, Eloise hadn't told Ida that not far behind them, Silas Dobbs followed. She had convinced Silas they could engage Father in their search to uncover the secret behind the disappearing bodies at the asylum. She had convinced herself that Father would care, if for no other reason than to know his own daughter's remains were unaccounted for. That Evania might somehow be mixed up in a body-snatching scheme would be an awakening for Father. Eloise just knew it would be.

Until, that is, she stepped into Father's study, which was just beyond the parlor in James Mansion. From here, Eloise could look out the east window and take in the expanse of lawn and welcoming flower gardens. But she didn't dare. Refusing to look Father in the eye would seal her fate. And that fate would be harsh. Eloise could see it in Father's expression, the way his shoulders were held stiffly, his nose tilted in the air.

At his obvious anger and displeasure, Eloise's words fled her.

Evania escaping the asylum?

Stolen bodies?

Illegal sales?

The asylum making a profit off their dead?

Silas's assumptions and deductions had made so much sense in the cemetery. But here? Here they sounded like wild accusations.

"Explain yourself," Father demanded.

Those two words felt like a slap across her face, and while that happened rarely, it *had* happened. She didn't wish a repeat of it either. Eloise was not invited to be seated, so she stood before Father as he positioned himself by the window she so desperately wished to escape through.

God help her if Silas appeared now, knocking on the front door as she had suggested. He would be coming ready to give testimony to Father of their wild story. She had not been thinking straight! She wished Silas away.

Do not come here. Do not come—

"I asked you a question, Eloise."

"Father, I—" She bit her tongue. "I wanted to be there for Evania. I wanted to bring her home and nurse her back to health here where she belongs."

His gaze never wavered. "And now you know the truth of it?"

She swallowed. "That she–"

"Died." Father said the word without compunction. "Yes."

"But Evania–"

"Evania what?" Father paced toward his desk and tapped his fingers on its top.

Eloise hated her meekness, and yet she had no idea how to overcome it. "I had hoped–" Again she cut off her words.

Father took a step toward her. "You had hoped to bring her home? You already stated that. But she was in the best place possible to receive the best care possible. That she passed away is simply fate."

"I don't believe Evania is dead." There. She'd said it.

Father's expression darkened, and he stared at her for a long moment before speaking. "Your sister is dead, Eloise, make no mistake about that. Do not encourage me to be concerned about your own state of mind now as well."

Eloise's breath caught, and she met her father's penetrating stare. There was an unveiled threat in his words and his expression. Still, somehow she needed him to understand. This wasn't her grief speaking. This was the story of the steward and what he'd seen. Evania faking her own death, being placed in a wagon next to other bodies, and–

Her father continued. "I trust Dr. Holzer implicitly. It is understandable that you don't want to believe Evania has passed, but reality must be recognized and accepted."

"But–"

"But?"

"*I* don't trust Dr. Holzer. There was a steward who–"

"Of course you don't trust the doctor," Father barked. "The impudence of your going there without my permission–on your own–and insisting not only to meet with the doctor but to insinuate now that he is mistaken in declaring your sister to be dead? The *audacity* of it is disgraceful." Father heaved an aggravated sigh as he moved to his chair, which creaked beneath his weight. Opening a drawer, he pulled out a piece of stationery, then reached for his fountain pen. "I shall write a letter of apology to Dr. Holzer for your impertinence. He will understand, as you are a woman grieving the loss of your sister, and what few wits you have about you have been strained by such a burden."

Eloise felt stung by her father's insult. She remained standing, desperate to tell him the full story but now afraid even of doing that. Afraid he would accuse her of lunacy. Afraid he would turn on her just as he had Evania.

"This is why you are not to take matters into your own hands. You act imprudently and ignorantly." The pen scratched across the paper as he wrote. As he composed the letter, Father launched into another verbal onslaught. "Are you wondering why I gave permission for them to bury Evania? Because she had taken ill, Eloise. Very ill, very quickly. Contagion was feared. Therefore, she had to be buried with haste to prevent a potential outbreak." He dipped the pen point in the inkwell. "But of course, you did not see fit to trust my wisdom, so you went traipsing off on feminine impulse."

"Contagion?" Eloise drew back. Dr. Holzer had said nothing of contagion. The steward had said Evania's illness was pneumonia. His story did not match Father's account of what occurred with her sister, not in the least.

He expressed no sympathy as he continued to scold Eloise. "You assume you understand the circumstances, but you are far removed from the truth. You paint me as a domineering father who has no affection for his children. That is utter nonsense. I do what I must for the James family name, and Evania needed care. While at the asylum, she took ill. I've no control over that, but I did have control over whether her illness would affect others." He jabbed the air with the pen. "Now that you've made a fool of us all by requesting to have your sister's remains *exhumed*—yes, I received a telegram from Dr. Holzer—I expect you to return to your rightful place in our home. And take heed, Eloise, that nothing like this happens again."

Eloise nodded, her tongue stilled by the intimidation.

"You are fortunate that Ida had the foresight to follow you or your reputation would have suffered from traveling alone. That would have been an entirely other sort of damage I would be forced to repair." He lifted his head, eyes drilling into Eloise's. "I knew Evania was a troubled daughter, but you? You have proven that I cannot trust you either. Do not test my forgiveness." The threat was barely veiled. "You may go now."

"Father . . ." Under his severe glare, Eloise ducked her head and gave a little curtsy.

"You are restricted to these grounds only. You will politely decline any social invitations for the next few weeks. I must ensure that your recent actions do not come back to haunt me or to cause further damage."

When he said no more, Eloise turned and hurried from the room. She closed the door to the study and leaned against it, her chest rising and falling from the intensity of the moment.

"Miss Eloise?" A voice to her left jolted her from one shock to another. It was their housekeeper, Mrs. Forrester.

"A young man is here to see you." Mrs. Forrester looked both confused and disapproving. "What shall I tell him?"

Silas!

Just as they had planned, but if Father even had an inkling of why Silas had arrived or who he was . . .

"I will take care of it," Eloise said, then hurried past Mrs. Forrester, praying the housekeeper would return to her duties and not try to eavesdrop.

She strode down the corridor toward the parlor and front entrance. Once there, Eloise glanced up the main staircase. She hesitated as she met the curious gaze of a workman. They were installing her father's latest claim to wealth—a stained-glass window on the east wall and another on the south wall. A ladder stood on the landing, but the south wall was already . . . Eloise frowned. Father must have decided against a window on that wall after all. The wall had been replastered where the window was to have been installed, and the workmen were now focused on the beautiful glass piece of artistry Father had commissioned for the east wall.

She hoped the workmen would cause her no trouble. She didn't want them overhearing her conversation with Silas.

Eloise opened the door.

Silas, his cap rammed over wayward curls, grinned at her. "You didn't tell me your father is the richest man in New Jamestown!"

"Shh!" Eloise waved him off. She squeezed through the door, causing Silas to step back and allow her space to close the door behind them. "You must go," she insisted.

"Go? But I've not told your father a thing yet."

"And you won't, Silas." Eloise tried to quell the panic rising inside her. "He believes my sister was contagious. He believes that's why they buried her so quickly. But aside from that, he thinks I am bereft and not of sound mind at the moment. If I press him and insist on this . . . this *story* we have little proof of, I'm afraid of what he will do to me."

Silas's grin faded, and his brows pulled into a deep v between his eyes.

"Please. I need you to leave," Eloise begged.

"Have you forgotten that the steward saw them take your sister away in a wagon? That Penny and Seamus disappeared just as surely as she did?"

"Silas—"

"And have you forgotten you were so beside yourself that you walked in your sleep and tore into the earth with your bare hands, tryin' to find your sister?"

"I know, but—"

He cocked his head, narrowing his eyes. "Does your father not care to know the truth?"

"Please stop," Eloise choked out, tears filling her eyes against her will. Why did men push and pull until she could barely form her own thoughts and opinions from the pressure of it? "I can't—please, just leave."

Silas's eyes gentled. "Aw, love, don't start cryin'. Tears are like fire to butter. They make me melt, and I'll have nothin' left in me to fight."

Eloise gave a watery laugh. She swiped at her eyes, still angry, still hurt, and yet touched by Silas's concern and caring words.

He took a step back and nodded. "I'll leave you be for now. I know none of this is easy. But I'm here. I'll be waitin' and I'll be investigatin'. This isn't over. I'm determined to find out what happened to Seamus and Penny. And now I'll be lookin' for your sister too. Send me a message at the Bigsby House. I took a room there. I'll wait for twenty-four hours, an' if you want me to come, I will."

"I'm sorry," Eloise choked out.

"Don't be, love. You're entitled to have your own mind. Just 'cause I don't share it today doesn't mean your feelin's don't matter." He reached out and, with a quick swipe, lifted a tear from her cheek and balanced it on his finger. His eyelid dropped in a wink. "For good luck." He made a pretense of tucking the tear into his pocket. "You know where I'll be."

Silas bounded down the front steps and hurried away, his whistling filling the air as he disappeared.

Eloise paced her room, a shawl wrapped around her shoulders, its silk tassels tickling her arms. Trying to make her thoughts cooperate and see reason was confusing her further. Her throat tightened with tears, and she held a corner of the shawl over her mouth to stifle her emotion. Should she trust Silas, a man she hardly knew, whose confidence in himself verged on irrepressible and whose passion to find his relatives was admirable?

He was known by the police, and it was obvious Captain Farber hadn't much respect for Silas. Was Silas who he claimed to be?

Or should she place her faith in her father and Dr. Holzer, both of whom were respected men of society? Men who led and who understood how things should be done.

Eloise stopped pacing and stared out her bedroom window at the flower gardens she'd dared not look at while in Father's study earlier. They had been her mother's gardens. Father paid Kenny, their groundskeeper, to keep them up, but it was for the sake of appearances. Father was not keen on Eloise spending long hours there, telling her it would worsen her grief. Mother had been dead for seven years now. There was no reason to wallow in missing her. It wasn't proper.

That emphasis on the family's reputation, on not asking questions, and her father's repeated observations on the ignorance of women were what had driven Evania away. They had fed into her rebellion, which gave no care to consequences—that is, until consequences arrived.

Eloise leaned her forehead against the windowpane. The gardens. Father didn't know what she knew. That the night Evania had given birth to her stillborn child, Father had ordered the illegitimate infant be taken away. *"It is not a James,"* he'd declared. But Eloise had stopped Kenny as the groundskeeper was carrying the babe away, wrapped in a blanket so that no part of it could be seen.

"Please, Kenny, I beg of you. Bury Evania's daughter in the rose garden. Where my mother used to sit and read. And tell no one."

Kenny, ever loyal, had done as Eloise asked. Now she stared into the darkness at the garden. Even Evania's unnamed baby girl had a resting place.

With a surge of determination, Eloise hurried to the door. Barefooted, she tiptoed so as not to awaken or disturb Ida in the next room, moving silently down the hallway to the front staircase. She paused as she reached the landing, carefully maneuvering her way around the ladder and tools left by the workmen. The boards across the window frame told her they'd yet to install the new stained glass. She wondered again why Father had decided against the other window, but that was not her concern now. Windows and newly plastered walls were frivolous in comparison to Evania.

Eloise padded down the remaining steps until she reached the parlor. Instead of going to the front entrance, she ducked behind the stairs to the narrow servants' entrance.

A few moments later, Eloise was standing on the soft, cold grass, her toes sinking into the earth. She walked toward the garden, toward memories of her mother and happier times when Mother used to recite nursery rhymes and play with long ribbons to make Eloise and Evania laugh. They had always found joy until Father returned home from his work. He never talked about his business, but Mother told them he was part owner of the railroad company and station on the west side of town. Evania had insisted that Father shoveled coal into the engine like she had seen another man do once. Eloise knew better. Father was the one who stared down at said man from his lofty office. Father was the kind of man who didn't allow anything to happen unless he wanted it to.

"Yes," Mother had whispered to Eloise, right here in the gardens, when Eloise had asked her about that.

"He wanted me to be a boy, didn't he, Mama? And Evania?"

"Yes, my darling." Mother had planted a kiss on Eloise's forehead, not shying away from a truth they all knew. "But you are exactly who God made you to be. Your father doesn't own our joy. Joy is what we hold in our hearts even when happiness drifts away or when we feel unwanted. Joy is a gift and a promise from God, whom you can always trust and depend on. And oh, my darling, I know as you grow, you will learn to trust in Him. You are wise in that way."

"Am I smart, Mother?" Eloise recalled asking.

"No, darling," Mother had whispered, "you are *brilliant*."

Eloise now found her way to the stone bench she had been sitting on when Mother told her these things.

After she died, Father had told Eloise and Evania, in no uncertain terms, that grief should be finalized like a loan that had come due. For a while, then, Eloise had blocked all thoughts of her mother. She had believed what Father told her about herself because that was her life after Mother passed away. Keeping the peace so that Evania and Father did not shout at each other, so that Evania did not anger him in such a way that it cost her.

Eloise had not been able to save Evania.

Now, as she lowered herself to the bench, the cold stone chilling her legs, she accepted the truth: she had not been able to save herself either.

"Honour thy father and thy mother," she'd been taught. It had been easy to honor Mother. It had been life-stealing to honor Father.

"What are you doing, love?"

Silas slipped from the shadows, his lean form a silhouette in the night. Somehow, Eloise had known he would be there. It seemed to suit this strange young man to lurk in the shadows. To wait and to watch. In a strange way, Eloise felt safer for it, though she couldn't explain why.

"I'm here to visit my mother," she answered, not mentioning Evania's daughter. Knowing her niece lay in peace only yards away beneath the yellow rosebush was sacred to her. Kenny had shown her, and then he'd promised her he would choose to forget it.

"Ah." Silas sat beside her. His knee touched hers, and Eloise looked at them. Then at him. Silas gave her a lopsided smile. "We need to stop meeting in the dark, don't you think?"

Eloise pulled her shawl tighter around herself.

Silas gave no indication he was irritated that he had come to New Jamestown at her behest, only to be met with her refusal to ask her father for his help.

"Do you think God expects me to honor my father when he sent Evania to that awful place?" There it was. Eloise felt the spark of bitterness rise in her. Or righteous indignation perhaps? She wasn't sure, only that Father would tell her she was out of line.

Silas countered with a question of his own. "Do you think God expects for all parents to be honorable?"

"I don't know," Eloise replied.

"Think on it."

She cast Silas a quick look. His remark startled her. Wasn't he going to tell her the answer? Eloise set her gaze on the yellow rosebush, its leaves a deep green in the night's shadows. "Honor is given when honor is due."

Silas nodded. "Sounds right to me."

"What should I do?"

"I don't know, love. I never had a parent to teach me the ways of the good Lord. Though can I offer somethin', if you don't mind?"

Eloise nodded, giving him permission to continue and feeling a little spark of reassurance that he respected her enough to ask.

Silas turned to her and reached for her hands. She was startled by his touch and uneasy at the way he bent close to her face so his eyes could seek out hers. "I can tell you have a good heart, love. And your sister didn't deserve what's happened any more than Penny or Seamus did. But you're smart too—I can see it in your eyes. And when goodness and smart come together, they're a right powerful thing. So you do what ya feel is best, but remember this: I may not know ya well a'tall, Eloise James, but you've a way of gettin' into a man's head and not lettin' go. If you love fiercely enough to want to bring your ailin' sister home, and if your father is so hard a man he don't see that, then he's the one losin' out."

He squeezed her fingers and leaned closer, his breath on her ear as he whispered, "I know you don't believe me when I say it, but when I told Captain Farber ye're the love of my life, I could at least see that one day, you'd be makin' a man a very lucky man."

Eloise jerked back, her heart lurching within her. Pounding rather. Taken aback by his boldness, she snatched her hands away.

Silas tipped the brim of his cap and stood, smiling down at her. "Just think, love. When we're old and gray and all this is behind us, you'll remember tonight and think to yourself, 'Ah, that sweet man, Silas, he is. Where would I be without him?' Now go inside and get some sleep. Remember why I'm here. We'll figure it out, and we won't stop until we do. And maybe your father will come around yet. Just like you'll come around to me."

With a chuckle, Silas disappeared into the night.

Eloise stared into the darkness where he'd disappeared. She'd never met a man so ridiculously sure of himself. She'd never met a man so charming and so terribly, wonderfully, achingly kind.

17

> Death, be not proud, though some have called thee
> Mighty and dreadful, for thou art not so.
>
> John Donne

She awoke with purpose. She also awoke with an unwelcome curl of delight in her stomach when she remembered Silas in the garden last night. The man was a complete fool, and she wouldn't be charmed by someone who had spent his growing-up years on the streets and his adult days sniffing out news for the next big story. No parents? No family? What did a man like that know about devotion? In the midst of such weighty circumstances, surely truer colors would be revealed. She'd been well versed on the stories of the lower classes. All of the bad of human nature was mulched by their poor circumstances. And yet, Eloise pondered, Silas had not yet proven to fit those prejudices. Instead, and in a humbling way, Eloise could almost believe that Silas Dobbs was a better man than her father.

Surely not. No. She refused to be charmed by Silas Dobbs.

Still, he had ignited in her a sense of rightness. More than that, a sense of confidence that she hadn't felt before.

Eloise stood in front of her mirror and examined herself. Her spectacles sat on her nose, round and gold, with wire frames. Her dress was sensible. Dark gray with pearl buttons. Ida had fixed her hair for her, thin-lipped and wordless. They had spoken little since Eloise returned, and she preferred it that way.

Today would be different. Although, as she drew a steadying breath, things were far shakier than she'd expected. It became clear to Eloise after she'd returned to her bedroom last night that before she could take another step, she needed proof of Silas's claims. Father would never believe her otherwise.

Body snatching? Stealing the dead from their graves?

Had the legislators of Indiana truly passed a law to bring more accountability to medical universities? It was, after all, almost the twentieth century. Surely the dreadful practices that had occurred for nearly a century were not still being carried out.

Yet if the steward at the Corinth Asylum for the Chronically Insane was being honest, and if Silas was correct in his theory that the unclaimed bodies of patients who died there were brokered in the back alleys, then someone somewhere had to have proof of it. There had to be more stories of graves being robbed, of dead people going missing. Surely anything that pointed to potential smuggling of the deceased would wind up in the newspapers. Silas couldn't be the only one with an eye for the sensational.

If it turned out that Silas was exaggerating, then Eloise would accept her father's word and disregard the tales of a conspiracy from a penny-a-liner she hardly knew. After all, stories bought off the street were known to be either slanderous gossip or inflated half-truths.

But if Silas's claims proved to be true, then she could only conclude that Penny and Seamus had in fact disappeared, either when they had passed away or in an attempt to escape like Evania.

Three missing people. And there were probably more.

Eloise lifted a gilded-framed portrait of her sister from her dressing table. She ran her finger over the image. Beautiful Evania. Her features were so fine, her hair so lavishly dark, her eyes sparkling, and her lips quirked in that familiar smile that said she was up to no good while she was as goodhearted as a sister could be.

Eloise reminded herself that she was doing all this for her sister—and for the sweet babe who lay in the garden just outside her window. What had happened to Evania—her imprisonment in the asylum amongst uncaring strangers—was unforgivable. And Father could have stopped all of it. He could have addressed Evania's waywardness differently. He could have allowed them time to grieve the loss of a child—illegitimate or not—instead of insisting the infant girl was not a James and consigning her to her own unmarked grave.

Eloise drew a deep breath. She was trembling inside. She could see it in her reflection in the mirror.

All she was planning right now was a trip to the basement. She wouldn't be leaving the house or running away. She was going to look through the piles of newspapers stored there for later use, such as for washing windows, stuffing a crack to seal a draft, or starting a fire.

But it was with the intention of looking beyond the walls of her home. That was why Eloise was anxious.

Attempting to find articles that might add credence to Silas and her claims was merely a place to begin. She wasn't sure what she would even look for, but Eloise's intuition urged her to study the past reports and scour the columns. It could be a difficult search to find truth, one that might help her to discover her voice as a woman. The way Mother had planted dreams for Eloise to become, and the way Evania had always been.

She was created for more than staying silent all the time.

Eloise lifted a shaking hand to straighten the cameo at her throat.

She was created to raise her voice, loudly, and be the woman God had intended her to be.

Eloise hesitated. She tucked a strand of hair behind her ear and adjusted her glasses. Perhaps she wouldn't roar too loudly quite yet. But even if she could release a tiny meow, it would be a victory won.

Eloise never went into the basement. There wasn't a reason to. But she knew the servants' practices, as she'd witnessed them haul old newspapers there. She was unimpressed by the basement's dankness as she descended the stairs by the butler's pantry just off the kitchen.

"Miss Eloise?" a voice called from above.

Eloise twisted on the stairs to look up. She saw the housekeeper, Mrs. Forrester, concern lining the woman's face.

"Do you need something, Miss Eloise?"

"No, no. I'm quite all right." Eloise glanced toward the basement. She could already sense the humidity trapped in the stone foundation and the hard-packed dirt of the floor. "I'm just in need of some old newspapers."

"Well, I can send Sam to fetch them for you," Mrs. Forrester offered. "You needn't bother yourself."

What to say? Eloise searched for an acceptable explanation as she stood on the wooden steps. "I'm looking for specific ones." It was all she could come up with at the time.

"Specific papers, miss?" Mrs. Forrester frowned.

"Yes. For a project I'm working on with the Ladies' Missionary Society. I need to review last year's mission reports in the Lutheran church column."

"Oh!" Mrs. Forrester's eyes widened in understanding.

Now that Eloise had broken one of the Ten Commandments and outright lied—apparently successfully—her courage grew a little even as her conscience was pricked. "I will be fine, Mrs. Forrester," she reassured the woman.

"Just a moment. Let me get you an apron. All that black ink from the newsprint will rub off with the moisture in the basement. You don't want that on your dress." She disappeared from view and then was back just seconds later, an apron hanging over her arm. She descended the stairs and handed the apron to Eloise, who took it gratefully.

Mrs. Forrester hesitated. "Are you sure you don't want me to have Sam bring the papers upstairs? They're in bundles, so it wouldn't be too much trouble. We could lay them out on a table on the back porch. Fresh air would do you good while you're looking through them."

It sounded far lovelier than poking about the newspapers down in the basement. But the last thing Eloise wanted was for Father to come upon her and ask what she was up to. He would not believe her falsehood about the Ladies' Missionary Society and lying to him would take far more skill than she possessed.

"I'm quite curious to visit the basement," Eloise answered quickly.

As if perplexed by this, Mrs. Forrester shook her head. "Very well then. There isn't a bell down there to ring if you need us, so do be careful."

"I will," Eloise reassured the woman with a smile. Be careful? She pondered the admonition as Mrs. Forrester left her to herself. How dangerous could her own basement be?

Eloise soon discovered, as she reached the bottom step, that it could be quite dangerous indeed. A mouse scurried across the floor in front of her, and Eloise stifled a scream, pressing against the wall and uttering a prayer that the mouse would not attack her feet. Somehow even mice became more threatening in a place like this.

The basement spanned the entire mansion and was divided into several rooms, including a coal storage room, furnace room, a food cellar, and additional storage areas. But Eloise hadn't far to go. The newspapers, she knew, were stored in a small cubby at the bottom of the steps.

She bent down and tugged on the cubby door. It opened, and

she peered inside. She would have to crouch low to enter the space. There were no windows to provide light. The newspapers were piled in bundles on the floor. It was wasteful to simply toss them, but how many did they need to keep for kindling and cleaning?

She half wished she'd taken Mrs. Forrester up on allowing the footman to haul the papers upstairs. Summoning her courage, Eloise ducked into the cubby. There was a lamp in the corner, and she made quick work of lighting it, also being sure to leave the cubbyhole door open for airflow.

At least she was able to stand, though the top of her head almost brushed the stone ceiling. Eloise eyed the newspapers piled in bundles on the floor, recalling that Silas had referred to increased activity of body snatching in the last year. So Eloise looked for newspapers that fit that time period and was pleased to see she wasn't going to need to dig very far.

The first few papers did not offer anything useful. Society news, columns on political issues facing Indiana, and Father had made the paper with reference to a business deal he had negotiated that would result in additional jobs for the railroad. So her father did do good after all . . . economically speaking.

Eloise reached for another newspaper, her fingertips already black from ink. But this one gave her pause. She moved closer to the lamplight and began reading:

> *Freddy Bains and Millie Harris, who were arrested for taking up the dead from the burial grounds in St. Matthew's Cemetery of New Jamestown for the purpose of disposing of them for financial gain, were accompanied to the jail for a hearing yesterday at 2 p.m. While Mr. Bains's involvement in the activity and sale of the remains is still under investigation, it has been ascertained that Miss Harris was assigned the duty to attend all funerals as a mourner for the purpose of locating the graves and studying the general surroundings. Her participation facilitated the nighttime thefts.*

Eloise set the paper aside. There was actual strategy involved in dealing with the selling of the dead! The audacity and utter shamefulness of pretending to mourn while planning to rob? How despicable! To think that friends and family had gathered to grieve the loss of a loved one, only to have a pseudo-mourner standing beside them determining if that very loved one was worth stealing and selling for . . . for their desecration!

Eloise looked around her. She needed to sit down. There was no chair, so instead she balanced on a stack of newspapers. She fingered through a few more until she came upon another story.

It is reported that a man by the name of Westchester worked out of southern Corinth. After interviewing the superintendents of cemeteries there and in the surrounding area, this paper has learned that a prominent physician in Indianapolis is at the head of Westchester and his ghouls. This doctor enjoys the protection of the police.

Skimming subsequent papers, she learned that only nine months prior, this physician and Westchester had been indicted for their crimes against the deceased.

Eloise shook her head. The cold and paralyzing truth was becoming clearer, and it appeared as though Silas had been correct. A horrified curiosity urged her forward.

Body snatchers' tools often consist of a wagon, a spade, a crowbar and grappling hook. Wagons tend not to arouse suspicions and can easily carry an adult corpse without the need to double them up or dismember them to transport them in barrels, which has been the case in other circumstances.

Eloise's hand flew to her mouth. She quickly glanced further down the page and resumed reading.

The grappling hook is a trademark tool used by resurrectionists. Once the coffin has been opened, its hook is fastened to the jaw, and the body is pulled from the coffin.

Enough.

Eloise flung the paper away from her as if it were evil itself. Silas had not been exaggerating. Why, even the newspapers seemed to revel in the lurid details of the practice. And surely her father was aware of this, seeing as he read the newspapers. While the gruesome truth applied an exclamation point to the end of Silas's overall claims, it did not provide any information that pointed to the asylum itself.

However, the possibility that many of the patients at the asylum had been victims of just such depravity was very real. Possibly Seamus and Penny and, God save her, Evania, if she'd been found out or died because of her illness while in their wagon. But how to prove it? And if these criminals had already been apprehended and charged in the last year, and a law had since been passed to increase the punishment of such activity, why was it continuing?

Eloise already knew the answer to that.

When man looked through the eyes of greed, all else was expendable. She thought of Father, of the way he'd prioritized and all but worshiped his business endeavors. They had always come first. His family seemed to matter only to the extent it contributed to his reputation and status.

She made her way to the door and bent to pass through it, shutting it behind her and grabbing for the stair railing to right herself.

Somehow she had to convince Father to look into the matter. She would appeal to his pride if need be.

The resurrection men were still at work.

And Evania was their potential victim.

18

Tilly Thompson

The mansions of the dead.—Roused from their slumbers,
In grim array the grisly spectres rise,
Grin horrible, and, obstinately sullen,
Pass and repass, hush'd as the foot of night.

Robert Blair

Present Day

"How did the entertainment center get moved?" Erik had come over right away when Tilly called him. He stood in the middle of the unused bedroom, surveying the situation after sweeping the house for an intruder. He measured the air with his hands. "That thing is at least ten feet long and six feet high. It covers the whole wall and the door." He checked behind it, not even commenting on the words scribbled on the wall. "It doesn't look like it was attached to the wall at all," he observed.

"But it's heavy," Tilly said.

"Yeah. Someone would have to manhandle it to push it out even this far."

"That means someone else was here." Tilly stated what was obvious to them already. No ghost had moved the entertainment center. One might be able to get away with blaming a spirit for chucking books onto the floor, but this?

"You didn't hear a thing?" Erik asked.

"No. But the mansion is seven thousand square feet."

"I know, but you heard the books fall. Why those and not this unit scraping along the floor?" Erik gave it a shove for good measure to gauge the sound it would make. When it made little, he frowned. Moving to the front of it, he toed the rug on the wood floor. "That maybe explains it."

"What?"

"The corner is resting on the rug. I push it, and the rug slides beneath. It dampens the sound."

"Should I call the police? Someone was in our home." She didn't need to repeat it to convince Erik, but for whatever reason, saying it out loud emphasized the point. There had to be steps to follow to address this.

Erik placed his hands on his hips. "Nothing was broken or stolen. I checked all the exterior doors. Did you know there are four separate entrances *plus* a cellar door to the outside that leads to the basement?"

Tilly nodded. She knew this. It'd never bothered her before, but now she felt like she should hire a guard to stand watch at each entrance.

"Whoever got into the house must have found one of them unlocked."

Tilly shook her head. Not with her nighttime routine. "I lock them all." She was quite religious about it. Mostly to deter Grandpa Don in the event he started wandering at night.

"Maybe they entered through a window. I don't think the police will do much more than file a report, though. Not when the crime is breaking and entering and moving an entertainment center."

Tilly didn't appreciate that conclusion. "There has to be something that can be done." First the vision outside her kitchen window, now this? She might sleepwalk and do weird things, and her brain might be working overtime, but common sense told her that she couldn't just accept this invasion and move on.

"We could look into getting an alarm system installed," Erik suggested.

It was a start. Tilly immediately pulled out her phone to begin searching for a home security company nearby.

Erik slipped between the shelving and the wall. He eyed the words there.

"'Help me. You are not alone,'" he read aloud, then glanced at Tilly. "Comforting. Those are words to go to sleep by."

"That's not funny," Tilly reprimanded.

"No, but . . ." He ran his hand along the wall. "Why move the entertainment center? To do what? To expose what's written on the wall? That's just weird. And how would they know those words are there?"

"Is there a secret door or something?" Tilly edged closer to look.

Erik shook his head. "This is an interior wall. If there was a secret door, it'd just lead back into the hall."

He was right.

Erik's phone rang. "What's this about? It's ten o'clock at night." A glance at his caller ID, and he answered, "Luke, what's up?"

Tilly stilled, watching her brother.

Erik's face grew serious. "Uh-huh . . . yeah, what else?"

Tilly mouthed a silent *what?* to her brother.

Erik waved her off. "Well, Tilly just had an incident here at the mansion too."

Tilly stiffened. Had something happened to Luke?

Erik nodded at whatever Luke was saying. "Sure, come on over. We need to get to the bottom of this . . . Okay, see you in a few."

He lowered his phone. "Luke's brother, Kyle, just gave him a call. There's more junk being posted on that online community site."

"Who is posting this stuff?" Tilly asked.

Erik shook his head. "Whoever it is, they're protecting their anonymity. But it's going to blow up. People feed off this type of thing. Not gonna lie. This latest event makes me nervous—you and Grandpa here alone."

"Small towns are supposed to be trustworthy," Tilly muttered.

Erik's expression was as grim as Tilly had seen in a long time. He patted the entertainment center more out of frustration than anything else. "Whoever is writing this has some sort of vendetta. If this house becomes mixed up in it? That's not cool. Now they're claiming the James family has been dealing in body brokering for decades. There's a lot of vitriol in their post, too."

"In *what*?" Body brokering was a new one for her.

"Dead bodies, Tilly. They're accusing the James family of being involved in selling corpses on the black market."

"Sorry to barge in at this hour." Luke entered the mansion, his hair disheveled from fingers raked through it many times over. Tilly stepped aside, catching a whiff of juniper and mint. He smelled good. He looked exhausted.

"You look awful," she said, giving voice to her intrusive thought.

"Thanks," Luke responded.

"It's good you're here." Tilly tried to sound encouraging. She had empathy, she just wasn't sure how to express it.

Luke stepped inside his childhood home, and Tilly closed the door. She motioned toward the train room. "We're in there with my grandpa right now. He's all worked up after the break-in."

"Yeah, Erik told me." Luke reached for her arm, and his touch stilled her. She looked down at his hand and pulled away.

He let her create some distance between them, but still he asked, "Are you okay?"

Tilly allowed herself the luxury of swimming in his brilliant-blue eyes for a moment. Then she blinked and said, "I'm fine."

Erik greeted Luke when he entered the room. Grandpa Don looked up from his model train as he positioned a miniature conductor by the track. He looked ready to run the conductor over with the train's engine.

"What are they sayin' about you now, boy?" he groused at Luke.

Luke's smile was crooked as he dropped onto an overstuffed chair and laid his head back against it. "Apparently, I come from a family of grave robbers."

"They need real proof to make that factual," Tilly stated.

The three men in the room all looked at her for a silent second, then seemed to accept her frank observation.

"Even theories can become supposed facts when people want them to be," Erik said.

Tilly digested his statement reluctantly. "That's just wrong," she replied.

Luke's wry laugh told her she was right, and it was unfortunate that Erik was right too. "I don't know who is behind all this, but they really don't want me to be the mayor."

"Could it be Morrow?" Erik asked, perched on a stool by Grandpa Don.

"I can't imagine it is," Luke replied. "Like I said, he's a decent guy."

"Sure, but he's running a campaign that's all about New Jamestown needing fresh blood," Erik argued. "His comments regarding the James family in leadership have been pretty negative."

Luke shook his head slowly. "I think whoever is doing this has a personal intent. It's like they want Kyle impeached and my campaign shut down. I don't mean to diminish the position's importance to the community, but it's a small-town mayoral seat. Not a seat in the Indiana Senate. Why would someone stoop to making such wild allegations unless there's something personal involved?"

Tilly couldn't disagree with Luke. "It doesn't make sense. No one robs graves anymore. Laws were passed that criminalized the practice, I believe around the turn of the century."

"You've studied grave-robbing history?" Luke's eyebrows winged upward.

"If it's historical, she's read about it," Erik interjected.

"Okay. Well, Kyle just called me," Luke said. "He told me he doesn't need this kind of stress right now. Not with everything he and his wife are facing. They want no part of some person's muckraking exposé on our family going back generations."

"Making them out to be grave robbers," Erik confirmed.

"Yeah."

"Sue for libel," Erik suggested.

"Even if I knew who was making the allegations and did sue, that would hardly make my family appear more innocent to the public," Luke laughed wryly.

"Being accused of stealing and trafficking bodies is very serious," Tilly inserted.

"It sure is!" Grandpa Don piped up, his attention on a plastic railway sign he was positioning. "When I was a boy, they caught two men stealing bodies from the funeral home. They intended to sell them."

"Dover Funeral Home?" Erik asked.

"No, the Horace Home," Grandpa Don said.

Tilly swapped looks with Erik. The Horace Home was in Fort Wayne. They knew this because a distant aunt had died last year, and the funeral service had been held there.

Grandpa Don's details weren't reliable, but maybe his story was.

Luke seemed to think so. "Your grandfather is right. I looked it up, and there's even a market for body parts today. In fact, some body brokers are doing business legally."

"How?" Tilly stared at Luke.

"It's been known for ages that for doctors and medical researchers to learn about the human body, they need cadavers."

"True, but people donate their bodies to science for that purpose these days," Erik responded.

Luke nodded. "They do, and it's noble of them. But keep in mind there's also an entire market made up of people who aren't licensed practitioners, and they also practice medical procedures but under the radar. They need bodies too. And they're not acquiring them legally."

"So how does that work?" Erik said. "I go online and contact a *body broker* and buy someone's stolen corpse so I can cut it up and study it, then turn around and treat patients?"

"And all of it done illegally if you're not licensed. That's one example, yeah."

Tilly sank onto the nearest chair. That was a repulsive concept on so many levels.

"What exactly does this latest post say?" Erik asked, his arms crossed over his chest. He hadn't bothered to pull out his phone to look it up. Neither had Tilly. She had no desire to feed the algorithm's hunger and make it even more popular.

"Well . . ." Luke leaned forward, resting his forearms on his legs and rubbing his palms together. "It claims the James family built our wealth on this practice."

"That and colluding with the Russians during the Cold War," Grandpa Don said.

The three of them turned to stare at him. Tilly couldn't tell if he was kidding or being serious. His eyes remained fixed on the model train.

Luke smirked and continued, "It also accuses the James family of using our influence and wealth to bribe law enforcement and others in leadership. They state that the unhoused woman who went missing when I was a kid is further evidence, as are the remains you just found here in the mansion wall." Luke raked his fingers through his hair. "The fact is, someone out there is trying to dredge up old stories and rumors and make them sound current." He paused before asking, "Do we know yet who the woman in the wall was?"

"No, her identity hasn't been verified yet," Tilly answered. "The DHPA said it could be two or three months before we hear anything."

"I hate to ask this, but . . ." Erik let his sentence hang.

Luke waved him on. "Go ahead."

"Do you think there's any validity to the claims?"

To Tilly's surprise, Luke gave Erik a meaningful look. He shrugged. "You know the answer to that."

Tilly looked to Erik, whose mouth was set in a thin line.

"Maybe you should do some digging of your own. Get ahead of whoever's been feeding this sensational story."

Luke leaned back in his chair, stretching his legs out in front of him. "I'm not even sure where I'd start."

Tilly studied the men in the room: Grandpa Don hovering over his trains, Erik standing cross-armed and staring out the window, and Luke brooding over his situation and picking at his thumbnail.

"You should probably look into your family's history some more," Tilly offered matter-of-factly, breaking the silence.

Luke met her eyes, and there was a shadow in his that dimmed the brilliant blue to a murky gray. "Family history is a pretty dark place to go," he admitted.

"Where's Luke?"

Daphne Dover stood just outside the door, a sheet of paper clutched in her hand, her foot tapping a rhythm on the stone. Her dark eyes snapped with fury, and Tilly knew exactly why. New Jamestown's social-media community group had exploded this morning with opinions. Red splotches of irritation dotted her neck and revealed Daphne's frame of mind. "I know he's here. I talked to his assistant," she pressed.

Tilly stepped aside, allowing Daphne to march into the house, her jean-clad legs shapely and her autumn-orange tunic a bright spot in an otherwise dreary and exhausting morning.

The truth was, Luke had never left last night. Erik had finally returned home to his family in the wee hours. Grandpa Don had fallen asleep on his bed surrounded by train cars, and Tilly had invited Luke to stretch out on the bed in the spare bedroom upstairs. At first he'd declined, but when he stumbled from weariness as he tried to leave, he'd accepted and made his way upstairs to a room he was probably far more familiar with than Tilly was.

"Well? Where is he?" Daphne didn't seem remotely curious as to why Luke was there. Maybe it felt normal to her, even after all these years.

"He's in the library up—"

Daphne pushed past her and headed for the staircase. She knew where the library was. Tilly made to follow her, noticing Daphne's hesitation as she passed the hole in the wall. She pointed. "The woman was in there?"

"Yes."

Daphne grimaced, then finished climbing the flight of stairs. "Luke," she called out.

Tilly hurried after her.

"Luke!" Daphne stormed into the library. He was sitting at the table in the center of the room, a mug of coffee his only companion besides his laptop.

"Hey, Daph."

"Don't 'hey Daph' me, Luke James." She dropped the printout on the table. "You've seen this. I know you have."

Luke reached for his coffee, and Tilly couldn't blame him. Anyone would need bolstering on a morning like this. She scanned the room. Where had she left her cup of coffee? Oh yes, she'd left it on a parlor table when she went to answer the door.

"Who's behind this?" Daphne demanded, waving her phone in the air.

"I have no idea," Luke admitted. "The post is anonymous, just like the last ones."

Daphne yanked out a chair and plopped onto it, looking more desperate now than irate. "It accuses my husband and me of brokering in body parts from our funeral home! That is the most ridiculous thing I have ever been accused of. I may have a few misdemeanors from back in college, but you're no saint either."

"I never claimed to be." Luke sighed.

"But drug use at a sorority party is hardly the same as selling *dead bodies* for scientific research!" Daphne let her head fall back, and she blew out a huge sigh. She suddenly brought her head back up. "At least this gets Will off the hook for posting these allegations. He wouldn't accuse his own family of such things just to win an election."

"I'm not sure what you want me to do," Luke stated. "I'm as victimized by the accusations as you are."

"Hardly!" Daphne threw her hands up. "The James family is used to warding off slander. Anything shady in the community seems to get blamed on a member of your family, and the Jameses always bounce back."

Luke's expression darkened.

Tilly wondered if she should go, but she didn't have the heart to leave Luke to face Daphne alone, although remaining in the doorway behind Daphne probably didn't offer him much support.

"Look," Daphne went on, "I get that the James family has been a cornerstone of this community for over a century. You can't tell me there was never any wrongdoing in all of that time."

"I never said there wasn't," Luke said.

"But to drag Mitch and our business into it? There is no way you and I are in cahoots to sell bodies in the black market!"

"I know."

"So? What do we do about it?"

"First, maybe stop with the insinuation that this is all somehow *my* fault."

Daphne drew a steadying breath. "I didn't mean to imply that, Luke. I just don't see how anything is going to be gained by hiding in your mansion and drinking coffee."

"Actually," said Tilly, "it's *my* mansion." She couldn't help herself.

Daphne shot her a look. "I realize that." She turned back to Luke. "We are a good family," Daphne insisted, her voice sounding watery now. She swiped at a tear that trailed down her cheek. "This scandal could ruin us. It could ruin Will's run for mayor just for being associated with us as extended family. Luke, you know how the rumor mill works in New Jamestown, the gossip. We have to put a stop to this nonsense at once before we're ruined."

"Too late for me," Luke mumbled. "Listen, Daphne," he said as he leaned forward and twisted his coffee mug on the table, the bottom of it scraping with the movement. "I'm sorry you're mixed up in all this. The entire story is a wild stab at something to bring down my family, and apparently you're getting caught in the crossfire. But—"

"Buuuuut," Daphne repeated, dragging out the word.

Luke looked up at Tilly, then back to Daphne. "But part of me wants to know if there's any truth to it. And maybe the James family has been in leadership for too long."

Daphne stared at him, her mouth hanging open.

Tilly realized she had probably much the same expression on her face.

"Don't let Will hear you say that," Daphne warned. "And what about Kyle? He wants you to pick up the baton and keep up the family tradition."

"Is that what you want, Luke?" Tilly asked.

Both he and Daphne turned toward her. She'd done it again. Been too direct. Tilly crossed her arms over her chest and considered not speaking ever again.

"I . . . I don't know," Luke answered after a long pause. "Anyway, what difference does it make what I think? I'm a James—this is what we do. It's what's expected."

"But that's not right." Well, so much for never speaking again.

"Thank you for that, Tilly." Luke's voice was grave. "But it's not that simple."

"Luke." Daphne reached out a hand, but he leaned away from her in his chair. "Whatever happened in the past, you can't answer for your family—for their decisions. My family can't afford to get wrapped up in it either. Once your brother, well, essentially you're the last of the James family, and this needs to get fixed."

Luke's gaze lifted and collided with Tilly's. "Yeah, well, welcome to the root of the problem."

19

Our very hopes belied our fears,
Our fears our hopes belied—
We thought her dying when she slept,
And sleeping when she died.

Thomas Hood

Luke reached across the library table to take the paper plate with the sandwich Tilly had made for him. He'd remained upstairs in the mansion all morning. For the most part, Tilly had left him alone, seen to Grandpa Don's needs, and then wrestled with the fact that she still had to deal with the issue of the suspected intruder the night before. Somehow that had gotten lost in the shuffle of the social-media post, which was still blowing up, and the administrators of the group refused to take it down, citing "free speech."

Luke took a bite of the sandwich. "Thanks." He lifted it in a salute to Tilly.

"It's just ham and cheese."

"It's food."

She wanted to ask Luke if he was okay. She wanted to say a lot of things to him, the first being that it wasn't his fault. He couldn't bear the weight of guilt of generations of Jameses and their deeds on his shoulders alone. But then saying it and convincing him to believe it were two separate things.

"I called one of the social-media group's administrators," Luke said.

"You did?" Tilly took this as her invitation to join him at the table.

"I asked if there was any way they could see who posted the information."

"And?"

Luke shook his head. "They can't. Which is why they offer the anonymous post option."

Tilly pondered that for a moment. "Can you report the group to the social-media site? For spreading false reports? Or what about posting a rebuttal?"

"Maybe. But I have to be careful. The mayoral race is almost one hundred percent grassroots in a small community like New Jamestown. That means I've had to hit the streets and go door to door, build relationships one by one, attend social functions and school events. When people vote next month, the last person they want to vote for is some guy who's been engaging in fights on social media. It's one thing to post your opinion, but it's quite another to go online trying to defend yourself. Such people don't come across as having integrity."

"So they get to post whatever they want, and you can't say anything to refute their allegations because you might come across as defensive and combative?" Tilly asked, incredulous.

"I don't know that I even care anymore," Luke said and took another bite of his sandwich, chewing slowly and then swallowing. "I'm tired, Tilly. I'm tired of striving to be what my brother thinks I should be. I'm tired of being a James. What's that old saying? 'There's an element of truth in every lie.'" Luke gave a sigh. "Who's to know if some of what's been posted isn't true?"

"Are you serious?" Tilly was confused.

He gave her a wan smile. "I've never been more serious."

They stared at each other for a moment before Luke broke the spell that hung between them.

"I've been doing some online research on my family this morning just like you suggested. I found a family tree that goes back to when New Jamestown was founded in 1818."

"By your ancestor?" Tilly leaned forward.

He nodded. "New Jamestown was founded by my great-grandfather six times removed, Wesley Price James. He moved here from Pennsylvania and settled with his wife, whose name was—" Luke punched a key on his laptop, and the screen lit up— "Eugenia Fitzgerald of Pittsburgh."

"I wonder what brought them to Indiana?" Tilly ventured.

"Opportunity probably. Land. And Wesley James made sure everyone who came later knew he was the first one to settle here."

Tilly couldn't help but laugh. "New Jamestown is like a play on the real, historic Jamestown in the Colony of Virginia. The first permanent English settlement in the Americas."

"No doubt intentional. And it was awfully subtle of him to name the town after himself." Luke rolled his eyes. "Humility isn't something the James men have ever been accused of."

Tilly couldn't help herself. "Well, at least you don't have to worry about being accused of that."

Luke's grin widened, and for a moment she saw what he could be like if he were unburdened of the James dynasty. If he could just live life on his own terms. If the hurt and the history hadn't impacted his life so profoundly.

He shifted back to his laptop. "Next up, my five times removed great-grandfather Price James. He was an interesting guy."

"How so?"

"Come here." Luke patted the chair next to him.

Tilly wondered why butterflies came alive in her stomach. He'd just asked her to sit beside him to view his computer screen. But when she did, she got another whiff of juniper and mint—deodorant? cologne?—and Tilly realized she was reverting to her high school self. The one who secretly crushed on Luke James.

"Okay. So . . ." Luke pointed at the James family tree displayed on a genealogy site. "Here he is. His wife gave him two daughters before she passed away when the eldest was fourteen. Eloise and Evania. He was also the one who built this mansion we're sitting in today. I've found a few records in the archives of the local historical society. His daughter Evania was committed to the Corinth Asylum for the Chronically Insane in 1879."

"So that did happen? Erik and Ashley and I were talking about that old rumor just the other night."

"Apparently." Luke grew quiet as he stared at the screen. "I wonder what her story was . . . why she ended up there."

"The article doesn't say?"

"No. Just that she was committed to the asylum, and her father refused to speak of it afterward."

"What about her sister, Eloise?"

"There's really not much on her."

"Don't genealogy sites include links to newspaper archives, birth records and such?" Tilly asked.

Luke nodded. "Only if a family member links them. As far as I know, no one in my family has bothered to do any family history research since databases like these came into being. We just know what we've been told."

"Which is?" Tilly drew back and turned to Luke.

"That you let sleeping dogs lie."

"Meaning what exactly?"

"Meaning . . . my father was mayor of New Jamestown, my grandfather before him, and great-grandfather before him. Everyone who predates them was either a leading businessman in New Jamestown or a lawyer, something high-profile and influential. No one in the James family questions their father's choices." His words were thick with insinuation.

"Or you end up in a dark cubbyhole alone with your thoughts and a journal?" Tilly bit her lip and quickly added, "I'm sorry. I shouldn't have said that."

"You're right, though." Luke nodded. His eyes were shadowed now, and any hint of lightheartedness had dissipated. "Never question Dad."

Tilly hesitated. She hadn't yet shown Luke the wall in the other room and the words written on it.

Help me.

You are not alone.

So ominous. So revealing of the kind of lives the people who had lived in this mansion had experienced throughout the generations. She couldn't imagine not being allowed to question her dad, to seek truth as it related to her family or to God or to anything. Don't question. Just obey.

She realized then there were different types of prisons. The kind with bars and locks and throwaway keys, and the kind where freedom was an illusion. Because even inside the walls of a carefully curated and prosperous home, the roots of love and grace could be yanked out, leaving behind desperation and soil that could produce nothing good.

It had been a long day. Luke hadn't left the mansion until after supper, and he'd spent a lot of the time on the phone with his campaign manager trying to do damage control. Tilly had made the mistake of going on social media, only to see the local community group had several active threads, all of them chatting about the recent allegation against the James family.

I'll never vote for him now.

We all knew that mansion was a house of horrors.

In 1973, my grandmother said there was a string of people who disappeared in a hundred-mile radius of New Jamestown. Bet they were farmed for their body parts.

Tilly hoped Luke wasn't reading any of it. Which also revealed something else about herself. A few weeks ago, she would've probably agreed with some of the accusations just because it was Luke James. But she knew now that that wasn't who Luke was. Erik was right. She had no idea what Luke had been through.

But she was beginning to see.

After a call from Erik to verify she'd locked all the doors and checked every window in the house to be sure it was locked, Tilly went to the train room to check on Grandpa Don. He had a little TV in the corner turned on to *Bonanza*, and Tilly caught a glimpse of a young Michael Landon. She was distracted for a moment. Even sixty years later, Little Joe was a handsome devil, although Tilly had better known him as Pa from her *Little House on the Prairie* days, watching the show with Grandpa Don. Another thing they'd shared together. What else was a girl to do when her grandpa was her best friend?

"Don't worry about tonight, Tilly," Grandpa Don reassured her as he tinkered with a motor that attached to his model train. "I aim to stay awake and keep watch on things, so that some hooligan doesn't break in again."

"Grandpa, I don't–"

"No arguments, missy." He raised his hand and his head.

"You're not a Cartwright, Grandpa," Tilly teased with a glance at the TV.

"Maybe not, but I did my time in 'Nam."

That reminded her. "Grandpa, you *did* give Erik your hunting rifle, didn't you?" The last thing she needed was her grandfather wielding a firearm in the middle of the night, thinking her trip to the bathroom was an intruder lurking on the floor above him.

"You leave that to me."

His cryptic response didn't bring her any comfort.

She noticed he'd glanced toward his bed. Tilly marched toward it and lifted the mattress. Between it and the box spring, her grandfather's .22 rifle lay ready to grab, and if she knew her grandfather, it was loaded and ready to use.

"This is a no." Tilly pointed at the gun.

Grandpa Don reared back. "Who put you in charge?"

"You did," she retorted.

"Worst mistake of my life," he grunted.

A pang shot through her at his words, even as she confiscated the .22. Tilly exited the room and hurried upstairs to her room where she checked the gun to see if it was loaded. It was. She quickly emptied it, hiding the bullets in a place Grandpa Don would never think to look.

He didn't really know what he was saying. His behavior wasn't consistent with the loving, gentle man she'd always known. But glimpses like these into his failing mind hurt her. She was losing him. Ever so slowly, but it was happening.

Coaching herself not to take his cutting remark personally, knowing it wasn't truly Grandpa Don speaking, Tilly tucked the emptied .22 in the back of her closet. She'd give the gun and bullets to Erik the next time she saw him.

Was Grandpa Don really going to play hero and stay up all night to guard her and the mansion? Tilly chose to dwell on that pledge from her grandfather. It was true to his nature. Protective.

Her gaze traveled to the drawer in her dresser where she'd stuffed Luke's journal. Had Luke ever known that feeling? A fatherly or grandfatherly covering of protection? Knowing that if something went wrong, the patriarch of the family would be there to save you?

She knew Grandpa Don wasn't physically capable of that anymore. But she also knew, if something did happen, it was in his warrior-like heart to try to defend her. Hence the reason why she'd taken the gun from him.

If she read Luke's journal, if she peeked a little further into Luke's past, maybe she could better understand him. Come alongside him during this rough time.

No.

Tilly held her hand up to the drawer as if it were speaking to her. Though her intentions might be honorable, she knew deep down that it would be a betrayal of confidence and trust if she were to open the journal again.

Instead, Tilly hurried from her room, shooting a glance at the doors on the second floor as she passed them. Closed. Closed. Closed. Closed. Good. Everything was as it should be. Windows were locked. Thankfully, there wasn't that niggling feeling she was being watched, not like the other night.

She bounded down the stairs and, for a second, stopped in front of the gaping hole in the wall. Tilly had called to get an estimate on repairs, but no one had followed up with her yet. Now she wondered if, after the social-media posts this week, anyone would. Or maybe instead of being frightened away, curiosity would inspire more people to offer their estimates for patching the hole.

Argh.

So much for her idyllic days spent with Grandpa Don building model train layouts in the historic James Mansion while enjoying the autumn breeze as it filtered through the grand home.

This place—though still beautiful in many ways—was becoming like a good book that you pulled off the shelf, only to get halfway through to find out it wasn't anything like what you were expecting. Instead, what you were reading was the type of bad story that kept you turning the pages only to see if it could redeem itself.

"Grandpa, I'm going to make some tea. Do you want—?" She rounded the corner into the train room.

Grandpa Don was no longer there with his model train cars.

"Grandpa?" she called.

When he didn't answer, Tilly hurried through a side door into the adjoining room that was now split into a laundry room and bathroom. The bathroom door stood wide open, and the room was dark.

"Grandpa!" Tilly called again, this time hoping he hadn't turned off his hearing aids, which he was apt to do from time to time.

Hoss Cartwright was punching some villainous cattle rustler in the face when Tilly rushed back into the train room. Maybe Grandpa Don had gone for a snack in the kitchen.

But everything inside Tilly was twisting with a growing feeling that something was not right.

And it wasn't.

The back door was wide open, the night beyond as black as could be with the moon covered by an overcast sky. Tilly raced onto the back porch.

"Grandpa!" she called again.

This was her worst fear. That he would wander off. It meant his care would need to be taken to the next level: heightened observation, better locks on the doors, an alarm system installed—not to warn her of someone breaking in, but rather someone breaking out.

Tilly ran out into the yard. As her eyes adjusted to the darkness, she sped around the back of the mansion to the front. When it became clear that Grandpa Don was nowhere to be found, she pulled her phone from her pocket to call Erik.

What seemed like hours later, Erik arrived at the mansion. He slammed his car door shut and sprinted to meet her at the edge of the woods, where Tilly stood shining a flashlight in case Grandpa Don had wandered into the pitch-black woods.

"Nothing?" he asked.

"No," Tilly said in a shaky voice. "I had just gone upstairs, Erik—I'd just taken his *gun* away."

"His gun!" Erik exclaimed, shock on his face.

"Yes, but what matters most right now is that when I came back downstairs, he was *gone*."

"I'm going to call the police. They can issue a Silver Alert." Erik was already dialing.

"I already did that." Tilly started for his car.

"Where are you going?" he shouted after her.

"Let's drive around and look for Grandpa."

"Hold on!" A new voice was added to the mix. Tilly spun around as Luke hurried up the drive. He'd parked on the street. She could see his car with its headlights on. "Erik told me to come."

"He did?" She had no idea why.

"Grandpa called Luke, thinking he was calling me," Erik explained. "He was talking gibberish, so Luke called me when he couldn't get ahold of you."

"I can go with Tilly," Luke offered, "if you want to wait for the police."

Erik nodded.

Tilly charged ahead of Luke, who jogged to catch up to her. Tilly whipped open the passenger side door, but before she could get in, Luke stopped her, a hand on her wrist.

"You're going to have to calm down," he said.

"I am calm!" she barked. She made a move to wrestle her arm from his gentle grip. His touch felt like sandpaper on her skin.

"I mean, you're going to need to think calmly if we're going to figure out where your grandfather may have gone."

Luke's voice was soothing, and it reached places inside her she hadn't known were wide open at the moment.

This was Grandpa Don!

Her grandpa.

The man who had always been there for her. The man who had bought her James Mansion. The man who'd been her truest friend for years. The sheer panic of his going missing was only compounded by the reality that she was losing him—if not today, then all too soon. And she was losing Grandpa Don long before death would come to claim him.

Luke might have his dysfunctional family history to deal with, but that wasn't hers. Hers was loving and supportive, everything a family should be.

She wasn't going to lose that. She *couldn't* lose that. Tilly wasn't sure she could keep going without Grandpa Don. But the problem was, she knew that soon—maybe sooner than she wished—she would have to learn to live without him.

IF WALLS COULD TALK

I saw the old man leave. He took with him his remnants of memories. All of the ones who have come and gone from here have taken their memories with them. They leave the worst behind, or in the mercies of old age, their minds steal from them and they are left with nothing.

I see them fight to retain their memory almost as belligerently as they strive to lose it when they are young and sharp. The questions linger, though. The whys, the hows . . .

Why is life like this?

How did it come to this?

I can tell them. I have seen. I have whispered *Help me* to those who listen and those who do not. I have called for truth to walk into the light and for the lies to cease.

But who am I to make it all stop?

I cannot.

I can only watch. Listen. Whisper. Then, I am silent.

Because walls cannot speak.

Even when we want to.

20

Eloise James

Lo! Death has reared himself a throne
In a strange city lying alone
Far down within the dim West,
Where the good and the bad and the worst and the best
Have gone to their eternal rest.

Edgar Allan Poe

October 1879
James Mansion

She sent word to the Bigsby House. A note to Silas. The very act of it heightened her sense of insubordination against Father. But Eloise didn't want to do this on her own. Silas was different from any man she had known before. He instilled courage into her just by his merry smile and ridiculous proclamations. He didn't criticize or demean her, and somehow that gave Eloise the strength to believe she *could* find Evania. That there was still hope. That maybe God had not been mistaken when He'd made her, not as a woman who *knew* her place, but a woman who could *create* her place.

And that place would be empty without answers about Evania. Everything inside of Eloise screamed that she wanted to pretend none of this had happened. She wanted to somehow reverse time and go back to the days when Evania's glee had been contagious. But as Eloise considered her sister, she couldn't deny the question that had begun to plague her. Was Evania ever truly filled with contentment and joy or had it all been a facade in order to survive?

Eloise had chosen to be diminutive and submissive, to avoid conflicts, to believe that she needed to remain in her place. Evania had chosen to dance and laugh, making those around her believe that life could not stain her happiness. But even that had been a lie. Evania's search to be loved and her quest to find herself in the arms of a man, who tossed her away when she no longer suited . . .

Eloise was becoming aware that she and Evania were more alike than she had realized. Each of them ached to be valued. Not just loved but *valued*. To know they could influence the world around them, and that it would benefit as a result. That they could inspire deep conversations and have intelligent insights. That they could be complementary to the men in their lives, not looked at as beneath them.

The penny-a-liner Silas Dobbs had shown Eloise in a matter of mere moments that he saw her. Truly *saw* her. That was a powerful sensation. So no, Eloise didn't wish for Silas to give her words to say or instruct her on how to approach Father. She merely wished to draw from whatever it was Silas saw in her—his belief that she was indeed worthy. This man who really didn't know her, but who already seemed to understand her more than any man ever had.

She and Silas were united in their cause to find their family members and bring them home. Or if the worst turned out to be true, then bring them to a place of eternal rest. If Seamus and Penny had vanished from the asylum because they had died of sickness—perhaps from a contagion as Father had inferred about Evania—and if their suspicions were correct, then the probability of finding their remains to lay them to rest was slim. The resurrectionists would have stolen their bodies, which would never be found.

Eloise hated the thought of it. If Evania had been seriously ill as the steward had said, her gumption might have helped her escape the asylum. But what happened after she was taken away in the wagon beside the bodies of her fellow patients? Had she slipped from the wagon and run into the woods only to die there alone? Perhaps she had found someone to take her in and nurse her back to health. Eloise was loath to entertain the very real possibility that her sister had fallen victim to the wiles and greed of the resurrectionists and met a similar fate as the others.

Still, if she could convince Father that this despicable practice of selling human remains was taking place, he could go to the asylum and alert Dr. Holzer of the fact—assuming the doctor wasn't also a part of the illegal scheme. Hopefully, those in charge at the asylum would listen to Price James. His very name yielded results. It was Father's one redeeming quality.

Eloise strode along the walkway toward the small park in the center of New Jamestown. She had slipped from the mansion and was grateful she'd succeeded in leaving Ida behind. Granted, she should be chaperoned, seeing as she was meeting a young man—and not a respectable one when it came to his family name. But Eloise couldn't risk Ida's presence.

She made her way to a cast-iron bench tucked at the edge of the park and away from the primary strolling area. Yet she was within sight of it, and she watched for a long moment as mothers pushed their children in buggies and little children ran out ahead only to be called back to their mothers' sides. A robin hopped on the lawn, and a squirrel scampered in front of her with an acorn in its mouth. Both animals were preparing for the coming winter. One would fly away, the other nestle in with his stash of food and sleep away the cold.

The park was peaceful. It was difficult to believe that underneath the quiet prettiness, something ugly lurked. Just beyond was St. Matthews Cemetery. A place that should bring solace and comfort to the grieving. It wasn't a garden to be harvested, but a bed in which to rest. Still, Eloise believed if she looked very hard, she could almost see a shadow hovering over it now, reminding her that the wickedness of men could touch even that.

"Good afternoon, love." Silas hurdled the back of the bench and landed next her on the seat.

Eloise yelped in surprise, then clapped a hand over her mouth.

"Did you miss me as much as I did you?" He winked.

Eloise had no intention of answering his question, but she did notice how her heart jumped a little, and not because of his rambunctious arrival.

"I know you're shy. Ya don't need to admit it aloud. You've been pinin' for me, I know." Silas nodded, whipping his cap off and shaking out his head of dark curls. "Now, what did you find to help our cause?"

Eloise pressed her lips together, averse to admitting he'd been right only because the truth was so awful. "Everything you said is true—at least about the body snatchers. I don't know how it may still tie to the asylum, but I know I need to go to my father about this."

"Ah, that's my girl." Silas dropped a peck on her cheek before she could pull away. "Listen," he said and grasped her hands, "I was thinkin' it might be a smart idea, before you go to your father, we get a better idea of who he'll be facin' when he visits the asylum and confronts them. Who's on the board there, and who might object to his accusations that the nefarious body snatchin' is happening right in their own hospital."

"All of them will object," Eloise said. She didn't pull her hands away from him. She was wearing gloves but suddenly wished she wasn't. "No one will want to admit that someone in their institution is involved in selling the patients' remains."

"Aye. And we don't have any proof as yet to show them. Just our word. *Your* word, that is."

Eloise flushed. "That's why it's important we go to my father first. He can provide the credibility we need."

"Assumin' he believes you."

She did not argue with that. It would be a miracle if he even listened to her all the way through. But if they were to inspire a thorough investigation of how the asylum handled the remains of patients who had passed away, they would need someone like Father to be their voice. Eloise knew beyond a shadow of a doubt that Dr. Holzer would certainly not give her the time of day again, let alone an audience with the board.

"I'm sayin' we need to be prepared. We find out who is on the board of the institution and then we can let your father know there's at least one worker who'll give testimony of what they have seen."

"The steward who talked to me," Eloise confirmed.

"Aye."

"But will he? It's one thing to tell me what he saw, but would he go before a room of powerful men who hold his employment in their hands?"

"We'll pray he's not easily scared."

Eloise nodded. Silas was right, but she could tell by the look in his eyes that the entire situation was an uphill battle.

They stood in front of the county clerk's office. Eloise reached up to make sure her hat sat properly on her hair. She adjusted her gloves and patted her collar.

"You're well put together, love," Silas assured her.

"I've never been in a county clerk's office," she admitted.

"There's nothin' to be afeared of. It's not a court of law."

"I know." Eloise shot him a sideways glance. "They keep public records."

"Right. And you can ask 'em for the list of the board of trustees. That's all you need to say. There's nothin' suspicious about askin' for it either."

Eloise stared at the door as though if she walked through it, she'd never be able to make her way out. "What if they know why I'm asking?"

"They won't." Silas's eyes twinkled, deep chocolate eyes with so much surety in them. Eloise was envious of his confidence. "You're not goin' to walk in and announce you're needin' to know the trustees so you can make a case to them that their patients' remains are bein' sold. You're simply askin' for the list of names."

"What if they ask me why I want the list?"

"They won't."

"You can't be certain of that," Eloise retorted, surprised at her irritated tone.

"Do you really want me to come in with ya?"

She eyed him, noting without discrimination his worn trousers and jacket, the frayed edges of his shirtsleeve cuffs, and the unruly curls beneath the brim of his cap. No. They would instantly judge him according to his appearance. Scrappy he might be, and to his credit, for it seemed to serve him well. However, she could see how even someone from the middle class might censure him.

"I-I'll be fine." Eloise couldn't help but lock eyes with Silas. This was ridiculous. She was so nervous to do something so simple.

"I've faith in ya," Silas said. "Just remember, you're doin' it for Evania."

"And for Penny and Seamus," Eloise added.

He nodded, then gestured toward the door. "On with ya now."

Eloise drew a deep breath and then went inside. She felt his absence instantly, but she still took his confidence with her. She lifted her chin.

"May I help you?" The man at the front counter lifted a kind face. His white shirt and green vest were professional yet welcoming. It put Eloise at ease.

"Yes. I need to get a listing of the members of the board of trustees for the Corinth Asylum for the Chronically Insane, please." Eloise waited with bated breath. She knew there was no reason the man would withhold the information, and yet she braced herself for a barrage of accusatory questions.

"Why?"

"Pardon me?" Eloise thought she had heard the question she'd feared most. She must have given the clerk a panicked look because he offered Eloise a reassuring nod and motioned to a row of chairs against the wall.

"I said, why don't you have a seat while I get that information for you."

"Oh . . . yes, thank you." Eloise sheepishly took a seat after a look out the window. She saw Silas on the sidewalk, crouching to scratch the head of a stray dog. He reached into his pocket and drew out a small paper bag. He opened it and broke off a piece of jerky, extending it to the dog. The poor creature looked hungry.

Silas. Eloise felt herself warm all the more toward him. That he had a penchant for jerky was news to her, but so was his gentleness with the dog. If it had been Father, he would have hooked his foot under the dog and given it a good toss out of his way.

She sat on a wooden chair, keeping her posture straight as she'd been taught, her purse in her lap, hands gloved appropriately. If Evania could only see her now. Out with a young man and no chaperone, gathering information of importance without consulting their father. Evania would be so proud of her!

Eloise knew there was nothing monumental in asking for a list of names, but for her, it was no small thing. She had left home, traveled the reasonable distance to Corinth by train, returned home to face her father, and even combed through the basement for old newspapers. Now here she was in a building she'd never imagined entering. She looked over her shoulder, and sure enough, Silas was still petting the dog. And she had met a friend—a young man, no less.

Eloise could picture it then. Sitting with Evania on her bed, their heads together, commiserating on Father's suffocating control while giggling over their dreams for the future.

"I'm going to meet a fine young man, and we'll sail to Europe. I want to see the opera in Vienna. I want to fall madly in love while floating down the Grand Canal in Venice."

"But first you have to meet the fine young man," Eloise had said, laughing.

A knowing look from Evania and then, "Perhaps I have!"

And she had.

Evania's "fine young man" had become inconsequential. He had vanished the moment Evania began to increase with child. She had been left to bear the ire of their father, the shame of her choices, and eventually the gutting of her grief.

Eloise closed her eyes, trying to memorize every curve and line of Evania's face. She tried to imagine what Evania would say now. If tonight they could sit on her bed and confide in each other again. This time it would be Eloise's turn.

"I have met a young man who is becoming a friend."

"You have?" Evania's eyes would light with anticipation.

"His name is Silas Dobbs. He is Irish."

"Irish?" A twinkle of rebellious mischief.

"He's spirited and handsome, and he calls me 'love.'"

Evania would fold her hands and clutch them to her chest, releasing a swoony sigh. "And Father? Will Father approve?"

"Never. He would abhor the very idea of me even entertaining a man like Silas as an acquaintance."

"Tell me all about him!"

"I-I don't know much. He is an orphan. He has no family."

"And?"

"And he . . ." She would search for words to explain him, and she would be reminded of how little she knew about Silas Dobbs.

Evania would grasp her hands then and press a sisterly kiss to them. "Oh, Eloise!" But then, in Eloise's imagination, Evania's eyes would deepen with a sadness she had not expected. "Be cautious with your heart."

"Cautious?" Eloise would inquire.

Evania would grow reflective, and her smile would fade. "Men can become a possibility, or a pastime, or a diversion from what pains us most." Tears would sparkle in her eyes as she squeezed Eloise's fingers. "But you must not be rash—not as I have been. You must search for character, just as our mother told us to do so many years ago. Look for a man with integrity over conceit. Look for a man who, when he sees you, sees the essence of you, not just a woman to grace his arm. The intoxication of attraction fades, and then you will find yourself trapped—like our mother did."

"I've only just met Silas . . ." Eloise would let her worry shake her voice.

"Shh, sweet sister." Evania would smile then with all the bravery and life she had in her soul. "First, you must believe that you have a purpose. And that purpose stands on its own between you and your Creator. As Mama taught us." Her smile would fade. "As I wish I had been more mindful of."

Of course, it was a made-up conversation, and so Eloise shook herself back to awareness of the present. Of the clerk who passed in front of her while she sat by the window. Evania never spoke like that, but Mama had. Perhaps in Eloise's imagination, she was merging Evania and her mother. Two women who had seen the darkness of abuses and knew their own insignificance in the eyes of the men they chose.

"Here you are, miss."

Eloise jerked from her thoughts.

The secretary stood over her, a sheet of paper in his hand that he extended to Eloise.

"Oh!" Eloise shot to her feet. She took the page and didn't bother to look at the names. "Thank you so very much."

"You're welcome, miss."

After they exchanged polite goodbyes, Eloise hurried from the county clerk's office. The door closed behind her.

She had done it. She had dared to act on her own again, and it felt almost euphoric. Especially when Silas met her outside, and his grin split his face.

"There's m'lady," he said.

Yes. Here she was.

Silas led her away from the office, allowing Eloise to hook her hand on his arm. She noticed a few people giving them glances, she in her well-tailored dress, fine hat and gloves, and Silas who was, well, Silas. Eloise had to admire the way he didn't seem to notice or care if anyone looked at him sideways. Eloise would feel better when they were in a less public place, though. She needn't take too many unnecessary chances with wagging tongues. It had not served Evania well.

They crossed the street, hurrying between carriages and finding their way to a small fountain with a bench beside it.

"Here you are." Eloise handed him the folded paper she'd received at the clerk's office.

"Did you recognize any names?"

She shook her head. "I haven't read it yet. I just wanted to—" She bit off her words. There was no reason to share how she had rushed from the office to escape the scrutiny of the man there.

Silas unfolded the page. "This is where we pray there are reasonable men on the board, those who will want to avoid a scandal. More'n that, we need men who are willing to listen to reason, or I'll have to resort to making these allegations in print."

"If they're like my father, we must appeal to their pride and their finances."

"Aye. An' there's the trouble. If even a one of 'em are a part of the scheme to sell bodies, then we'll need to be careful. They won't want to be exposed or lose money because of allegations by riffraff like m'self and a lady like you."

Eloise worried that it was all for naught. But again, that was where Father came in. If they could win his confidence, he would do all he could to protect their family name.

Silas skimmed the names written on the page. He tapped the second one down. "Jonas Barnaby. I've heard that name before."

Eloise nodded. "He's an attorney in New Jamestown and quite prominent."

Silas continued to study the names on the page. "I don't know these other fellas . . ." Then there was a shift in his expression.

"What is it?" Eloise shifted to view the list, but Silas pulled it away.

He looked at her with confusion.

"Silas?" she pressed.

"Did ya know?" His voice lowered, doubt lacing it.

"Know what?"

After a moment, as he searched her face, Silas concluded, "You don't know, do ya?"

"Silas, you're frightening me."

His chest heaved as he blew out a breath. He moved the page back into her line of sight.

Eloise looked at the list of names. A few sounded familiar. Dr. Holzer, of course, and the attorney, but there was another businessman from Corinth she had heard Father refer to once, and then—

Her eyes flew up to meet Silas's.

"Aye." He nodded at her disbelief.

"*Father* is a trustee?" Eloise had not expected to see that. Father, a trustee, on the board of the very asylum he'd committed his daughter to. She considered the implications of this new development. "He will be furious when he learns the hospital he helps to oversee has mishandled Evania."

"Will he?" Silas didn't sound very sure.

"Of course," she said. A new hope flooded her thoughts. Any shadow cast on Father or anything he was involved in was tantamount to the highest of offenses in his eyes. Whereas she'd previously worried that she would have to present a story to engage his interest in investigating the asylum, now he would be personally invested, even without the connection to Evania.

"Silas!" She turned in her seat and grabbed ahold of his forearm. A smile touched her lips. "Do you know what this means?"

He eyed her cautiously. "What do you think it means, love?"

"It means we're sure to find out what happened to Evania. To Penny and Seamus. If my father is on the board of trustees, he will not want any stain on the institution he represents."

"No stains?" Silas asked curiously.

Eloise waited, unsure why he was so hesitant.

"Love, if what we are afraid of is true, it will ruin the asylum, sure as a fire will burn down a forest. If your father has an investment in the place, he may want to keep it all under the table. Which means he could shut ya down before you have a chance to find out more. You know that, don't ya? Your father may have to decide who he's most loyal to, your sister or sparing the hospital a scandal."

21

What has this bugbear Death to frighten man,
If souls can die, as well as bodies can?

Lucretius

Evania was there. Eloise could see her in the corner of her room. She rubbed at her eyes, sleep weighing them down. Had she walked in her sleep again? Or was this like the night the drapes in her bedroom had reached for her?

"Evania?"

There was no answer.

Eloise sat up in bed, already having tossed and turned. The very fear of approaching Father tomorrow left her agonizing with worry. But troubled enough to see her dead sister?

The form in the corner shifted from shadow to nothingness.

"Evania!" Eloise swung her legs from her bed. She sprinted across the floor of her bedroom until her hands met the wall, hard and cold beneath her touch. There was no Evania. No being.

Dreams were a wicked thing. She spun around, still sensing Evania behind her.

"Evania?"

There was no one. Shrouded in the depth of night, her bedroom remained as empty of life as it had when she had retired. Without light, it brooded in its melancholy.

Eloise clutched at the ribbons that had come untied at her neckline. Her nightgown was damp with sweat. Her hair stuck to the sides of her face.

The floor creaked outside of her room, like the footsteps of someone hovering just outside the door, as if considering whether to knock and disturb her.

Eloise could still sense her sister's presence. Irrational as the idea was, she flew to the door, flinging it open. "Evania!" she cried.

A tiny flicker of light at the end of the corridor was snuffed out. For a moment, Eloise saw the form of a woman disappear on the stairs.

Eloise hurried after it.

She didn't concern herself that there was little light.

Her bare feet padded along the floor, and she turned to the stairs.

The flicker of light glowed in the parlor below—a pinprick. Eloise hurried down the steps to the landing where she stopped in surprise. To her left, the new stained-glass window sparkled in the moonlight, the colored panes begging her to admire them.

But she couldn't. Not now.

Nor could she examine the disappointment she felt—without good reason—for the fact that there was no window added to the south wall as initially planned.

A shadow passed across the floor. It beckoned to her, but even as Eloise rushed into the sitting room, its fireplace cold, its bay window overlooking the front lawn empty, the room was devoid of any person. Eloise braced against the doorframe to steady herself.

Where was she?

How had she gotten here?

Oh yes. The shadow. Evania. Confusion clouded her mind,

making the world blurry around Eloise. The night was like a heavy blanket, causing her to perspire. She could hear herself breathing. The air around her was thick and cold.

"Evania?" Eloise's voice cut through the stillness. "Was that you? Where are you?"

Her cheeks were wet, and tears trailed down her face and neck.

Eloise opened a door. Her father's study. Hadn't she just been in the sitting room? Confusion made her spin around, trying to gain her bearings. Her stomach clenched, anxiety overwhelming her. This room was even darker, heavy and oppressive. The smell of Father's tobacco permeated her senses, then dulled them, and then . . .

Eloise awoke. She didn't know how much time had passed, only that her dreamlike state had led her here. Sleepwalking. Again.

She was on the floor at the feet of a velvet-covered chair. Using it for support, Eloise pushed herself onto her knees, her nightgown tightening around her neck as she did so. With one more unsteady shove, Eloise stood, tripping on the nightdress and landing awkwardly on the chair.

Eloise trailed her hand around her neck, feeling the dampness of her skin. She had been dreaming again. Of Evania. Of shadows. Her dreams had inspired her to come to Father's study. This was a place she never came to alone, never *dared* to trespass when she was in her right mind. Now she was alone in her father's private world, surrounded by everything that reminded her of him.

She needed to leave. To retreat back to the simplicity of her rooms. Father would be livid if he were to find her here. He would be—

Eloise caught sight of the wall behind Father's desk. A painting had been moved from its usual place, revealing Father's safe. Its door was ajar. She maneuvered around the desk, trailing her hand along its top to steady her steps.

It was so dark. So very dark. Eloise could barely see into the safe as she pushed the door fully open. She was invading his privacy, and yet the compulsion to know him—to understand his role in all that comprised her and Evania's lives—gave Eloise the tenacity to put her hand into his safe. She felt a small book and drew it out.

Eloise opened the book, staring down at handwriting that was not her father's but someone else's. She strained to read the words in the dim light . . .

May 10—Dr. Holzer called at the house for me this afternoon. We took the train to the asylum and discussed further resurrecting next winter.

May 11—Called to see Dr. Holzer at his office regarding furnishings for his classes on dissection.

May 22—Went to the asylum and stayed for dinner. Dr. Holzer and I went for an evening walk, as there was a cadaver on hand. But we could not get it.

May 23—We got a subject this evening.

May 24—Stayed at the asylum last night with Dr. Holzer and took breakfast there. Went to the college this morning and injected our subject.

June 8—This has been a beautiful day. I stayed at the asylum and then took a walk through the cemetery.

June 12—It rained a good deal last night. Dr. Holzer and I found three fresh graves at the cemetery, but the ground was too wet to remove them.

June 17—Sent two subjects to Pennsylvania this morning. I'm to meet with our investor in the morning.

June 18—Met with our investor. More subjects are required for university. Went with Dr. Holzer to get a subject, but then abandoned it, as it was too much work and because one came in this evening from the asylum to be interred on the morrow.

Eloise closed the book with solemnity. She could not breathe. The air was stolen from her lungs. However this journal of business had arrived in her father's safe, it was apparent that he already knew what it was she'd planned to discuss with him and Silas tomorrow.

Eloise whirled around, the journal flinging from her hands and landing on its pages in the middle of the floor. A woman stood there, her features unrecognizable in the semidarkness. She bent to retrieve the book.

"Say nothing," she whispered as she straightened. The words came too late.

Eloise sank to the floor, the room spinning, and her eyes closed against the fright of it all.

She could feel herself rocking with the motion of a carriage. Her body felt heavy, her eyelids impossible to open. Disoriented, Eloise tried to speak, but a gloved hand covered her mouth.

"Silence."

A woman's voice.

Nausea filled Eloise, and she had no choice but to succumb to the dizzying sensation of floating while being securely supported.

Where was she?

Eloise tried to open her eyes again and to gather her wits, but the oppressive weight of an addled mind and a body that spun without moving proved insurmountable.

"Hold her feet."

They were the next words Eloise heard. Someone was holding her shoulders while another hoisted her legs.

Eloise moaned, wanting to protest.

"Be still." Again a command spoken softly so as not to disturb.

But disturb whom?

Eloise attempted to wriggle free of the arms hooked under hers and the hands that held her ankles.

"I said *be still.*" This time the command was hissed and more urgent.

A door opened.

Eloise managed to get her eyes to cooperate and open into narrow slits. She saw the nighttime sky. Stars twinkling overhead. And then she was passing through a doorway.

"In here." It was a man's voice. He was holding her shoulders.

A deep fog hovered over Eloise.

Her body was lowered.

A bed. The softness of it unexpected but not unwelcome.

"Keep her here," she heard a woman say from farther away. "You cannot bring her home."

A rumble of a man's voice again.

A door closed.

Murmuring outside the door as the voice rose in intensity.

"I've done all I can to protect her."

"I cannot explain."

"Until we know . . . not safe . . . Evania's demise should not be hers."

Eloise strained to sit up, to move even, but she couldn't do so.

She resigned herself to the reality that her body was not allowing her to fight, to come into full awareness. She could not resist the heaviness.

Eloise opened her eyes.

Morning sunlight spread across her face, her body, and a quilt was pulled up to her shoulders. Her head hurt, but in a dull way that was manageable and not debilitating. The room was simple, unfamiliar, and she could feel cool air on her face. It wasn't heated nearly as well as James Mansion.

Eloise struggled to push herself off the bed. She had been home last night! Her father's study. The journal.

"Lay back, love."

Silas appeared by her side. His hand pushed her shoulder with gentle pressure, urging her to lay back on the bed. His eyes were deep with concern, and as he bent over her, she noticed a brown curl flop onto his forehead.

"You're safe with me," he reassured.

"Where am I?" Lying on a bed with Silas Dobbs crouching beside it was unseemly! She tried to sit up once more, grabbing at the blanket that covered her. "I need to leave. I shouldn't be here." Eloise scanned the room in a panic and then leveled horrified eyes on Silas. "Is this your room? Your bed?"

"Shh." Silas urged her to lie back again. "You'll wake the dead." He flinched.

It was not the best choice of words, but Eloise ignored them. "How–?" Eloise tried to ask, but her words congealed in her mouth.

"Your lady's maid, Ida–she brought you here to me at Bigsby House last night. You're to stay with me now."

"I was in my father's study." Eloise struggled to remember. "There was a logbook of business . . ." The woman who had entered. Had that been Ida? Eloise couldn't remember after that. "What happened to me?"

A flicker of disapproval flashed in Silas's eyes. "Your maid is a force to be reckoned with. She brought you here. All by herself too. She knew you'd fight her, so she used chloroform to keep you under."

"Ida administered chloroform to me?" Eloise couldn't help the shrill shock in her voice.

"Shush, love." Silas waved at her to be silent. "Her methods leave much to be desired, aye, but you're here now, and you must stay with me."

"Stay with you?" Bewilderment overwhelmed her. This was ludicrous. This wasn't the plan. To be knocked out and hauled to Silas Dobbs's room in the middle of the night by Ida? It was highly out of character for her lady's maid. She'd been disapproving of Silas, and so to bring Eloise to his quarters? "What was Ida thinking? Father will be–"

"Aye, he'll be worried, but you'll be safe." The mattress dipped under Silas's weight as he lowered himself onto the edge of the bed. "There's more goin' on than we knew. And your father—"

"He already knows about what's happening at the asylum. There's a journal that describes events, but it's not my father's handwriting. He must have found it or confiscated it. Perhaps he is already investigating, and he'll help us stop—"

She was interrupted by a knock on the door. Then it opened, and Ida herself slipped into the room, shutting the door firmly behind her. She met Eloise's astonished gaze.

"Good morning, Miss Eloise."

"You—you gave me chloroform." It was an accusation, not a question.

Ida approached the bed, not bothering to give Silas the time of day. "It's not safe for you at James Mansion. Not after Evania has been taken away, and your sleepwalking is becoming worse. Someone in that house is involved in nefarious activity, and I had to get you out for your own safety."

Eloise blinked in surprise. She exchanged looks with Silas, then returned her attention to Ida. "And it required chloroform to do so?"

Ida didn't seem perturbed in the slightest. "Miss Eloise, I'm not sure you quite understand how incoherent and unmanageable you are when you're in that state. I tried to convince you to come with me, but you were like speaking to a ghost. You looked right through me. And that was after you'd removed the painting on your father's wall, and goodness knows how you got that safe's door open." Ida folded her hands primly in front of her.

"What?" Eloise tried to piece it all together.

"She's a smart one, Miss Ida is," Silas interjected, oblivious to Ida's discerning scowl. "An' she's seen and heard things over several months. Says there's someone in James Mansion who's tied up in all of it."

"All of what?" Eloise tried to keep up.

"Stealing bodies from the asylum," Ida answered. "And if you continue to get in their way, I fear for your safety."

"It's not my father." Eloise instantly defended the man who so intimidated her. He was a hard man, but he would never have subjected Evania to *that* potential fate.

"But someone there is," Ida insisted.

"Then my father must be under duress," Eloise concluded, tossing a panicked look between Silas and Ida.

"Under duress?" Silas parroted.

"Someone must be blackmailing my father, maybe was even behind all that happened to Evania. And my father is powerless to refuse. It could be they've got something on him . . ." Evania let her protest drain away. She had no sudden affection for Father, but she could hardly comprehend the idea he'd subject Evania to the care of such wicked people.

Silas spoke before Ida could say anything. "Aye, he might've seen somethin' or stumbled on it, I suppose. But your sleep-walkin' has you goin' places you shouldn't be alone at, that's for sure. An' that journal? The foolhardy devil who put to pen every step of his crimes, if he knows you've seen it, he'll be after you to kill you. We're tryin' to keep you out of it. You can't go back to James Mansion, Eloise, you just can't."

"But where will I—?"

"You'll stay with me, love. I'll see to it you're kept safe."

"Absolutely not!" Eloise shot an appalled look at her prim and proper lady's maid. Ida's gray brows were drawn in a frown, but she didn't affirm Eloise's outburst either. Eloise looked to Silas. If he thought she would agree to sleep in his room . . .

"Of course not *here*." He broke into her rebuttal and swung his arm to emphasize the room they were in. "We'll get you a room next door."

"That's still hardly appropriate." Eloise found herself capitulating to the reason behind it—her safety—while still believing she needed to adhere to propriety.

"Under normal circumstances," Ida interjected, "I would agree. However, your life is more important to protect at this moment than your reputation."

"But I was going to talk with Father," Eloise attempted.

"We're past that," Silas stated. "This is bigger than just one or two people takin' bodies from the asylum or diggin' up a grave. An' your father seems to be caught up in the midst of it."

"What about you?" she asked, directing her question to Ida. "What about your safety?"

"I will return to the mansion. And I must do so soon or my absence and your disappearance will raise many unwelcome questions. I will keep an eye on things."

"Keep an eye on . . . what do you hope to see?" Eloise was baffled.

Ida sighed as though tired of the conversation and not wanting to waste time discussing the details. But perhaps the fact that she had chloroformed Eloise made her feel like she at least owed her an explanation.

"Several months ago," Ida began, "a detective working with the local police came to me with suspicions that pointed to someone connected with James Mansion possibly being involved with the surge of grave robberies in the area. He requested that I tell them if I noticed anything or heard anything. I have maintained a watchful eye for the safety of yourself and Miss Evania." Ida's features were troubled for a moment. "I was not able to help Miss Evania."

In her shock, Eloise sank deeper into the mattress. Her naivete. Her ignorance. "What do we do now?" she finally managed to ask.

"You need to get the journal to the investigator." Ida directed her instructions to Silas. "I've packed it in a bag with some of your things and brought them along. When your father discovers the journal is missing, I'm not sure what will happen. It doesn't appear to be in his handwriting, so why he has it and how he got it is unknown."

Silas gave Eloise a conspiratorial wink. "But that book proves Dr. Holzer, at least, is part of the scheme to steal and sell the dead. An' that adds weight to what we thought all along." He drew back and hefted a determined sigh. "I'm fearing for my cousins and for your sister."

"We need to find them!" Eloise couldn't hold back her cry of desperation.

A shadow overtook Silas's face. "I'm afraid . . ." His unfinished sentence hung between them like a guillotine waiting to be released.

Eloise wouldn't say the words herself. She didn't want them to be true.

"I'm afraid we're not going to find the answers we're wishin' for. They're like ghosts. They vanished, just like the steward says others have."

"But Evania . . ." Eloise started to argue.

"Where is she then?" Ida asked. "If she truly escaped, why haven't we heard from Evania? A message at least, but there's been nothing from her."

Eloise didn't want to believe what Ida was insinuating. "You think she's dead."

Ida averted her gaze. "I'm saying I know Miss Evania. If she were alive, wouldn't she be trying to get back to us?"

Eloise turned away from Ida and Silas. Her eyes burned with tears. She had thought that many times, but never said it aloud. The last time Evania had been seen, she was *alive*, even if struggling to stay so. That was Eloise's last shred of hope. If Evania hadn't made it—and if this horrendous scheme was true—then Ida was right. Seamus and Penny, Evania . . . they were all gone. Forever.

No one resurrected bodies from the grave more than once.

22

Tilly Thompson

Old Yew, which graspest at the stones
That name the under-lying dead,
Thy fibres net the dreamless head,
Thy roots are wrapt about the bones.
Alfred, Lord Tennyson

Present Day

"Do you have any idea where your grandpa might have wandered to?" Luke asked.

Tilly shook her head, then said "no" aloud when she realized Luke probably couldn't see her in the unlit interior of his car.

"Maybe some old places he used to hang out at?"

In another time and place, Tilly would have laughed at the words "hang out" attached to Grandpa Don. "Not really. He's always been a family man. He mostly stayed home with my family and me after Grandma passed away. He kept busy building his model trains, helping out with church projects, and attending the church members' monthly meetings—called Silver Saints, for retirees."

"Does he have an old friend he might be trying to find?"

"I don't think so. His best friend died two years ago. They used to drink coffee together and smoke cigars, but they always did that on Grandpa Don's back porch."

Luke shot her a glance as he peered through the windshield in search of Grandpa Don, strolling down the sidewalk maybe or loitering in someone's front yard. The car's headlights provided some means of seeing, but at the moment, Tilly would've given anything for a pickup truck and big spotlight in the back like some hunters used to illegally scope out deer during hunting season.

"Where's the house your grandpa used to live in? Maybe he got disoriented and is trying to go back home."

It was a good thought. A surge of hope shot through her. "His old house is on the west side of town. Maple Terrace."

"The subdivision?"

"Yes."

"Let's go check it out." As Luke turned the car on their way to Maple Terrace, Tilly kept scanning the area outside her window for her grandpa. "Is there anywhere else he might want to go?" Luke asked her.

Tilly racked her brain trying to think of the possibilities. She thought of Grandpa Don's favorite nighttime snack. What if he had gone to the kitchen to grab the box of graham crackers, crunch them up like cereal in a bowl, and saw there was either no milk or graham crackers? "He may have gone to the grocery store," she said.

"Okay. That's on the way to his old house."

Or Grandpa could have been in a sentimental mood. He always became so when watching *Bonanza*. He told her once that he used to watch the television show with Grandma in the early years of their marriage. She'd always had a thing for Michael Landon—that was probably where Tilly had gotten it from.

"Grandma . . ."

"What's that?" Luke rolled to a stop at a stop sign. Rain started to sprinkle, dotting the windshield.

"Sometimes he misses my grandma," Tilly said. "He could have gone to the cemetery." Yes, Grandpa Don's sentiment may have awakened with force. Enough to make him think he needed to visit Grandma's grave.

"Which cemetery?"

"St. Matthew's."

Luke flicked the left turn signal. "That's my family's cemetery."

Tilly tapped Luke's arm. "We need to go there first. I think it makes the most sense."

"And it's only a few blocks from the mansion," said Luke. "We'll check the cemetery, and if that's a bust, we'll drive to his old house."

Tilly nodded, straining against her seat belt. Eagerness and concern had her wanting to scoot to the edge of her seat.

"We're not far," Luke reassured her.

But "not far" felt like a hundred miles.

At last, the cemetery's wrought-iron fence came into view. There were no gates to lock anyone out at night, so Luke turned onto the narrow asphalt lane. "Where's your grandma's grave located?"

The cemetery was large, and it was hard enough to find a grave in the daylight. In the dark, Tilly assessed as best she could where they were. The gravestones intermingled with large oaks and maples, all appearing as shadowy guards in the night.

"Up there." She pointed to where the cemetery sloped up a gentle hill. "That's where Grandma's grave is."

"Hold on." Luke slowed even though the car was already crawling at ten miles per hour. "I think I see . . ."

Tilly leaned forward, looking in the direction Luke was studying. "Yes! It's Grandpa Don!" Adrenaline surged within her, and she pounded the dash.

"Careful there!" Luke's laugh was laced with relief.

Sure enough, the form of Grandpa Don stood over a grave, his head bowed.

"Whose grave is that?" Tilly muttered. "That's not Grandma's."

Luke pulled the car over and hadn't even put it into park when Tilly threw open the door and unbuckled simultaneously.

"Grandpa!" She waved as she hurried across the cemetery toward him.

Grandpa Don lifted his head. "What are you doing out here in the middle of the night?" He sounded as if he had his complete wits about him.

Tilly knew he didn't, though she treated him like he was well aware of his actions and whereabouts. "First, what are you doing out here, Grandpa?" She came up beside him and tried to temper her frustration while heaving an enormous sigh of relief.

"I was watching *Bonanza*." He said it as though it were obvious how that had led him to come to St. Matthews.

Tilly wasn't sure how to respond to that.

Grandpa Don seemed to understand that his statement needed context. "That episode with Mary Wharton, remember?"

Tilly shook her head. "I'm sorry, Grandpa, but I don't—"

"You know, the episode where Ben Cartwright helps that poor woman with the alcoholic husband? Her name was Mary."

"Okay . . ."

"Reminded me of Mary Franks."

"Who's Mary Franks?" Luke's voice behind Tilly startled her. She looked at him, and he whispered, "I called Erik to let him know we found your grandpa."

Grateful for Luke's thoughtfulness, Tilly nodded.

"Mary Franks!" Grandpa Don turned toward them and away from the gravestone. "You really don't remember her?"

"I have no clue who Mary Franks is, Grandpa," Tilly admitted.

He shifted his attention to Luke. "What about you?"

"No, sir, I'm sorry."

"Well, if that don't beat all. This here is her grave."

Tilly moved closer and looked down at the stone. It was hard to read at night, but she managed to do so.

Mary Franks
B. November 11, 1972
D. August 3, 2006

"I was only six years old when she died," Tilly observed.

Grandpa Don sniffed and then proceeded to educate them. "In *Bonanza*, that gal Mary had a husband who knocked her around and drank like the devil."

Tilly sensed Luke shifting restlessly beside her. She didn't dare look at him.

"I got to thinking," Grandpa Don continued, "about that homeless woman who used to wander all over town. Mary. Your grandma and I tried to help her a few times. Sweetest gal. She got mixed up with a man who drank and knocked her around. Folks say she disappeared, but that's only half the story."

Tilly stilled.

She couldn't help but look up at Luke. His face was expressionless.

"She did disappear, but her remains were found four years or so later. I can't remember exactly. It made the news, but enough time had passed that no one really cared. That's the sad thing about it." Grandpa clucked his tongue. "Mary Franks."

"But why did you come here to the cemetery, and at night? Why didn't you tell me you were leaving the mansion?" Tilly had to know. It didn't sound as though he'd had a relationship with this Mary Franks, aside from her grandparents trying to help Mary years ago. For Grandpa to leave with no warning, walk to the cemetery in the dark . . . it made no sense. But then, she reminded herself, a lot of what was to come with Grandpa Don's behavior would make no sense.

"You should know the answer to that!" Grandpa nodded to Luke.

"I-I don't," Luke answered. The stammer in his voice had Tilly turning her attention to him. He *had* told her that he'd seen his father arguing with the unhoused woman before she disappeared. At first, he had thought the remains found in the mansion wall had the potential to be hers.

The gravity of it fell on Tilly in a way she hadn't explored before. If Luke had thought the girl in the wall could have been this woman, then he also believed someone in his house could have been responsible for killing her.

"Sure you do!" Grandpa Don busted into Tilly's deductions. He reached over and yanked on Luke's shirtsleeve for emphasis. "Your dad and her . . . not to speak ill of your father, but he wasn't a nice man."

Even in the dark, Luke's face looked ashen.

"Police thought he might even be responsible for Mary's death. But her remains were too far gone. The case went cold," Grandpa Don finished.

"But why did you come here?" Tilly insisted, trying to put aside the fact Luke was unresponsive to Grandpa Don's story.

"I helped pick this plot for Mary since she didn't have anyone to fight for her when she was alive or after she passed." Grandpa Don patted Luke's shoulder. "Your mama was a big help too."

Luke's jaw worked back and forth.

Grandpa Don continued, clueless to the fact he was revealing things Tilly had a feeling were as new to Luke as they were to her. "Your mama paid for this plot."

"Why?" Luke choked out.

Grandpa Don shrugged. "Not sure about that. But she was a good woman, your mama, and she was married to a tough man."

Luke turned on his heel and hiked through the night toward his car.

"Luke!" Tilly called.

Grandpa Don moved to stand beside her. "Something about that *Bonanza* episode made me think of Mary. You know, for years, women were supposed to keep silent, even when they were taken advantage of." He wrapped an arm around Tilly's shoulder, and she knew he had no idea what impact his words had had tonight. "Your grandma was a strong woman, Tilly. She tried to help Mary Franks. Tried to help that boy's mama too. But some people just can't be helped. Seems like the devil gets his teeth into their lives, and the only peace they can find is beyond this world."

The car ride back was silent. Grandpa Don appeared content and pleased with himself, having given into whatever had made him leave in search of Mary Franks's grave. Tilly kept stealing little glances at Luke, who stared straight ahead, his hands gripping the steering wheel at ten and two like his life depended on it.

When Luke pulled up the drive to the mansion, Grandpa Don gave a tired groan. "Well, I think I'd best be getting to bed." He exited the car as Erik jogged up to greet them.

Tilly gave her head a slight shake in an unspoken plea to her brother not to ask questions right now.

"C'mon, Grandpa, I'll walk in with you," Erik offered.

"No need. I can put myself to bed. I'm not *that* elderly."

"I know, Grandpa," said Erik. "I need something to drink, though."

"Ah, well, I think we've got some apple juice in the fridge."

Their voices faded as they headed for the mansion.

Tilly sat in stillness, the car shrouded in the blanket of night, but also in something more. Something heavy.

"Thank you for coming to help find Grandpa," she attempted.

Luke seemed to snap out of his thoughts. He offered her a wan smile. "Yeah." He took a deep breath as if pulling himself together. "Yeah, no problem. I'm just glad he's safe."

Tilly looked at Luke.

Luke looked back at her but without expression. He was waiting for her to leave the car so he could leave.

Something told her that would be a bad idea. "Why don't you come inside for a bit?" she suggested gently.

A wry chuckle was her answer.

"Please?"

Luke shook his head. "I don't think I want to step inside that house ever again."

"What my grandpa said tonight—"

Luke let the truth fall like a hammer. "My dad was the most frightening person I've ever known." His admission didn't seem to make him feel any better.

Tilly stayed quiet.

Luke looked through the windshield toward James Mansion. "My mom suffered the most. Then me. Kyle managed to avoid him most days." He turned to gaze out the side window. "Of course, Kyle did what he could to protect me. At least he tried." Luke's voice became quiet. "I owe Kyle a lot."

Pain squeezed her. Despite the narcissistic corruption the residents of New Jamestown had suspected of the James family with their power-filled personalities, their attitude of entitlement, somehow the charming aspect of the family still influenced people. Did anyone know of the physical abuse the James children suffered? And for how many generations had it been going on?

Luke's hair curled at the back of his collar. The strong column of his neck and his shoulders were tense. He hadn't dared to look back at her, not after his admission.

"Is that why . . . ?" she started but then stopped. It wasn't her place.

Luke's head swiveled to face her. In the darkness, Tilly could see the pain in his eyes. "Is that why I used? Why I went to Morning

Song for rehab ten years ago? Quit my job as HR director?" He nodded. "It was that or lose my mind."

"Is that where you and Erik patched things up?"

Luke sniffed. "It wasn't that I didn't like your brother"—he winced, his eyes locking with hers—"or you." Disgust with himself was evident. "I lashed out in my hurt. I was sick and cruel, and I was becoming my dad." He choked up, swallowed, and cleared his throat. "I'm sorry, Tilly, for the terrible things I said and did to you back in high school."

And there it was.

Tilly had waited twelve years to hear those words from him, and while she was glad to finally hear them, they didn't affect her like she thought they would. Not because Luke didn't mean it, but because she'd never really needed his apology. She realized that now more than ever. Yes, he'd been a jerk to her. But her entire life, in spite of the cruelty, she'd always known she was loved. Treasured by Grandpa Don, by her parents, by Erik. So even though at one time she'd wanted an apology or even revenge at times, Tilly still remained confident in who she was. Who God had created her to be.

Luke had never had that. His foundation had been cracked and broken from his early days. His little boy self, hiding in the alcove in the basement. He'd written that he wished his worst monster would go away. He'd watched his father mistreat his mother, even mistreat a poor homeless woman living on the street.

"Luke . . ." Tilly whispered. She had no words really, because in times like this, what could she possibly say that would offer comfort or resolution? There was no easy answer, no logical progression from step A to step B. Instead, she reached across the car's console between them and laid her hand on Luke's arm. And kept it there.

He stared at her.

Neither of them spoke.

Because, in that moment, there was nothing to say.

23

What is it men are shrinking from?

It would be easy to be clever
And tell the stones: Men hate to die
And have stopped dying now forever.
I think they would believe the lie.

Robert Frost

Tilly stared at the newest anonymous post in the community's social-media group. So it had come to this.

Mayoral candidate Luke James has a past with Morning Song Recovery, a rehab center. Here are the details . . .

His run for office was over. Maybe Luke would be relieved by that, though certainly not by the way it ended.

Tilly sank onto a chair at the table in Grandpa Don's train room. He was oblivious to what had happened the night before. Little connections. Lost connections.

Her eyes went back to the post, skimming the words.

Who here has heard that mayoral candidate Luke James was treated for substance abuse during a period of eight weeks in 2016 at Morning Song Recovery? If you dig into it, records reveal that he relapsed in 2017 and spent another stint at Morning Song before leaving the state to be treated at a California-based rehab center where he lived for six months. He never returned to his position working in Human Resources, and now the community wants him to lead the city of New Jamestown?

Oh, Luke!

Tilly deposited her phone on the table.

It never stopped. How could anyone expect to heal or amount to anything if no one extended any support or forgiveness for mistakes in the past? Luke was sober now. He wasn't "that guy" anymore.

She could only imagine what the town was saying today.

It might have been hours later, but eventually Luke found his way to James Mansion. He had the appearance of a man who had been through emotional warfare and back again. Tilly didn't understand why he chose to come back here. He had friends. A brother. There was Erik. Maybe it was the mansion itself. But no, for last night he'd stated he never wanted to set foot in the place ever again. It held memories for him—bad ones.

Tilly knew she had a perplexed look on her face. It wasn't that she didn't *want* him here. She did, and that realization also gave her pause. Yet she wanted to understand the reason behind it. What it was that had motivated a person to act a certain way.

"I need you today," Luke said plainly when he saw the question in Tilly's eyes. "I mean," he continued, "Erik encouraged me not to be alone. My brother is occupied with doctor appointments, and I . . ."

That was it. Tilly nodded as understanding washed over her.

Even years after his last stint in rehab, the need was still there. He couldn't and *shouldn't* be alone.

"Of course. Stay as long as you need to," she said.

Luke stared now out the bay window overlooking the front yard, at the people sauntering by on the sidewalk. "Life just carries on. They read something that ruins a person's life or career, and they continue on as if it were ripped from a novel. Entertained, intrigued, and disassociated." Luke's phone buzzed. He looked at it and quickly swiped at the screen. "My campaign manager."

"Do you need to go into the office? I can come with." As soon as she said it, Tilly regretted it.

"No," Luke replied, squelching the idea, "but thanks anyway."

His phone buzzed again, and he glanced at it. Tilly could see the name on the screen: *Kyle*.

His brother. The man was finishing his last few weeks as mayor before he finished his remaining months on earth. Luke swiped the screen again, then shoved the phone into his front pocket. "I can't do this. Not right now."

"Won't he be upset?" Tilly asked.

"Upset? No. He'll be *supportive*. He'll tell me New Jamestown will be fine without a James family member at the helm."

Tilly frowned. "Then why did you decide to run for mayor?"

Luke shrugged, his attention still captivated by the view outside the window. "For Kyle. For our legacy. He told me I didn't have to, but I know how important it is to him. This town. Ever since our dad died, Kyle has wanted to redeem our name. To show others we are good and honest men. But his chance at that has been cut short, and so I felt it was up to me to pick up the baton for his sake. I'm thirty years old, Tilly, and I don't know what I want to be. I just want to . . . *be*."

She nodded.

"But that's not possible with someone out there smearing the family name, digging up all this negative stuff."

"Is there more they haven't exposed yet?" She realized as soon as she asked it that she probably shouldn't have.

"A century-old corpse hidden in the mansion's wall. An unhoused woman who went missing when I was a kid. Alcoholism and drug addiction." Luke considered the list. "An abusive father. Let me see . . . I don't know, murder? Theft? God only knows what else my family has been involved in over the decades." Luke looked around him. The spirits of his ancestors seemed to permeate the place, his childhood home. "If only these walls could talk . . ."

"I don't think we should want them to," Tilly concluded.

"You're probably right. But it's not going to stop." Luke's voice was filled with resolve. "I need to find out if there's more I don't know. I mean, what's going to pop up online tomorrow? Whatever it is, I need to be prepared."

Tilly caught a whiff of Luke's scent, peppermint and juniper. "How about we take a closer look at your family tree?"

"For what purpose?" he asked.

"Well, let's look at each person and see if there are any old family stories or secrets you can remember. And there's still the big question of Mary Franks and how she died. The fact that Grandpa remembered all those details tells me it made an impact on the community at the time. It's worth looking at, don't you think?"

"Who killed her, you mean?"

"Yes," Tilly said.

"I suppose." Luke abandoned his position at the window and retreated to the couch. He motioned for Tilly to join him. She did so, making sure to leave a sensible amount of space between them so the couch didn't dip so far as to dump her into his lap.

Placing his computer on the coffee table in front of them, he booted it up. He soon had the James family tree displayed onscreen.

"All right," he said, pointing to the tree. "In the 1800s, we've got Price James, son of the founder of New Jamestown."

"His daughter Evania was committed to an asylum." Tilly hadn't forgotten this unusual detail.

"From what I could find, yes." He clicked a link.

"According to the family tree, you descended from Thomas James?"

Luke nodded and clicked back to the family tree.

"Who is that person?"

Luke eyed where Tilly was pointing. "Good question." He scrolled down. "Here's Evania James, deceased in 1879. Eloise James . . . that's weird. There's no date of death or of marriage."

Tilly frowned. "But her name attached there isn't a confirmed connection."

"Eloise?"

"Yes. She's grayed out as only a *possible* relation."

Luke's brow furrowed. "Eloise James. Died in 1918."

"Maybe she doesn't actually belong here. Could it be a mistake?"

"I have no idea." Luke cast her a sideways smile. "Welcome to the curiosities of the dysfunctional James family."

"Maybe she's a distant cousin."

Luke didn't reply but followed the family tree down. "There's my dad." He pointed to the name. "Then Kyle and me."

"So the family tree lines up with what you know?"

"All except for Eloise." Luke tried clicking on Eloise James's name. "It's like no one wanted to remember her."

"Or maybe she wasn't actually a part of your family," Tilly offered. "I'll do some research on it."

Luke blew out an exasperated breath. "The hits keep coming, you know? It feels like people in my family haven't been honest about our history for decades."

Tilly didn't answer him. She couldn't. There was nothing concrete on which to form an opinion, only that seeing a lone name tucked away to the side of an otherwise familiar family tree was extremely odd.

IF WALLS COULD TALK

Eyes follow them.

My eyes.

They have for over a century. I have watched them all searching. A quest, if you will, to discover what I know. When their newspapers fall short of the truth. When their boxes that send them information hide pages of reality that would shed light.

But it is coming.

For the first time in a century's breath, I can feel it.

Truth.

It is boiling up from inside me. It has swollen and demands to be released.

She demands that it be released.

She is the woman I concealed in my frame, hiding her from the evils that placed her there.

She is the woman who stood staring at me from the outside, wondering what it was like inside and wishing for a horror she didn't know she wished for. Until she found it.

She is the woman who first ran through my halls, a little girl, desperate to please and to obey, and in doing so, she helped to hide the truth that even now pounds against me to be let out.

She is all of them.

A victim and a participant.

A truth teller and a liar.

A mother and a daughter.

She is powerful.

She is weak.

This is what my eyes have seen. And if I could, I would weep for them.

24

Eloise James

Under the wide and starry sky,
Dig the grave and let me lie.
Glad did I live and gladly die,
And I laid me down with a will.
Robert Louis Stevenson

October 1879
James Mansion

St. Matthew's Cemetery was familiar to her, but not by the light of the moon. Eloise questioned her reasoning, and not for the first time, as she hurried behind Silas. They dodged between bushes, and her skirt caught on one. She paused to tug it free, very aware of the small rip it left in her black mourning dress.

They were in the fancy part of the cemetery, the section that included the crest of a gently sloping hill. She knew she had already passed graves familiar to her. Her mother's, her grandparents', the

James family members who had left their mark on New Jamestown before she'd been born.

Nothing was peaceful tonight in the cemetery, and their desperate, harebrained idea to stake out a fresh grave in order to catch grave robbers red-handed frayed Eloise's already raw nerves. An entire twenty-four hours had passed since Ida had whisked her away to Silas's boardinghouse. Though they had stayed quite far apart from each other, Tilly moving to her own room next to Silas's, she knew that Mrs. Bigsby, who owned the place, was very curious. Once word got out that Price James's daughter was missing, Mrs. Bigsby would put two and two together.

Why, Miss James ran off with a scamp of an Irishman! I saw the two of them. Had I only known, I never would have rented a room to the likes of Silas Dobbs.

Adding more coal to the fire, she was now traipsing about in the dark like a body snatcher. If caught, there would be further scandal, she was sure of it. Oh, that God would smile down on her tonight and say, "I understand your motives are good." But for now, it took every ounce of her fortitude to stay by Silas and follow his lead.

A note had arrived at the boardinghouse for Silas. Written in Ida's hand, it stated that Father was beside himself to know where Eloise had gone—though, Ida had added, she assumed his volatile state was just as much due to the missing journal as to Eloise.

Have you turned it in to the police yet? she'd inquired in the note, then encouraged them to do that as soon as possible. Something was happening. She had caught wind of someone in the house the night before and heard mention of St. Matthew's Cemetery. Of "bodies to be acquired" there. Because the person remained hidden, Ida's missive stated she could not identify who had reported this to another unknown soul within James Mansion. But after looking into it, Ida learned that a Mrs. Geraldine Kaufman and a Mr. Spencer Jenser had both been interred there yesterday in two separate funerals. She could only assume these were the bodies the intruder had referred to.

Turning the journal over to the investigator should go a long way toward ending whatever deceit had infiltrated James Mansion and cobbled Mr. James into some sort of sordid cooperation.

If only Silas had done so immediately.

Eloise ducked down as he motioned her with his hand. She shrank behind a bush.

"We'll hide here," he whispered in her ear.

Eloise nodded, petrified at the very idea Silas had concocted. Of course, it suited him. He'd been almost delighted at the prospect.

"We'll catch 'em in the act," he'd told her. "Then we'll know who's hauling the bodies away. We can inform the investigator when we give 'em the book. All this together should be enough."

Enough for what? she wondered. To end the body-snatching ring? Or just to stop two men low on the ranks of those profiting from the sale of the dead? The journal mentioned Dr. Holzer by name, yes, but who was the investor? And there had to be others. Would bearing witness to the gruesome exhumation of two recently deceased souls really give Eloise and Silas the information they needed to bring to justice all those involved in the scheme?

Eloise swiped away the sweat that trailed down her temple. It wasn't a warm October night by any means, but she was nervous. Anxious. Her entire life had been upended, and now here she was, tucked up next to Silas in a bush mere yards away from a fresh grave for Mrs. Kaufman.

Silas lifted his finger to his lips, then tipped his head.

Sure enough, the midnight hour was interrupted as a wagon rolled up the hill. Two men sat on the front seat, and as soon as it stopped before Mrs. Kaufman's grave, they hopped down.

"I'll keep a lookout," one growled.

The other eyed the grave. "Shouldn't take too long. Six feet and I'll hook 'er like a fish."

Eloise felt sick.

The shoveling began, each jab into the earth a sickening sound that curdled her stomach. Silas's hand rested on her shoulder, encouraging her to remain still. She knew they just wanted to see faces. If they didn't recognize the men, they could at least provide descriptions.

After some time had gone by, a thud sounded as the shovel hit the lid of the coffin. Within seconds, Eloise heard the sound of metal smashing into wood.

"Shh," Silas whispered.

She must have whimpered at the sound.

"Do you recognize them?" he whispered again, so quiet she could hardly hear him even as his mouth brushed her ear.

Eloise shook her head. But then she'd not gotten a good look at them. The one keeping watch wore a hat tugged low. The other's back was to them, but he was tall and thin. They could be anyone.

Another sound of cracking wood and then, "All right. She's here and ready." The man was quiet for a bit, maneuvering, until he added, "And she's hooked. Let's haul her up."

The next awful moments were filled with grunting and the hoisting of Mrs. Kaufman's corpse to the top of the grave. It was apparent when he'd succeeded, as Mrs. Kaufman's arm hung over her head. The man dragged her onto the earth as the one on lookout brought a canvas tarp and laid it out on the ground.

"You grab her arms, and I'll get her legs. An' don't pull off an arm this time."

Eloise turned away from the horrible sight, burying her face in Silas's arm even as she struggled to place the voices. They sounded familiar. She strained to hear more.

"I can't help that that body was so ripe for the earth!" the other man protested with a grunt as they hoisted Mrs. Kaufman onto the canvas. "There. See? All in one piece."

"Better'n havin' to chop it up to fit in a barrel."

This time Eloise retched, and it landed on Silas's shoe. He jolted back, trying to stay silent as Eloise pressed a hand over her mouth to avoid vomiting again and the subsequent cough that followed.

"What was that?" Both men froze, one of them holding the edge of the tarp intended to wrap Mrs. Kaufman for transport.

Silas grabbed for Eloise just as a voice boomed out from the tree just to the left of them.

"Don't move!" A new form emerged, and then another, and another. All of them wore the very distinct uniform of policemen.

"Ah! They beat us to it!" Silas turned to Eloise with a look of glee.

And then gruff, meaty hands grabbed Eloise and Silas from behind, and they were hauled to a standing position. Eloise strained to see the face of her captor.

The beady eyes of a police officer stared back at her, and he gave Silas a shake. "The lookouts, eh?" he said.

"No, not the—" Silas started to protest, but the officer gave him another shake and ordered him to be quiet.

The officer turned to Eloise. "It's a sad day when we find a lady taking part in grave robbing."

"C'mon."

Eloise followed the policeman down the dingy hallway to the meeting room of the jail. A man stood at the window, along with another portlier fellow who appeared to be the captain. Both men turned as Eloise was told to enter. Her gaze crashed into the cold and controlled face of her father.

"Thank you, Officer Pitts." The captain nodded. He motioned for Eloise to have a seat at the stark wooden table in the center of the room.

She did. Avoiding Father's glower of judgment.

Eloise knew she looked a mess. Her dress was soiled from kneeling in the cemetery, torn from the shrub, and made dusty from being thrown in the back of the police's jail wagon. She had no idea where they'd taken Silas. He'd been quite vocal, proclaiming their innocence, even as they jostled about in the wagon next to the two men who had been digging up poor, dead Mrs. Kaufman.

When Eloise met the eyes of the man across from her—the man who had "hooked" Mrs. Kaufman and hauled her to the surface—she held her tongue.

Kenny. Their groundsman. The kind soul who had helped her bury Evania's baby! The horror of it washed over Eloise, and she locked accusatory eyes on him.

"Did you bury her?" she hissed.

Kenny refused to look at Eloise.

"Did you bury Evania's daughter like I asked you to? Beneath the rosebushes?"

Kenny had looked at her then, a pained expression on his face. "Who do you think I am, Miss Eloise? I wouldn't hurt a babe, dead or alive!"

"You have standards then?" Eloise bit back.

Kenny looked away.

The police had hauled off Kenny and his cohort, and now she faced her father.

"What were you thinking?" Father growled, demanding Eloise's attention as they sat in the bare room.

The captain gestured to Father to sit down.

Father shook his head. "My apologies, Captain Rutter, but I prefer to stand." There was no apology in his voice, but the captain didn't seem offended in the slightest.

"Very well." Rutter nodded and stood back as though Father were in charge.

Father bent over the table, arms extended, palms pressed flat. "I asked you what you were thinking? Grave robbing!"

What should she say?

"Running off with a vagabond and having an illicit affair!" Father continued.

"Silas isn't . . . I didn't—"

"Say nothing more." Father held up a hand. He turned to Captain Rutter. "It's obvious I have a *second* daughter with the same bent toward immoral behavior. Eloise was overwhelmed by the unsuspecting charms of that *man*—Dobbs is his name?"

The captain nodded.

"Dobbs is to blame here," Father spat. "You cannot hold my daughter as guilty when it is so apparent she has been taken advantage of. Coerced and manipulated by a man of no account."

"He's a reporter, or so I heard from my associate, Captain Farber of Corinth. More of a wannabe newsman," Captain Rutter added.

"Corinth? Then send the man there and let them deal with him. But I request that you show my daughter leniency. As a woman, she cannot comprehend the dark designs of men. I will address her behavior in the privacy of our own home. I'm asking you not to hold her responsible for something as deplorable as stealing a body from the cemetery."

"She *was* there," Captain Rutter said.

"Observing, yes, I cannot deny that. But was she caught handling the corpse?"

Eloise blanched.

"No, she wasn't." Captain Rutter shook his head.

"Then we can only conclude that she is a victim of these men and their heinous attempt to make money off the misfortune of families still mourning their deceased loved ones."

Captain Rutter looked at Eloise for a long moment. "Miss James, can you tell me anything about the men you were with tonight?"

Eloise caught Father's eye. There was caution in them.

"I-I . . ." She would not reveal a thing about Silas. Dare she speak of Kenny? It stood to reason that the police would soon discover that Kenny worked for James Mansion. "I know one of them. Kenny. He is our groundskeeper."

"What!" Father bellowed.

Captain Rutter blustered. "We, uh, hadn't gotten around to telling you that, sir."

Seeing as the captain already knew about Kenny's association with them, Eloise decided it was good she had admitted to her familiarity with Kenny.

"Was it Kenny who lured you into such bad company, Miss James?" Captain Rutter inquired.

"Not at all," Eloise said. "I've reason to—"

But Father spoke up before she had the chance to finish. "It's obvious he did. And through him, my daughter became mixed up with this Mr. Dobbs fellow."

Silas.

Before the wagon had come to a halt at the jailhouse, he had whispered to Eloise, "Don't say anything about the journal. That may be our ticket out of jail, so let me take care of it."

She vowed she would, mostly because Eloise had a distinct feeling Father was going to get his way when it came to Captain Rutter.

25

She knows her misery and her majesty,
And recks not if she be to live or die.

Emma Lazarus

"Do you have any idea what you've done? The danger you've placed us in?"

Father had sat in stony silence in the carriage the entire way back to James Mansion, but now he shoved Eloise into the parlor, not seeming concerned in the slightest when she lost her footing and careened into a table. A pot of ferns wobbled, then crashed to the floor, erupting into shards of porcelain and mounds of dirt and greenery.

Sam, the footman, hurried into the parlor, as did Mrs. Forrester, the housekeeper.

"Leave us!" Father bellowed.

Both obeyed immediately. They did nothing to stop Father as he hauled Eloise up with a painful hold on her arm. She whimpered, trying not to anger him further but feeling the sting of her skin being twisted beneath his hand.

He dragged her toward his study. For a brief second, Eloise considered breaking free and running down the corridor to the back door that was just beyond his study. But she didn't dare. Father would catch her, she was sure of it.

He shoved Eloise into the study, shut the door, and pushed her into a chair.

Eloise fell, catching herself as she careened into it.

Father spread his arms wide. "I have not built all of this just to have your wanton behavior bury us!"

"I didn't do anything with Silas, Father."

She should not have spoken.

Before Eloise could react, Father slapped her face. The stinging sensation was almost as painful as the cut to her heart. The desperate act told Eloise he was indeed in dire straits, a man who had been forced into a corner.

"You have brought scandal to the James name a *second* time!" he shouted. "But worse than your sister, you have made it public by being *arrested*." Father's glare was unyielding.

"Father, I . . ." she tried to explain, yet how could she? Father was correct. He had told her from the start to leave Evania alone at the asylum, to accept his wisdom in allowing the institution to bury her body there. He had been adamant that she carry on without her sister, and if she had . . . Father was right. Even if he was in serious trouble for whatever reason with the group of conspirators smuggling remains in cooperation with Dr. Holzer, she had most definitely made things worse. And who knew if the capture of Kenny and this other man would bring an end to the illegal practice.

"I'm sorry, Father." Eloise found no relief in taking the blame.

"Sorry isn't enough!" He rounded his desk, pounding his fist on its top.

Eloise jumped at the sound.

Father faced her. "I need that journal, Eloise. Where is it?" His voice was chilling.

"I–"

"Don't lie to me. I know you have it."

"Is it Kenny's? Is he using the journal to blackmail you into cooperating?" Eloise didn't know what in her decided to question her father instead of telling him where it was.

The study doors opened. Ida stood in the doorway, her birdlike features placid. "I heard a disturbance, Mr. James. Would you like me to accompany Miss Eloise to her room? She appears to have hit her face on something."

Ida's feigning ignorance became apparent when Eloise locked eyes with her. Eloise couldn't miss the concern she saw there.

Father straightened. "No. My daughter will remain here with me. You may go."

Ida didn't leave but stepped farther into the room. "You have company coming tonight, remember, Mr. James?"

Father blanched.

"Miss Eloise will need a bath before they arrive. I don't mean to be impertinent, Mr. James, but she will be quite unready to make a good impression if she's unable to prepare."

Though Ida was speaking out of turn, Eloise was grateful for her boldness.

Father looked to Eloise, and his countenance darkened. Ida's words had hit their mark. "Go. Clean yourself up. Be ready for our guest this evening."

Eloise wasted no time. She sprang to her feet and hurried to Ida's side.

"Eloise." Father's voice caused her to stop and turn to look over her shoulder at him. "Do not disappoint me."

She shook her head and scurried out of the room.

"Who is coming tonight?" Eloise asked as she trailed behind her lady's maid.

Ida's hand lifted. "Not here."

As they climbed the stairs, Eloise glanced at the newly installed stained-glass window. The new plaster of the windowless southern wall smelled sour. She skipped up the steps behind Ida, in part out of fear that Father would suddenly charge from his study and haul her back.

Her face still stung from his slap, and when they arrived at her room, Eloise caught a glimpse of herself in the mirror. Her cheek was apple-red. She worried it might bruise.

Ida shut the door, and Eloise heard the latch click. "What is going on?" she asked in a whisper.

Ida moved to the open door that led to her adjoining quarters. She shut and locked it as well.

"Who is coming tonight?"

Ida moved to the wardrobe and opened it. "You must do exactly as I say."

Eloise nodded. She had no intention of arguing with the woman who was proving her worth far more than Eloise had ever imagined.

Ida continued, "I never intended to become as deeply involved as I am now. When I was asked a year ago to report to Captain Rutter anything suspicious going on here, I had no idea it would come to such an end."

"Captain Rutter?" He had just allowed Eloise to come home. *He* was the one Ida had been working with?

"Yes." Ida reached for a sensible green dress that was appropriate for dinner with company, but also one that leaned toward the subdued. "You will need to bathe first."

Eloise didn't care about bathing. Silas was in jail for a crime he did not commit, her own father had struck her, and Ida was advising her to pretend as if all that lay ahead was to entertain a dinner guest!

"I don't know the man coming to dinner," Ida explained. "All I know is that he is associated with Dr. Holzer from the asylum. I believe it is he who has cornered your father and caused him to panic."

"And he's coming here? What does this have to do with me?" Eloise sank onto her bed.

Ida faced her, hands on her hips. "I don't know. Truly, Miss Eloise, I don't."

"What *do* you know, Ida?" Eloise asked. "Tell me."

Ida faltered for a moment, then nodded. "About a year ago, I was approached by Captain Rutter, who asked me to let him know of anything I found or heard that might give him insight into an investigation he was running in cooperation with the police in Corinth. It had to do with the asylum, and they were interested in the goings-on at James Mansion because of your father's involvement as a trustee. No one suspects your father is involved, mind you, just that he may inadvertently be assisting."

"Yes. That makes sense." Eloise nodded.

Ida took a breath and folded her hands in front of her. "Over the course of this year, there have been hints that Kenny is somehow involved. He disappears at night from his quarters over the stable and comes back in the morning, sometimes with mud on his boots. And Kenny was very aggravated when he learned Miss Evania had been made to live at the asylum."

"So Kenny and Dr. Holzer are working together. Kenny was afraid that if Evania saw him at the hospital and then later returned home at some point, she would likely tell Father, and Kenny would be in trouble."

"Which is what I thought too." Ida nodded. "I shared my suspicions with the captain. But then Miss Evania became ill, and we discovered your father had agreed to have the asylum bury her—supposing she had indeed passed away. But what could I do? I couldn't go behind Captain Rutter's back and tell your father I believed Kenny was working with Dr. Holzer to steal bodies here and in Corinth. I couldn't tell him I was afraid, which could also affect Miss Evania's fate."

"But you *could* have!" Eloise tried not to blame Ida, but she was frustrated that Ida had stayed silent.

"I was afraid for you as well," Ida said. "It doesn't help that you have always walked in your sleep. Much as you did that night in Corinth and again the other night when you discovered that book. Unless you want to be sent away, you will keep quiet about your sleepwalking and your vivid dreams. Those can be used against you." Ida held up her hands as if to inspire Eloise to remain calm and listen. "If Kenny has been arrested, he will try to implicate Dr. Holzer. He will not take the fall for any of this—not alone. And after reading the entries in the journal, well, once Captain Rutter has it in his hands—"

"Silas left the book in his room at the boardinghouse," Eloise interrupted. "He wanted to be an eyewitness to the crime to add credibility."

Ida squeezed her eyes shut, then opened them, resolve settling in them. "We can do nothing about that now. We must focus on preparing you for dinner and the guest."

"But what has this guest to do with any of this?" Eloise pressed.

Ida hesitated, then asked, "Do you remember in Kenny's book, that he mentioned an investor?"

"Yes."

"It is my belief that your father stumbled on this and was made aware of the ring of deception. And when he confronted Dr. Holzer about it, the doctor held something against him to buy his silence." Ida caught Eloise's eyes with a severe warning in her own. "I'm afraid that investor is coming to dinner tonight to collect whatever it is your father owes him."

26

Tilly Thompson

I dare not let it languish,
Dare not indulge in memory's rapturous pain;
Once drinking deep of that divinest anguish,
How could I seek the empty world again?

Emily Brontë

Present Day

Luke had gone home. He assured her he would be all right, but Tilly couldn't help herself. She had called Erik. Grateful for her call, Erik promised to look in on Luke later. He would not be left alone.

Tilly bent over Grandpa Don's sleeping form. She kissed his cheek and pulled his blanket up higher around his shoulders. He had been exhausted today. This evening he'd even skipped his restocked graham crackers and milk. The TV had been his entertainment, though Tilly had advised him to watch a classic football game replay instead of a show that might inspire the urge to go wandering in the night again.

She'd called for a security system to be installed in the mansion. Until then, Tilly planned to sleep nearby on the first floor. With the number of exits in the house, she would have her work cut out for her, and she knew Grandpa Don would be very cranky if he found she'd slept in the train room with him.

"I don't need you hovering over me," he'd argue. Or "It isn't right you're in my room. A man needs his privacy."

So Tilly had called Ashley with an idea, and sure enough, her sister-in-law had arrived with the contraband. Tilly hurried down the hall to the front door after hearing Ashley's knock. She unlocked the door and let Ashley in.

Hands extended, Ashley deposited a cardboard box into Tilly's hands. "Two baby monitors and charging bases, as ordered."

Tilly smiled. "Thank you!"

Ashley followed Tilly into the sitting room. "They're already linked. You only need to turn on the base in the train room and then bring the monitor with you wherever you are. That button there." Ashley pointed to a red button. "Press it if you want to talk, and Grandpa will be able to hear you." She gave Tilly a look of consternation. "If only I had a nanny cam."

"This will be fine." Tilly held the white receiver in her hand. "It's just to get us by. The security system will have cameras I can access with my tablet. Grandpa will never know I'm keeping track of him." She waggled her brows.

They shared a laugh, but then Ashley grew serious. "I wish we could help more. Erik is going to stop by Luke's place and check on him tonight when I get back from here. Just to make sure he's okay."

"Good," Tilly said.

"And what's this I hear about the James family tree?"

"Erik told you about that?" She'd filled Erik in on literally everything that had occurred that day. "How incomplete it is?"

"Well, yeah." Ashley waved her hands. "That's not something you overlook, especially with the James family."

"That's what I'm afraid of." Tilly set the box of baby monitors on the sofa. "Someone has it out for Luke. It seems personal. We spent the day digging, trying to find any other events from the past that could be dredged up to dog him."

"So did you find anything?" Ashley asked.

"Nothing in particular. But to learn there's a James member in the family tree with no details or records of her is strange. She's only there in the margins."

"I don't get it."

Tilly shook her head. "Luke and I don't either. But after he left, I did more research into ancestry sites. Half the family trees shown are built by regular people doing their own ancestral searches. If you submit your DNA, it can be cross-linked with others' DNA, so descendants can build their family trees. Sometimes the site will make a suggestion that a person *might* be related, and the descendant could just accept it as fact and add the person to their tree without verification. It can become sloppy fast if the one building the tree doesn't do thorough research. It leads to broken branches on family trees."

"I'm not sure I understand."

Tilly tried to simplify it. "Basically, someone else out there shares a DNA match that links directly to Luke James's family tree. And for whatever reason, that person added Eloise James to the site but didn't identify any connections. Who was she? A sister? A daughter? It's unclear."

Ashley nodded. "Ancestry can be confusing."

"And . . . what if Eloise James has been forgotten? Like the woman in the wall or like Mary Franks." Tilly shrugged. "Why does it seem like the women in the James family weren't valued or treasured?"

Ashley's eyes widened at what Tilly was implying. "Are you saying this Eloise James was disowned?"

"I'm saying, what if Eloise James was the key to understanding the James family, and that's why she was all but erased from the family's history."

Eloise

October 1879
James Mansion

Father waited at the bottom of the stairs.

Eloise descended, her nose twitching at the smell of partially wet plaster. Cleaned, freshly dressed, primped, her wounded cheek powdered, she was ready now to meet their guest, although everything in her told her to flee. It was also all she could do not to worry herself sick over Silas.

A younger man stood beside Father. Eloise had never seen the stranger before, but he was pleasant-looking enough. Mustache, brown eyes, hair parted smartly on the side.

"There you are, my dear." Father's endearment fell flat on Eloise's ears. It was for show, of course. He extended his arm toward their guest. "I'd like you to meet Thomas, a business partner of mine."

This was the man Ida believed might be the investor mentioned in Kenny's journal? Somehow, Eloise had expected someone older, more menacing. More like Father.

"How do you do, Miss James?"

"Very well. Thank you, Mr. Thomas," she replied. It was a lie. Such was the case in polite society. People pretended, spoke of good health and well wishes, all while keeping mum about the hard truths hovering just below the surface.

What was true about Mr. Thomas? What did he hold over Father?

She wished Silas were here beside her. Her thoughts came back to him as though he were a magnet. If only she could have slipped out, retrieved the journal, and taken it to Captain Rutter. Hopefully, he would listen to reason and believe that Silas was innocent of grave robbing. Silas was guilty only of inserting himself into an investigation neither of them had known was ongoing.

Instead, here she stood playing the role of dutiful daughter and leading the men to dinner.

Sam served roasted duck, baby red potatoes, and candied carrots, along with wine. The air in the room felt stifled, and Eloise found herself suffocated to the point of not wanting to eat. She stopped sipping the wine, opting instead for her glass of water.

The conversation was mind-numbing.

"Hmm?" Eloise lifted her eyes from her plate when she heard Father address her.

He did not look pleased. "I asked you to tell Mr. Thomas about your work with the Ladies' Missionary Society."

"Yes, of course." In truth, she hadn't been to a meeting in over three months, not since Evania had been taken away. She scrambled to recall their last gathering. "The ladies and I took donations of tea bags to send to the missionaries."

"Didn't you say Mrs. Abernathy suggested they all dry their used tea bags so that the missionaries could reuse them?" Father led.

"Yes, she did. We had piles of dried tea bags to send," Eloise added, surprised her father had remembered this detail.

Mr. Thomas dipped his head politely. "A brilliant idea."

She found it rather stomach-turning—and cheap. Couldn't wealthy benefactresses do better than to send used tea bags to poor missionaries in Africa and China? And didn't much of their tea come *from* China? Surely the Chinese would have tea of better quality. But the ladies had felt good about themselves. That was, after all, the point of the society. In Eloise's opinion, it wasn't so much about the missionaries as it was about congratulating one another for their generosity and goodwill toward others.

After more horribly dull conversation, an ever-heightening question rose in Eloise's mind as to why Father was so at ease and why this man was sitting at their table. Eloise felt relieved when dinner was finally completed and Sam began clearing their plates.

"You may leave us, Sam," Father stated abruptly. "You can finish with that at a later time."

This caused Eloise to lift her eyes from where she had just put down her folded napkin.

Sam hesitated, unused to being dismissed rather than Father reconvening to another room and allowing the staff to clean up after dinner. He gave a stiff bow, replied, "Yes, sir," then disappeared into the butler's pantry, shutting the door behind him.

"I had plans, Eloise, for this evening, but recent circumstances have made me alter those plans."

She didn't miss his reference to the day's events. Grateful Father hadn't embarrassed her in front of their guest, she still couldn't shake the uneasiness that saturated her from the instant she had laid eyes on him.

Father leaned back in his chair and studied her. Why was he so focused on her and not Mr. Thomas?

He worked his jaw back and forth in thought, his eyes sharp. "You have been a bit of trouble lately, my dear."

Eloise stared at him. She dared not look in the direction of Mr. Thomas.

Father continued, "As you know, your sister also caused trouble, although it was of a different nature. To a degree," he added. She knew he was hinting at Silas.

She grew pale and was absolutely chilled.

"Mr. Thomas here knew your sister at the asylum."

Eloise's eyes shifted to meet Mr. Thomas's.

"That's right," he said. "I had several conversations with Miss Evania."

Eloise shifted her gaze between the men.

After a pause, Father said, "Your sister continued to cause problems while at the institution. Mr. Thomas sought to help her with her . . . behaviors in hopes of getting her to cease them."

Given what Eloise knew of Evania attempting to escape from the asylum, she frowned and said, "I don't understand, Father—"

"That isn't important," he said, cutting her off. "What *is* important is for you to understand your place in this family, Eloise. Which is something Evania failed to do. I'm afraid, however, you may be choosing to follow your sister's same path."

"What path is that?"

"She didn't listen to me or to reason," Mr. Thomas interjected.

Father did not appear the slightest bit offended by the stranger's insertion into their family business. Since when did Father allow another person to take control in his home?

Mr. Thomas settled his gaze on her, and for a long moment the two of them stared at each other. His look one of assessment, and hers one of utter fear.

"It was a pity your sister took so ill. But she was quite persistent, wasn't she?" Mr. Thomas's eyes narrowed.

"What did you do?" Eloise hissed. She looked to Father. "What did he do?"

Mr. Thomas leaned back in his chair, making a show of folding his napkin and laying it neatly on the table. "When she returned here—after her little escapade to break free from the institution—she was in very bad shape."

Eloise couldn't breathe. She couldn't move. She looked at Mr. Thomas and Father with incredulity. "When . . . when she returned *here*?" Had Evania come home? The idea that she might have crossed paths with Evania—her on her way back to James Mansion and Eloise on her way to rescue her sister—was disabling. She sagged onto the table, leaning on her elbows so she didn't collapse. "Father, did Evania make it home?"

He looked away, but before he did so, Eloise thought she glimpsed regret in his eyes. But it fled as fast as it came.

"I took care of her," Mr. Thomas went on. "She was never going to make it anyway. Coming back home was a very unwise decision on Evania's part."

"Are you saying she's—?" Eloise couldn't say the word. It was all unraveling like a terrible tale that not only confirmed Evania did not survive but implicated Father in her death as well. Father wasn't being blackmailed into silence. That was only a desperate attempt to distance himself as if innocent of the business of selling bodies. Yet it was becoming clearer now—appallingly so—and the truth of it was heart-wrenching. No! From the beginning, Father had full knowledge of the goings-on at the asylum—especially if Evania had made it home after being taken out with the dead, driven away as the illicit inventory of smugglers.

Father cleared his throat. "Eloise, there comes a time in every family when loyalties must be tested. Your sister was ill. That is what ultimately took her life."

Hot tears filled Eloise's eyes. Tears of repulsion. Of disbelief. The crushing blow of lost hope.

"She would have gone to the police. That was Evania's intention," Mr. Thomas stated. "She wanted to garner your father's support in exposing what she believed she'd uncovered at the asylum. We argued. She was so unwell . . . there was an unfortunate accident, and I'm afraid she fell from the balcony to the parlor floor."

Eloise's mouth opened in a silent, agonizing cry. Had this man *killed* Evania? Father had allowed him into their home to orchestrate a disgusting business, and he had stood idly by while Mr. Thomas confronted Evania, his actions resulting in her death!

"How could you?" Eloise managed. She turned accusing eyes on Father. "You allowed this man to aid in the death of your daughter?"

"It was never supposed to happen like that. Evania was never supposed to come home from the asylum. Her behavior threatened to damage our good name, our reputation. Mr. Thomas has worked diligently to get us where we are, and Evania was reprehensible in her conduct. She refused to stay in her place, not even at the institution where they were treating her ailments. She wasn't supposed to try to escape!" Father raised his voice, and he sounded so insistent that Eloise could almost understand the logic behind his thinking.

But in the end, there was no logic for her to understand. Only greed. Greed and pride, and for whatever reason, a severe detachment from his daughters, who were mere interruptions in his corrupted world.

"You are profiting from the loss and grief of families! From your own daughter's death!" Eloise's voice shook with rage. "To think you even sent Evania to that place to begin with, knowing that if she died there, she would be . . ." It was too awful to put into words. Too sickening. Eloise snatched up her napkin and held it to her mouth.

Mr. Thomas raised his hands as if to calm her. "Now, now. Don't judge Father too harshly. Our intention was never for Evania to grow ill, nor to die, and certainly not to try to free herself and, in doing so, literally fall into the middle of it all."

"Father?" Eloise heard Mr. Thomas's reference. "*Our* intention?" Bewildered, her mind scrambled to keep up with what was being revealed.

"Oh yes. That." Mr. Thomas's smile did not reach his eyes. "I forgot, Father, that you never told them of me."

"Their mother knew. That was enough." Father gave a curt nod.

Mr. Thomas offered Eloise a regretful smile. "You see, our father was married before your mother came along. I'm your elder half brother. When my mother died, Father arranged for me to be raised in boarding schools in order to have a proper education and be able to come alongside him when the time was right."

"You had a son by a prior marriage? Why, Father, did you keep it a secret all these years? Why did you never say anything?"

"I didn't keep Thomas a secret, Eloise. Your mother knew, and she also agreed that neither you nor Evania needed to know until the timing was best. After your mother passed, there was never any need to mention Thomas. My first marriage was short-lived. My wife never moved to New Jamestown and was fragile of health. After Thomas was born, she passed away. The details are of no further concern. What matters is that I've entrusted Thomas here with the future of our family. He is my rightful heir."

Eloise didn't realize she had risen from the table even as she gripped its edge.

Mr. Thomas rose to his feet, as did Father.

"I am so pleased to meet you, dear sister," Mr. Thomas said with an air of disingenuous politeness.

Eloise's knees gave way, and she dropped back onto her chair. Her eyes flew to Father's.

He smiled grimly. "You must learn to trust those in authority over you. There was never any reason for you or Evania to concern yourself with such matters. If you had both just stayed in your places, I would have eventually introduced you to your brother. But there was no reason to do so until now. Your mother wanted nothing to do with poor Thomas, and I was afraid you and your sister would feel the same."

Father leveled a disheartened look that implied Eloise would not have welcomed Thomas with an open heart. Would he make this her fault also?

"None of this has evolved according to my choice, but here we are, Eloise. Your sister suffered the consequences of her poor choices. But we have your brother, and he has been pivotal in the financial endeavors of our family."

"Kenny's journal . . ." she choked out, then bit her tongue. She could not reveal they still had possession of it. It was incriminating evidence. It had to be!

Thomas waved her off. "When I discovered that book among Kenny's things, I confronted him about it. He was an idiot to have ever written anything down. I helped myself to a good read of it before Father put it in his safe. My intention was to hang on to it in the event Dr. Holzer ever decided to renege on our business arrangement. It was foolish for Kenny to have written it, and yet it may end up being beneficial to us. That said, it's unfortunate you were privy to it—and stole it." He smiled. "Bravo, sister. But the book names neither me nor Father. Therefore, the only thing left on the table to address tonight is *you*." He glanced at Father. "You and your nosy friend, Silas Dobbs, and the attention you've brought to the asylum and Dr. Holzer with your talk of grave robbing, well, it's turned into far more than just an annoyance."

"But Kenny has been arrested!" Eloise struggled to see why Father and Thomas weren't more frightened. "He'll tell all!" And she hoped he would. She hoped he would expose Thomas and Father for the heartless men they were. That they would be dealt justice for what had been done to Evania and likely to the bodies of Seamus and Penny too.

"Perhaps," Father said, "but Thomas has reassured me this afternoon—and I must say, I was becoming quite rattled—that he has kept the James name carefully protected."

"Protected?" Eloise was not concerned at all that the family name be saved any shame.

A banging sounded on the front door.

Thomas and Father exchanged glances.

Eloise jumped to her feet once again.

"Ah." Thomas gave a thin smile. "Good. They're here. Let us be done now with this entire charade."

27

Tilly Thompson

Can it be you that I hear? Let me view you, then,
Standing as when I drew near to the town
Where you would wait for me: yes, as I knew you then,
Even to the original air-blue gown!

Thomas Hardy

Present Day

Sleeping on the sofa in the sitting room wasn't the most comfortable. Still, even with the assurance of the baby-monitor system, last night's race to find Grandpa Don had left Tilly without the ability to relax. Now she tossed and turned on the sofa, trying to find a comfortable position where her hips didn't become sore and throb in a matter of minutes.

By the time Ashley had finally left, the two of them had blown through at least an hour scouring the internet to find more associations between the James family and Eloise James. They'd found a few odd references to Eloise of Corinth, Indiana, which had raised more suspicion that Tilly's theory might be correct. Yet there were no articles or references to her anywhere that they could find. The ancestral site returned to one username who had inserted Eloise James into the tree. It showed that user's profile to be disconnected, and there was no way to reach out to someone with the username James101.

Tilly rolled onto her back, staring at the ceiling as she listened to Grandpa Don's fuzzy snoring through the monitor.

The fact was, if Eloise James was somehow related and even in Luke's direct line, what difference would it make? That was over a century ago. Nowadays, most people could barely cite the names of their great-grandparents, let alone those that went back three generations. That Eloise's name was *there* was what bothered Tilly. Luke had been vaguely familiar with the name Thomas James, even Evania James. But Eloise? Who was this relative, and why the mystery?

A dull thump invaded Tilly's thoughts.

She sat up straight, instantly on alert. Tilly slipped from her place on the sofa and padded to the doorway to peer down the hall.

Nothing.

She looked straight ahead up the stairs to the stained-glass window.

The stairs were empty.

A quick recollection reassured her that she'd locked the windows. The back door, the servants' entrance, the front door, the door off the kitchen, all locked. The cellar doors were padlocked from the outside, and in the basement she'd . . . Tilly's heart pounded. She'd failed to ask Erik to install a more secure lock on the cellar doors. She'd been worried that a simple padlock was insufficient to keep out intruders. With everything that had taken place since the night with the entertainment center, she'd completely forgotten to talk to him about it.

Hearing no more thumps, Tilly's breathing returned to normal. Yet it nagged at her that the cellar doors might have been breached by someone. She would never fall asleep now until she went and checked it for herself. She was reluctant to go outside, though, because she'd have to unlock a door to do that, leaving Grandpa alone in the house at two in the morning.

The image of the face and the palm against the windowpane came back to her in force, creeping her out. An overactive imagination was no help when your nerves were shot.

Tilly walked to the front entrance and grabbed a flashlight she kept near the door. She'd head down to the basement and check the cellar doors from the inside. Down into that awful, dank, eerie basement where she'd envisioned bodies hanging from the rafters or mobsters yanking out teeth.

Mustering her courage, Tilly knew she just needed to reassure herself that the cellar was secured. Then she would hurry back to the sofa.

She opted to cross the parlor and access the servants' entrance. The small entryway was dark, but the flashlight's beam more than made up for it. The stairs remained a deep, gaping mouth leading to the pit where everything terrifying in her imagination lived.

Thankfully, the cellar wasn't too far away. A quick peek and she could sprint back upstairs like a twelve-year-old girl running from the bathroom after flushing the toilet in the middle of the night. She made it to the doorway of the cellar, the stone floor beneath her feet cold. She raised the flashlight to check the doors that opened to the outside . . .

Tilly froze, staring at the doors. One of them had been lifted and opened. The cool night air wafted toward her. She could see stars beyond the open door.

That was it. She was calling Erik. Or maybe 911. Yes, definitely 911. She reached for her phone in the back pocket of her jeans but felt her pocketless pajama bottoms instead.

"No, no, no, no . . ." She'd left her phone upstairs on the sofa.

Whirling around, Tilly hurried through the basement, clutching the flashlight to direct her way back up the stairs, also considering it would be a good object to hit an intruder over the head with if needed.

She made it back to the parlor, breathing heavily.

All was dark save the flashlight's beam.

All seemed normal.

Until it wasn't.

From the bottom of the stained-glass window facing the staircase, a man leaped from the shadows. He hit her solidly with the bulk of his body. Tilly flew backward, the flashlight falling from her hand and rolling across the floor of the sitting room. She cried out as she wrestled beneath the man's weight.

The only thing familiar about him was his eyes. They were narrow. She'd seen them before. They were very, very blue. Just like Luke's.

Eloise

October 1879
James Mansion

Captain Rutter was at the door, as were several policemen. They barged in past a flustered Mrs. Forrester and entered the sitting room just as Father and Thomas met them. Eloise hung back, holding on to the doorframe.

They were here. Here to arrest Thomas. And Father?

The truth hit her again. Father was not being threatened or blackmailed or maligned. He was an integral part of, if not the one financing, the cadaver-selling business. Whatever his exact role, she knew now that he had profited from it. Profited greatly. And he worked with her half brother, whom Father had kept to himself like a prized possession all these years. Thomas had usurped Father's affections—if you could call them that—from his daughters. In Thomas, Father had the only child he ever really wanted.

"Ah! Captain Rutter! To what do I owe this interruption?" Father addressed the man.

Captain Rutter looked between him and Thomas and then saw Eloise in the background. He brought his attention back to Father.

"It is my duty to inform you, sir, that my associate in Corinth is placing Dr. Holzer of the Corinth Asylum for the Chronically Insane under arrest. The doctor has been working with your employee, Kenny Blunt."

"You have got to be mad!" Father's feigned outrage sickened Eloise. "Working together in what way?"

"In a grave-robbing scheme. They've been selling the remains of asylum patients while also desecrating the burial sites of other deceased victims. In fact, we believe care may have been withheld from the hospital patients in order to increase the amount of, well, opportunity." Captain Rutter cleared his throat uncomfortably.

Eloise steeled herself for his next words: *And you, sir, are under arrest for your role as investor and as the person behind this unsavory enterprise. You and your son, Thomas James.*

Instead, Captain Rutter continued with different words. "A journal has come into my possession by way of Mr. Silas Dobbs."

"That hooligan?" Father chuckled as if entertained, but also acceptably appalled.

"Mr. Dobbs is not a hooligan, sir. He has been quite pivotal in helping us get to the bottom of what has been taking place. After he told us where this journal was, we were able to obtain it. It lists a detailed log of the goings-on of the grave-robbing scheme."

"That's horrific." Father exchanged looks with Thomas.

Eloise held her breath.

Captain Rutter continued, "Is there a Samuel Tanner in your employ?"

"Sam?" Eloise blurted in surprise, releasing her hold on the doorframe and stepping into the conversation.

"Yes, Miss James." Captain Rutter gave her a little nod. "He is mentioned in the journal as one working alongside Kenny."

"No!" Eloise threw a shocked look at Thomas. At her father. "No, Sam is just our footman." Captain Rutter had it all wrong!

"How dreadful." Thomas shook his head, clucking his tongue.

Father's expression fell at the news. "This is quite the shock. I hired both Kenny and Sam a few years ago. They came recommended from Dr. Holzer himself. Now I see why."

A commotion at the front entrance demanded their attention. A policeman held Sam by the back of his collar. "He tried to run, Captain!"

Sam struggled. "You should arrest him too!" He pointed at Father.

Father took a step back.

Captain Rutter hesitated.

Sam swore.

"We've no evidence that Mr. James has had any part in the scheme," Captain Rutter said.

Eloise felt the life seep out of her. She looked to Thomas, who remained impassive.

Father blustered, "I am *appalled* at all of this! Absolutely appalled!"

"What?" Sam cried. "You're the one who told me where to go and who to take the messages to. You're the one who pays me! You have Kenny doing your dirty work!" He shifted shocked eyes to the captain. "You mean to tell me you're not going to arrest Mr. James?"

Captain Rutter looked uncomfortable, and then he pointed to his officers. "Take him away."

Sam was led from James Mansion, kicking and cursing.

Captain Rutter turned back to Father, his brows drawn and his eyes narrowed. "I apologize, sir, but I'll have to investigate those allegations."

"I completely understand," Father agreed with carefully measured approval. "Do what you must."

"Miss James?" Captain Rutter directed his attention to her.

Eloise bit down on her tongue. Nothing she could say in this moment would do anything to implicate Father or Thomas. They had cleaned up their involvement. Evania was dead. Saying anything now would only paint her as an emotional, unstable daughter with wild claims.

"I apologize for the misunderstanding today, miss," Captain Rutter continued. "You and Mr. Dobbs have been cleared of any charges."

"Thank goodness," Father breathed.

Eloise nodded, grateful for that at least, and grateful that Silas was now free. But she was shaking uncontrollably, her breath coming in tight, fast gasps. Kenny's and Sam's involvement was awful enough. Father and Thomas and their charade of innocence left Eloise feeling shredded inside. And Evania? If what Thomas had declared was true, then Evania was dead. Eloise stifled a sob.

Thomas eyed her while Father led the other men to the foyer. Once the captain and his men left, Father closed the door with a resounding click. He stepped back into the room.

"While this *investigation* ensues, Thomas," said Father, "I believe you and I have business to tend to. I'm assuming that won't take long. Perhaps a trip to Europe is in order." His glance at Eloise revealed he wanted distance from all this. The scandal at the asylum would be in the papers, and Kenny's and Sam's names would be included as his employees. If her father and Thomas were lucky, they'd be linked by association only. But distance and time would help everyone to forget. They were Jameses, after all. They could *pay* people to forget.

"Of course." Thomas gave a confident nod. "I'll make the travel arrangements right away." He exited the sitting room and strode down the hallway toward Father's study as though he had been there a thousand times. Perhaps he had.

Father turned to Eloise.

She could see a storm brewing in his eyes. She didn't understand it. But she understood the feeling that had been growing in her since dinner.

Anger.

Outrage.

Eloise met her father in the parlor. She faced him as he stood with his back to the stairs, the new stained-glass window above him looking so beautiful in a home so darkened by evil.

"I believe there must have been a dead animal—perhaps a mouse—caught behind the wall when they plastered it." Father's general observation was so in character. He was going to overlook it all. Evania. Thomas. Even her. Father rubbed his finger under his nose. "Perhaps I shall go to Europe even sooner," Father concluded. "You'll be fine here with Mrs. Forrester and Ida, Eloise," he added. "You've no need to come."

Eloise stared at him. What words were adequate enough to confront a lifetime of lies and manipulation? She had never confronted her father before. But he had allowed Evania to die at the hands of—whether intentional or accidental—his own son! She'd long thought Father was cruel. Now she knew he was *wicked*. Would their family ever be free from such abuse and darkness? The scars would remain well past Father, Eloise was afraid.

"How could you?" It was all she could think to say.

"How could I?" Father countered.

"Where is Evania?" Eloise asked. She was desperate to know once and for all.

Father offered her a grim smile. "Thomas had your sister's remains interred in the cemetery."

Eloise fought to maintain control of her emotions. Her eyes burned with tears, betraying her fury and her grief. "Next to Mama?"

"How am I to know?" Father snapped.

"How could you *not* know?" Eloise challenged.

"I trust my son." His eyes leveled a bold honesty that drew a solid line between Eloise and her older brother. "Thomas is a James man. It's his privilege to make decisions that will benefit our family and our legacy."

In that moment, it all became very clear to Eloise. She took a step away from her father and made no attempt to hide her utter revulsion of him.

"Then I am grateful I am *not* a James man," Eloise said, her voice low and threaded with steel. "You are shameful." If her father winced, Eloise was certain she only imagined it. "You disgust me, and if God has mercy on your soul, I shall never understand the why of it."

28

Tilly Thompson

He did not love me living; but once dead
He pitied me; and very sweet it is
To know he still is warm though I am cold.

Christina Rossetti

Present Day

It wasn't Luke. But it was the face she'd seen in a blur in the window. It was the hand that had dragged along the glass as if taunting her.

Tilly rolled away from the man, clambering to her feet. "What do you want?"

He was tall, lean, his face clean-shaven and his hair dark. "I'll leave. Just let me leave, and you won't be hurt," he said with a gravelly voice.

Tilly knew if she tried to call for help, he was only one step away from attacking her and silencing her. His body looked to be built like a powerful spring.

"What are you doing in my house?" she demanded. Tilly wished she had her phone with her. Better yet, she whispered a 911 prayer to God.

The man held up his hands. "Just let me go."

"Go then." Tilly gestured toward the door of the sitting room.

But instead of leaving, he took a step toward her. His towering height was menacing.

"Did you not hear me? I said *go*."

He eyed her. "You're Tilly."

She backed up a few steps, and her backside collided with a table by the wall just outside the sitting room. She grabbed for it to steady herself, catching sight of the stained-glass window that faced the main staircase behind the stranger. "This isn't the first time you've broken into my house, is it?"

He took another step toward her. Apparently, his offer to leave had been an empty one. "I can't believe they sold this place—the James Mansion—and after all the years they left it empty." He flung his arms wide like a ringmaster in a circus. "Funny how Luke has been spending so much time here recently after selling it. Who knows? If his brother Kyle wasn't half dead, he'd probably be hanging out here too."

There was no respect or empathy in the man's words. Instead, it was all bitterness. The resentment of someone who believed he had been wronged.

Tilly edged toward the front door, but he shot her a glare of warning.

"Don't run. I just want to talk."

"Talk?" Tilly didn't want to talk. She wanted to sink through the wood floor. She wanted to run to Grandpa Don.

Grandpa Don!

O Lord, please don't let him wake up.

She could only imagine what he might do. She didn't want him to risk getting hurt.

"Do you like it here? Finding dead bodies in the wall? Digging up old secrets?"

She didn't respond.

"Did you know, I've been in here several times? There are so many ways to get inside, and this house likes to speak to your soul. I don't know what it is, but I swear it has a voice."

"It was you who moved the entertainment center, wasn't it?" Tilly asked.

"Yeah. I thought it was odd they put it in front of a door. Maybe something interesting was behind it. But there wasn't much I could post since the words there didn't make any sense. 'Help me. You are not alone'? What does that even mean?"

Tilly's eyes widened. This was the person posting online about Luke and his family.

A smile stretched knowingly across his face. "Figured it out, huh? The more a person digs around someone's childhood home, the more they figure out about their family." The man reached into his coat pocket and tugged out a book.

Tilly shrank back against the table as she recognized it.

Luke's journal.

The man had gone through her dresser and found the journal. Why hadn't she been more careful with it?

"There's some good stuff in here, isn't there?" He circled Tilly slowly, his eyes never leaving her face. "I heard you and that other lady talking about DNA and family trees. You have me to thank for that link to Eloise James. I figured everyone needed a little James family 101."

She recognized the ancestry site's username instantly. "Who are you?" Tilly pressed. She couldn't demand much of anything. At the moment, she was about as helpless as she'd ever felt.

"You haven't figured that out?" He clucked his tongue. "See, that surprises me. You're pretty smart. You see things others don't. I thought you might figure it out. But apparently not."

Another burst of laughter. "Mary Franks?" He lifted his brows as though the name would help her to connect the dots.

Tilly scrambled to do just that.

Mary Franks. The homeless woman. This man was of a similar age to Kyle James, or maybe in between Kyle and Luke.

He lunged toward her.

She yelped.

He stopped inches from her, laughing at the fear he'd inspired. "Good grief. Do I have to spell it out for you?"

When she didn't answer, he obliged. "Luke's father had an affair with my mother, Mary Franks. After I was born, she told him about me, and then we lost our home. And life sucked after that. Then she just disappeared. Convenient for the James family, if you ask me. I was sent to live with my aunt and uncle, who never talked about my father. It wasn't until five years ago that I did a DNA test. It linked me to the James family."

Looking at his features, it wasn't hard for Tilly to believe this guy was related to Luke. Yet there were holes in his story. "You're a James?"

"James Mansion has been unoccupied the last several years. I've spent a lot of time here, finding family treasures and secrets that speak of our past. Secrets I could ruin the overprivileged James family with. Like the fact that Price James had a daughter named Eloise who no one included on any family tree, except for one. I found that ancestral chart in the basement of all places, along with a whole stack of old James business documents. Did you know Eloise all but disappeared after 1879? One daughter was sent to an asylum, the other vanished, leaving him with his precious son. Sons are very important in this family, unless of course they're illegitimate like me."

"Who are you?" Tilly was still trying to piece it all together.

"Actually, I want nothing to do with the James family or this house. I just want their father exposed for what he did to my mother. He abused her, and then he threw her away to end up dead somewhere." He flung his arm up. "This place is a living tomb—fitting for a family that destroys anyone and everyone in their wake."

Tilly froze as he leaned in close, his breath hot on her face.

"My name is Brandon Franks. I may be Luke's half brother, but I will always be one hundred percent Mary Franks's son."

Headlights illuminated the parlor as a car pulled into the drive.

Hope flooded her. Then came fear. Whoever it was would be walking into danger.

Brandon's face darkened. "Who did you call?"

"No one! I don't have my phone with me." Tilly lunged for the front door, reaching for the lock, hoping to release it and call for help.

Brandon flew at her and yanked her against him as the door at the back of the house banged open. With the stairs behind him, Tilly thought that if she pushed him, Brandon might lose his footing and his grip on her. She shoved him backward, but he was too strong and too tall. He jumped up a step, his arm encircling her throat.

Tilly heard footsteps pounding on the floor toward them.

"Be careful! There's an intruder!" she screamed.

Luke barreled around the corner, running headlong into Tilly and Brandon, who released her instantly. Luke shoved Tilly away from Brandon and slammed into him with all his weight.

Tilly sprinted into the sitting room, diving for her phone on the sofa. She punched in 911 but was startled when she heard sirens outside the mansion. The blue-and-red lights of squad cars coming up the drive flashed in the windows.

Still battling it out, Luke and Brandon rolled across the parlor floor.

Luke's foot hooked the table Tilly had just been gripping a moment before, and it toppled over.

The front door flew open, the police surging inside and announcing themselves.

There was a scuffle of bodies, and Tilly, afraid to move, hovered by the sofa. She needed to get to Grandpa Don. The fact that he'd been so silent this whole time was raising a whole new level of fear in her.

Had Brandon done something to him? Hurt him?

A police officer manhandled Brandon onto his stomach on the floor, yanking his arms behind him and cuffing him.

Another officer had Luke in a hold. Tilly cried out, "He's the good guy!"

Luke, his nose bleeding and with a cut on his temple, wasn't struggling.

The officer looked between them, his eyes settling on Tilly. "Are you the owner of this house?"

"Yes!" Desperation choked her.

"You know this man?" He jabbed a thumb toward Luke.

"Yes, please, let him go. He came to help me."

As the officer released him, recognition flooded his face. "Luke James. Oh!" He stepped back, stunned that he'd almost cuffed a candidate for city mayor. "My apologies, sir."

"It's okay." Luke held up his hands.

Brandon cursed and shouted at Luke as the officer escorted him outside.

"Grandpa!" Tilly pushed past the other officer and Luke, beelining for the train room. She skidded around the corner and pulled up short.

Grandpa Don sat on the edge of his bed, looking as contented as a Cheshire cat. He glanced up at her. "You took my gun, didn't you?"

"I . . ." He'd seen her do it. He'd obviously forgotten.

Grandpa Don smiled and waved her off as though he'd just watched an episode of *Bonanza*. "It's all right." He raised his phone in the air. "I called Erik for help and then let him inside."

The pieces of how Luke knew to come and to call the police fell into place. Apparently, neither she nor Erik had made it a priority to correct Grandpa Don's contact entry in his phone to call the right person.

Tilly bent at her waist, grabbing her knees, allowing herself to breathe deeply. "*Luke*, Grandpa. You called Luke."

But he didn't seem to comprehend her correction. It didn't matter. They were safe now. They were all safe.

And that was the most important thing.

Eloise

October 1879
James Mansion

Father and Thomas left the following day for business out of town. Plans for a European trip were in the making. They wouldn't be back for some time, Father had indicated, but if Captain Rutter needed to speak with him, he could contact Father's solicitors. They would be able to get ahold of him. And then, with little compunction, Father had told her that he expected she would find it a good idea to relocate. Having lost Evania and all, living in James Mansion would be too difficult. He promised to set aside a sum of money for her to get situated elsewhere.

This was the end. The end of her and Father. He had chosen Thomas. He had always chosen Thomas; she just never knew it until now. But Mama had. Oh, Mama! How she had tried to teach Eloise and Evania their value and worth as daughters, as women. Father's voice had always been louder, though.

Eloise hadn't slept and therefore sleepwalking was not a threat. Ida had made sure to leave open the adjoining door between their bedrooms, but it was for naught. Eloise had sat facing her window, staring out at the night sky and the blue moon. There were no tears. There were no words. For the first time since she'd last seen Evania in the same position by her window, Eloise understood her sister. Grief and betrayal and rejection . . . they felt as though insurmountable.

Eloise remained silent in her room while hearing Father and Thomas moving about the house, gathering what they needed and preparing to put space between them and any potential scandal.

Now they were gone.

No one questioned them. No one knew *how* to question them. She was sure that Captain Rutter, in spite of his intentions to investigate, would find it difficult to successfully do so against a man as well situated and powerful as Price James.

An hour away by train, Dr. Holzer was being arrested, and the asylum was most likely spiraling into chaos. Captain Rutter would write his reports, document the sordid details of Kenny's and Sam's involvement with Dr. Holzer in stealing and selling dead bodies for profit. Captain Rutter would never know that Price James and his secret son were the masterminds behind it all, even if he had his own suspicions. Thomas had seen to that.

Thomas. Her brother.

Evania.

Eloise ran her fingers across the bedcovers in Evania's room. Less than two months ago, Kenny had placed a ladder against that very window frame, and she had determined not to hold it against him. Now she held far more than that against him. Father and Dr. Merriweather had knocked on the door. Evania had accepted her fate. At least for the moment.

Her hand trailed along the bedpost to the chair in which Evania had sat that day. Her throat became sore as the watery lump grew larger, making it difficult to swallow. Evania had made it out of the asylum! Her strong-willed sister had literally feigned death and allowed herself to be tossed next to deceased patients and driven away.

Eloise sank onto the chair, burying her head in her hands. And somehow Evania had made it home to James Mansion. Had she looked for Eloise? Slipped into Eloise's room only to find it empty? What had given her away? Had she collapsed, ill as she was, and been laid in this room?

"Of course you would have confronted Thomas," Eloise whispered, lifting her head to look out the window. The day was bright, and the sun smiled down as though the world were beautiful and all was well.

Had Evania truly fallen or had she tripped from the balcony over the stairs? It was possible. In the heat of an argument with a brother of whom Evania might have just become aware. With the ladders and the mess from installing the stained-glass window, yes, it was possible. But deep in her soul, Eloise knew it wasn't likely that Evania had tripped. In her mind's eye, Eloise could see the moment Thomas realized if Evania was no longer alive, she would be one less hassle to have to deal with. Father might have sent Evania away. Perhaps that was his small mercy. But Thomas and mercy? Eloise believed he had none.

She rose and moved to Evania's dresser. Much was still as it had been the day Evania was taken away. A yellow ribbon. A tatted bookmark. There was a locket lying on a mirrored tray. Evania's locket. She had worn it for years, ever since the day Mama gave it to her when she was a young girl.

Eloise lifted the locket and opened it. A watercolor miniature of two yellow roses lay inside. She remembered then. Mama . . .

You are my roses. My special and beautiful garden. I am so proud of you both. You will grow, and life will threaten to make your petals droop, but remember always that your worth is not in who you are on your own, but in who you were created to be together. A garden is more beautiful where two or more roses grow. God did not create you to walk alone.

Eloise wiped tears from her face as she closed the locket.

She was alone now.

Lifting her eyes, she looked at her reflection in Evania's mirror. She met her gaze, framed by her gold spectacles. Or was she?

Something had been awakened inside her. A voice. *Her* voice. There were others who might need to hear Evania's story. The story of those who suffered behind the locked doors of asylums. To hear of the grief and the loss of loved ones.

No. She was not alone. She had been given purpose, and she would not allow this place—this house—to keep her hidden any longer.

Eloise sat in the garden, staring at the yellow rosebush. Knowing Evania's locket was there, buried next to her infant, soothed her. There would always be an empty space in her heart. It belonged to Evania. It would always be Evania's.

But somehow, in the darkness, Evania seemed to live again, in Eloise. In her memories. And no matter where she was now, where her body had been taken and what had been done with it, that wasn't Evania. Her body had never been Evania. Evania was the spirit that God had given her, and the spirit that God would allow to rest in peace.

Eloise shifted her gaze to the heavens.

So much pain.

So much horror.

So much unresolved.

And what of her? Of Eloise James? She wished she could return to James Mansion, close the door on the world outside, and start life anew. Fresh. Clean.

But she couldn't. Father would come back one day. Thomas would take over James Mansion and the James holdings, and the future of the James family name. He would become the next in a line of James men who would continue to pass down the seeds of pride and greed, but worst of all, a sickness of the mind that convinced them they were kings over the little kingdom they had created in New Jamestown.

Eloise fingered the yellow petal of the one straggling rose that tried to stay alive as the cold of late October settled in. Mother had told her years ago that God would look down and smile on her because she was His precious creation. Even if everyone else saw her as nothing, God had proclaimed His creation to be good.

She wanted to believe that.

Eloise wanted to believe there was beauty to be had. Like this rose. The chill seeped in and stole life from the blossoms, but somehow this one remained. And the bush would bloom again next spring when the snow melted.

She felt a hand slip into hers. Silas.

She had known he was there. She'd known he'd been there for quite some time, giving her the moments she needed, making sure she was safe.

Gone was Silas's cheeky grin. In its place was a solemnity she hadn't expected.

"I'm sorry, love," he said.

"Sorry?"

"For your sister."

"And Penny and Seamus," Eloise added.

"Aye."

"Will this ache ever stop? I can't change what has happened, but somehow I feel guilty, like I've been a part of it. I am a James, after all."

Silas drew her to his side, and Eloise didn't resist. He was perhaps the only real thing she had left that held any possibility of promise in the midst of darkness.

"Ya aren't to blame for the sins of your father. And ya won't always be a James. Come with me. I'll help ya find your way. I can't afford to pay your lady's maid, but if she wants to come too, then so be it."

"Leave my home?" Eloise lifted her eyes to the mansion. It held their stories. It held the memories of Mama, of Evania, and now the memories of these awful circumstances.

"Aye. Leave this place to Thomas. Let the James men figure it out. Maybe one day, one of 'em will wake up and see that the good Lord didn't create them to live in a way that profits from the sufferin' and dyin' of others, that glories in lordin' it over other people." Silas turned, bringing Eloise with him to look up at the outline of James Mansion as it stood beneath a cloudless sky. "Maybe one day, love, there'll be a man who grows up here an' says 'enough is enough,' an' seeks what is good and true."

"I don't know what I'd do if I left here," she admitted. "Although I know Father does not want me here when he returns."

"Then don't be. Start fresh." Silas's eyes held the promise of new life. With him? Perhaps one day, though how a man like Silas Dobbs would ever settle down and support a family was beyond her. And yet her father had never supported his family, not in the way that mattered.

"Look for a man with integrity."

"I will," Eloise whispered to the memory of her sister. To the memory of her mother. And to the future of those women who would come after her.

Silas put his mouth against the base of her ear, and his whispered words wrapped around her, lighting the tiniest pinprick of hope. "Ya see, love, sometimes in the bad, God does a wee good thing like droppin' a woman in a man's life, and suddenly everythin' changes. An' the man knows, he just knows, that if he listens to the good Lord, blessin's will fall from heaven."

Tilly

PRESENT DAY
TWO MONTHS LATER

"Evania James."

Luke announced the findings to the occupants of the room. Erik and Ashley, Grandpa Don, and Luke's brother, Kyle, and his wife were all there, seated around the sitting room of James Mansion.

Kyle's oxygen tank puffed, and he was horribly thin, but Tilly had been grateful to meet with him over the last two months. That he believed in Luke was so evident. And when Luke had officially dropped out of the mayoral race, there had been no disappointment. It was pressure Luke had applied to himself.

"For sure?" Kyle's voice was hoarse. He read over the copy of the DNA results, sharing with his wife.

Tilly averted her observations from Kyle back to her own copy of the results.

"The remains in the wall were those of Evania James. Mitochondrial DNA is far more resilient than nuclear DNA, which was used in forensics until recently." Luke offered a sheepish grin. "Look at what I've been able to learn."

"You always sucked at science," Erik interjected.

Tilly squirmed in her seat. She didn't want the results to be derailed by humor. She tried not to sound like she was interrupting but hurried on to keep them focused. "The testing they did on the woman's remains in the wall were a match to Luke and Kyle in that it verified a relation. But then a Y-DNA test was done on Luke. This tests the chromosome passed down from father to son in an unbroken line. Because Luke comes from Thomas James, who we discovered was a half brother to Evania James, the Y-DNA was important. The mitochondrial DNA is from the maternal side so—"

"Hold on." Erik held up a hand. Tilly could see she was losing him. "What's the short nonscientific version?"

Tilly shot Luke a disappointed look. The facts were important, for they proved the woman in the wall was indeed Evania James.

"It's okay, Tilly. Simple is okay," Luke reassured her.

She gave him a small smile. Their friendship had grown in the past several weeks. She never expected that the boy she couldn't trust in high school would become the man who was beginning to understand her as well as Grandpa Don could.

Grandpa Don was sipping coffee and observing. Tilly glanced at him. He did a lot of observing these days. She wondered if he was slipping faster than he was letting on.

"The short version . . ." Luke's voice interrupted her meandering thoughts. "DNA is advanced enough to trace down the line, and when merged with historical and genealogical records, many old remains—even the Russian Czar and his family, the Romanovs—can be identified down to a specific name. This is how it was determined that the woman in the wall is in fact Evania James."

"The daughter who was sent to an asylum?" Ashley frowned. "How did she end up in the wall back here? And who does that?"

"While we were searching the records, we uncovered more old articles about a complex moneymaking scheme in the area. An *Eloise James* helped to expose it." Luke looked around the room. Tilly thought he might be enjoying the attention, and she was glad to slip into the background.

"Brandon Franks was right about Eloise James. She *was* removed from the family tree," Luke said. "For whatever reason, when Evania was no longer spoken of, neither was Eloise. From then on, our records come directly from our great-great-great-grandfather's line. Thomas James."

"But who put Evania in the wall?" Ashley asked again, unrelenting in her curiosity.

"We don't know." Erik reached out and tweaked a strand of his wife's hair playfully.

"Actually . . ." Tilly should have been prepared for the entire room's sets of eyes to turn on her. This time it was Luke who registered surprise.

"We don't know how she got there, right?" Luke asked.

Tilly shook her head. "Remember those words written on the wall behind the entertainment center?"

Luke frowned, listening intently.

"I think Evania wrote those words. 'Help me. You are not alone.' I believe she left them as a message for her sister. But I don't think Eloise ever saw them."

"That's a lot of conjecture," Kyle inserted. He wasn't trying to be rude, Tilly could tell, and she nodded.

"It might seem so, but I was going through one of the boxes in the basement, and I found this." She pulled a folded piece of stationery from beneath the page of DNA results that lay on the table in front of her. "It's a letter written by Thomas James, almost a month before he died in 1946. Should I read it?"

"YES!" was the cumulative chorus from everyone in the room.

Tilly opened the letter and started reading:

I've never spoken of this, but when a man is facing death, he looks back on his sins. I have only a few to record of any great measure. But one, and only one, begs me to question my fate once I am dead.

She should have been buried by her mother. My father always believed I had arranged for Evania to be laid to rest in their family plot, though he never returned from Europe to verify this with a visit to her grave, which did not exist. When Price James, my father, died overseas, I returned. The house had been closed. My half sister, Eloise, had disappeared with some rapscallion, and I had no care for her. I still do not.

But my sin is that I wanted no repose for Evania in her death. I would no longer share my father with her. I would not share him even with her memory. Father had changed his mind to put a window in that wall, and so it was an opportunity to be rid of Evania quickly, and where she would be forever forgotten.

But even after, and before we closed James Mansion, Evania would not leave me in peace. I took her room as my own to sleep in, which was a mistake. That first night after her death, I found her words on the wall. A message she was determined would not be missed. I knew it was for Eloise. But I would share my father with Eloise no more either.

I hung a painting over the words. Months later, on my return, I had shelves built.

The curious thing, I suppose, is that although the dead may rest in peace, those of us still alive do not. My life has been haunted by the souls of many who were disinterred from their eternal rest. May I somehow find peace in my dying confession. Honestly, I don't believe I shall.

Six Months Later

Luke threw a tennis ball in the backyard, and Pickle took off after it with a gusto that belied his diminutive size. James Mansion overlooked their playing. Of late it had been a quiet, peaceful place to be. Tilly thought they could all get used to this.

Erik stood at the sizzling grill, the smell of hamburgers wafting over the summer grass. Ashley was inside the mansion, and Tilly could hear her nieces giggling as they played in the hall, pushing toy cars up and down the original hardwood floor. Children. Laughter. Loved children, healthy and secure, not questioning their safety as their loving daddy cooked burgers and their mama cut carrots into sticks.

Tilly sat next to Grandpa Don on the back porch. He was watching Luke and the dog, a quizzical look on his face.

"What's Erik doing with a ball that big for a dog that little?"

Tilly didn't bother to correct him. These days he was forever swapping Erik and Luke. Eventually, he'd forget one or the other altogether. But for now, Tilly went with it, tucking her hand into her grandpa's.

"I think Pickle likes the tennis ball, Grandpa."

"Pickle? Who names a dog after a cucumber?"

Tilly laughed. "I guess Luke does."

Grandpa Don squeezed her hand and then released it. "Well, one of these days, I want to see you find yourself a man with a dog. Men whose dogs like them are a good sign of a good man."

"Oh, but you'll always be my first man, Grandpa," Tilly whispered as she planted a kiss on his cheek.

His smile was all she needed for an answer.

Tilly left him and walked across the yard to visit with Luke. He watched Pickle as the dog rolled the ball between his paws, then bounded across the lawn.

"You doing okay?" She hugged Luke's arm.

Kyle had passed away the week before.

In two weeks, Brandon would undergo his first legal proceeding for his crimes against Tilly and James Mansion.

Tilly had excavated the James family history in the past few months, and she'd found all sorts of old newspaper articles. Along the way, she'd run across a wedding announcement for Eloise James and a Silas Dobbs.

"Yeah. I'm good. I feel at peace." Luke sighed. It was a contented sigh. He'd gotten through these past months without any relapses, leaning on his faith, his family, and a big side helping of Tilly. He leaned over now, and she met his lips with a soft kiss. It would never stop amazing her that they were here together at this moment.

"You start your new job tomorrow," Tilly said, giving him a proud smile.

"I do." Luke's grin echoed his contentment. "Morning Song Recovery is where I belong. Only this time in a different position. It will be great to work alongside Erik."

"What, you don't want to be mayor?" Tilly's attempt at teasing earned her another grin from Luke.

"Absolutely not. Will is doing a good job of it. And in spite of all the hometown gossip about Brandon Franks, any potential bad rap from social-media false reports about selling cadavers from their funeral home has thankfully died down for Daphne and her husband."

"You should be proud of yourself," Tilly said.

"No. I'll never be proud," Luke replied gently. "I'll just be grateful. That the old can be made new. That there can be redemption. That I can end a cycle, and new growth can come from it."

Tilly hugged his arm tighter.

They would grow together.

James Mansion would be patched and its dark crevices fixed. Pain would be alleviated, and healing would follow. Luke had Evania James buried beside her mother finally in the historic James portion of St. Matthew's Cemetery. It had only seemed right.

The woman in the wall had witnessed so much from her vantage point, and yet she could never speak about what she'd seen. Maybe it had been her voice Tilly had heard all those nights ago.

Help me.

Probably not, but Tilly was thankful that she hadn't sleepwalked for some time now.

Still. Evania James was a reminder that in their darkest hours, in the moments when the world failed them, and the pain was agonizing, and death inevitable, the grave was not their final resting place. Because they were held. Through it all. And yes, as Luke had said, redemption could be found.

IF WALLS COULD TALK

I watched him place her there. When his father was out pretending none of it had happened. I embraced her as her brother hid her here. And when it was finished, I held her in my frame.

I watched her father as he stood unaware she was mere feet away, looking up at the beauty of his stained glass.

I witnessed pride. I witnessed generations of men who were not broken. Of women who tried to be heard. Of redemption always just out of reach. Because when a heart is hard, one cannot hear the whispers of hope.

But they are listening now. The past has found its voice, and I no longer need to try to reveal what I know or what I've seen. Most don't believe their lives today are touched by one who lived a hundred years before them. That's not true. They have been touched, as well as formed and influenced.

It is like a pool of water. When a stone is tossed in, ripples travel outward until eventually they touch the shore, but it is forgotten where they started from. Legacy is like that.

Legacy is the memories that live in its children. The memories that become the choices and the consequences and the blessings.

A legacy can be one of broken pieces, or a legacy can be one of faith.

If walls could talk, then that is what I would say.

Author's Note

I've often wondered, *What if walls could talk?* What if we didn't have the power to suppress that which we want to remain hidden forever? What if our memories could determine when they wanted to speak and influence the ones living?

And then it struck me. Memories *do* speak. They are the unhealed portions of us we hide behind the walls we make in our hearts. We block up the holes, we let them rot and decay, we pretend they aren't there, until generations later, it is our great-grandchild or someone else who discovers them, who says, "The sins of the father will carry on to the generations." We stifle the trauma, the hurt, the brokenness, the abuse, and our memories understand why we do it. Because it is pain-filled, and it not only hurts but it tears, and claws, and slices until we cannot bear the torture. The torture is brutal, and to spare ourselves, we hide our memories.

Until they speak.

Because they will.

Whether in our time, our children's, or our grandchildren's.

Because pain cannot stay hidden without staining the walls it hides behind. Until one day, memories find their voice, and someone must listen. Someone must unravel them. Someone must seek to find healing or renovate the wall and restuff the memories there, only for another generation to uncover them.

In the end, as I wrote this book, it became an allegory of sorts. The woman in the wall is the memory we cannot face. The woman in the wall is the memory we *must* face. We must walk through the pain, barefoot on shards of glass, our hearts exposed and vulnerable in our hands, before new life can be breathed into our battered souls.

We must decide that no more will thieves break in and steal our peace, our healing, our hope. They will not dig up our graves and disassemble who we were created to be. Instead, justice will be delivered by way of our Creator, healing will be administered because of His Son, and life will give memory more than just a voice.

Life—true life—will give memory a song.

Our legacy.

One of faith, forged in the past, claimed in the present, gifted to the future.

Here's to your legacy of faith!

Historical Note

This story was inspired by two books: *Daughter, Doctor, Resurrectionist: A True Story about Medical Body Snatching in 19th Century America* by Edmund Michael Van Buskirk; and *American Body Snatchers: Merchandising the Dead in 19th Century New England and Washington, D.C.* by Richard S. Ross III.

The first book highlights the selling of the dead to medical schools and the robbery that took place in cemeteries, most specifically in Fort Wayne, Indiana, in the late nineteenth century. When in my story, Silas Dobbs mentions a newly passed law, he is referencing the 1879 law passed in Indiana designed to bring tighter regulations to prevent the abuse and theft of the dead. This law still allowed some leeway because it recognized that studying the dead was necessary to improve medical treatment for the living, but it had to be done honorably.

The graphic story Silas shares with Eloise in the graveyard regarding the wealthy woman stolen from her grave, leaving only the remains of her dead infant in the casket, was in fact taken from real American history. As in this book, asylums and poorhouses were known to be places where patients who had died were farmed for their remains, mainly because many died unnoticed.

Likewise, the journal Eloise finds in her father's safe detailing a resurrectionist's day-to-day tasks in acquiring cadavers was also based on a similar diary. The entries featured here are original but closely resemble the entries from a diary used in a court hearing against a man who had made a career of this appalling practice and decided it was a smart idea to write about it.

Astronomically unbelievable as it might seem to find a body in a wall, I was inspired by the story of a skull discovered in an Illinois home that was identified through advanced DNA methods, linking the deceased person's story with a great-great-grandson. The skull was that of a woman who had died in 1866 in Indiana at the probable age of seventeen. Authorities believe she was a victim of grave robbing.

Reading Group Discussion Guide

1. During the eighteenth and nineteenth centuries, grave robbing was often driven by the medical community's need for research subjects. Today, some people choose to donate their remains to science to help advance our knowledge of the human body, although there still exists a black market for stolen remains. Where do you draw the line between medical research for the sake of the living and desecration of the dead? How would you articulate the Christian ethic or moral principle in support of your view?
2. Historically, women were committed to asylums by husbands or fathers for exhibiting strong emotions like grief, anger, or even opinions considered dangerous at the time. In what ways do you think this tendency might still influence modern medicine and family relationships? Have you encountered this dynamic in other books you've read? If so, can you give a few examples?
3. Old houses have been found to contain hidden rooms, sealed-off passages, and even human remains within walls. What do you think compels us as readers to want

to enter a world where a building becomes a keeper of secrets? In such cases, is the house a type of character, a villain or antihero perhaps, or is it something else entirely? Why or why not?

4. When we talk about "dysfunctional" families, we often contrast them with the ideal of a "healthy" family. But how realistic is that ideal? Do you believe every family carries some measure of dysfunction hidden beneath their surface? If so, how does this apply to the novel's main characters?
5. Consider how, throughout much of Western history, grief was at times treated as madness in women, while typically being thought of as noble suffering in men. How does this double standard shape the family narratives passed down through generations, particularly the stories families choose to share with others versus the ones they bury and keep silent about?
6. If a body were discovered behind the wall of a home that had housed multiple generations of the same family, what might that mean for each generation as they sought to reckon with the discovery? How does the passage of time affect one's complicity, guilt, and/or responsibility?
7. "Generational trauma" is a term used frequently today, and yet countless families in the past have experienced similar cycles of silence, control, and buried pain without ever naming it. At what point does a family's loyalty to its own narrative become a destructive inheritance, and what does it take for a person or a family to break this cycle?

For more from Jaime Jo Wright,
read on for an excerpt from

The LOST BOYS *of* BARLOWE THEATER

Available now wherever books are sold.

Keep up to date with all of Jaime's releases
at JaimeWrightBooks.com
and on Facebook, Instagram, and X.

1

Greta Mercy

October 1915
Kipper's Grove, Wisconsin

Sometimes death came quietly. A phantom swooping in and siphoning the last remnant of a soul from one's body, leaving behind a shell of a person who once was and would never be again. Other times, death decided that dramatics coupled with terror were its preferred method of delivery. Tonight, that was the chosen form death took.

Screams echoed throughout the theater's golden, embellished auditorium and drifted upward to the domed, hand-painted ceiling, where putti flew as angelic, childlike spirits over the mass of onlookers.

A shoulder rammed into Greta's arm as a husky man, far too large for the narrow seats, pushed his way past her toward the center aisle.

"Let me pass!" he barked. Urgency spurred him forward. "I'm a doctor, let me pass!"

The vaudeville lights on either side of the stage boasted letters *a* through *g*, with the *g* lit and distinct over the other letters.

"I'm letter *g*!" the doctor shouted while those in front of him jostled to the side or hurried ahead to move out of his way. Doctors were assigned specific letters from the vaudeville lights, and if they were lit, a doctor was needed—either at home, on call, or in the vicinity.

The vicinity was here. It was now.

Onlookers continued to gasp and protest. Women in beautiful silks and satins hurried to the back to find respite in the upstairs ladies' room. Men in evening wear catapulted over seats and to the floor on the far left of the auditorium.

Greta was frozen in place, her seat having flipped up against its back so she could move. But her eyes were fixed with horror on the scene unfolding. They lifted to one of the box seats above the floor, where men, including the doctor, were congregating en masse. The gilded box was a flurry of activity. A man embraced a woman, who fought and clawed at his hold. Her screams had many onlookers staring at her, including the performer in her violet gown and befeathered hair. Moments before, her vocals had swirled around them all in a cadence of beauty and refined music. Now, her mouth was open, her face pale, her entire pose aghast. She had captured an enthralled audience, all whose gazes toward the stage had kept them from seeing what Greta had seen. Greta, who shouldn't have been here to begin with. She didn't belong with the pomp and circumstance, the heady scent of perfume and cologne, which made her mind thick and her eyes wander. They'd wandered to the box seat, and she'd witnessed what no one else had. The white hands stretching, reaching over the side, dangling . . .

"It was a *child*!" The horrified cry slipped for the third time from Greta's lips. She could hear herself screaming and was unable to stop. Her screams had ripped through the performance as the child in a white nightdress plummeted into the shadows of the floor's obscure corner.

The woman in the box seat had been pulled from view, its red velvet curtain shut swiftly.

"It was a baby!" Greta rasped out as horror strangled her.

"Greta. It's all right." The reassuring voice of her friend, Eleanor Boyd, as well as the comforting grip on Greta's arm finally stilled her.

Greta focused again on her friend—her wealthy friend who should not be her friend at all.

Eleanor's blue eyes were round with fear that must mirror Greta's own. Her blond curls swept upward and were twisted with pearls. Her dress was a baby-blue silk. Any other moment, Greta would have soaked in the awe that tonight she, Greta Boyd, who could barely keep her family fed and clothed, was sitting among the elite, pretending to be one of them. But now? It hardly mattered. The borrowed corset that tucked in her waistline, the aged but wearable pink dress she had borrowed from Eleanor, and even the gloves she wore on her dry, cracked hands—none of them mattered now.

"What happened? What did you see?" Eleanor clutched at Greta's arm.

Greta couldn't reply. The sheer magnitude of the moment, the honor of being in the audience of the Barlowe Theater had been overwhelming . . . until she'd seen it. The *baby* launched over the side of the box seat. Like a cherub from the mural above, it had taken flight before it disappeared.

Greta's knees gave out, and she fell to where her seat should have been had it not folded in on itself. Her hip struck the polished wood arm.

"Greta!" Eleanor reached for her.

Greta felt Eleanor's brother on her other side, grabbing for her waist to give her support. But it was too late. She had collapsed to the narrow walkway between the seats. Her knees hit the carpeted floor.

Was she the only person who had seen death's swift visitation tonight? The only one who had witnessed its evil intent as it ripped the babe forcefully from its mother's arms?

It wouldn't survive. It could not. The fall was too far, too great.

Death had decided to match the theater's reputation for drama and awe. Greta couldn't tear her gaze from where she'd seen the small form disappear on its way to its resting place on the floor of the Barlowe Theater.

The babe had slipped. No, it had been *tossed*. Its mother's screams still echoed from the hallway beyond the curtain. Those in the crowd cried "Accident," "Traumatic mishap," and other such things. But Greta knew differently. She had known before she came tonight, and she should have stayed away.

Barlowe Theater was not a place that brought joy and entertainment, as was its supposed purpose. No, it had already taken lives in the construction of it, tortured the ones who dared stand in its way, and now it was hunting those innocents who had happened into the shadows of its deadly interior. The theater was cursed.

Kit Boyd

October, Present Day
Kipper's Grove, Wisconsin

Death stuck with a place. Once the blood had seeped into the carpet, the flooring, the walls, it stayed there, long after the stains were removed. They were the testament to lives robbed of their rightful journey through time. Cut short. Obliterated. Bludgeoned into nonexistence. Smothered by the grave, burrowed into by the worms–

"Hey!"

Fingers snapped in front of Kit Boyd's face, and she startled out of her staring into the dark, narrow stairwell that led beneath the stage of the Barlowe Theater.

"Get with it, bruh." The fingers snapped again. Kit looked up at the taller man beside her. He was overweight and smelled like pizza, but he had a nice face. His name was Tom, they'd told her, the crew from the TV show *Psychic and the Skeptic*.

"Sorry." Kit offered him a wince. She'd paused on the first concrete step while her best friend, Madison, the psychic medium, Heather Grant, and the skeptic investigator, Evan Fischer, disappeared into the bowels of the theater. Tom the cameraman was held back by her hesitation. She gave him a warning look, though the theater's darkness in the midnight atmosphere probably hid most of her expression. "You *do* know people died here . . . have disappeared here."

"That's the point." Tom waved her forward, the camera on his shoulder blinking a red light. "But I need to catch them on film if I can, and you're in my way."

Fabulous. She was on camera. That would probably make the show too. Kit Boyd, the quirky sidekick to Madison Farrington, the historical activist, the beauty, the granddaughter of the town's ambitious CEO of all things expansion, modern, and money-making.

"Hello?" There was definite irritation in Tom's voice.

"I'm *going*! I'm going." Kit hurried down the steps. She'd taken them many times before. Anyone who was native to Kipper's Grove, Wisconsin, had grown up in the Barlowe Theater at one point or another. Dancers had tapped and glided across its stage in recitals, high school glee clubs with dreams of Broadway had warbled off-key through its hall, and the local theater guild had put on such plays as *Arsenic and Old Lace* and *The Music Man*. Kit hadn't been in any of those. Instead, she was the one backstage handing bottles of water to the performers, smiling and cracking jokes to encourage the stage-frozen little six-year-old dressed in a yellow tutu with glitter on her cheeks.

"Oh, *c'mon*!" Tom hissed, his irritation past the point of being hidden. How he'd gotten behind her anyway was a faux pas for filming. He was supposed to stick close to the stars of the show, Heather and Evan. And boy, did those two get along famously—*not*.

"Whew!" Kit wheezed under her breath, not caring if Tom heard. "I'd try to avoid those two if you could."

"Yeah, well, I have a job to do." Tom squeezed past Kit as she hugged the cement-block wall at the bottom of the stairs to let him through. He elbowed her arm and didn't bother to apologize. He probably felt as if she owed him that luxury. The luxury of being annoyed.

Okay, fine. She did.

If she was being honest, Kit wasn't a fan of the Barlowe Theater past dark. Which was the cliché of all theaters built just after the turn of the century. It was dark. Haunted. The place was like a tomb. Crank up some vaudeville music and the place became a literal haunted house of horrors for Halloween. And Kit hated Halloween. The darkness, the Gothic look and feel. Halloween was for morbid people who thought Edgar Allan Poe was romantic in his mystery and lore instead of macabre and bleak. Hadn't he died questionably? She'd heard a podcast once that claimed the poet might have been murdered, contrary to the popular belief that his death had been the result of some fatal malady undiagnosed.

Kit shook her head to clear her thoughts. Mom said cobwebs couldn't possibly gather in her head because she had too many ideas. Mom was right. Kit would never be accused of having an underactive imagination.

A finger jabbed into the back of her shoulder.

"Stop it!" Kit spun to glare at the offender.

No one was there.

Her skin began crawling. "Gahhhhhh!" She waved her hands wildly at the unseen ghost finger. Probably her imagination, but whatever. She had let Madison sucker her into a ghost hunt for the popular ghost-hunting television show. This was her penance? Getting poked by an elusive spirit?

"Sorry, God." Kit mumbled an apology to the Almighty, who was probably rolling His eyes at their attempts to mess with the spirit world. But this was Madison. She believed *anything* was possible. Kit had been raised to believe that this type of *anything* was probably demonic. There had to be a middle ground. Hadn't there?

Kit hurried around the corner, stubbing her toe on a bolt that rose half an inch up from the floor. Dampness and time had warped the theater's floor, making it uneven. She leaned against the wall, rubbing her bare toe. Flip-flops on a ghost hunt. Bad idea.

She looked around—well, as best as she could. The basement was dark, as were the dressing rooms to her right, sized like prison cells. The short hall to her left leading directly below the stage was also dark.

"Hello, darkness," Kit crooned quietly, craning her neck to peer ahead. "Hello?" she tried again, this time louder.

No answer.

"Seriously, someone?" Kit was beginning to share Tom the cameraman's annoyance now. Two argumentative television stars, her best friend, and a cameraman didn't just vanish within minutes. The basement wasn't *that* huge.

But it was Barlowe Theater.

"*Tom?*" Kit hissed, daring a few steps into the dank blackness. "Madison?"

Again, no one answered. The only light was a flickering bulb that had to be a wattage short of worth having at all. It buzzed too. Of course it did. If this stunt was for show dramatics . . .

"Madison!" Kit shouted. In the ten years since they'd graduated high school, she had followed this woman around. She was owed some loyalty in return. "If this is for ratings, it's unkind of you!" Kit yelled. Her words echoed back at her.

"Madis–"

Light slammed into her face, blinding Kit. She raised her hands as the flashlight's beam collided with her eyes.

"They're gone!" It was Tom.

Kit could see the whites of his eyes just beyond the flashlight he swung around wildly.

"What do you mean?" Kit tried to take captive Tom's arm as he flooded the hallway with the light, then a dressing room, then the ceiling. His camera wasn't on his shoulder.

He wasn't filming.

Kit's throat tightened. Okay, that wasn't a good sign. "Where's Madison?"

Tom swung the light back in Kit's face. "Where's Evan? Where's Heather? Where's my *team*?" His voice shook with undisguised concern, turning fast into panic. "How big is this place?"

"Not *that* big." Kit pushed past him. Concerned now. This had gone too far. Madison and her harebrained schemes to keep her own grandfather from ruining the historic downtown. Make it famous, she said. Put it on TV, she said. Make viewers defend Kipper's Grove, she said. "Madison!" Kit shouted, anxiousness seeping into her voice. "Stop this! It's not funny!"

Tom's light bounced on the floor in front of them as Kit spun around and marched back toward him. She shoved past his husky chest and down the short passage to the door leading under the stage. Her fingers curled around the doorknob, its old mechanics making it wobbly beneath her grip.

Kit jerked it open.

She fell back with a shriek, colliding with Tom, who had come way too close behind her.

Heather, the medium from the show, stood stock-still facing them. Her eyes were wide and unfocused, her skin white in the flashlight's glow.

"She's gone." Heather's monotone voice filtered through the passage.

Kit's words were stolen from her as her stomach dropped.

"Who's gone?" Tom demanded.

"Madison." Evan Fischer, the cohost, the skeptic, and the all-around grumpy hero of the show strode past his partner. Heather's expression didn't waver as her eyes remained fixated on . . . whatever she was staring at in the spirit world beyond. "Madison's gone."

Evan left less than a few inches between his face and Kit's as he bent his six-foot frame down to meet her five-foot-four one. "Where is she?"

"I don't kn–"

"Where. Is. She?" He cut off Kit's answer as unsatisfactory.

Her breaths came shorter, faster. She could feel Tom behind her. She was sandwiched between him and Evan, with Heather staring into the great abyss.

"I told you. I don't know." Kit heard the quaver in her voice. She shoved her trembling hands into her pockets.

"She's gone." Evan slapped the wall, glaring at Tom, who was speechless. "Is this a scam? A stunt?"

Kit couldn't answer. Of course, the show would think it was a ploy by Madison. A publicity ploy. But it went deeper than that. Far deeper. Kit sagged against the wall, the air not reaching her lungs as it should.

She prayed then. Prayed that Madison really was messing with them. That she had simply gone too far ahead beneath the stage and left them behind.

But the theater was hungry, and everyone in Kipper's Grove knew it was only a matter of time before this hunger added to the stories of death and spirits. That's how the theater was, after all. Drama. Suspense. And the unearthly way that such things drifted through its rafters.

Jaime Jo Wright is a *Publishers Weekly* bestselling author of sixteen novels and three novellas, including Christy Award–winner and ECPA bestseller *The Vanishing at Castle Moreau*, Christy Award– and Daphne du Maurier Award–winner *The House on Foster Hill*, and Carol Award–winner *The Reckoning at Gossamer Pond*. She lives in Wisconsin with her family and fabulous felines. Learn more at JaimeWrightBooks.com.

Sign Up for Jaime's Newsletter

Keep up to date with Jaime's latest news on book releases and events by signing up for her email list at the website below.

JaimeWrightBooks.com

FOLLOW JAIME ON SOCIAL MEDIA

Jaime Jo Wright

@JaimeJoWright

@JaimeJoWright